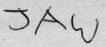

JAW

DESIRE'S SURRENDER

Lathe knew he was in danger. Leona could be his emotional undoing, but he was unable to resist temptation. . .

He pulled her gently into his arms. Eager to feel the warmth of her soft body against his, he circled her with his arms and crushed her to him.

Leona was too surprised and too pleased to offer immediate protest when Lathe's hand slipped behind her head and brought her parted mouth downward to meet his. It was an instantly passionate kiss, and a warm, jolting sensation shot through her.

Truth was, she should be pushing him away. Chastising him for daring to be so bold. But by the time any real thought of protest occurred to Leona, it was too late. She was already acknowledging how much she desired the man, and she was much too enthralled by the fire that was building inside her to think of anything else . . .

D0976440

ROSALYN ALSOBROOK

Endless Seduction

ZEBRA BOOKS
KENSINGTON PUBLISHING CORP.

A special thank you to my editor, Alice Alfonsi Kane, and to my agent, Ruth Cohen, for not pressuring me in times of personal duress and allowing me the time I so desperately needed to help my family through not just one but *three* successive family crises.

ZEBRA BOOKS

are published by

Kensington Publishing Corp.
475 Park Avenue South
New York, NY 10016

First printing: July, 1992

Printed in the United States of America

Chapter One

Leona Stegall paused to study her reflection in the store window and quickly adjusted her collar. Although her dark blue tailored dress had been purchased well over two years ago and was more suitable for late fall than early spring, it was the most stylish, businesslike outfit she owned.

Continuing to assess her appearance, she thrust her chin higher to give herself that look of authority she felt she needed. She also took a deep, fortifying breath to steady her nerves and at the same time drew herself to her fullest height of five feet five inches before turning sideways to view her trim profile.

Leona decided the dress made her look considerably older than her twenty-four years, and far more mature—more like the businesswoman of the 1870s was supposed to look.

Or at least she hoped it did.

Her shoulders sagged again when she realized the dress really did nothing for her other than accentuate her tiny waist and the gentle flair of her hips. She considered returning home to change clothes again, but knew that it would be yet another attempt to put off the inevitable.

It galled Leona to have to go to the bank and ask Beb-

5

ber Davis for the business loan she so desperately needed, yet she could not stall any longer, not if she wanted to save the family business from eventually falling into total ruin. She should have asked for the loan months ago, but that Stegall pride of hers had kept her from it. Leona was too accustomed to handling her problems herself because until now, she had never had to rely on anyone's help but her own.

Until now —

Wincing against the sharp, twisting pain, she bit deep into the tender flesh of her lower lip then turned and with short, purposeful strides, and headed quickly down the street. Now that the decision had been made, she was determined to put the matter behind her.

Within minutes after entering Little Mound's only bank, Leona was ushered into Bebber's elaborately furnished office. Anxiously, she sat and waited for him to finish writing a quick note to one of his tellers. Her dark brown eyes followed the rapid movements of his hand while he quickly scrawled the message then handed it to his secretary, who stood, also waiting.

"Now, then," Bebber Davis said after he watched the secretary leave the room. He leaned back in his oversized upholstered chair to give Leona his full attention.

Bebber Davis was a tall, imposing man in his early fifties with a thick head of silvery white hair that reflected the morning sunlight streaming in the multipaned window behind him. "What can I do for you?"

Leona sat ramrod straight in one of three small, cushioned chairs facing his desk.

"As you know, Stegall's Mercantile is going through a pretty rough time right now," she stated in her most businesslike tone, eager to get right to her reason for having come.

"Yes, and it is a pity — circumstances being what they are," Bebber expressed, nodding to indicate his sympathy. Then he glanced at her hand as she nervously fingered the strings of the bonnet she had slipped from her fashionable twist of dark curls and allowed to dangle loosely down the middle of her back. "That drought hit this whole area pretty hard."

"Which is why I am here."

Aware of what had attracted his attention, she quickly dropped her hands to her lap, folding one over the other to help keep them still.

"Because of last year's drought, many of my farming and ranching customers have not been able to pay last year's bills and yet have had to charge even more supplies to get their new crops underway for this year. Of course they will pay everything they owe just as soon as their crops are harvested and sold; but until they do, I am left with a severe cash shortage. One that seems to get a little worse each day."

It was not easy to keep the desperation from pulling at her voice, but somehow she managed. She was proud of how calmly she spoke about such a serious problem.

"I can well imagine your dilemma," Bebber acknowledged. He continued to nod his understanding, though his hazel eyes sparkled with deep satisfaction. "Several of our business customers have allowed credit to the local farmers and are having a hard time of it this year. That drought put a big dent in our entire East Texas economy. It really is a pity something like that had to happen, especially when we were just getting over the problems caused by that April freeze three years ago."

Aware that he was deriving great pleasure from her predicament, Leona curled her hands into tight fists then moved them to her sides to remove them from Bebber's sight so he could not see how angry she had become. She was too accustomed to being in total control of her life — a fact of which Bebber was *well* aware.

And he did not plan to make this any easier for her.

"Which is why I am here," she repeated, simmering over the obvious fact that he thought her plight so amusing. Somehow she continued to keep the resentment out of her voice when she quickly broke through to the bot-

7

tom line. "I need a temporary loan of three thousand dollars. I need to pay that money I still owe on last year's taxes and I also need to replace my inventory so I can keep the Mercantile functioning."

"By temporary, you mean until after first harvest," he surmised. He studied her through the bottom half of his spectacles.

"Exactly. After the first crops have been marketed, most of my customers should be able to pay the full amount they owe me, and I in turn should be able to repay you."

Bebber paused to study her hopeful expression. "I'm afraid not."

He leaned forward in his chair, laced his long, lily-white fingers together and rested them on the gleaming surface of his massive oak desk.

"Oh, but they *will*. All that most of them need is one good crop; and with the rain we've had thus far this spring, this should be a bountiful year for both corn and cotton."

"That's not what I meant," Bebber corrected, his quiet tone more like that of an undertaker than a banker. "I'm afraid I can't give you the loan."

A sharp pain sliced through Leona's stomach causing her to cross her arms and double slightly forward.

"Why not?" Her voice became suddenly sharp and accusing. "Because I'm a woman?"

"No, of course not. I've loaned money to women before, although I'll admit not often."

"Then why won't you loan me the money? You know I'm good for it. I realize we have had our differences in the past, but I thought, overall, you were my friend."

"I am your friend, but I am first a businessman. And as a businessman, I cannot in good conscience provide you with a business loan of that magnitude." When Leona opened her mouth to again question why, he held up his hand to stop her. "You don't have the collateral necessary to back such a loan."

"But what about the building? Isn't it worth three thousand? If not, I'll put up the house instead. I really do need that money."

"You don't understand. You don't happen to be the legitimate owner of either the Mercantile or the house," he quickly pointed out. "In your parents' will, it is clearly stated that both the house and the business were to be left to your brother with the simple stipulation he would take care of you until you marry."

Again, Leona opened her mouth to speak and, again, Bebber cut her short by presenting his palm. "*And* because you have never had Ethan declared legally dead — something my son and I have both encouraged you to do for several years now — technically, Ethan is still the rightful owner of both the Mercantile and the house. In essence, you are nothing more than the caretaker. As it stands now, you are merely managing the business and minding the house in your brother's absence." He thrust his chin at a lofty angle. "Therefore you personally do not have the collateral we require for a business loan."

"Then what about a personal loan?" she asked, still hoping to find a solution to her problem. "You know I'll pay it back the first opportunity I have."

"I'm sorry. I can't risk it. And it is not because you are a woman or because I don't trust you. It is because legally your brother could return at any time and demand to take over everything, leaving you nothing with which you could repay a loan. All your parents' will indicated was that Ethan had to provide you with food, shelter, and clothing. It said nothing about money. Ethan might decide he wants all the money for himself."

"He wouldn't do that."

Bebber sighed with frustration. "The truth is, he *couldn't* do that because he is dead. In your heart, you *know* he is. We both know he is. This whole blasted town knows he is. Granted, his body was never returned, nor was the exact location of his grave ever found; but we all know Ethan Stegall is dead. Even the captain he fought under admitted he has to be dead because he never returned to camp after a particularly bloody battle. And until you decide to stop being so blamed mule-headed about it all and finally have that brother of yours declared legally deceased, there's nothing I can do to help you."

"And if I do have him declared dead, then you will give me the loan?" She lifted her hand to play absently with a tiny curl near her temple while she thought more about it. Her brown eyes became distant with thought.

"Probably," he answered carefully, just as eager as his son to see the deed finally done. He paused to study the pained expression on his future daughter-in-law's beautiful face for a moment, wishing the young woman did not have such a fierce streak of independence, then quietly added, "There is one other way you might be able to work around your current dilemma."

"What's that?" Letting go of the tip of her brown curl, she glanced at him again. Her eyes sparkled with renewed hope.

"You could always agree to marry John. I imagine if you would finally become his wife, he'd feel obligated to help you however you wanted him to."

Knowing how determined Bebber was to have her marry his only son, she should have expected him to say that; but she hadn't.

"Bebber, you know as well as anyone that your son and I are in no way romantically bent toward one another. We are nothing more than a couple of good friends who spend some time together now and then. We are not now and never have been in love with each other." She spoke firmly then sighed with renewed annoyance, aware that her continued refusal to marry John was probably the real reason Bebber had denied her the loan. Bebber had never kept his desire to have grandchildren a secret and for some reason he and John both had it in their minds that *she* was the only woman in all Little Mound worthy to be John's wife.

"Love or not, John has asked you to marry him several times and all you ever do is find ways to put him off." Bebber's oversized chair squeaked when he again leaned back and looked at her as if she were a young child in need of parental guidance. "Fact is, unless you finally decide to have that brother of yours declared legally dead—something my son has told you he can have done in a matter of weeks—then marrying John is really the only alternative you have. That is if you honestly want to save your family's Mercantile from ruin."

"You know I do. Why else would I be here?" she asked, exasperated that he could suggest anything different.

"Well, I will agree that you were right about one thing: if you hope to stay in business, you will have to have something to sell. If you don't keep a good stock, your regular customers will be forced to take their business to Porterfield's. His location may not be as good as yours or his prices quite as fair, but at least he's keeping his store filled with the sorts of things the people here in Little Mound need. The last time I was in your store, those shelves of yours looked pretty bare. Even with fair prices and such a good location, right across from the courthouse and all, your customers will soon quit coming in at all if they know they won't find what they need when they get there."

"And you won't loan me the money to restock," she stated, more to herself than to him. She held her head proudly erect while she considered what she should do next.

"I can't," he said with finality. "I'm sorry, but that's just the way it is."

Angry that she had put herself through such a humiliating experience for nothing, Leona quickly stood, holding her arms stiffly at her sides.

"Then I guess I will have to find some other way to keep my doors open." She tried to sound as if it were really a simple matter.

11

"Good luck," Bebber stated, leaning forward again to fold his arms across his desk rather than rise from his chair to see her out. Clearly, he was annoyed. She had not embraced his sage advice with the enthusiasm he had hoped. "You are certainly going to need it."

"It's not luck, I need." She narrowed her gaze while her throat constricted with painful outrage. "It's money."

"No, what you need is to come down off that high horse of yours and marry my son. You are twenty-four years old. It is high time you stopped being so blamed stubborn about the way you live, and settle down." He wagged a slender finger to emphasize his words. "You may not think you *love* my son enough to marry him, but you definitely *need* him enough. Now more than ever."

"You're wrong. I don't *need* anyone. I have managed to get along on my own just fine until now — in fact, I've done just fine since my parents died five years ago. And I will continue to do just fine on my own for at least ten times that. It's true, I am suffering an unfortunate financial setback because of last year's drought, but I can assure you, it is only a temporary problem. I will find some way to get the money I need without either your or John's help."

Just *how,* remained to be seen.

Frustrated to the point of tears, mainly because she knew Bebber was right about her brother, Leona spun about on her booted heel and marched proudly out of his office. Although it hurt dreadfully to admit it, deep in her soul, she knew Ethan was dead. If he hadn't died, he would have returned years ago; and it did no one any real good to pretend differently.

Slipping her bonnet back over her head, more to shield herself from the curious stares of those around her than from the late morning Texas sun, Leona continued along the dusty boardwalk toward the Mercantile. She reached up to dash away an embarrassing tear just seconds before she stepped onto the gravel and dirt street that ran through the main part of town. Quickly, she glanced in both directions to make sure nothing was coming, then hurried across to the opposite side.

When she stepped up onto the opposite boardwalk, she met her mother's old friend, Josephine Haught, coming out of Nadine's Dress Shop. She quickly dropped her gaze to the rough planked flooring and hurried along on her way. She did not want anyone to see her cry. Tears were a sign of weakness and she refused to be weak, not when the future of the Mercantile depended on her remaining strong. *Strong enough to make the right decision, no matter how much it hurt.*

Perhaps she *should* gather the forbearance needed to have her brother declared dead. By doing so, she would finally gain the legal control she so desperately needed to save the store.

It was either that or agree to marry John Davis.

Her slender nose wrinkled at the thought. Even though she truly believed John Davis did love her—in his own lofty sort of way—and she did like him well enough as a friend to keep company with him on occasion, the thought of spending the rest of her life with someone that dull and that pompous made her stomach feel as heavy as if it were weighted with lead. True, being one of the area's most prominent lawyers, John Davis had more than enough money to rescue the Mercantile from its present dilemma; but there had to be another way.

There had to be.

Still, whatever she decided to do to save the store, she should do it soon because the longer she put it off, the longer it would be before she could restock her empty shelves and regain the confidence of what few customers she had left.

The thought of the family business falling into total ruin after all the years of hard work her parents had put into it—not to mention the countless hours of work she had put into it—hurt more than she cared to admit. Something had to be done. And soon.

13

She agreed to give herself until the following morning to make a decision.

Lathe Caldwell's boots connected soundlessly with the hard surface of the ground while he slowly made his way down the dark alley toward the street. Having circled the back of Porterfield's Dry Goods undetected, he positioned himself in the late evening shadows, across the street from the Golden Eagle Saloon.

He pressed his back against the faded clapboards of the small store, only a few feet away from the brightly painted false front. He had a good, clear view of the saloon across the street yet was able to remain under the protective cloak of darkness.

With his right hand, he eased his pistol out of the worn, black leather holster that hung low on his hip and he tipped the weapon against his shoulder in readiness. With his left hand, he felt for the handle of the buckknife tucked neatly into the special band sewn to his belt. He then felt for the long piece of rope that dangled loosely from his belt loop. Reassured everything was where it was supposed to be, he lowered his left hand back to his side. His fingers flexed with nervous anticipation.

He kept his gaze trained on the batwing doors of Little Mound's most popular saloon, and waited — afraid even to blink, for fear he would miss his chance.

Finally, after all these years of relentless searching and tracking, Lathe had located Zeb Turner again. He had seen the man for himself, standing up against the bar, holding a tall glass of whiskey, and laughing with two other men as if he hadn't a care in the world. Obviously the fool thought he had successfully shaken him back there in Jefferson.

But he hadn't.

Lathe's mouth curled into a cold, malevolent smile that matched the hard gleam in his pale blue eyes. He could hardly wait to see Zeb's expression when he finally

14

caught him off guard and alone.

That was exactly what he had to do. He had to wait until Zeb had finally had enough to drink and came out of there. He had to wait until Zeb was outside, well away from any occupied building, where he could get a clear shot at him. And most importantly, he had to wait until he was alone. But how long would that take?

He glanced toward the sky. A trace of grey lingered, dulling the twinkle of the half-dozen stars and the tiny streak of a moon overhead.

He guessed the time to be around seven o'clock, maybe later. No telling how much longer before Zeb finally left that saloon. But then it did not really matter how long he stayed in there. Lathe would wait. This time, he would not make any mistakes. Zeb was not getting away.

Zeb Turner had already lived five years too many.

"Scraps!" Leona called loudly while walking along the dimly lit streets of Little Mound. Her gaze darted about in search of the crafty mutt that had eluded her yet again. Although she had no idea how the animal had escaped, when she had walked into the back room where he liked to lie on a mat near the back door, she had discovered him missing. A quick search had proved he was nowhere in the house.

She could not understand how he could have gotten away. The only two means of escape in the entire house had been those two windows upstairs that no longer had wire screens covering them, but she had closed the door to that room earlier. Surely the dog did not have enough sense to open and close that door; and even if he did, he would have risked breaking his neck to make a leap like that.

But how else could he have gotten out? All the other windows had screens to keep out the insects and both of the outside doors had been bolted shut. The animal cer-

15

tainly could not work an iron bolt mounted four feet from the floor. She wondered how he had managed to get out, and how he always managed to make these daring escapes while her back was turned.

"Scraps, where are you?"

While muttering several suggestions concerning what she should do to that dog, she continued to scan the dark shadows and shapes scattered beneath the awnings and alleyways on both sides of the street, eager to catch sight of the mangy, good-for-nothing canine.

She patted her skirt pocket to make sure she had remembered to snatch up the piece of rope she would need to drag the stubborn animal back home.

While carefully watching and listening for some clue that might indicate where Scraps might be hiding, she heard someone whistling an oddly familiar tune somewhere in the distance. She turned her head to listen better and decided the lively sound had come from the general direction of the hotel just ahead.

For several seconds she tried to place the tune, then it dawned on her where she had heard it before. It was the same sprightly tune she and Ethan had made up back when they were both still children — the tune they'd put to a naughty little lyric describing their least favorite schoolteacher, Mr. Jones.

Although in her heart, Leona had finally accepted the fact Ethan was dead, for a brief moment she truly believed the whistler had to be her brother. With her next breath lodged deep at the base of her throat, she gathered her skirts high above her ankles and hurried down the street to find him.

When she neared the man whistling the jaunty tune, he was bent forward, searching for something in his saddlebags, his back toward her. Although the man looked only a few inches taller than she, which was *much* shorter than she remembered Ethan to be, and he also appeared broader across the upper portion of his back and even a little thicker through the waist and hips, she held tightly

16

to her hope. She clasped her hands together and pressed them against her heart when she cried aloud his name.

"Ethan?"

There was a moment's hesitation before the man turned to face her. Breathlessly, she awaited his response and for a moment, her hopes were reinforced because the man did look the way Ethan might have looked if he had grown a thick, heavy beard and allowed his hair to grow wild and put on about twenty or so pounds.

The man studied her for a moment, his thick, dark brows drawn low, as if uncertain what he should say, then he glanced around to see if there was anyone else nearby. "Ma'am? Was you speakin' to me?"

He even sounded a little like Ethan, though his voice was decidedly deeper and his grammar poorer than Ethan's. Ethan had finished high school with high marks and had been about to enter college when the war broke out.

Leona blinked back her tears and took a small step toward him, trying desperately to get a better look at his face, partially obscured by the late evening shadows. "Y-you're not Ethan Stegall?"

Whether intentionally or not, he kept his face low and turned away from the glow of the nearest street lamp, which stood across the street in front of the bank. He barely met her gaze and appeared extremely uncomfortable over the prospect of talking with her.

"No ma'am, I'm not. The name's not Ethan, it's — George." He grimaced the very second he'd said it, knowing why that name had been so quick to pop into his head. But now, he needed to think of a good last name, and he didn't dare use the name Martin. "George *Parkinson*."

Disappointed, Leona realized how foolishly she had behaved. Of course he was not Ethan. He couldn't be. Sadly, she swallowed to relieve the ache filling her throat, then apologized for having bothered the man. "I'm very sorry. For a moment, I thought you were my

17

brother, Ethan. Yet at the same time, I knew you weren't. Ethan was killed several years ago during the war."

Saying it aloud caused a slight grimace, but she finished her explanation in as cheerful a voice as she could muster, "Besides, Ethan would be much taller than you. Why when he left here, I hardly came up to his shoulder." But then, she had barely been fifteen and he had already reached eighteen by the day he left. "And Ethan certainly didn't have a scar like that." She indicated the deep, jagged disfigurement that ran horizontally across his upper cheek then dipped at an angle into his beard.

Self-consciously, he reached up to touch the thick scar with his fingertips then nodded absently. He lied to keep her from guessing the truth. "Sure hope this thing don't scare you none. I've had it since I was near on to nine years old."

Because of the dangerous nature of the business he had there in Little Mound, he did not want his sister or anyone else to recognize his true identity. It was better for Leona to continue to believe him dead than to learn the truth.

He felt the pain tightening in his chest, causing him to look away. If only he could have avoided an encounter altogether. How it hurt to see her after all these years. He fought back the overwhelming urge to take her into his arms and hug her, as well as the powerful desire to ask about their parents. Were they well? Were they over his supposed death yet?

Leona continued to stare at Ethan with a sad look of bewilderment for several seconds. Then she suddenly remembered why she had been out walking along Main Street so late in the day. She glanced around at the surrounding shadows again then asked, "You haven't seen a dog about this high with a dark brown collar running around here loose have you?"

She held her hand several inches below her hip to show where the top of Scrap's head usually came—when

18

he wasn't crouched low, poking that skinny snout of his where it did not belong.

"A dog? What kind of dog?" he asked, relieved to have her attention move on to something else — anything else.

"Part collie, part thief."

Ethan blinked as if he had misunderstood.

"More thief than collie actually," she admitted. Her mouth flattened into a grim line when she looked back into the shadows covering Ethan's face. "I happen to be the reluctant owner of a young dog named Scraps. His hair is mostly black but he has large patches of gold and white across his chest and face. When he appeared unexpectedly at my door one cold night last winter, he was a lanky little pup with huge sad eyes. He looked like he hadn't seen a meal in days."

"So you took him in and fed him," he concluded with a knowing nod, remembering how she had always taken in strays when she was a child, much to their parents' continued dismay.

"Yes, I made the mistake of feeding him a hot meal and giving him a place to sleep that night, thinking he would be on his way the next morning. Only he never left. And that lanky little pup has grown into a rather sizable young dog who has turned out to be a notorious and quite nonreformable thief. To avoid trouble, I usually keep him either locked inside the house or chained to a large tree in my side yard. But somehow, he slipped away from me tonight. I have to find him before he gets into something he shouldn't. He has about as much sense as a moth does when there's an open candle flickering. He always seems to find some sort of trouble to shove his nose into."

"But should you be out here searching for your dog all alone like this?" It was clear by his scowl that he thought it a bad idea.

"Well, it's not really the sort of thing one would round up a posse for," she explained, then smiled. "But if you mean am I taking a big risk by being out on the streets alone after dark, the answer is no. Little Mound is a pretty peaceful little town. As long as I stay clear of the area surrounding South Jefferson Street where all the saloons are, no harm will come to me. Now, have you seen my dog or not?"

"No, I haven't seen no dog," he admitted then glanced around as if hoping to catch sight of the animal. Suddenly, his eyes widened and he pointed toward an alleyway across the street. "Is that him over there?"

Leona turned in time to see the furry bandit dash off into the darkness with something large and white protruding from his mouth.

"Yes, that's him," she muttered, then immediately took off after him. Lifting her skirts just high enough to be out of her way, she hurried toward the alley where she had last spotted the furry renegade. "Come back here, you thieving little outlaw. Come back here before I decide to hang you by your scraggly paws and skin you alive."

Sadly, Ethan watched his sister's silhouette disappear into the shadowed alley across the street. He heard her scolding voice long after she had left his sight. He closed his eyes and took a deep breath to relieve some of the tightness pulling at his chest, then turned back to his saddlebags. Finally, he located the folded piece of paper he needed. He dropped the flap across the leather pouch then yanked his wide-brimmed hat off his saddle horn and slapped it down across his head.

Immediately, he stepped up onto the boardwalk and entered the hotel.

Unfolding the well-worn sheet of paper while he strode into the brightly lit lobby of the Traveler's Hotel, he approached the desk clerk with a friendly smile.

"You haven't happened to have seen this man around here lately, have you?" he asked, trying to sound as if he was only casually interested. He turned the faded sketch so the clerk could see it better. "The way I heard it, he was last seen headed in this direction."

The desk clerk looked at the drawing, blinked with obvious recognition, then tried to mask that recognition when he looked back at Ethan. "I don't see no badge. What are you? A bounty hunter or something?"

"Yeah, somethin' like that," Ethan answered, then nodded toward the sketch again, too eager to find the man to put up with a lengthy conversation.

He reached into his pocket and brought out a small coin and held it just out of the clerk's reach. "So have you seen him or not?"

After a few seconds of chewing his lower lip and studying the sketch more closely, the clerk finally nodded. "I think so. That looks an awful lot like a man who came in here earlier today, about midafternoon. I think his name was Creel. Jonathan Creel."

"Did he have on a gold ring with a fancy lookin' letter *C* carved into it?" Ethan wanted to know, not surprised Lathe had used a false name.

"Yes sir, I believe he did," the clerk answered, keeping his eye on the coin still in Ethan's hand.

Aware that it had to be Lathe, Ethan asked, "Is he still here?" His gaze moved to the steep, narrow stairwell just to the left of the desk.

"No. Although he did take time to get himself a room, all he did after I gave him the key was put his saddlebags up there then headed straight on out."

"But his saddlebags are still in his room?" Ethan wanted clarified. His heart raced with anticipation, aware that after all these years, he had finally caught up with the very man he had been sent to capture. That long, frustrating search could very well be nearing an end.

He swallowed his apprehension while he considered his next move. He had to be careful. "Did you happen to notice if he was armed when he went out of here?"

"Sure did. He was definitely totin' a pistol," the clerk responded. His eyes stretched wide at the memory. "This is a pretty quiet little town most of the time. Not

21

too many people walk around with their pistols strapped right to their legs like that. My guess is he was headed for one of the saloons over on the next street near the south end of town. That type fellow usually likes to hang around those kind of places and in this town they are all bunched up there together. My guess is, he'll probably end up at the Golden Eagle, since it is the wildest in town."

"Which direction is this Golden Eagle?"

"That way. One block over and a couple of blocks south." He pointed off in the general direction of the front door. "This time of night the saloons is about all that's open over there on Jefferson Street and the Eagle is the biggest saloon we got, so I don't rightly think you'll go missin' it."

"Thanks for all your help, friend." Ethan tossed the coin onto the counter but when the clerk made a grab for it, he quickly slapped his massive hand down over it and looked at him with hard, penetrating brown eyes. "If anyone asks, you haven't seen me or anybody who even remotely looks like me."

"I ain't seen nobody," the clerk agreed, shaking his head hard while he gazed up at the man with sudden fear.

"Good," Ethan said then smiled again as he lifted his hand off the coin and tugged gently at the brim of his hat. "Glad to know you are so cooperative." Refolding the sketch and tucking it into his vest pocket, he headed for the door with long, determined strides.

He had to get to Lathe Caldwell before Lathe Caldwell got to Zeb Turner. He just hoped he was not already too late.

Leona had lost sight of Scraps for the third time and was becoming increasingly annoyed with the bothersome canine. He was undoubtedly hiding from her so she could not take away whatever bounty he had stolen,

22

so she continued to walk ever so slowly down the narrow alley behind Soape's Furniture Store. She bent low while she quietly searched every potential hiding spot, hoping to catch a quick glimpse of that worthless mutt.

While inspecting every possible cranny in which a dog of that size could hide, she quietly slipped from one alley into another, wondering if she would have to search them all before she finally found the mischievous critter. She tried not to make any noise that might alert the animal to her presence.

It was after she had entered the cluttered alley that ran between the furniture store and Porterfield's Dry Goods that she first glimpsed something moving near the street. As she was narrowing her gaze to see better into the surrounding darkness, her heart quickly jumped to her throat.

There, only a few dozen yards away, near the street yet well hidden within the shadows of the alley, stood a man clad in dark clothing. He had what looked like a pistol held tipped back against his shoulder, pointed toward the blackened sky. If he had not reached up to push his hair back out of his face when she had glanced that direction, she would never have noticed him at all.

Although there was not enough light to make out more than a dark silhouette, she could tell that a tall, muscular man faced the street, intent on ambush.

While her heart throbbed at a frantic rate, she tried to think of some way to stop him. But what could she possibly do against a man so strongly built — a man already holding a gun?

Chapter Two

Aware that the danger was too great to try to handle alone, Leona cautiously retraced her steps. Her heart hammered violently deep in her chest while she took several steps backward until she entered the small street that bordered the north side of the furniture store, parallel to the darkened alley where the gunman stood waiting, and perpendicular to Jefferson Street, where he obviously expected to find his prey.

Clutching her skirts, she hurried along the side of the furniture store until she finally reached Jefferson Street. From there, she could see the sheriff's office, still more than a block away. Fortunately, the office stood in the opposite direction from the alley where the gunman waited.

Thinking she was far enough away from the alley to be well out of the gunman's sight, she lifted her skirts even higher and hurried across the dimly lit street, crossing at an angle. She was near the opposite board-walk, where she hoped to blend into the spotted shadows created by the huge, spreading trees that cloaked the courthouse yard, when she glanced back to see if the darkly clad gunman had entered the street yet.

She did not see him, but seconds before she turned to face forward again, she noticed another man coming out of one of the saloons across the street from the alley where the gunman stood. The man from the saloon stopped to take a deep breath of cool, night air then started down the boardwalk in her direction.

When Leona glanced back again seconds later, she saw the dark shape of a man move out from the blackened shadows near the alley entrance. The dark specter stepped slowly into the street, until he stood even with the sidewalk in the front of the furniture store. She could tell he still held the pistol in his right hand, the barrel pointed skyward while resting lightly against his shoulder.

She froze within the dappled shadows of the courtyard trees, unable to do more than watch in horror while the culprit slowly and carefully lowered the gun until the barrel pointed directly into the back of the tall, thin man who had just come out of the saloon. The intended victim was still headed in Leona's direction. He was now less than a block away and he appeared to be unarmed.

With the quiet, agile movements of a cat stalking its prey, the dark gunman took several slow, deliberate steps toward the other man, following him at a distance of forty feet, the pistol still leveled at his back.

Knowing the poor man from the saloon had no idea he was being stalked by a cold, decisive gunman, she shouted a strangled warning, directing the hapless stranger to run for cover.

Puzzled by the woman's wild cry, Zeb glanced back over his shoulder to see what she might be shouting about, and saw Lathe with his weapon already drawn. Then Zeb made a wild dash in Leona's direction. One shot was fired and kicked up a puff of dirt just inches from his moving feet.

Before Leona realized what had happened, Zeb had her by the hair and had slung her around for protection, facing her forward in an attempt to use her as a human shield. Leona was confused and frightened

25

when suddenly she felt the cold blade of a knife press firmly against the throbbing base of her throat.

"Don't shoot again, Caldwell." The man cried out, so close to Leona's ear the harsh sound made her cringe. "You do and this pretty little lady gets her throat cut wide open. You're not the type to live with something like that on your conscience, are you?"

Lathe did not respond. Nor did he make a threatening move. He simply stood there, his pistol trained on the two, an evil hatred glinting from the pale blue pools of his eyes. Only his breathing could be heard above the trickle of music and laughter that drifted from the saloons beyond, and that breathing came out in sharp, rapid gusts.

He waited for Leona's captor to make another move.

"What are you anyway?" the man who held Leona in a painful grip asked, his tone disbelieving. "You part bloodhound or somethin'? How the hell did you find me so quick? I figgered it would be several weeks before I had to worry about you again."

"When I realized you'd spotted me, I knew you'd make a run for it. The ruse with that plump little saloon girl in Jefferson just didn't work. I knew she was just pretending to be entertaining you in her room all that time. That's why I decided I'd do better to watch the back window instead of the hall door."

"If that's what you did, why didn't you just go ahead and get the drop on me the minute I slipped out of Heather's room? After all, last night was the closest you've come in quite some time."

Lathe's blue eyes glinted with the anger that consumed him, offering a glittering contrast to his black clothing. "Because I didn't make it outside into the back alley in time. You were already down the drainspout and running toward the river like a rabbit with its tail on fire by the time I'd rounded the

26

building and caught a clear view of you."

The muscles in his finely honed jaw pumped in and out while a black fury slowly consumed him.

"I admit I was in a hurry," Zeb chuckled, obviously delighted at how it must have frustrated Lathe to have come so close yet again. "Too bad you was so slow at gettin' outside—too bad for you, and too bad for this here little lady." He gave Leona's hair another sharp tug to indicate whom he meant. Her hairpins fell out and scattered down upon the planked boardwalk at their feet. "Now you just toss that fancy pistol of yours over here real gentle-like so me and her can be on our way."

At that moment Sheriff Lindsey appeared from another alley a little further down the street. The rifle he carried was also pointed toward Zeb and Leona. He never moved his gaze off Zeb's face while he made several slow, steady steps toward them. When he stopped, he was about as far away as Lathe, but on the opposite side of the street, facing them.

"Better rethink your situation, Turner," Sheriff Lindsey called out, his voice deep and deadly calm. Though he was several inches shorter than the other two men, his shorter height in no way hindered his determination. "So happens, there are two of us out here. You see, Caldwell had a lot better sense than to try to take you alone this time. Now drop that knife before I decide to blow that ugly face of yours well into the next county."

It was then Leona realized just how badly she had misjudged the situation. The man who held the knife to her throat was the bad one and the tall stranger who stood glaring at them with an almost demonic expression on his darkly handsome face was working with the sheriff in some effort to apprehend him.

Zeb pressed the flat of the knife blade harder against Leona's throat while he considered his options.

27

He didn't much like the odds, now that there were two against one, especially when both of his opponents were armed with heavy firearms and all he had with him at the moment was one lousy buckknife and a frightened female hostage. Still, he knew that a hanging rope waited for him if he did what they wanted and simply gave up.

He frowned when he realized he could become just as dead either way. And because he was as good as dead no matter what he did, there was not much point in simply giving up and letting them haul him off to jail. He would rather go down fighting. If only he had thought to carry his rifle into the saloon with him. But how could he have known Lathe would be back on his trail that quick?

"You'd better rethink your own situation, sheriff," Zeb responded, still frantically searching for a way out. "If you shoot me, you'd be the same as killin' this here innocent bystander because I'm sure goin' to slit her pretty little throat wide open if I see as much as a finger move on either one of you."

Aware that he had caused the sheriff a moment's pause, Zeb stepped backward, dragging a terrified Leona with him. He pulled her toward one of several horses that lined the west side of the street. With the knife still pressed firmly against Leona's throat, he ordered her to climb into the saddle.

"And set yourself astride," he added in afterthought. "None of that sideways sittin'. We've got us some hard ridin' ahead of us."

With the steel blade against her tender flesh, Leona felt no inclination to argue. She put aside any modesty as she quickly lifted her skirts to her knees then swung herself into the saddle. While attempting to do exactly what he wanted, and without acquiring any new openings to her throat, Leona noticed that the large bearded man she had spoken to earlier now stood at the opposite end of the street, a block and a half away. Motionlessly, he stared at them in horror.

She noticed that he also now wore a pistol, but there was not much good it would do anyone still stuffed in his holster. But in all fairness, he was too far away to get a clear shot anyway. If he tried to shoot at them from there, she could end up being the one with an unexpected hole in her side.

After she settled into the badly worn saddle, she noticed a rifle jutting from its holster, held in place by only one, thin leather tie. She also noticed that the knife had been lowered from her throat and was now pressed against her side, where it would have to go through three layers of clothing before causing any real damage. Yet before she could summon enough courage to make an attempt for the rifle, Zeb had the reins in his free hand and had swung up behind her.

He immediately returned the knife to his favored spot near the base of her throat and Leona felt his hot, liquored breath against her neck when he bent forward to get a tighter grip on the reins. In the next second he had turned the horse and prodded it into a fast gallop toward the outskirts of town.

After they had traveled one block beyond where Lathe and the sheriff stood watching helplessly, Zeb glanced back to be sure they had not moved. When he did, Leona felt the knife drop away from her throat again. He now held it several inches in front of her.

Fearing what the man might do after they were alone, and sensing that this would be her last chance to escape while there were people still around to help her, Leona bent forward and bit into the gritty wrist, just inches above the hand that held the knife. The second Zeb jerked the arm back, yelping with pain, she threw herself from the horse. Angered that she would try such a thing, Zeb made a wild slash at her as she fell.

29

The blade sliced deeply into her back.

Leona screamed, shocked that he had managed to react so quickly. In the next second, she felt the side of her head and her right shoulder strike the hard ground simultaneously. Dazed from the fall and from the realization that she had just been stabbed, she did not move.

Instead, she lay on the gravel street, staring in stunned silence at Scraps, who was squatting between a hitching rail and the raised boardwalk, only a few dozen yards away, chewing happily on a large soup bone. He stopped his incessant gnawing long enough to glance at her, his head tilted to one side as if unable to understand his mistress's sudden inclination to lie in the middle of the street.

Lathe watched the incident in horrified silence, undecided what he should do next. A part of him wanted to climb onto his horse and chase Zeb into the night, aware he had never come quite that close to apprehending him; but another part of him felt obligated to stay and see how serious the woman's injuries might be.

Seeing that the sheriff was already headed for his horse only a half block away, and knowing he would be right behind Zeb while he tried to flee town; and believing the woman's injuries were partly if not entirely his fault, Lathe made his decision. He hurried to where the young woman lay crumpled in the middle of the street, dust still settling around her.

Noticing that the upper back portion of her dress was soaked with blood, he knelt down to examine that injury first.

Without moving her for fear she could have broken bones with jagged edges, he reached for the ragged tear near her right shoulder and ripped the garment wider so he could get a better look at the wound. He was so lost in thought, still wishing he had not felt so obligated to help this woman, it did not occur to him he should speak.

"How dare you!" Leona gasped, coming immediately out of her daze as effectively as if she had been slapped. Propping on her right elbow, she tried to wrench herself from his grasp but his grip tightened on her uninjured shoulder until it was almost as painful as the burning sensation from the knife wound. For the moment she gave up the struggle and simply glowered at him, still too confused to realize he meant only to help.

The sheriff had already climbed onto a tall buckskin horse similar to Lathe's and had headed off after Zeb. George Parkinson, the man she had mistaken earlier for her brother, Ethan, was racing toward them as fast as his stocky legs would allow, to see if he could help in any way. Several people inside the saloons had heard the commotion and now stood in knots near the front doors, trying to figure out what had happened.

"She obviously doesn't have any broken bones or she could never fight me like that," Lathe observed to the husky newcomer who had just asked if he needed any help. "But she does have a pretty bad cut there."

Without warning, Lathe then reached beneath Leona's skirts and tore away the ruffled hem of her cotton petticoat. He was so immersed in his efforts to stop her bleeding, he ignored her shrieks of indignation and quickly folded the white strip of cloth into a large square then pressed it firmly against the wound. He would have to stop the bleeding before he could get an accurate assessment of the damage.

When the small cloth filled immediately with blood, he glanced at Ethan, his expression drawn with mounting concern. The wound looked to be only a few inches wide, but was bleeding at an alarming rate. "Does this town have a doctor?"

"Used to," Ethan answered before realizing that

such an answer would indicate he had been there before. "I remember Doc Owen used to have an office over on the next street, right between the bank and the undertaker. I reckon he's still there."

Having thought the man a stranger to Little Mound, Leona wondered how he knew that, but at the moment she had too many other concerns to question him. "No, Doc Owen died last fall. We don't have a doctor anymore, although we are trying to get one," she said.

"Well, this wound needs immediate attention," Lathe stated grimly, wishing it had been a minor cut so he could have felt right about leaving her in someone else's care. He was eager to head out after Zeb. But because he still felt the incident was as much his fault for having confronted Zeb in town as it was hers for having interfered the way she had, all he could do was hope the local sheriff proved competent enough to capture the killer alone. If only the deputy hadn't gone out of town this week. Then there could have been two of them on Zeb's trail. But as it was, one would have to do.

Aware that Zeb's capture was out of his hands now, Lathe glanced again at Ethan, a deep frown still etched on his face. "She's losing a lot of blood and fast. The wound doesn't appear to be all that deep, but it still needs to be cleaned, stitched closed, then tightly bandaged so she will stop all that bleeding."

"Stitched closed?" Leona cried out in alarm. She stretched her neck to try to see this gruesome wound herself, grimacing when the movement increased the sharp burning sensation near her shoulder.

"Yes," Lathe continued. He pushed against the edges of the wound, trying to see if he could close it with just the gentle pressure of his fingers. "I'll need a sturdy sewing needle and some very stout sewing thread."

"You plan to sew it shut yourself?" she asked, staring at him over her shoulder with a look of horrified disbelief. The man had not bothered to shave in at least two days and was dressed in a pair of dusty black trousers, wore a threadbare black shirt, and smelled as if he had ridden a sweating horse for several months without once stopping for a much-needed bath. Clearly, he was not a doctor and she certainly didn't want him pretending to be one with her.

Anxiously, she looked at Scraps, hoping the flea-bitten mongrel might realize her distress and come to her rescue, but the worthless beast had turned his attention back to the large bone he had purloined.

Knowing that the normally protective animal would prove no help to her that night, and eager to get as far away from this madman as possible before he did something to cause her even worse injury, she twisted just hard enough to free her shoulder from his grasp. Without pause, she pushed herself to her feet. She *had* to make a run for safety.

When she glimpsed the crowd still gathering on the sidewalk, she decided to go there for protection. Surely someone among them would do something to save her.

"Stop! Don't try to stand," Lathe warned her. His frown deepened when he realized she had no intention of listening to him. "You're only going to make your injuries worse. You have already lost a lot of blood. You very well could—" He broke his warning short and stumbled to his feet in time to catch her just when her legs gave out.

Having lost consciousness, she had become so much dead weight causing Lathe to ease his rebellious patient back to the ground. He was careful to position her on her left side so the knife wound did not touch anything.

"Mule-headed woman," he muttered, thinking she

33

would do far better and probably live a lot longer if she would stop to think through matters before acting on them. "Well, since there's no doctor around here, we probably should carry her on home and try to do something for her ourselves," he commented, then glanced at Ethan and asked, "Do you happen to know where she lives? I wonder if she has any parents or perhaps a husband we should send for."

Realizing that he was not supposed to have such information, Ethan quickly shook his head. "I only met her a little while ago. I don't even know what her name is. All I know is that she's got a brother named Ethan that's dead, and a dog named Scraps that's not."

As if the mere mention of his name had been a summons, Scraps picked up his bone and moved several feet closer, but remained cautiously out of reach. He continued to gnaw happily on the oversized bone, but at the same time kept a curious watch on the two men hovering over his mistress.

By that time, several of the people from the gathering crowd had moved closer, eager to find out what had happened.

"Hey, mister," Ethan called out to one of the closest bystanders, all the while keeping his head low and his face turned away and protected from the dim glow of the nearest street lamp so his hat threw a dark shadow across his face. "This young lady has been badly hurt. Do any of you happen to know where she lives?"

"Sure do," the man answered, stepping a few feet closer. "That's Miss Leona Stegall. Everybody knows where she lives. She lives over on Maple Street." He pointed to a nearby cross-street and gave further directions, and added, "It's a big white house with dark blue shutters and a tall wrought-iron fence that stands about as high as your head. It's been painted dark blue to match. Hard to miss."

Lathe's eyebrows drew into a questioning frown.

"Since you know the way, maybe you could help me carry her. That way I could get her there safer and a lot faster," he suggested, not certain he had understood every turn and aware that one person could never carry the woman that far without causing further damage. Her injured shoulder needed to be braced against something solid while she was transported, therefore it would take at least two people to get her there.

The man's eyes widened at the thought of having to help carry a bleeding Leona Stegall all the way to her house. He glanced around to see who was close enough to hear him try to get out of it.

"Nah, that won't be necessary," Ethan quickly put in, saving the man from embarrassment. He wanted to help Lathe carry her himself.

Even though Lathe was the very man he had been sent to capture, and Ethan knew he should be looking for a means to do just that, right now, his first concern was for his sister. "The house shouldn't be that hard to find. I'll help you tote her."

The dark, burly man would be much stronger and undoubtedly more steady than the man who had just stumbled out of the nearby saloon, so Lathe quickly agreed. "All right, friend. But we need to hurry. Grab her feet."

While Ethan moved to do just that, Lathe glanced again at the man who had given them directions. "Will there be anyone at the house to let us inside?"

" 'Fraid not. Miss Leona lives alone. But chances are the door won't be locked anyway. Nobody on that side of town ever locks their doors. No real need in it."

Ethan thought it odd that Leona now lived in the house alone but did not dare ask the man where her parents had gone. He did not want to appear overly curious about a young woman who was supposed to be little more than a stranger to him, especially after having already recognized three of the dozen or so faces in the crowd.

"Hurry up and get hold of those feet," Lathe complained, already having sat Leona up and turned her so she faced away from him. "We don't have any more time to waste. She's losing too much blood. She may be as stubborn as a twenty-year-old mule when it comes to accepting help when it's offered, and awfully quick to put her nose in where it doesn't belong, but she doesn't deserve to die because of it."

Lathe eased his muscular arms under hers then gripped his wrists in front of her to form a strong, human band. He supported her injured shoulder with his chest while he waited for Ethan to bend down and help carry her.

Ethan gave the studious dog a wary look. "We're goin' to take her on home now," he said in a loud voice, as if he thought it best they explain every move to the watchful canine. Slowly, he bent forward again, wrapped his massive hands around Leona's ankles, and stood at the same time Lathe stood. With Lathe supporting most of her weight, keeping the shoulder pressed firmly against his chest, Ethan adjusted her skirts so they would not drag the ground nor would her ankles show. Then he turned to face forward and they began the awkward trek down the street.

Several onlookers followed as far as Cypress Street, but only a couple proved curious enough to accompany them as far as Main. By the time they had reached Pine Street, there were just the four of them: Lathe, Ethan, Leona—and Scraps.

When they finally reached the house, Ethan transferred both of Leona's ankles to one massive hand then used the other to turn the doorknob. Frowning to discover that the front door was indeed locked, he reached above a nearby window frame and instantly produced a small key.

"How'd you know where to find the key?" Lathe asked, thinking it odd a stranger would know such a thing.

"Ethan's eyes widened when he realized what he had done. "I didn't know for sure that's where I'd find it. It's just that my Aunt Nell has a big fancy house like this one and she keeps her key hidden above the ledge on the window frame so I figured that might be where a lot of people kept their keys."

Lathe decided that made sense enough. "Then hurry up and unlock that door so we can get her inside." He was eager to do something to save this young woman's life. Although he still resented her earlier interference, he could not bear the thought of letting her die. A woman as beautiful and full of spirit as this one deserved a long, healthy life.

While Ethan slipped the key into the lock, Lathe wondered who else would hate to see this beautiful young woman die. If she lived alone, there was no husband; but what about a sweetheart? As beautiful and spirited as this one was, she probably had several sweethearts who would mourn her death for years to come. He had to save her.

Ethan breathed a quick sigh of relief when he heard the lock give way but when he turned the knob again, he discovered the door still would not budge. "Must be bolted from the inside."

"Then how'd she ever get out, climb through a window?"

Ethan stared at the stubborn door with a puzzled frown. "Must be somebody in there after all. Probably why so many lights are on."

He knocked loudly, but there was no response.

"We don't have time for this," Lathe muttered, aware by the warm spread of stickiness across his chest that his own shirt was completely soaked with her blood. Every precious minute counted.

37

"Kick the door in. We can repair the damage later."

Ethan glanced around to see where that dog was, afraid the animal might not take too kindly to having his mistress's door kicked in; but a quick scan revealed that the animal had gone. Relieved, he gently set his sister's feet down then lifted his boot high and with one swift movement, kicked the door open with a loud, splintering crack.

Tossing the key onto a small table inside the door, he bent to grab Leona's feet again then proceeded to help Lathe carry her inside.

As soon as they had entered the entrance hallway, they discovered that same dog sitting in the middle of a nearby doorway, his head cocked at a curious angle.

"I guess the back door must be open," Ethan observed, grinning back at Lathe. "We're probably going to have a hard time explaining that busted front door to this gal after she's come to."

"We only broke the bolt latch. She can still lock the thing if she wants," Lathe muttered, thinking that the least of his worries. "See if you can figure out where the dining room is. I could work a lot better if we could put her on a table," he ordered. Then as if the man knew right where to find the room, Ethan turned toward the door nearest where Scraps stood and started walking. Since Lathe still supported the other end of the patient, he had little choice but to follow.

After Ethan quickly cleared the dining table with his free hand, they placed Leona face down so Lathe could examine her injuries more easily.

"See if you can find a sewing basket," Lathe said, already rolling his sleeves to his elbows.

Within minutes Ethan had returned with Leona's sewing basket. "Anything else?"

When Lathe glanced at him questioningly, Ethan

shrugged. "All I had to do was find the parlor. Didn't you know that most ladies keep their sewing in the parlor?"

"Never gave it much thought," Lathe muttered as he flipped the sewing basket open so he could look inside. "Go wash your hands. All the way up to your elbows. With soap. The kitchen is right through that door. Then come back here and help hold her still while I try to stitch that wound closed."

Normally it would have bothered Ethan to be ordered around like that, but considering the circumstances, he did exactly as he was told. He hurried into the kitchen and was momentarily taken back when he noticed the familiar canisters on the cabinets and the familiar plates sitting in the sink.

He remembered the day his mother had brought those dishes with the matching canisters home. How proud she had been of her new dishes. They had come all the way from England and had a thick edge of gold.

Ignoring the ache that filled his heart while again he wondered about his parents, Ethan hurriedly stopped the sink and pumped the water he needed to wash his hands.

He considered wiping his wet hands on the curtains just above the sink, but remembered how angry that had always made his mother. Instead, he flapped them in the air to dry them while he hurried back into the dining room.

When he entered the well-lit room, he found Lathe methodically stripping Leona of her clothing. At first, he felt annoyed that the man thought it perfectly all right to take such liberties, but he soon realized that Lathe's concerned gaze remained on the seeping wound near her shoulder.

"Help me get these filthy clothes off her," Lathe muttered, awkwardly trying to lift her off the table and remove her clothing at the same time. "That wound needs a clean environment."

Ethan quickly took over the task of holding Leona up off the table while Lathe finished peeling away all her outer clothing. When they had her down to just her blood-soaked camisole and her bloomers, Lathe ordered Ethan to let her back down. "Gently."

Taking the scissors from the sewing kit, Lathe then cut away the ruined camisole and began to cleanse the skin surrounding the wound using fresh water and one of the dish towels he had located in the kitchen. Soon the large bowl of water he had drawn earlier was bright red with Leona's blood.

And still there was blood to be wiped away.

"The only way I'm going to get that thing to stop bleeding is to cauterize it," Lathe finally said, then reached for another small hand towel. Quickly he pressed the folded cloth over the wound. "Here, hold that tightly against her while I find something I can cauterize it with."

Ethan put his massive hand over the folded towel and held it pressed firmly in place while Lathe disappeared into the kitchen.

"Hurry, mister," Ethan called out, aware he should not call Lathe by name nor should he know that he was a trained doctor. They had not yet taken the time to introduce themselves. Lathe had been far too concerned over his patient's welfare to offer any small talk. "She's still bleedin' awful bad."

"It will be a few more seconds," Lathe called back. His voice revealed his frustration. "I have to get this knife red hot first."

When a minute later, he did reenter the dining room, he carried a large carving knife. The blade was black from having been held over a wood flame.

"Glad she didn't bother to put out the fire in her stove after she'd heated that kettle of water," he muttered while he hurried across the room to apply the heated metal before it had much time to cool. "It would have taken forever to get this utensil hot enough to do any good over a regular lamp flame."

Ethan had to close his eyes when the doctor slowly removed first his hand then lifted the stained towel away from Leona's shoulder. He kept them pressed closed while Lathe quickly placed the dull side of the hot blade against the wound. Ethan could not bear to see something that painful performed on his own sweet sister.

When he smelled the acrid stench of searing flesh and heard Leona whimper despite her unconsciousness, his stomach clenched and he became so unsteady that he finally had to sit on a nearby dining chair to keep from passing out. He thought it odd he should react like that when he had seen far worse injuries during the war.

"Did that do the trick?" he asked after several deep breaths of air, not yet ready to look at the wound in order to make his own assessment.

"I think so. She's not bleeding nearly as badly as she was. But I still need to secure it with several stitches." When he looked at Ethan and saw how pale he had become, he frowned. "I'll need you to help hold her down. Judging by the way she jerked when I put that hot blade to her, she will probably try to fight every little stitch I take."

Ethan swallowed hard then stood to help; but rather than look at the wound, he watched the concentration that drew Lathe's face into an intense frown. He was impressed by the man's professionalism and wondered how someone could seem so truly concerned for his patient and also be a murderer.

It just didn't make sense to Ethan. Instead of taking off after Zeb as he'd undoubtedly wanted to do, Lathe had stayed to help save Leona's life. And rather than take advantage of Leona's partial nakedness, which he easily could have done, Lathe had concentrated solely on her injuries. He had never once allowed her breasts to be exposed to either's view. Since entering that house, Lathe's sole concern had been to try to stop Leona's bleeding.

Ethan felt strongly grateful. Had it not been for Lathe, Leona would have bled to death by now. As it was, she still could die; but not because this man had not tried his very best to save her.

Ethan thought that in itself was commendable, considering she was the very person who had caused Lathe to lose Zeb yet again. Still, Lathe had shown no real resentment toward her. Only concern. That heightened Ethan's opinion of the man considerably.

Although Ethan would still have to follow through on his orders to capture Lathe and hold him against his will until the captain had time to arrive, he would be forever grateful to Lathe for what he had done. He would try his level best to convince the captain not to kill him outright — but instead allow him to stand trial for the terrible thing he had done. Perhaps there were extenuating circumstances no one yet knew about, circumstances that could be brought out during the course of a real trial.

"The laceration itself isn't nearly as deep as I thought it would be," Lathe commented while quickly threading a needle. "But it still needs a few stitches to make sure it stays closed while it heals. Better keep one hand on her good shoulder and one across the small of her back. If she tries to fight the pain, it will be up to you to hold her still."

Chapter Three

Lathe bent low to take his third stitch then glanced up at Ethan with a curious expression while he gently pulled the thread through her skin. Now that the bleeding had stopped, he felt more relaxed and started to notice his surroundings more. "You know, you look awfully familiar to me. Have I see you somewhere before?"

Ethan blinked. It had been over two years since that night Lathe had come out of his room and bumped smack dab into him. Could he possibly remember such a short, momentary meeting? And if he did, did he also remember that just a few hours later, someone had tried to jump him in the very same hallway of that very same hotel?

Ethan grimaced at the memory of his second failed attempt. If only that little girl had not come out of her room at the exact wrong moment and then screamed her fool head off. He had already knocked Lathe out with the butt of his rifle and had already started to drag him down the hall toward his own room. Had that little girl not come out and caused such a commotion when she did, he would have been able to turn Lathe over to the captain that very next morning and been done with it. As it was, he *still* didn't have him. Not really. And he sure didn't plan to make another move on the man until he was absolutely certain his sister's life was completely out of danger. Leona's well being was far more important than fulfilling his duty to Captain Potter.

"Not unless you've spent some time up in the Ozarks," he finally answered, thinking that an unlikely place for Lathe to have ever been. "Although I spent most of my time up in the mountains themselves trappin' wild game, I did manage to come to town now and then to sell the hides I'd tanned and to get me a woman. Man can't go too long without the comforts of a good woman. Ever been up to the Ozarks?"

"No, I've never been up that way," Lathe admitted, his brows still pulled together as if still wondering why Ethan looked so familiar. After looping the black thread into a tiny knot, he reached for the scissors and clipped it close to the wound. "But I can't get over the feeling that I've met you somewhere before."

"Probably because most mountain men tend to look a lot like me," Ethan said, gesturing to his long hair and thick beard with a quick wave of his hand. Because Lathe had set the needle aside, he no longer felt it necessary to continue holding Leona's shoulder. "Men who spend most of their time up in the mountains don't bother gettin' their hair cut or their faces shaved too often." *Neither do men hot on the trail of a murderer,* he thought, though he wisely kept that remark to himself. "The name is George. George Parkinson."

He decided to stick to the same moniker he had used with Leona.

"My name is Lathe Caldwell. I'm originally from Alabama," Lathe said, bending low again to examine the tiny black stitches.

Ethan wondered why he had bothered to tell him the truth when he had used the name Jonathan Creel at the hotel then realized his reason for secrecy was seated on a horse, riding hard, already headed for the next county.

"What is it that you trap, George?" Lathe asked while he carefully tested the wound's tolerance with a gentle touch of his finger to an area nearby. He wanted to be sure the stitches would hold.

"You mean what *did* I trap," Ethan corrected him. "I don't trap no more. Gave it up a few months ago. Decided it was time I saw more of the world."

"Well then, what *did* you trap?"

"Bear and bobcat mostly," he answered, thinking those two animals to be as likely as any.

Aware he was finished with the needle, Lathe picked it up and put it back into the sewing kit then slowly stretched the taut muscles in his back. "Is there a good market for bear and bobcat hides?"

"Sure there is. There's also a good bounty on the bobcats. Paid me good enough I could afford to pack up and head south. Always wanted to see what Texas was like." Then to turn the focus of conversation away from him—before he said something that might signify he was lying—he looked down at his sister's pale, lifeless form and asked, "How is she?"

"Hard to say," Lathe admitted. "As you well know, she's lost a critical amount of blood." He pulled at his own wet shirt to prove it. "But at least we've managed to stop any further bleeding and her pulse rate is still pretty strong." He then turned her head to face the opposite direction and pushed her hair back with his fingers to examine a large bruise he had noticed earlier on her right cheek. Now that the main crisis was over and his own heart rate had settled into a more normal rhythm, he took the time to

45

notice not only her scratches and bruises but also how extremely attractive she was.

Except for the slight swelling around the main bruise itself, she had perfect features. Her slightly upturned nose was delicately shaped as was her chin and narrow jawline, and she had a high, aristocratic forehead. Her skin was pale from the loss of blood but smooth as silk and her hair was a rich, lustrous brown, although now, the strands that had fallen where the pins had held them in place were splattered with her blood. He then noticed her long, feathery dark eyelashes that lay against the high curve of her delicate cheekbones and he wondered what color her eyes might be.

He also wondered why such a beautiful young woman dressed in such tasteful clothing, who lived in such a nice house in what appeared to be a respectable part of town had been out alone in the most bawdy area of Little Mound so late in the evening. She certainly wasn't a saloon girl, nor did she look the type who would ever step inside one of those places for any reason.

"I will need a sheet or something thin like that to tear into bandages," he said, still wondering why she had been out on South Jefferson after dark. "Since you seem so adept at finding things, why don't you make a quick search and see if you can discover where she stores her linens. I'll clean up some of this mess and try to wash some of this blood out of her hair while you are gone."

When Ethan returned several minutes later, he was unfolding a clean white sheet. "Turns out she keeps her sheets downstairs. Although there are two big bedrooms upstairs, she evidently uses the one that's downstairs." He knew why—it had been her bedroom when they were growing up. Evidently

46

she had never found a reason to leave it.

"Then that's probably where we should put her after I finish with the bandages." Lathe took the sheet, picked up the scissors, then clipped the hemmed edge twice. He then tore the sheet straight across until he had two long strips of cloth several inches wide and several feet long. He quickly rolled the two strips into small cylinders so he could manage the cloth more easily then took several straight pins out of the sewing basket and notched them into his sleeve where he could get to them more easily.

"Hold her up off the table while I bandage her," he said, waiting until Ethan had obliged before reaching around Leona and quickly wrapping her with the cloth. Although her breasts had been momentarily exposed, neither Ethan nor Lathe had taken advantage of the fact. They both focused their attention elsewhere.

As soon as the improvised bandage was in place, covering her breasts as well as the freshly stitched wound just below her right shoulder, Lathe asked Ethan to turn her over gently so he could examine the front of her body for further cuts and bruises.

Quickly and adeptly, he felt her arms and legs, and although he found several more bruises and scrapes, he decided his original assessment had been correct. There were no broken bones.

"Pretty tough little lady," he said, his voice reflecting his admiration when he remembered how bravely she had reacted to the very frightening situation. Most women would have fainted dead away, but this one had kept a cool head and when she saw her one opportunity to escape, she took it.

"Yes, she is," Ethan agreed, smiling proudly at his little sister. He wanted to comment that she always had been the brave sort, but caught himself before

47

the revealing words actually came forth. "Think we should put her to bed now?"

"I suppose we'd better. Which way is that bedroom?" he asked, then frowned at the thought of putting her clean bandage against his still sticky wet shirt. "Maybe you'd better carry her." As an added precaution, he draped what remained of the sheet over Ethan's shirt before he bent forward to lift her off the table.

Several minutes later, they had Leona tucked away into bed, a cool compress over the swollen bruise near her cheek.

While Lathe slowly removed the last of her hairpins then gently brushed her hair away from her face to make her more comfortable, Ethan glanced around at the painfully familiar room. He bit deep into his lower lip when he noticed one of the letters he had written to Leona shortly after he had joined the Confederate Army. It had been placed in a glass frame and was hanging on the wall near the door.

How close they had been when they were younger. There had never been anything they couldn't confide in each other. Until now.

It took all the resolve Ethan had to keep the tears from his eyes.

With the work finally done and him still very close to tears over the sudden realization of everything he had lost, Ethan decided it was time to get the heck out of there—before any more painful memories were forced to the surface. Quickly, he mumbled a few inane excuses and started for the door.

"Wait a minute," Lathe called out, aware he was about to be left alone with his new patient. "Just because she's resting peacefully right now doesn't mean something can't go wrong later tonight.

Somebody needs to stay here with her."

"Can't be me," Ethan stated adamantly, then quickly searched his brain for a plausible lie. "I was supposed to meet an old friend of mine at the hotel hours ago. I'm going to have a hard enough time explaining the reason I'm so late as it is. Why it's almost midnight."

"But I need to go to the sheriff's office and find out if he caught the man who did this to her." He had to know what had happened.

Ethan took a quick breath at the unsettling reminder that Zeb had been the one to do this terrible thing. "Sorry. I can't stay."

"Can you at least drop a note by the sheriff's office for me?" he asked, hurrying toward a small desk in the far corner of the room. Quickly, he searched the drawers until he found a sharpened pencil and a scrap of paper.

"Here," he said when he had finished, then quickly folded the page in half and handed it to Ethan. "If the sheriff isn't there, pin it to his door where he'll be sure to spot it." He then handed him one of the straight pins still notched in his sleeve.

Aware that it was the least he could do for the man who had just saved his sister's life, Ethan accepted the note and promised to see that the sheriff got it. When he headed out the door, he wished there was more he could do for Lathe, but knew he would be putting his own neck on the line if he did not fulfill his duties exactly as they had been given him.

While he hurried along the empty street toward the sheriff's office, he continued to ponder everything that had happened that night. Lathe's decision to stay and help Leona had truly baffled him. Why hadn't he gone off after Zeb instead? After all, Lathe

49

Caldwell had been chasing after that man for nearly five years now. Why had he allowed his concern for Leona's welfare to get in the way of that? Why should he have cared if she lived or died? Why should he have cared about anything but the fact that he had finally caught up with Zeb?

Yet instead of chasing after Zeb Turner as most men would have done, he had stayed behind to save a life. Leona's life.

It was simply hard for Ethan to believe that Lathe Caldwell, whom the captain had claimed to be a cold, heartless murderer, was the same man who had just fought so intensely to save a stranger's life.

Ethan decided there must be some good in everybody. And there was just enough good left in Lathe Caldwell for Ethan to allow him to remain a free man a little while longer — at least until his sister was out of danger. From what he had learned about the man in the many years he had been tracking him, Lathe really was a doctor. He had graduated from Yale at the top of his class. He had also served as a surgeon in a prisoner of war camp during most of the Civil War, taking care of the sick and the wounded. That meant he was probably the only person in Little Mound who would know what to do for Leona should any complications arise.

Because of that, Ethan decided not to send word to the captain just yet. He would wait to announce that he had again caught up with the man who had killed the captain's younger brother, at least until he was certain Leona would not need any more medical attention.

Lathe paced the floor restlessly. He was torn between the obligation he felt toward his unwanted patient and the duty he felt toward his dead brother.

The doctor in him believed he should stay with

the injured woman until he was certain she was out of danger, but the vengeful brother in him wanted to leave her behind to fend for herself—at least leave her long enough so he could find out if the sheriff had managed to capture Zeb Turner.

Although George Parkinson had agreed to leave a note with the sheriff, informing him of Lathe's whereabouts, Lathe really did not trust George. There was just something about the man, something about the way he had refused to look him in the eye that made Lathe think him unreliable.

"Damn," he muttered while continuing to pace the floor, returning to the window often to see if anyone might be riding along the street.

Several hours later, only minutes after the clock in the main hall had struck twice, he heard a lone horse clopping up the street. He hurried to the window and sighed with annoyed relief when a horse and rider appeared along the small section of road that could be seen from Leona's bedroom.

Finally!

Eager to know what had happened, he hurried to the front door and jerked it open.

"Well? Did you get him?" he asked even before the sheriff had entered the house.

"No, I'm afraid not," the sheriff admitted as he pushed his hat back, a dismal frown on his tired face. The sheriff was a stout, middle-aged man, probably in his early forties, with greying brown hair and a wide, friendly smile—when he used it. At the moment, he did not have the strength nor the inclination. "He got away."

Lathe closed his eyes to keep from screaming aloud with frustration. "But you were right behind him. You left just minutes after he did."

"I know and I did get close enough to plug him

once, but even that didn't stop him. I'm not quite sure exactly where I hit him but I do know that I plugged him at least once."

"How can you be sure?" Lathe asked with intense disappointment.

"Because after I lost him I backtracked to the area where I shot at him and I saw the blood. Big splotches of it. And as bad as that man is bleeding, he's not goin' to get very far and should be leaving us a very easy trail to follow. First thing in the mornin', I'll be roundin' up a posse to ride out after him. If you want to be a part of it, you need to be at my office by seven o'clock. *Sharp.*"

"But I don't dare leave that woman alone," Lathe explained, gesturing toward the far end of the hall where Leona still lay unconscious in her bedroom. "She could become delirious and try to get up, which could cause her to fall and split that wound open again. It may not be a very deep wound, but it is definitely a bleeder and she just can't risk losing any more blood."

He ran his hand through his thick, tousled hair while he considered his predicament further. "If she was already awake, I could explain to her how very seriously she has been injured and how important it is that she stay in that bed. I wouldn't worry so much then. But I'm afraid when she wakes up she won't realize how very much blood she's lost, and will try to get up. She'll probably faint dead away if she does." He looked at the sheriff with an almost pleading expression. "Do you think you could find someone to stay with her so I *can* go with you?"

"I can't think of anyone offhand, but I'll see what I can do," he promised, then turned to leave. "Surely one of the men's wives will come look after her. I'll ask while I'm rounding up enough riders for the posse."

Lathe waited until the sheriff was back on his horse before returning to Leona's bedroom. When he did, he could not resist stopping by the bed and gazing down at his beautiful patient. A powerful surge of tenderness and protectiveness rose within him while he peered down at her sleeping face. If only she would wake up. If only he could be certain she was all right. Then he could leave that house and join the sheriff's posse with a clear conscience. But as it was, he felt trapped.

Restlessly, he moved on past the bed toward the window, believing that if the sheriff did not send someone to relieve him soon, he would surely lose his mind. He glanced at the clock and noticed the hands coming around to three o'clock and knew that in just a little over four hours the posse would leave town.

By five o'clock, Lathe had stopped his incessant pacing. He stood with his shoulder jammed against the window frame, staring determinedly at the street, as if willing someone to appear. His only movement was the constant tapping of his thumb against the side of his leg. What was keeping that sheriff? He had expected him to find someone by now. *Anyone*.

When a feeble groan sounded behind him, he turned away from the window and saw that Leona was finally waking up. He hurried to her bedside.

"Don't try to get up," he cautioned her in a soft voice when he noticed she had reached to pull back her cover, even before she had her eyes open. "You have to stay in bed."

Leona's eyes flew open with startled surprise when she realized she had heard a man's voice. For a mo-

53

ment she stared at him, confused both by her pain and by the fact there was a strange man in her bedroom.

"Who are you?" she asked, blinking while she tried to bring her blurred vision into focus. Her brown eyes then widened as her thoughts were stirred by horror-filled memories of what had occurred. She quickly tried to sit up, only to discover that any movement she made caused a sharp, burning pain to shoot through her shoulder and made the whole side of her head throb mercilessly. She bit deep into her lower lip while she eased her head back down onto her pillow. Her vision slowly cleared, but she felt as if the entire bed jumped with each pulsebeat of her heart.

"Lie still," he said, holding her in place by gently putting his hand against her uninjured shoulder. "You have some pretty serious injuries."

"You are the man from the alley," she stated matter-of-factly when at last her pain had eased enough for her to speak. She looked at him amazed. In the light of her bedroom he looked far less menacing and she decided that if he would just take the time to shave and comb his hair, he'd be downright handsome.

"Yes, I am. I am also a doctor and I had to cauterize that knife wound then stitch it closed just to get it to stop bleeding. Any abrupt movement could open it up again," he cautioned.

"A doctor? You?" she scoffed, eyeing him with immediate suspicion. Again she noted his dark attire and decided he was anything but a doctor.

"Yes, believe it or not, I am a doctor," he said, smiling in an attempt to reassure her.

Leona felt so oddly drawn to his smile, she looked away so as not to be unduly influenced by it.

54

"You're no doctor. Doctors try to save lives not take them. And doctors certainly don't go around trying to gun down people in the street."

"I wasn't planning on gunning him down. Neither was the sheriff. We just wanted to capture him and put him in jail."

Leona frowned while she stared at the ceiling and tried to remember what had happened more clearly. It was true, the sheriff had been in on it, too — and it was also true, they hadn't shot him on the spot. Finally, she looked at him again. "But why did you want to capture him? What did that man do?"

"He's wanted for murder," is all Lathe was willing to tell her. "Killed an unarmed man in cold blood."

"And I botched your attempt to capture him," Leona said, feeling wretched for her own stupidity. All her earlier hostilities drained out of her, leaving her plenty of room for regret. "I'm sorry I fouled things up like that, but when I saw you stalking the man with that gun, I thought you were the bad guy." Her gaze became dark and distant while she thought more about it. A tiny shiver skittered over her when she realized exactly how much danger she'd been in. She'd fallen into the hands of a real murderer.

"I suppose I do look pretty sinister at that," Lathe said, then grinned again when he glanced down at his trail-worn, blood-splattered clothing.

Leona focused on the long, slender dimples that embraced his wide, compelling smile and again realized that under the several days' growth of beard lay a very handsome face. She then noticed how incredibly blue his eyes were and how long his dark lashes were, before she slowly followed his distracted gaze downward, curious to see what had his attention.

When she glimpsed the hardening brown stain on his shirt and realized it was blood, her eyes widened

55

with instant alarm. "Did he hurt you, too?"

Aware of her misconception, Lathe shook his head. When he looked back into her huge brown eyes and saw how truly concerned she was, he smiled again then explained, "No, that's your blood, not mine."

Leona stared at him for a few seconds, surprised to learn she had lost that much blood. "How badly did he cut me?"

"Badly enough so you will have to stay in that bed for several days," Lathe answered truthfully.

"But I can't," she argued.

"Sorry, but you really don't have a choice."

Leona tried again to sit up, only to be met with another stab of pain so severe it forced her to lie down again. She was almost in tears when she tried to explain, "But I have to get up and get dressed. I have to open the store."

Fighting both her pain and her panic, Leona tossed her covers back, ready to prove him wrong. She gasped in horror when she realized all she had on other than her bandages was a pair of blood splattered bloomers. Quickly, she jerked the covers back into place and grimaced from both the resulting pain and mortification. "Where are my clothes?"

"In the trash. I'm afraid you ruined them."

"But, but I don't understand," she said, her eyes darting about the room in a desperate search for someone else. "Who undressed me?"

Aware of the reason behind her outrage, and knowing it would probably outrage her more to know he'd had the help of another stranger, he gave her only half the truth. "I did. I had to get to your injuries. Besides your clothes were covered with blood and dirt. You'd have wanted them off."

"You brought me here all by yourself?" she asked,

finding that hard to believe. He appeared to be strong, but not strong enough to have carried her several blocks, much less to have opened the back door with one hand while holding her with the other.

"No," he answered honestly. "I had help carrying you. A man named George Parkinson helped me bring you here. He also stayed and helped hold you down while I cauterized and stitched that wound."

She glanced around again. "Where is he now?"

"He left hours ago."

"And he didn't help undress me?" she asked, narrowing her dark brown eyes suspiciously while she continued to glare at him.

"Well, he helped a little," Lathe admitted then quickly went on to reassure her. "But we both diverted our eyes. We did nothing that would dishonor you, I assure you."

But Leona wasn't assured. She wasn't assured at all. She didn't know either man well enough to be assured by mere words that they had that much collective honor. Her faced reddened at the thought of what they might have seen, or what they might have *done* during the time she was unconscious.

Quickly, she turned the subject back to what it had been. "Even so, I still have to get up. I have to go on to the store. I at least have to open my doors. If I don't, I'll lose what few customers I have left. What time is it anyway?" She glanced toward the window to see if there was any daylight yet.

Lathe turned to look at the small clock that rested on a nearby mantel. "It's about five-thirty."

His expression hardened, aware the sun would be up soon. "Isn't there someone else you could have open this store of yours for the next few days? One of your employees perhaps?"

57

"I don't have any employees," she answered, her tone clearly bitter. "I am too far in debt right now. I had to let them all go. Occasionally a friend of mine sits with the store while I run a few errands, but I can't even afford to pay her right now. She does it because she was such a good friend of my mother's. That, and I give her scraps of material for her quilting."

"What's her name?"

"Mabel Sanford. She's an older woman. Too old to be running the store for more than a few hours at a time."

"Well, sounds to me like it's either her or no one," he pointed out, then added with finality, "You are *not* getting out of that bed."

"Oh, yes I am," she said and lifted her chin with renewed determination.

"No you *don't*," he tried again to convince her. "Give me the key to the front door and tell me where this Mrs. Sanford lives and I will see to it she opens the store for you. I will even pay her out of my own pocket," he offered, then waited. When she did not immediately reveal the whereabouts of that key, he let out an exasperated breath. "It's really the only option you have, because you are *not* leaving that bed."

"And what is to keep me from getting up the second you leave?" she asked, narrowing her dark gaze defiantly.

He had thought the pain she must surely be suffering would be enough to keep her in that bed, but obviously he had misjudged the woman's stubbornness. "The sheriff is supposed to be sending someone over to stay with you during whatever time I can't be here. That person will make sure you do exactly what you are told."

58

"And what if Sheriff Lindsey doesn't send anyone?"

"Then *I* will find someone. Either way, you will not be allowed out of that bed for several days."

"But you have no right to keep me here," she muttered, still glaring at him angrily. She was too accustomed to doing exactly what she pleased and resented his unwanted interference.

The eastern sky had already started to turn a deep dusty grey, shot through with small splashes of dull pink, and this stubborn woman was certain to get out of that bed the moment his back was turned, so Lathe finally gave up trying to be nice and told her in no uncertain terms, "I happen to have every right to keep you there. I happen to be the man who just spent several long, tedious hours cleansing and caring for that wound and I am not about to let you do anything to reinjure it. I don't relish the idea of having to redo all that hard work."

"No one asked you to do anything for me," she pointed out, narrowing her gaze and lifting her chin with childlike resentment. She knew she should be grateful for what he'd done, but for some reason all she felt at that moment was frustration and anger.

Rather than continue arguing with such an obstinate female, Lathe tossed his arms into the air and spun about to stare out the window again.

"What is keeping that sheriff," he muttered angrily. "He should have sent someone by now."

Lathe was tired from having gone two nights without sleep, and the blood-stiffened shirt felt uncomfortable against his skin. But what bothered him the most was the fact it would soon be seven o'clock. The sheriff had said they would leave at seven o'clock *sharp*. If only he could trust that fool-headed woman to have enough common sense to stay in that bed. Why couldn't she see that it was for her own good to stay put for the next few days?

When he turned to look at her again, some of his earlier anger had abated. "Look, why don't you just give me the keys to the store and tell me where to find your friend, Mrs. Sanford."

"Because it is *my* responsibility to open that store," she answered, wishing he could understand why it was so important to her. The Mercantile was now *her* obligation. It was up to *her* to see that it prospered again.

Sighing to reveal his aggravation, Lathe spun around to face the window again, and saw that the sky had now turned pale blue. Noises indicating a new day had begun to drift in through the open window.

He was rapidly running out of time. The muscles across the upper portion of his back bunched with mounting tension. He raked his hand through his hair while trying to decide what to do. He desperately wanted to be a part of that posse, yet he didn't dare leave this woman alone.

Finally, he spotted a young man who looked about eighteen or nineteen walking down the middle of the street toward town. Lathe's heart pounded with renewed hope.

"Hey, you," he shouted, startling Leona, who could not see the street from where she lay.

The young man shrugged then stepped cautiously toward the tall, wrought-iron fence that surrounded Leona's yard. "What do you want?"

"If you would like to earn five dollars for just one day's work."

"Five dollars?" he asked, his eyes widening at such an amount. He pulled off his short billed cap and tucked it under his arm when he stepped closer still.

"For just one day's work? Why that's more than I usually earn in a whole week at the feed store. What would I have to do?"

"Come inside and I'll tell you," Lathe shouted, then glanced back at Leona and smiled victoriously. "Come all the way inside. As you probably can tell, I'm in one of the back rooms."

Within seconds, the young man stood at the door to Leona's bedroom, embarrassed when he realized she was still in bed. His face reddened when he then looked at Lathe. "What is it you want me to do that pays so well?"

"I have to go into town for a little while. All you have to do is keep *that* woman from getting out of *that* bed while I'm gone," he said, already tucking the hem of his shirt back into his trousers.

"But I don't understand. Who are you?"

"I'm Lathe Caldwell, her doctor." He flattened his eyebrows when he heard Leona's derisive snort. Evidently she did not yet believe he was who he said he was. "I know I don't look like it at the moment, but I *am* a doctor. And she *is* my patient. And as her doctor, I don't want her getting out of that bed for any reason," he explained as he reached for his holster, which was draped over a nearby chair. "All you have to do to earn the full five dollars is make sure she stays put. Simple as that."

"But how?" he asked, looking at Leona's determined scowl doubtfully. "And for how long?"

Lathe also noticed Leona's obstinate glower and his expression darkened. The beautiful little hellcat was still bent on getting out of that bed, even if it killed her — which it damn well might. "I'll try to be back before nightfall. If I'm not, I'll pay you double for having to stay after dark. I'll even go by that feed store where you said you work and explain

61

things to your boss. Is it the one over on Market Street?"

He nodded that it was.

"By the way, what's your name?"

"Tony. Tony Newland."

"Well, Tony, I want you to do whatever it takes to keep her in that bed." He then took his pistol out of the holster and handed it to the boy. "Shoot her if you have to." He met her determined gaze with his own. "At least that would give me something *new* to work on when I get back."

Then, deciding even that might not stop her, he hurried about the room, muttering while he jerked bureau drawers open and snatched clothes out of them. He was still muttering when he then tossed the huge pile out the window, letting them fall into a large heap outside. "There, that ought to help keep her where we want her. All she has on at the moment are a flimsy pair of summer bloomers and her bandages."

"But I have to open the store," she complained, as frustrated as she was angry by what he'd done. How dare he make her a prisoner in her own bed.

"Where's the key?" he asked, giving her one last chance to show some common sense. "I'm still willing to run by this Mrs. Sanford's if you want."

It was her only choice and also aware her shoulder was throbbing painfully from the exertion she had placed on it during the past few minutes, so she finally admitted defeat and told him where to find the key.

After tucking the key into his pocket, he again cautioned her against attempting anything that could reopen her wound. "Take my word for it. You can't afford to lose any more blood."

Because her pain had become almost unbearable,

she knew she would never make it to the Mercantile even if she did manage to get out of that bed. But she refused to let *him* know that. She was so frustrated by her present physical limitations that she felt very close to crying, but she didn't want him to know *that* either. She wanted him to think she was tough as nails, that she didn't need him or anyone else telling her what to do. All she needed was for her shoulder and head to quit hurting.

"Don't expect to find me here when you return," she said, thrusting her chin forward in a defiant gesture. The sudden movement caused another jolt of pain so severe, it was all she could do to keep her eyes open and her gaze focused.

Lathe glanced up at the ceiling and sighed with exasperation, then returned his attention to the young man. "Remember, Tony, she is to stay in that bed the entire time I'm gone or you won't be able to collect the full five dollars. That means staying right in here with her. Therefore, before I head out with the posse, I'll —"

"Posse?" Tony responded, his eyes rounding with curiosity and awe. "You going out with the posse?"

"Yes, to catch the man who stabbed Miss Stegall last night."

"Stabbed? She's been stabbed?" He looked at her with a startled expression.

"Yes, she has. And before I leave with the posse the sheriff said will be departing at seven, I'll pay someone to bring over some pain powders. I'll also send someone with some soup or something else she can easily tolerate for lunch. I'll send enough for you, too, so you won't have to scrounge something. I don't want you leaving her alone any longer than you absolutely have to." He then glanced away to glare at Leona. "That woman does not have the good sense God gave a jackass. She's determined to get out of that bed even if it means bleeding to death."

Having said that, he spun around and stomped noisily out of the house, leaving behind a gape-mouthed young man and a scowling, but exceptionally beautiful young woman.

He had less than an hour to do everything he'd promised and still make that posse.

Chapter Four

Because Ethan was so worried about his sister, he awoke early, ate a quick breakfast at the restaurant next to the hotel, then headed straight for the freight office, which doubled as the local telegraph and post office.

Because it was important to report to the captain every few days, and it had been nearly four days since he had last sent a wire indicating his situation, Ethan decided he had better take the time to send word back to Alabama. It was part of his duty to keep Captain Potter informed of his whereabouts.

But because he did not want to get the captain's hopes up too early — still bent on waiting until Leona was completely out of danger before making any new attempts to capture Lathe — Ethan decided to keep his message vague.

"Think I have finally located our man." The telegraph operator read Ethan's message aloud to make sure he had the wording correct. "Waiting for the right moment. Will keep you informed." After Ethan nodded that it was exactly the message he wanted sent, the operator looked up at him again and asked, "You a private investigator?"

"No, I'm more like a bounty hunter," Ethan answered, thinking it was really none of the little man's business what he was, but at the same time knowing he would be rewarded for his efforts. Maybe not in money, as a real bounty hunter might, but he would be rewarded all the same.

"And what name should I put at the end?" the operator asked, lifting his pencil to insert that information at the bottom of the page.

"George Parkinson," Ethan answered quickly, already used to the name he'd given himself, then realized the captain might not know who had sent the telegraph if he signed off like that. But he didn't dare use his *real* name. Not in Little Mound. "Sign it, George *Ethan* Parkinson."

"All right Mr. Parkinson," the operator said, quickly scribbling the added notation at the bottom. "That will be eight cents."

Telegrams were always cash in advance. Ethan dug deep into his pocket for the coins. "And if there's a return message, you can leave it for me at the Traveler's Hotel. Looks like I'll be staying there for the next few days."

"Will do," the operator said with a cordial smile while he quickly tucked the change into his metal box. "Always eager to accommodate strangers."

Thinking the short message should be just enough to appease his boss, at least for now, Ethan headed next for Leona's house. *His* house, too, he thought with a distant smile, then again he wondered where his parents had gone. Why had they moved out and left the house to Leona? Was business so good these days that they had bought themselves an even nicer house? If so, where? Maybe over on Pine Street, near where Judge Thomas and Bebber Davis lived. Those were certainly nice enough houses there.

With his head filled with wistful images of his parents, Ethan decided to take a longer route back—by way of the Mercantile. Although he fully intended to keep his hat pulled low and would not go close enough to be noticed, he wanted to catch a glimpse of his mother and father. But only a glimpse. Just enough to assure himself that they were all right.

He wouldn't dare go inside. Although his appearance had changed dramatically during the past five years, he doubted it had changed quite enough to fool his own mother. He might manage to get by his father without being recognized, but never his mother. They had been too close.

Minutes later, when he passed along the boardwalk across the street and quickly glanced inside, he did not see either of his parents. The only person he noticed was an elder woman seated behind the main counter, deeply engrossed in a small book. Although she looked a little like his mother's good friend, Mabel Sanford, she was too far away to be certain.

Dismayed to find his parents gone, he next noticed how terribly understocked the shelves facing the windows looked and felt a cold fear rise from the very pit of his stomach. Suddenly he *knew*. He knew the reason his sister lived in the family house alone and the reason the store was so poorly stocked. His parents were dead. A trip to the small cemetery near the Baptist Church just outside town would undoubtedly confirm his suspicions; but he knew that was not necessary. His father would never have allowed the store to become so understocked. He would have sold everything he owned before letting that happen.

Tears sprang to Ethan's eyes. He felt suddenly weak and terribly vulnerable inside. Rather than go on to Leona's as planned, he leaned against one of the fat, angular posts that supported the awning in

67

front of Shelly's Bakery directly across the street from his parents' store. While he stared forlornly at the Mercantile, he could not stop the memories from pouring forth.

Suddenly he was eighteen again. He was young, spry, and smart as a whip, or so his father had always claimed — but far more impressionable than someone his age should have been.

At age eighteen he had faced a bright and very secure future. The money for college had already been set aside and he had an entire summer ahead of him. A whole summer in which to do nothing but gather together what items he would need for college and help his father run the Mercantile, the same Mercantile that was to be his one day. He glanced up to see if the name Stegall still hung overhead. It did. He saw the very same sign he had helped his father hang a dozen or so years earlier.

Smiling sadly, Ethan remembered the day they had hung the sign and all the trouble they'd had making it stay. His memories then drifted forward to the day George and Jason had come bursting into the store, eager to talk to him, all excited because the South had finally decided to stand up and fight for what was rightfully theirs. They were not about to let those Northerners tell *them* what to do. They were all three tired of the federal government's continued oppression and pleased to hear about the decision of the members of the Confederacy to stand their ground.

Thinking that the Civil War would be little more than a temporary inconvenience and could end up being the adventure of a lifetime to boot, the three boys joined the Confederate Army that very same afternoon, eager to do their part. In their hearts, they had truly believed that joining their neighbors

68

in the battle for justice was the right thing to do. It was the patriotic thing to do.

If only they could have seen into the future.

Ethan shook his head to dispel the bitter memories that followed. He needed to get to the house. But first, he wanted to stop off at the hardware store and buy a new latch and a handful of nails. Knowing Leona's temper, she was going to be pretty upset when she found out they had kicked her front door in, especially when she had left the back door unlocked the way she had. He hoped to have the door fully repaired before Leona ever found out what they had done.

It was a little after nine o'clock by the time Ethan finally entered the front gate. He thought it a bit odd when he glanced off into the yard and discovered Scraps sound asleep atop a large, colorful pile of clothing, but decided there had to be a logical reason for Leona to have provided the animal with such ample bedding. Leona rarely did anything without first having a logical reason. She was the type who always thought matters through. Always had been.

Although Scraps lifted his black, shaggy head long enough to find out who had entered the yard, he evidently decided Ethan offered no threat, and the dog did not even bother to bark. Instead, he lowered his hairy chin back to his folded paws, closed his eyes, and went right on back to sleep.

Ethan grinned, thinking the dog about as useless as they came, then hurried on up the front steps and knocked loudly on the front door.

He expected Lathe to be the one to open the door for him and he was surprised when instead, a strange voice called out to him from somewhere around back. He walked over to the side of the veranda that stretched across the full width of the house and looked to see who had done all that hollering.

He was further surprised to notice a young man he'd never before seen pop his head out a lower window, just above where Scraps lay snoozing. By counting back from the edge of the house, he realized it had to be one of the windows to Leona's bedroom.

"Come on in," the young man shouted again after glimpsing the small sack in his hand. "We're in one of the back rooms."

Finally, Scraps found the energy to bark, but more with annoyance from having been so rudely disturbed than from any deeply rooted desire to alert anyone of possible danger.

Shrugging, Ethan did as told. He entered through the front door, which he discovered had been pushed shut but not locked, then tossed his hat on a table near the entrance and headed straight for Leona's room.

An eerie feeling crept over him while he walked along the familiar hallway and passed the different rooms, all filled with familiar furniture, easily seen in the daylight. It felt almost as if his heart could not decide whether he had a right to be there or not.

Years ago, when he had realized that he was no longer worthy of his parents' love—nor even of Leona's love—he had sworn he would never return to Little Mound again—never see his family nor enter his family's home again. And he should have stuck to that vow. After all, he was supposed to be dead. Dead men did not return home—unless they felt they had a very good reason to haunt the place. He shivered then swallowed hard. Suddenly he felt like a spook creeping through a house where he did not belong and it was hard for him to shake that feeling.

When he first entered the bedroom, he noticed Leona lying in bed with her rumpled covers pulled to her chin, sound asleep. The pained expression pulling down at the corners of her mouth let him know that her slumber was not peaceful.

Ethan next noticed that Lathe was gone, yet in his place was a young man who appeared to be no more than eighteen. The lad stood looking at Ethan expectantly, as if waiting for him to speak.

"Did you bring the medicine?" Tony finally asked, eyeing the sack again, his expression hopeful.

"What medicine?" Ethan asked, also glancing down at his sack as if that might help him figure out what the boy meant.

"The pain medicine Dr. Caldwell was supposed to have sent over. She's been hurtin' somethin' fierce. Moans and groans a whole lot."

"No, all I brought is a door latch," Ethan answered then set the sack aside.

Tony looked at him strangely. "What good is a door latch goin' to do her?"

Rather than explain, Ethan stepped closer to the bed and gazed down at the dark, swollen area that marred the perfection of his dear sister's face and at the grim creases near the compressed corners of her mouth. The boy was right. She was clearly in pain. She twitched her arms and tossed her head to one side while he stood watching her.

Stroking his heavy beard, he wondered if she had awakened yet or if she'd been lying unconscious like that since he'd left. He also wondered how long Lathe had been gone.

His brown eyes narrowed with resentment when

71

he realized how badly he had misjudged Lathe Caldwell. He should have listened to the captain's urgent warnings instead of acting on instinct. Lathe Caldwell was not to be trusted. He was a cold-hearted killer concerned with no one's welfare but his own.

Despite Leona's obvious pain and the critical nature of her injuries, Lathe had deserted his patient to save his own skin. Ethan wondered when it had finally dawned on Lathe who he really was and how soon after that he'd fled town.

Angry with himself for not having foreseen Lathe's escape as a very real possibility, Ethan turned to look at Tony, his expression grim. "Where'd the doctor go?"

"Off to find the man who did that to her," Tony answered, moving to stand beside him, but not looking down at Leona because during the last few minutes of tossing and turning, the sheet had slipped down past the tops of her creamy white shoulders.

"Then Lathe's not gone for good?" Ethan's eyebrows arched with renewed hope. Maybe he had judged him right after all.

"No," the boy answered then blinked at the thought. His thin body tensed. "At least he'd better not be. He's going to owe me five dollars for staying here with Miss Stegall." Then just as suddenly as he had tensed, he relaxed. "But I know he's comin' back. He left his pistol here with me."

"His pistol?" Ethan glanced around until he spotted the weapon lying on a table near the window. "Whatever for?"

"He told me to shoot her with it if she was to try to get up," Tony said, then chuckled. "She was acting pretty ornery about wantin' to get out of that bed when he left. Of course he wasn't really serious about me shootin' her, but he left the pistol all the same. I reckon it was his way of makin' a point. Claimed he had another one at the hotel he could use in the meantime."

Ethan felt better. If Lathe had left a fancy Colt like that behind, then undoubtedly he would be coming back. "You say he's off lookin' for the man who did this to her? Didn't the sheriff catch up with him last night?"

"I suppose not," Tony answered then sank back into the chair where he had been sitting for the past couple of hours. "Or he wouldn't have been out roundin' up no posse to go lookin' for him early this morning."

Although at first Ethan worried for Zeb's safety, he remembered what Zeb had done to Leona and decided that maybe this time the hothead deserved to have Lathe catch up with him. With the sheriff right there beside him, there was no way Lathe would try to kill him in cold blood. He'd be safe enough and maybe, just maybe, it would be better for everyone involved if Zeb did spend a few days cooling his heels in jail. The captain would see to it that Zeb was eventually released. He always did.

While Ethan continued to mull over the possibility of Zeb's spending a few days behind bars to atone for what he had done to his sister, there was another loud knock at the front door and Tony glanced at Ethan with an uncertain look.

"Dr. Caldwell told me not to leave her side unless I absolutely have to. Says she might try to get up even while she's asleep. Could you go see who's at the door for me? Maybe it's whoever Dr. Caldwell was goin' to send over with the medicine. Most stores have been open for well over an hour. Someone should be here with it by now."

When Ethan returned just a few minutes later, he carried a large black bottle with fat brown cork and a white and red label.

Setting the bottle and cork on the small bedside table, Ethan hurried to the kitchen to find a spoon. When he returned, he ever so gently shook Leona to wake her. When that didn't bring her around, he shook her a little more firmly, but not hard enough to hurt her injured shoulder. Slowly, she opened her eyes and blinked — groggy with pain.

"Who are —" she started to ask then suddenly remembered and changed her question: "What are *you* doing here?"

There was no resentment in her voice, only surprise.

"Came by to see how you're doing," he said, smiling happily while he studied every detail of her startled expression, amazed at how very much she had changed during the past nine years, yet she had somehow remained the same. His grin broadened when he realized how extremely beautiful she had become in such a short time.

He even smiles a little like Ethan did, Leona thought sadly while she also studied him, although she remembered Ethan's smile to be much broader, revealing more of his teeth.

"I was the one who helped the doctor bring you here, then I helped him hold you still while he sewed up that knife wound you got last night." Ethan then picked up the open bottle and showed it to her. "Got some pain medicine for you, too."

"Pain medicine?" She lifted her head just a few inches off the pillow in an attempt to see the label. She gritted her teeth against the resulting explosion along the back of her head. It did not matter what was in the bottle, if there was any chance at all it

74

would help ease her pain, she wanted some. "Give it to me."

Ethan chuckled silently, wanting to comment that she had certainly changed, because when she was younger it had taken three of them to hold her down and administer any medicine the doctor said she needed. "I plan to do just that. In fact, I've already gone and got the spoon and a glass of water to help wash away the taste with." He could tell by the awful smell that the medicine was going to taste terrible.

After Leona had taken the medicine and had lain back down with the sheet pulled to her chin, Tony finally relaxed enough to ask Ethan, "Are you a doctor, too?"

"Not hardly," Ethan answered with a chuckle then extended his hand. "My name's George Parkinson. I'm just someone passin' through. I was there when it happened."

"You were?" Tony asked, eager to know the details. "Who did that to her? Did you know the man?"

"No, never saw him before," Ethan lied. "But then you have to remember, I'm not from around here."

"Neither was he," Leona put in, startling them both because they had expected her to drift immediately back to sleep.

"Then you got a pretty good look at him?" Tony wanted to know, leaning forward in his chair. "What did he look like?"

"I really only got a quick glimpse of his face," she admitted. She focused her gaze on the ceiling while she tried to remember. "I was too busy studying the other man because I thought he was the bad one."

"What other man?" To Tony, this was more exciting than any dime novel because it had happened right there in Little Mound, just a few blocks from

75

the feed store where he worked. "Did he have a partner?"

Aware how eager the boy was for details, Leona then described everything that had happened the evening before, feeling at first angry then guilty when she told about her part in the mishap. But because the medicine she had taken had already begun to take effect, making her feel extremely drowsy, she did not finish her tale by detailing the argument she and Lathe Caldwell had exchanged after she finally awoke. Instead, she slowly drifted into a deep, painless sleep while Tony and Ethan discussed what they thought about such a terrible event happening in a peaceful little town like Little Mound.

After awhile, Ethan grew weary of talking with the boy and decided to repair the broken latch and hammer the shattered door frame back into place. When the promised soup had not arrived by eleven, he located a clean jar under the kitchen sink and went into town to buy some himself.

While Mattie Davis ladled a generous amount of her cafe's famous vegetable soup into the jar, he noticed a freshly baked apple pie sitting on the counter and bought it, too, thinking he and Tony would need something besides soup to get them through the day.

When he returned, he was told that some lady had brought a small jug of chicken and noodle soup by while he was gone. Tony had encouraged Leona to eat a bowlful right away and by the time Ethan had returned with yet more soup, she had already eaten her fill and was sitting up in bed, propped up by a half dozen pillows—scowling angrily at anyone who entered the room.

"Well, I'm certainly glad to see you're feelin' so much better," Ethan commented, trying not to chuckle at her murderous expression. "I guess the medicine did whatever it was supposed to do."

"I guess so." Her mouth flattened with annoyance at having had to admit it because although she still hurt whenever she made any abrupt movements, the constant throbbing she had experienced earlier was indeed gone. As long as she didn't move her head, her right arm, or her right shoulder, she felt fine.

"Is there anything I can do for you?" he asked, truly wanting to help.

"Yes, there is." She nodded sharply, then grimaced. "You can go outside and bring in my clothes. I am tired of lying in this bed. I want to get dressed."

"Outside?" he asked, confused, then glanced at Tony to see if he knew what she meant. He felt certain he would have noticed any clothes on the clothesline.

Tony grinned. "Before Dr. Caldwell left here this morning, he rounded up all her clothes and tossed them right out that window." He nodded toward the window. "Said it was the only way he knew to make sure she stayed in that bed like she was supposed to."

Ethan chuckled, thinking Lathe was probably right. Leona was not the type to lie around recuperating when she thought there was work to be done. "Pretty smart man that Dr. Caldwell. Looks like it worked."

"Are you planning to bring me some of my clothes or not?" Leona interrupted, not wanting to hear any more praises sung on behalf of anyone as arrogant and domineering as Lathe Caldwell.

"I'll go out there and bring everything inside for you, but only to save them from that dog of yours. I won't be bringin' any of it in here for you to put on."

"Scraps?" Leona had not thought about her dog

77

since last night just before she'd fainted. "Where is he?"

"Outside sleepin' on a big, comfortable-lookin' pile of clothes," Ethan said while stretching his hands out in opposite directions to approximate just how large that pile really was. He tried to look as if he hadn't yet made the connection between that particular mound of clothing and the clothes Lathe had tossed outside earlier.

Leona shrieked with dismay, then winced again. A spot along the side of her head had started to throb again, and she reached up gently to touch the swollen area near her temple. "That stupid dog will have fleas and dog hairs all over my clothes," she muttered, angered as much by her pain as she was by the fact no one would bring her any clothes.

"You're probably right. I guess I'd better put 'em in a big pot and boil 'em first," Ethan said, wrinkling his nose.

Although it had been years since Ethan had done his own laundry, he managed to recall the proper procedure. By midafternoon, he had Leona's entire wash and his shirt hanging out on the clothesline to dry. He closed the front gate so Scraps could not return and help himself to yet more of her clothes and then he sat down in a fat wicker chair on the front porch to wait.

Thinking the clothing safe, he closed his eyes and tilted his head back against the chair so his neck could catch as much of the afternoon breeze as possible. It wasn't until a sharp, audible gasp pierced his sleep that he realized he had dozed. To his embarrassment and that of the woman who had entered the yard with yet another jug of soup for Leona, not only did he still not have on a shirt, but Scraps had returned and lay at his feet chewing happily on a

78

freshly laundered piece of clothing.

"Excuse me, ma'am," he said, reaching automatically for something—anything—to cover his chest. When he snatched the material out of Scraps's mouth, thinking to use it, he was further embarrassed to discover he held a pair of shredded bloomers. He reddened immediately and shoved the bloomers behind him, wondering what he should do next. "I—I didn't hear you come up." He blinked rapidly when he finally remembered his manners and stood.

"Obviously," Mrs. Haught responded in a terse voice before diverting her gaze to the dog, who had sat up and was now eyeing Ethan with annoyance. Her hands fidgeted nervously around the base of the small brown stoneware jug she carried. "I am here with more soup. After finding out that Tony Newland was staying here, too, I thought perhaps that one jug might not be enough to last the entire day." She then returned an accusing gaze to Ethan. "Are *you* also staying for supper?" Immediately reminded of his bare chest, she quickly returned her attention to the hapless dog.

Ethan was pleased that Josephine Haught felt no desire to study his face, for she had known him well during his childhood. She had been his Sunday school teacher for over a year. "No, ma'am. I just came by to see how Leon—" he coughed to cover the mistake he had nearly made, "how Miss Stegall was feelin' and decided to do her wash for her so she'd have some clean clothes when the time came for her to get out of that bed again."

To prove his words, he nodded in the direction of the clothesline, which could be partially seen from where they stood then went on to explain, "I was there last night when Miss Stegall was injured. I was the one who helped the doctor bring her back here so he could stitch up her knifewound. I guess that's why I want to do everything I can to help her. I feel sorta responsible for her welfare."

Knowing Mrs. Haught to be a notorious gossip, Ethan hoped the older woman would not read anything scandalous into his being there — *shirtless* of all things. If she did suspect something amiss, he just hoped she would keep those unfounded suspicions to herself for once. Leona certainly did not need that sort of talk circulating around town.

"The doctor?" Mrs. Haught asked with a skeptical tone, glimpsing his face again. She lifted her nose higher as if to indicate she had just caught him in a bold-faced lie. "We don't even have a doctor in Little Mound. Haven't since Tom Owen died."

Aware she doubted his word, Ethan struggled to conceal his resentment. "The man who asked you to bring the soup is a doctor."

"That handsome young man? A doctor?" she asked, still clearly skeptical. "Why he can't be more than thirty years old."

Thirty-one, thought Ethan, but he refrained from giving out that information. "I don't know exactly how old he is, but he is definitely a doctor. The way I understand it, he doesn't have a practice yet, but that doesn't make him any less of a doctor. He may not be from around here, but he was willing to take the time to care for her injuries anyway. His name is Dr. Caldwell."

"And just where *are* her injuries? When I came earlier, she was still asleep and Tony Newland didn't really know where all she'd been hurt."

"Her worst injuries were a blow to the head and the cut on her back, about where her shoulderblade is," he quickly supplied, eager to divert her attention

80

to something other than his or Lathe's identity.

"And you two took care of the cut on her back without a woman present?" she asked. Her slender nostrils flared wide with further dismay. "It's appalling enough to find out that an impressionable young man like Tony Newland was the one chosen to watch over her while she lies unconscious in her own bedroom; but for you two men to have taken care of such a private injury with no woman present was very inappropriate."

"We didn't have no women around to watch," Ethan pointed out. "Besides no woman I know would have been able to stand all that blood. Miss Stegall bled something fierce. The doctor said she came very close to bleeding herself right to death."

Mrs. Haught thrust her chin forward, still not convinced they had done the right thing. "And what makes you so sure that man *is* the doctor he claims to be? How do you know he isn't some sort of degenerate who just wanted the chance to gaze at Leona's naked shoulder?" She then narrowed her eyes as if asking the same question about him. "No telling what all happened before you two decided you were finished."

Ethan grimaced, aware Lathe had seen much more than a shoulder, but far less than he might have had he not displayed such prudence. He had acted with far more decorum than many professionals do. "If you had seen the stitches Lathe Caldwell took when closing that wound, you'd know he was a doctor. As for what else went on while the doctor worked so hard to stop her bleedin', nothin' did. All we did was take care of her injuries."

Josephine Haught narrowed her gaze further and tipped her head to one side, causing her elaborately feathered hat to flutter awkwardly above her head.

"You look familiar to me. Do I know you from somewhere?"

"I doubt it," Ethan quickly assured her. "I'm just a drifter passin' through." He dropped his face away from her probing gaze by reaching down to pet Scraps on the head. "Why don't you go on in and talk with Miss Stegall yourself. She's awake now and feelin' much better."

"I plan to do just that," she said, giving Ethan a self-righteous wave of her head. "Meanwhile, why don't you see if you can locate your shirt? It won't do Leona's reputation any good for you to be gallivanting around her front yard half-naked like that."

Feeling properly chastised, Ethan did exactly what she suggested. He waited until he had every button securely fastened and his shirttail properly tucked into his waistband before entering Leona's room to say goodbye to her.

"I'll stop by to see how you're feelin' tomorrow," he promised, then ducked out of the room before Mrs. Haught could make any further disparaging comments concerning him.

The posse had followed the spotted trail of blood as far as Stone Creek, which was a small, shallow river, several yards wide, that emptied into the Cypress Bayou three miles north of town. There, they discovered Zeb Turner had led his horse into the water near a low, sloping incline and then must have ridden down the middle of the slow-moving waterway for a while. With no more splotches of dried blood and no horse tracks to follow, they lost all trace of him.

After searching for the location where Zeb might have come out of the water and finding nothing to indicate he ever did, Sheriff Lindsey ordered the posse split up. He told two of the men to continue searching Stone Creek for clues while the rest of the men divided into two groups of three riders each for a house to house, barn to barn search of the area. Judging by the amount of blood Zeb had lost, the sheriff reasoned he could not have ridden much further. He had to have taken refuge somewhere in that area.

After having seen how much blood Zeb had lost, he and Lathe both doubted the man would have enough strength to ride all the way into the next town. But when a quick search of the caves and abandoned buildings in that area brought them up empty-handed, the sheriff sent two of the riders on into Karnack to warn the sheriff there to keep an eye out for the injured man. It was Sheriff Lindsey's theory that someone might have found Zeb and, after seeing that he was so badly hurt, taken him on to the doctor there.

Having lost all trace of Zeb, the posse eventually returned to town later that afternoon feeling defeated, tired, and hungry. There was little Lathe could do alone, so he told the sheriff where to find him, then stopped off at the hotel to shave and bathe the road dust off his skin with a wet wash cloth. He then changed into a set of fresh clothes and headed back to Leona's. He was eager to see if his patient had stayed in that bed as she'd been ordered to do.

When he got back to the house shortly after six, he was pleased to find not only that she was still in bed, exactly where he had left her, but that the bandage he'd made from torn sheets was still in place. Because Tony was too tired to stay any longer, and there was still nothing Lathe could do about Zeb until the sheriff finally heard something, he decided to take over the night watch himself.

When he reached deep into his shirt pocket to pull out a five-dollar gold piece, he told Tony to go home and get plenty of rest because he wanted him to come back early the following morning and sit with Leona again.

Although he had cooled down enough to realize what an exorbitant amount he had offered the boy for one day's work, he was willing to pay another five dollars for the second day. Anything to free his time so he could continue to help search for Zeb.

When he walked Tony to the front door, he was surprised to see the new latch but not too surprised when Tony told him who had replaced it. Evidently George still felt responsible for having broken it in the first place.

When he returned to Leona's bedroom, he paused halfway between the bed and the chair, wondering what he should do first.

"You really don't have to stay here all night," Leona said, aware that he had taken off his gunbelt and unfastened the top buttons of his shirt in order to make himself more comfortable.

She also noticed that he had shaved and changed clothes at some point during the day. He did not look quite as threatening dressed in a pair of dark blue trousers and a pale blue shirt as he had while dressed in black. Truth was, if she hadn't been so determined to disapprove of the impertinent man, she might be forced to admit he was really rather handsome. "There are not that many places I would care to go this late in the evening," she added.

She glanced at the clock, aware that it would soon be dark outside.

"That may be true," Lathe responded. "But even so, you, young lady, have already proven you are not to be trusted. It may be true that you are willing to stay in that bed for the rest of the night, but what about in the morning? You are just mule-headed enough to try to get up and get dressed along about daybreak."

"But that's because I feel a lot better," she reasoned, thinking it should be perfectly all right for her not only to get dressed but also open the store that following morning. "The medicine you sent over really helped a lot."

"I'm glad to hear it. But you still lost a lot of blood last night, a lot more than I think you realize. You may be feeling better, but trust me you are not yet ready to resume your life the way it was. That's why it is important that you stay in that bed, at least for a few more days."

Leona glowered at him from over the top hem of her bedcovers, which she kept pulled to her chin since she had yet to convince anyone to bring her any clothes. "I am a grown woman. I should be able to judge if and when I'm ready to get out of this bed."

"You would think so," he nodded while he studied the determined expression in her large, almond-shaped brown eyes. Such stunning eyes. Set in such an exquisite face. A pity she did not have a pleasing disposition to go along with all that outward beauty. "But obviously you are too stubborn to realize how weak your injuries have left you."

He walked closer to her bedside and stared down at her mutinous expression. "I guess I should let you try to get up out of that bed right now just to prove how very weak you are, but it just so happens I'm too tired at this particular moment to want to spend

85

the next half hour stitching that same wound closed again should you fall. It happens to have been a long, hard, disappointing day."

He ran a hand through his thick black hair while he glanced around the room, trying to decide the most comfortable place to rest his weary body. "If it helps, I stopped by the Mercantile to see how Mrs. Sanford was getting along and she said to tell you not to worry, she has everything well in hand."

"But that woman is in her seventies. She's too old to be doing so much work."

"How hard can it be to sit behind a counter and read books or crochet booties?" he asked, too tired to argue the point. "It's not like she has to get up every few minutes to wait on customers. There have only been a few in there all day." He hoped the sting from that comment would be enough to shut her up once and for all. He grimaced when that turned out not to be the case.

"The store is suffering through a very difficult time right now," she said with a proud thrust of her pretty little chin. "Last year's drought left many of my customers unable to pay what they owe me." Her face hardened with firm resolve. "But as soon as I can scrape enough money together, I fully intend to fill those shelves with everything my customers could possibly need. My customers will then come back in droves."

"That may be so, but meanwhile, it appears there are very few customers coming in to try to buy what little merchandise you do have. Therefore you have no worthwhile reason to risk getting out of that bed."

"Yes I do," she tried to explain. Having had the entire day to think through her predicament, her mind was set. "I need to see John Davis about having my brother declared legally dead. It is the only way I can get the money I need to save the Mercantile."

Guessing John Davis to be her lawyer, Lathe shook his head. "You will have to ask Mr. Davis to come to your house to discuss the matter. You are not getting out of that bed."

Leona pursed her mouth into a thoughtful pout. It was true, she could send Lathe into town to ask John to come to her house. John would respond by coming immediately. In fact, she was surprised he had not stopped by anyway. Surely he had heard about the incident by now. According to what Josephine Haught had told her, nearly everyone in town was talking about it. The only reason she could figure John had not yet stopped by was that he was too busy with some important legal matter—either that or he was out of town.

"So, how about it?" Lathe asked, tired of waiting for her to volunteer a response. "Do you want me to go find this John Davis fellow and bring him here or not?"

Thinking that was exactly what she wanted him to do, since she was obviously not going be allowed to go to him, Leona took a deep breath and met Lathe's expectant gaze. But when it came to actually voicing the request, she simply could not say it. Not yet. Maybe tomorrow when she felt stronger.

For now, she would follow Lathe's advice and stay right there in that bed and rest.

For now.

Chapter Five

While Leona slept after having taken yet another dose of the foul-tasting medicine shortly after supper, Lathe sat in a nearby chair and brooded over the infuriating situation surrounding Zeb Turner. It was frustrating to know the man had again gotten away from him. It became hard for him to concentrate on anything else.

After all these years, he thought he finally had him, finally had the man who had murdered his only brother, and then Lathe had ended up losing him again. Slipped right through his fingers.

It was almost as if Zeb had his own personal guardian angel. But that was preposterous. No celestial spirit worth its wings would bother to protect the likes of Zeb Turner. No, it made far better sense to believe that if he was indeed being protected by some unseen being, it was by the very devil himself. It had to be the devil to have provided him such easy means of escape and then to have offered him so many places to hide.

The sheriff had proved to be at a loss as much as Lathe was when it came to trying to figure out where Zeb might have gone. He claimed that he and his men had checked every possible house, barn, cave, cavern, or hollow that looked large enough to hide a man and a horse in the Stone Creek or Cypress Bayou area. But none of them had found the slightest trace of him. Nor could they locate anyone else who claimed to have seen him. It was as if Zeb had ridden into the shallow depths of that shallow river and promptly vanished off the face of the earth.

But that was impossible.

Zeb had to be somewhere; and he had to be somewhere fairly close, probably hiding in some thicket of woods just long enough to tend to his wound and regain some of his strength. But where? And in what direction would he head next?

The sheriff claimed he knew of nowhere else in that whole area where a man and a horse could hide. But, in all honesty, Lathe knew that the rolling landscape was filled with possibilities. East Texas was covered with small hills and dense pockets of underbrush. Even around the cultivated areas, there were thick, brushy windbreaks dividing the fields. The sheriff and his men had searched as many thickets as they could while making their farm to farm search; but it had been impossible for them to look everywhere.

Lathe's best bet was to forget where Zeb was hiding and try to figure out where he might head next.

Knowing the ex-Confederate had a tendency to exploit dead soldiers' families in order to obtain free food, shelter, and even a little extra spending money, Lathe wondered if there were any such families in that area—families of young boys who had been killed during the Civil War—families always eager for any scrap of information concerning their dead sons, whether true or not.

When Leona awoke again shortly before midnight, Lathe asked if she knew of anyone in that area who had lost a son, a father, or possibly a brother during the war.

"Of course," she answered, staring at him with a raised brow, thinking it an odd question. The Civil War was no longer a current topic. The fighting had ended nearly five years ago. Only the old-timers who sat around the courthouse with nothing better to do, and the veterans who were still bitter over the abrupt way the war had ended continued to discuss the horrible incident. Most people preferred to forget it ever happened. "There are quite a few people around here who lost a loved one during the war. I happen to be one of them."

"That brother you mentioned wanting to have declared legally dead? He was killed during the war?" Lathe asked. He wondered then if Zeb could have been headed for her house the night fate had brought them all together on the street.

Leona swallowed to ease the constriction in her throat then nodded. "His name was Ethan. He died in battle, but his body was never recovered." She blinked back the burning sensation in her eyes. Her grip tightened on the sheet she still held beneath her chin until her knuckles became as white as the fabric.

Ever since that incident in front of the hotel in which she had mistaken George Parkinson for her brother, Ethan's image had again become very distinct in her mind. She could visualize his boyish grin and that mischievous gleam that dominated his glittering brown eyes so clearly. It was as if she had seen him just yesterday. But it had been nine years. Nine *long* years.

How dreadfully she missed her brother. Especially now. And how desperately she needed him. Needed not only his calm and his reassurance, but his wis-

90

dom and strength. She knew that if Ethan were still alive, he would know what to do. He would find some way to save the family business from ruin.

"Anyone else from around here lose someone to the war?" Lathe asked, unaware her mind had wandered to other matters. He wanted no names left out. He had to investigate all possibilities.

Leona quickly reined in her painful thoughts. Her grip on the sheet weakened until her knuckles were no longer stark white. "Several families in this area lost sons or brothers during the war. A large group of local boys joined at about the same time and went off together to become a part of the same company and I suspect nearly half of them were killed. Let's see, there's the Martins, the Seguins, the Philers, the Sobeys . . ."

"Hold it," he said as he hurried to the desk for a pencil and paper. "Give me those names again more slowly then tell me exactly where they live."

"Why do you want to know where they live?" she asked, thinking it an even stranger request. She studied his somber expression for a long moment. "Why does it matter to you where those people live?"

Lathe kept the pencil poised over the paper while he explained, "The man I am after has a bad habit of preying on the grief of any family who lost a son, a father, or a brother during the war. I am not sure how he finds out exactly where to locate these families, but it seems he has a very good memory for those he saw killed during the war. He uses whatever information he remembers to gain these families' confidence, then he maneuvers them into putting him up for a few days, sometimes for weeks. How long he uses these people usually depends on how close he thinks I am to catching up with him again. Then when he does leave, it is almost always in the middle of the night and he usually takes most of the family's valuables with him."

Lathe continued to sit forward, prepared to write. "I figure the reason Zeb chose this direction after he left Jefferson the other night was that he had somehow discovered that another bereaved family from his company lives somewhere in this area. That might be where he is hiding right now—at some dead soldier's house, playing upon the family's lingering grief and earning inappropriate sympathy for himself. What I want to do is talk with anyone around here who may have lost someone during the war. I'd like to warn them against some of the things Zeb is likely to do or say and ask them to come and tell me or the sheriff if he does show up at one of their homes."

Thinking that made sense and believing Lathe meant them no real harm, she repeated the names slowly then gave him clear directions to their houses. Everyone but the Wilcoxes lived outside town, mostly on small farms and ranches, some several miles out. The Wilcoxes, though, lived just down the street.

While Lathe carefully wrote down the last of her directions, Leona's face drew into a pensive frown. "Did that man you said you are looking for actually know the soldiers he claims to have seen killed or does he just make that up?"

"A little of both, I suppose. I was told he did serve in the Confederate Army during nearly the entire war. I'm sure in that time he saw a lot of men die. But I find it hard to believe he knew them all as closely as he pretends. He's just not the sort of person most people would want to warm up to."

Leona fell silent. She stared at where her feet caused two small mounds beneath the bedcovers, wondering if Zeb could possibly have known Ethan, but then quickly pushed the thought aside. It had been a huge war. There had been hundreds of thousands of men killed. The chances that Zeb had known her brother were very slim.

"He must be a very cruel man to be willing to prey on people's emotions like that," she said, then lifted her dark gaze to meet Lathe's.

When he saw how intense her sadness was, he set the pencil aside and moved to the bed beside her. Gently, he reached out to stroke her cheek with the inner curve of his palm while his thoughts became lost in his own sorrowful memories.

"He is a very cruel man. A very cruel, very *bad* man," he told her, his voice deep and his expression distant.

Leona felt a strange, warm, oddly invigorating sensation wash over her and knew it was the result of Lathe's gentle touch. For the first time since he had entered her bedroom that night, she smiled. "And I thought you were the bad one."

When Lathe noticed her smile, the delight stretched wide across his handsome face. Leona found the returning smile to be so attractive and so very captivating, it sent more of those same exhilarating sensations splashing down her spine, kindling a deep inner warmth like none she had ever experienced. While she stared, awestruck, at the amazing transformation in his face, fascinated by the long, curving indentations that had formed along his lean cheeks, she only vaguely heard him as he spoke again.

"*Me?*" Lathe chuckled when he realized she had every reason to believe the worst of him. Normally, whenever an armed man dressed in black slipped out of a dark alley after having lain in wait for

93

hours, he could rightfully be considered up to no good. "And do you still think I'm a *bad* one?"

"Perhaps," she admitted with a soft laugh, pleased with how very attractive he looked when he smiled. He was handsome enough when he bore no smile, but when he did deign to stretch his mouth and offer a playful smile, the effect was devastating. It made it hard for her to concentrate on the content of their conversation. "Actually, I think there's a little bad in everyone."

Lathe's blue eyes sparkled at such a cynical remark. "And is there bad in you, too, Miss Stegall?"

Leona laughed again. The color rose in her cheeks while she contemplated her answer. "Like I said, Mr. Caldwell, there is a little bad in *everyone.*"

Certainly that would explain her explosive temper and her relentless determination to do exactly what she pleased. There was definitely a bad streak in this one, but suddenly that fact didn't bother him. "Please, don't keep calling me Mr. Caldwell. First of all, I'm not really a mister, I'm a doctor," he corrected. "And, second, I'd really prefer that you call me Lathe."

"Oh, but there are so many *other* names I would enjoy calling you," she bantered. Her brown eyes glimmered with impish delight, surprised at how much fun it was to goad this man. She liked how her teasing directly affected his smile, making those deep, curving dimples sink further into his cheeks.

While she continued to study the many attractive features that shaped his strong face, she decided Lathe Caldwell was not nearly as cruel and domineering as she had first thought. Fact was, he could be very friendly when he wanted and had the type of smile that could enter and warm even the coldest heart.

Surely there had to be a kind and understanding person hidden behind such a charming smile. Perhaps he would prove understanding enough finally to let her up out of that bed—if she played on his sympathies just right.

"Oh? And what is it you think you would prefer to call me?" he asked, his shoulders shaking with the need to laugh at such an outrageous remark.

Leona stared at him a long moment, her eyes glittering with sheer deviltry while she considered some of the names she had mentally called him during the course of the day. "On second thought, I think it would be a lot safer if I agreed to Lathe instead. At least for now."

"And may I in turn use the name Leona?" he asked, when she did not immediately reciprocate his proposal to use his first name.

"No, Leona doesn't fit your personality," she taunted. "You'd better stick with the name Lathe."

"You know what I meant," he said with an arched eyebrow, bringing her attention back to his glittering blue eyes. "May I call you by your given name."

"Yes, I suppose that would be all right," she responded agreeably, pleased he would want to.

Aware that Leona had finally begun to drop whatever barriers she had earlier erected between them, Lathe glanced at the bedsheet she still held pulled to her chin. He had put off examining her injuries earlier because he had been too tired and too preoccupied with his concern about Zeb to argue with her about the need to be examined.

When he had first entered the room that evening, it had been enough to notice that there were no blood stains soaking through the outer layers of her bandage. Nor were there any noticeable stains on the sheets. At least she was not bleeding as heavily as she had been.

"Would you mind if I checked that wound now? I just want to make sure none of the stitches have pulled loose and that no infection has started to set."

When she pressed back against the pillows behind her, as if uncertain whether she should allow it, he offered another gentle, reassuring smile then explained, "I *am* a doctor. And because I am a doctor, I have seen plenty of bare shoulders in my time. Including yours."

Maybe none quite as soft and silky as yours, he mused while he gently tugged the sheet from her grasp then dropped it to her waist, *but plenty of bare shoulders nonetheless.*

Still facing him with a cautious expression, Leona watched while he slowly eased the straight pins out of the material then gently began to unwrap the outer bandage. She ran the tip of her tongue nervously across her upper lip when she felt the material slowly slacken, aware that the larger the coil of material in his hand grew, the less fabric there was covering her upper body.

When the backs of his fingers lightly brushed against the sensitive sections of bare skin near where an extremely skimpy portion of the bandage still covered her breasts, she gasped and quickly jerked the sheet back up to cover the front of her body barely seconds before the last of her outer bandage was tugged away. With her eyes stretched to their limits, she held the sheet firmly against her breasts while he slipped one hand behind her neck and pulled her forward so he could examine the wound on the back of her shoulder. She tried to ignore the tiny bumps that sprang to life just beneath the surface of her skin.

Careful not to jar her, Lathe rose up on one knee and leaned over her, his shoulder touching hers while he slowly peeled away the small patch of folded cloth he had used for an inner bandage. He frowned when a tiny portion of fabric refused to come loose.

"I guess I'll have to soak it for a few minutes." He reached for the small towel he had used for a cooling compress earlier and redampened it with water from her drinking glass. Gently, he pressed the wet cloth over the section of bandage that still adhered to the wound and waited for the dampness to soak through.

While he continued to sit so very close to Leona, facing her with one knee still on the bed and his right arm curved around her shoulder, holding the damp cloth in place, Leona's heart hammered wildly. She had never allowed a man quite *that* handsome to sit quite *that* close while she was quite *that* unclothed.

Even though she now believed he was a doctor, just having him close enough to feel his breath fall warmly against her skin had caused another wild array of tingling sensations to cascade through her body. Her toes curled in response.

"Am I going to live?" she asked hoping to dispel the sudden giddiness she felt. She tensed with fearful anticipation when he bent forward and gently pulled the bandage free but she relaxed again when there came no immediate resurgence of pain.

"Looks like you might live," he admitted, though he was having a hard time keeping his attention focused on the injury while he continued to lean over her. He had become too distracted by the vast expanse of delicate white skin exposed to his view to

97

concentrate fully on the matters at hand. Judging by what he could see of it, Leona's body was as beautiful and tempting as her face.

Drawing on his deepest inner strength, Lathe forced his attention back to the wound itself while he gently pressed against the surrounding area with his fingertips. "There's no sign of puffiness. No obvious surface infection. And as much dirt as I scrubbed out of that wound last night, I really did expect to find some level of infection."

Leona grimaced at the thought of having her wound scrubbed. "And did your handiwork stay in place or have I managed to pull a stitch?"

"So far, so good. But then what else could you expect? I happen to have done a very good job of stitching that thing closed." He grinned and sat back so he could look into her face better. Such a truly beautiful face it was. He wondered then why someone so extremely beautiful was not married, but immediately remembered her sharp temperament. "You wouldn't happen to have a bottle of whiskey around here would you?"

"Why? Am I so vastly improved that you feel it cause for celebration?"

He chuckled then explained, "Not exactly. I want to rinse the wound before I put on a fresh bandage. Just because there is no infection now, doesn't mean that wound can't become infected in the future. Where's the nearest place I can buy a bottle this late at night?" He glanced at the clock. It was after midnight.

"Would brandy do?"

"You have brandy?" he asked, looking at her with a raised brow, surprised to think a woman of her social standing might indulge in a little after dinner drink now and then.

98

"My father liked to drink brandy," she explained, aware of his surprise. "There are several bottles still in his liquor cabinet in the library."

"You have a library?" For some reason, he hadn't expected that either.

"Well it is more what you might call a study than a library, but yes, we do have one," she said, then realized she had just used the term *we*. Though her parents had been dead for four years, sometimes it felt as if they were still there. "I mean, yes, *I* have one."

Delighted with the prospect of having something to do other than pace another night away while waiting for some word from the sheriff, Lathe stood. "Tell me where this library is and where I'll find the brandy."

He was pleased to learn the books and brandy were in the very next room.

When Lathe returned several minutes later, he carried an opened bottle of brandy and several books. After he finished tending Leona's wound, he tore up the rest of the sheet from the night before for fresh bandages, but this time he tied the ends into place instead of using the pins. Now that she was awake and moving around, he was afraid she might prick herself. He also decided she could get by with a smaller bandage, since the wound had already shown signs of healing.

Careful not to touch her in a way she might find unwarranted, he wrapped the long strips of cloth around her, working beneath the bedsheet she kept drawn to her chin.

After he finally had the bandage in place, he examined the bruise on her cheek and was pleased to see that the swelling had gone down and that the discoloration had already begun to fade. He finished by giving her another dose of medicine to help her sleep.

Believing it would be impossible for him to fall asleep, especially as frustrated and angry as he was over having lost tabs on Zeb again, Lathe sat in a nearby chair and began to leaf through one of the books he had found. It was not until he was startled awake by a sharp knock at the front door that he realized he had fallen asleep.

Blinking groggily, he set the book aside and glanced at the clock, surprised to see that it was nearly seven o'clock.

Unable to believe more than six hours had passed, he glanced at the window and felt further confused to see that a new dawn had risen.

Rubbing his stubbled face to help clear his head, he hurried to the door. When he opened it, he discovered a young man with a shiny badge prominently displayed on his chest. The town's deputy had obviously returned from his trip to Shreveport.

"Sheriff Lindsey said I was to tell you that he's sent a telegraph to every town within a day's ride warning them about that man you two tried so hard to capture. He gave a pretty detailed description, including that scar on his left hand. We should hear something pretty quick if he's foolish enough to turn up in any of the neighboring towns. Sheriff also plans to put together another posse and go looking for him again, this time a little further out. It really gets his goat that a wounded man was able to get away from him as easily as that one did."

"What time is he planning to ride out?" Lathe asked, frowning when he remembered how early they had left the day before. He had hoped to have time to stop by the hotel and change back into his riding clothes.

"About nine," the deputy answered. "He's got a few other matters to take care of first, but he plans to go out at least early enough to check some of those same farms and ranches that were checked yesterday and he also wants to ask around at some of those a little further out. He's pretty determined to find that man."

Lathe was glad to hear it. "Tell him I'll be there in time to join them." He patted the list he had placed in his shirt pocket earlier—the list of local families who had lost someone in the Civil War. "And tell him there are a few places I would like to check on myself."

When Lathe had closed the door and headed back down the hall toward the rear of the house, he was in a much better mood. With the sheriff again sounding as eager as he was to find Zeb, he had renewed hope.

When he returned to the bedroom, he was also pleased to find Leona sitting up in bed. Her long hair cascaded about her shoulders with wild abandon and her brown eyes looked droopy from having slept so soundly.

"Good morning," he said, smiling cheerfully. "How's that shoulder?"

"It feels fine," she answered, then glanced at him hopefully. "In fact, I feel well enough to get out of this bed. I really do."

Lathe arched a skeptical eyebrow when he came to a halt near her side. "Don't you ever give up?"

"Not when it is so very important I don't," she admitted, then remembering how agreeably he had behaved toward her the evening before, she smiled sweetly. "Surely you don't intend to make me stay in this bed again today, not when I am feeling so much better."

101

"I most certainly do," he said, unconvinced. "That's why I asked Tony to come back again today. To make sure you continue to stay in that bed even while I'm gone."

"While you're gone? And just where are you off to today?" she asked, then blinked, aware that her question had come out sounding very much like that of a complaining housewife and was not at all like her.

"I plan to visit those families you told me about last night. I want to warn them about Zeb. It's bad enough they had to lose their young men to such a foolish war. They don't need to be exploited, too."

"Foolish war?" Leona's eyebrows dipped low over instantly narrowed brown eyes, not sure she had heard him right. "You think the Civil War was *foolish?*"

"I think any war is foolish," he admitted, aware by her expression, he had struck a nerve. He watched while her whole body tensed.

"Let me get this straight. You believe it is foolish for someone to stand up for what he truly believes is right?"

"If it means having to kill people to get the point across, yes, I think it is foolish. Damn foolish."

Leona's expression hardened more. "Don't use language like that in my home, Mr. Caldwell," she demanded, her voice filled with resentment. "I won't allow it. And I also won't allow you to belittle the very war that took my brother's life."

Lathe let out a weary sigh, aware she had reverted back to calling him *Mr. Caldwell.*

"That in itself should prove to you how very foolish that war was. Your brother *died* in that war. And for what? What did the South gain by having fought the North?"

"For one thing, we managed to keep a good, strong hold on our dignity," she said, refusing to believe her brother had died for nothing.

"What dignity? The South was crushed. Our land was ravaged and our economy destroyed."

"But we came away from it with our heads held high and our shoulders erect, knowing we had been right to have fought such a war."

Lathe stared at her, unable to believe anyone could feel that way about such a ruthless and unnecessary war, especially someone who had lost a brother. "And how was it right?"

"How?" she asked, outraged to think he really did not know. Where was the man's sense of reason? "Why we were constantly being told by those uppity Northerners exactly how we should run our lives. What was worse, the federal government was always taking their side against ours. We were slowly losing every right we ever had to those ruthless tyrants."

"But there were other ways to handle the problem besides fighting a war."

"We'd tried those other ways. They got us nowhere." Leona thrust her chin forward and eyed him warily, thinking his traitorous words belied his deep, Southern accent. "Just what are you, a Northern sympathizer?"

"No, I was never sympathetic to the North. Nor was I particularly sympathetic to the South. I'm simply a man who believes the South never had a chance and would have fared better had they been more willing to compromise."

Leona coughed to show her contempt, then glowered at him. "I'll venture you didn't even bother to fight in the war. I imagine you hid out somewhere nice and safe while all that fighting was going on. If you had the money to go to medical school, you

103

probably had the money to pay someone else to fight for you."

"Yes, I had the money; but I didn't use it. The truth is, I did serve in the war, as a surgeon."

Leona's gaze narrowed further while she tried to decide if it was true or not. "For *which* side?"

He heaved another annoyed sigh. "The South."

"The South?" she countered, then crossed her arms triumphantly. "If you joined the cause like everyone else, then it stands to reason that you were just as big a fool as the rest."

Lathe stared at the mutinous set of her chin for several seconds before deciding to explain, "I didn't join because of any particular cause. I joined because I thought I might be able to save a few lives."

"Oh, how very noble of you," she bantered, her voice dripping with sarcasm. "Tell me, how many of those poor, foolish men did you save?"

Lathe let out another exasperated breath then gritted his teeth in an effort to contain his mounting anger. "Did you know that you happen to be one of the most annoying, most provoking, most *pig-headed* women I've ever had the misfortune to meet? Can't you see even now that the Civil War was a mistake?"

"No," she responded vehemently and thrust her chin even higher. "My brother would never have given up his life for anything that was a mistake. Fact is, the only real mistake the South made was waiting as long as we did before finally standing up for our rights. We gave the North too much time to prepare."

"Preparation had nothing to do with it," Lathe argued, thinking it a lame excuse for having lost. "The North was better manned and better supplied right from the beginning. But the Southern army was too blinded by its own foolish pride to see that."

"The only thing foolish about our army was that it allowed traitorous men like you to join its ranks." she retorted, glaring at him with the same degree of anger she had felt at the onset of the war.

Lathe shook his head and stared at her defiant expression, his voice edged with impatience. "It certainly is a good thing you never married, *Miss* Stegall. You'd make some man a miserable wife."

Leona glared at him with fury darkened eyes. "Well, that's something you won't ever have to worry yourself about, *Mr.* Caldwell, because I would never marry someone like you—not even with the delightful prospect of making your life *thoroughly* miserable."

"Which you undoubtedly would."

"Yes," she agreed with a scornful smile. "And I would take great pleasure in it."

Wondering how their argument about the war had degenerated into little more than a personal argument, Lathe snatched up his gunbelt and headed for the hall. Wanting only to get away from her, he continued toward the front door with long, determined strides.

Thinking she had won both the argument and the right to get out of bed, Leona immediately flung back the covers and swung her legs over the side. It was not until she was halfway to the door, eager to impart one last comment, that she realized how very grave her mistake was.

Her last thought before she fainted was of how pleased Lathe would be when he discovered she had proved him right. She *was* too weak to be out of that bed.

If only he wouldn't be the one to find her.

"How long was I out?" Leona asked when she

105

came to and found Lathe kneeling at her side, cupping her face in his hands. She was surprised to find he looked more concerned than pleased.

"About a minute," he answered, then slipped one of his hands behind her neck and lifted her high enough off the floor to glimpse the back of her bandage to see if any serious damage had been done.

Leona expected his next words to be a harsh reminder of his repeated warnings not to get out of that bed and was baffled when his only question was if she had hit her head during the fall.

"I don't think so," she answered and tried to focus on any pain she might have in that area. "My elbow smarts a little and my shoulder sure does hurt again, but my head feels all right."

Lathe slipped his hand inside the outer bandage and pulled the inner bandage away far enough to see that the wound was sticky with fresh blood but was not bleeding profusely. He sighed with relief then inhaled with annoyance. "Exactly what did you hope to accomplish by getting out of bed like that?"

"I had hoped to get dressed as soon as I could find out where George Parkinson had put my clothes after he washed them," she answered honestly, her anger now subdued. "Since you were obviously on your way out and Tony had yet to arrive, I saw what might be my only chance to prove to you that I am indeed ready to go back to work."

"And do you think you proved that to me?"

"No," she admitted then glanced away from his accusing glare. When she did, she caught sight of her scanty attire and quickly folded her arms over as much of her nakedness as possible. "Would you please help me back to bed?" she asked, not certain she had the strength to make it on her own.

"Only if you promise to stay there this time," he

106

muttered then slid both arms beneath her and lifted her off the floor with one lithe, easy movement.

Leona let out a startled gasp that had nothing to do with any pain. By help, she had meant give her something to lean against while she stood. She had not expected to be suddenly swept into his strong, masculine arms. Nor had she expected to feel his taut body pressed so warmly against her own.

Again, she was reminded of the fact that all she wore was a pair of summer-weight bloomers and a thin layer of bandages. Her cheeks burned a bright crimson.

"The next time a doctor tells you that you have lost far too much blood to be getting out of bed, I hope that you will have enough sense to listen to him," Lathe commented while he gently lowered her onto the top mattress, in the same spot where she had lain just minutes earlier. Aware her gaze was temporarily focused on his, he fought the overwhelming desire to glance down at her scantily clad body. "I know it is hard for you to believe, but there are times when other people do know more than you."

Believing she deserved that cutting remark, Leona did not retaliate with one of her own. Instead, she reached for the sheet and hurriedly pulled it up over herself. "Did I tear the wound?"

"I don't think so, but I won't know for sure until I've completely removed the bandage and gotten a better look," he answered, and immediately began to undo the tiny knots he had just tied. "But if it turns out you have torn that wound open and I have to take the time to put a whole new set of stitches before I can leave this house, don't expect much sympathy from me."

Chapter Six

When Zeb woke, it took a few minutes for him to realize where he was and another couple of minutes to remember how he got there. Although nothing about the room struck him as familiar, the dull, throbbing pain in his left thigh soon reminded him of his injury.

Vaguely, he remembered the incident in town and how that blasted sheriff had immediately taken off after him. He also remembered how terrified he had been when the sheriff finally got close enough to put that bullet through his left leg, just inches above the knee.

Despite some very close calls over the past few years, Zeb had not felt a bullet pierce his body since that one unfortunate incident during the war. He still had problems controlling two of the fingers on his left hand and all because that one lousy Yankee had got off such a lucky first shot.

And now that fool sheriff had managed to hit him square in the leg.

Zeb shivered when he realized how much more serious the damage could have been had that sheriff's aim been any better. He had gotten close enough so that bullet had gone clean through his body. If that same bullet had struck him in the lower back or in the head, no telling what might have happened.

He pressed his eyes closed when he realized how close he had come to being killed. He was fortunate. Shortly after he'd been hit, he had cut through a dense patch of woods and had managed to lose the sheriff within minutes, giving him the chance to examine the wound more closely.

If only it had not turned out to be such a bleeder, he could have made a clean getaway. But as it was, he had been forced to look for a place to hide, at least long enough to try to stop his bleeding. He knew from his many experiences during the war that a man didn't last very long at all if he continued to lose blood.

When Zeb remembered how unfortunate his plan had been to climb down from his horse while it was still dark and send the animal on its way by placing a good, hard swat on its rump, he grimaced.

His intention had been for the animal to follow a dirt path that stretched up the side of the sloping bank, thus leaving another false trail for Caldwell to follow. But the stupid horse had turned just short of the footpath and had continued along the creek, splashing wildly but leaving no real trail to lead Caldwell and that sheriff away from him.

Aware no one would be able to track him until after daylight, Zeb had then taken the time to examine his wound carefully. To help slow the bleeding, he tied his neckerchief around his thigh then immediately began searching for someplace to hide. He was too concerned with the fact that it would be dawn soon to concentrate on his pain, which had been considerable.

He knew that as soon as it was light enough to ride, a posse would be after him. They would track him to that shallow river easily enough, so he decided to make do with a small cave he had discovered just about the time the sky had started to turn a dull, lifeless grey.

Curling into a ball, he discovered he fit into the tiny hole just right and by pulling a large branch in after him, he prevented the hole from being seen from the river. He then waited until he had heard the posse pass by twice, each time headed in opposite directions. Finally he came out of hiding.

He would have stayed longer, but the pain in his leg had gradually grown worse and despite the tourniquet, he was still losing too much blood. He realized he had to find someone willing to help him before he bled to death, and he already knew just who that someone would be.

Recalling the directions he had gotten while consorting with some of the ladies in town, Zeb had headed immediately for the Martin farm. It turned dark only a few hours after he had started the three-mile trek and it was probably close to midnight by the time he finally had the house and its outbuildings in sight.

He remembered his elation when the house met the general description which the talkative little whore, Patricia, had given him for the price of a drink.

He had finally reached his destination. Help lay only several hundred yards away.

Somehow, Zeb had found the strength to break into a run.

Despite the pain that crippled his leg, he managed to make it halfway across the small pasture before he felt the last of his strength slowly slip away. He had immediately slowed to a staggering walk and had even tried using his rifle as a crutch, hoping that would help him make it the rest of the way to the house; but neither had helped.

He remembered his frustration when he stumbled over a rock hidden in the tall grass and toppled forward. He also remembered closing his eyes against the pain when he hit the hard earth and not being able to open them again until he heard someone shouting hysterically nearby.

There was no way to know how long he had lain there, but when he again broke his eyelids apart, he discovered that the sun was already high in a cloudless blue sky. He remembered how hot the rays had felt against his fevered skin and despite all the shouting someone was doing, he had heard the faint sound of flies buzzing around him. Flies meant certain infection. He just hoped someone would hurry and get him up out of that pasture and into a house.

He waited to see if whoever was doing all that shouting would turn out to be that someone.

He remembered trying to lift his head, but because the grass surrounding him was nearly three feet deep and he was too weak to sit up, he had not been able to see whoever was doing all that shouting. Still, he had known by the high tone, it was a child.

"There's a dead man out here," the voice shrieked repeatedly. "Somebody come quick. Come quick. There's a dead man out here."

"I ain't dead," Zeb had finally found the strength to say, hoping that it would stop the child from all that incessant screeching, then winced when his comment had brought an even louder shriek.

Although his memory became even more hazy after that, Zeb did recall that two women and a young boy eventually helped him into a wagon. He also remembered them helping him from the wagon into a house. He had felt hot from having lain too

111

long in the sun when they had first placed him in a bed and then started to tend to his injury. So hot, he had barely been able to stay conscious.

"This man has been shot," he remembered the older woman exclaiming just seconds after she had cut away the leg of his pants. Although he could not remember exactly what her face looked like, he could recall that she had possessed very gentle hands. "Sam, ride over to the Ewan's and get your papa. Tell him what we've found and to get back here right away. Then I want you to ride on to Karnack and find the doctor there. If you ride hard, you can be back before dark."

"No ma'am," Zeb had found the strength to say. "No, ma'am. No doctor. Please. I don't want no doctor. Please. Promise me. No doctors. All I need is some rest. That's all I need. Some rest. Please. No doctors."

Clearly against her better judgement, the woman had finally agreed. "Okay, Sam. You don't have to go for the doctor. But you do need to ride over to Mr. Ewan's and bring your papa back. Tell him to hurry."

Relieved there would be no doctor coming, and thus no sheriff, Zeb had sighed aloud his thanks. "And please, boy, don't tell nobody I'm here. Not just yet. There's a real bad man out trying to get me for something I didn't even do. He'll be lookin' for me. He'll kill me if he finds me."

Sam had glanced at his mother, who had then nodded in agreement. "Just tell your papa I need him to come home and to hurry."

Zeb could not remember anything that happened after that. All he knew was that he now lay in a soft feather bed, wearing a clean, white nightshirt, his leg neatly bandaged, and his face freshly shaved. Al-

though he could not recall having had his clothes removed, nor could he remember that anyone had
gone to the trouble to shave him, he was pleased to
discover they were taking such good care of him. He
was also pleased to be resting in a soft bed, surrounded by such a comfortably furnished bedroom,
and not in some dingy jail cell.

"Oh, I see you are awake," a young woman who
looked about twenty-three or twenty-four said when
she entered the room, a bright smile on her pretty
face.

Zeb noticed the smile was warm and sincere when
she came forward to set the hand towels she carried
on a nearby table. He took an immediate liking to
her. She was attractive in a way no saloon girl could
ever hope to be.

"Where am I?" he asked, though he had a pretty
good idea where—that is if he had followed those directions right. "And who might you be?"

"My name is Sarah and this is my parents' house,"
she explained, her tone cheerful as she stepped even
closer.

In all his thirty-one years, Zeb didn't think he had
ever seen eyes so blue or cheeks so naturally fair. He
felt his blood stir hotly inside him causing his leg to
throb.

"My little brother found you out in our pasture.
You were so weak from the loss of blood, you
couldn't walk and could barely talk. At that time we
had no idea what had happened to you, but after we
brought you into the house and tore your clothing
away, we discovered you had been shot."

"How long have I been here?" Zeb reached up to
scratch his head and discovered someone had not
only washed his hair but had gone to the trouble to
comb it neatly away from his face. He couldn't re-

member ever feeling so blasted clean. It was a downright eerie sensation.

"You've been here since day before yesterday. That first night after we found you, you developed quite a fever and started talking out of your head. We worried then you might be dying and Mother stayed awake all night keeping cool rags on your forehead. But luckily, the fever broke early that next morning and you calmed down shortly after that. You have been sleeping pretty peacefully ever since. By the way, I think we may have also found your horse."

"My horse?"

"Yes, while my brother was on his way back from a neighbor's ranch, he spotted a saddled horse standing right in the middle of the creek, munching on fishweeds of all things. Since that was the same direction from which you had obviously come and because he found several bloodstains on the saddle, he realized the horse had to be yours so he brought him back here. We have him in our barn and are taking very good care of him."

Zeb could tell by the way she talked and by her mannerisms, that Sarah was an educated, somewhat genteel young lady. She was also a woman who took to regular bathing and laundering. He wondered then if she had a husband, though it didn't matter much to him if she did. Husbands could be gotten around.

"What time is it?" he asked and next reached to scratch his whiskers only to be reminded he had none. Why there wasn't even any stubble hiding in the cleft of his chin. Someone had sure done a number on him while he was asleep.

"It's about four o'clock I guess. This room isn't used very often so we don't keep a clock in here and I don't have a watch to know the exact

114

time. Would you like for me to find out?"

She sure was a helpful little thing, Zeb thought, then heard a clattering noise in the next room and became immediately cautious. He quickly propped himself on one elbow and stared past her into the hallway, too concerned to notice the resulting pain in his leg. "Who else is here?"

"Just my mother and my father—oh, and of course my little brother, Sam. That was probably Sam making that noise," she explained then frowned briefly. "Sam is always making noise."

"And where are all these people?"

"Let's see," she said, tapping the corner of her mouth while she considered her answer. "Mother is in the kitchen starting supper and Papa is outside cutting and baling another field of hay. After last year's drought, hay became so scarce around here, everyone is trying to harvest as many cuttings as possible this year. Can't afford to feed the livestock straight feed anymore."

"Anyone else here?" he asked, watching her carefully for a reaction. He had to know exactly what he was up against. "A husband perhaps?"

"No, I have no husband," she said with a quick smile as if thinking it an absurd suggestion. "There's just Carlito and Thomas. They live out in the bunkhouse and help Papa work the farm. Right now, they are out in the field helping him with the hay."

Zeb mulled over everything she had told him and decided he was in no immediate danger. "Who bandaged up my leg so nice and pretty?"

"Mother did. We'd have sent for the doctor, but you seemed dead set against it."

"I can believe that. I don't trust doctors," he said, hoping to justify what must have seemed like pretty bizarre behavior. The last thing he needed was to

115

make these trusting people suspicious of him. "I'd rather take my chances with common fate than let a doctor anywhere near me."

"Obviously," Sarah laughed. "You certainly didn't have anything kind to say about them. Fact was, you were cursing one doctor in particular during the worst part of that fever."

The muscles in Zeb's chest tightened with instant apprehension. "Why? What did I say?"

"You seemed to think some doctor was hunting you down just to hurt you. You were very frightened and very confused. You also kept calling out to some captain for help."

"I did?"

"Yes, you kept crying out things like, 'Captain, Captain, I need help. Captain, Captain, I got to have some men. Can't face 'em alone, Captain. Please, Captain, send me some help.'" She then looked at him curiously. "Were you in the war?"

Aware she had provided the perfect opportunity to bring about George Martin's name, Zeb nodded. "Yes, and it was a terrible experience."

"That's what Papa thought. That's why he decided not to tell anyone you are here."

Not understanding the logic, but aware of the implication, Zeb asked, "Why? Did someone come by here lookin' for me?"

"Yes, twice. Once yesterday and once earlier today. Both times Papa told them that he hadn't seen anyone and didn't have the time to be talking to them about it. He had to get his hay crop in."

Zeb was so relieved, his whole body trembled. "But why? Why did he protect me like that? I'm a complete stranger to him."

"Because he feels he owes you that much. He had you figured for a Civil War veteran right off, what

116

with all that talk about a captain and needing help. He also knew by your accent that you had to have fought for the South. The way he sees it, you may have fought right along side my brother, George. Therefore, he thinks we owe it to you to protect you."

"George?" he asked, priming her. "You have a brother named George who fought for the Confederacy?"

"I did." Suddenly Sarah's expression became very solemn. "He was killed several years ago. During the war." She then abruptly changed the subject. "I suspect you are probably pretty hungry by now. I'll go see if Mother has anything cooked that you could eat."

Frowning to realize she had just ruined the perfect opportunity to mention he had known her brother, Zeb sank back into the fat, feather pillows and muttered quietly while he watched her disappear, "You just do that. Tell her to bring me a big, fat juicy steak with a big, fat buttered potato standing off to the side."

Then, aware she was well out of hearing range, he added with a perverse sneer. "And for dessert tell your sweet mother I'd like to spend the rest of the night in this very bed enjoying her lovely daughter's most pleasurable attributes. Bullet wound or no bullet wound, I still got what it takes to let you know what the best part of being a woman is."

His evil smirk widened and he decided that if he wasn't in too big of a rush when the time came to leave East Texas, he would do just that. He would show Miss Sarah Martin what glorious pleasures could be found in the confines of a single bed.

"You are one lucky woman, Miss Sarah Martin," he chuckled happily. "Before I'm through teachin' you all about the pleasures of womanhood, you'll be beggin' for me to take you with me. Too bad, I travel alone."

Raymond Lindsey reached just below his badge into his shirt pocket and pulled out a rumpled blue bandanna. He shook it once to open it then turned to look at Lathe.

"I'm starting to believe that this Zeb Turner fella either managed to ride that creek all the way to Caddo Lake where there are at least a half dozen tiny communities where he could have found help or else he crawled off into some hiding spot somewhere close by where he eventually died from his gunshot wound."

He mopped his sweaty brow with the bandanna then sank heavily into his desk chair. "Nobody has seen hide nor hair of the man or his horse since the night I shot him. And we never did find one single place along that creek bed where it looked like a rider might have come out. Of course it's possible he came out at any of the usual crossings and his horse's tracks would have been lost with the rest, but I don't think that was the case. The roads around here are too well traveled. Even at night. Someone would have seen him."

Lathe hooked his hat over the wall peg then ran his hand through his damp hair, frustrated that the sheriff sounded ready to give up after only three days.

"You are wrong about Zeb Turner being dead. But you are probably right about the main roads. If he had risked traveling along any one of them or if he had risked going into any of the local communities or towns, I think you'd have heard something by now. You've sent telegrams to many towns warning people to keep a watch for him. No, he's still out there and he's still very much alive. He's just well hidden at the moment."

"Nobody can hide that good for that long," the sheriff commented, thinking it very unlikely. "Especially when he's bleeding from a bullet wound and has no food."

"Let me assure you, this person can. He's a pretty crafty and determined man when it comes to saving his own skin."

"Well, I can't spend any more of my time riding around the countryside looking for him. I've got an entire county to take care of and no matter where this Zeb fellow may be hiding, he doesn't really seem to be much of a threat to us anymore," the sheriff said, obviously searching for a worthwhile excuse to give up the hunt. He was hot and tired and rightfully so. Both he and Lathe had been in the saddle for most of the past three days and neither had gotten much sleep in between.

Aggravated by the sheriff's pitiful excuse to quit, Lathe visibly tightened his jaw.

"You don't seem to understand. As long as that man is out there running loose, he is a threat to anyone he comes into contact with," Lathe explained, still hoping to convince him not to quit. Not yet. "Anyone who can slit a young man's throat for no apparent reason other than his own obvious lust for blood is capable of doing just about anything."

He decided not to mention that the young man had been his brother. It was too painful to say aloud.

"Still, I've got other responsibilities. You keep on looking for him if you've a mind to, but I've got to turn my attention to other matters. I just hope you

119

understand. I did give it my best shot. I just can't stay on this forever."

Knowing it would do more harm than good to alienate a man he would probably need again in the very near future, Lathe tried not to reveal his frustration. "Yes, I do understand. You have your duties. Just please be sure to let me know if and when you do hear anything concerning Zeb's whereabouts. Anything at all. I'll be staying at the Traveler's Hotel until I finally can find out in which direction Zeb went."

"You're staying at the hotel?" the sheriff asked with a raised brow. The corner of his mouth turned as if he were trying to conceal his amusement. "I heard you were staying over at Miss Stegall's."

Lathe frowned at the implication. "I was staying there until earlier today. But I was only staying until I saw evidence that Miss Stegall had finally gotten some of her strength back, which she has already started to do. When I stopped by this morning, I discovered she had managed to get dressed all by herself and was sitting in a chair in the front room taking care of some of her book work. I figure by tomorrow, she'll be moving around the house with little trouble so she really won't be needing anyone watching over her. And because she did get over her fainting spells so quickly, I plan to move my things back to the hotel later this afternoon."

Besides it was far too frustrating to be around a woman that beautiful and that alluring, who looked so incredibly angelic yet proved to be so downright aggravating and pig-headed about things. Ever since he had allowed his opinions about the Civil War to be known, *nothing* he ever said suited her.

"Mighty pretty lady that Miss Stegall," the sheriff commented, eyeing Lathe carefully, wondering why

Lathe seemed so distracted. "I think if I was a single young doctor who had such an excuse to stay right there in the house with her, I'd use it for as long as I possibly could."

"Well, you are neither single nor a doctor," Lathe reminded him. "And you don't know how truly exasperating that *pretty little lady* can be."

"Oh, but I do. I've had a few run-ins with her myself. I guess the best word to describe that one is *opinionated,* and strongly so."

"That is only *one* of many words that comes to my mind," Lathe said then grinned. "Obstinate and irritating also suit her very well." He then shook his head. "All I can say is that I'd sure hate to be her husband. Can you imagine what that would be like?"

"Oh, I don't know," the sheriff commented, also grinning while he tucked his handkerchief back into his pocket. "Life might prove to be downright interestin' married to an attractive little spitfire like that."

"Interesting?" Lathe repeated with a disbelieving lift of his eyebrows. "Infuriating is more the word that comes to my mind."

The sheriff chuckled, indicating he agreed. "Well, at least there'd never be a dull moment. Whoo-ee, I remember the time that little hellion took on our entire Little Mound Baptist congregation all because they were tryin' to keep a large family of black folks from buying a house that was just inside the town limits. She sure was quick to remind us of the new rights them black folks now got. Even threatened to bring in a federal marshall if the town didn't quit harassing those folks. Fixed it so I had no choice but to protect them. It wasn't long before a second family of them moved in. Now we got a whole street

121

of Negroes living inside the town limits."

"She did that?" Lathe asked, finding it hard to believe she had done anything so noble. "But I thought she was a strong advocate of slavery."

"Naw, not that one. She treats black folks like they was just as good as the rest of us, which I guess some of them are. But she's taken it a might too far. She lets them shop in her store anytime they want and lets them buy whatever they want, even lets them have first pickin's if they happen in at the right time. Why she even lets some of them have credit—which might have something to do with the reason that store of hers is in such pitiful shape. The woman can't have much business sense."

"I don't understand," Lathe said more to himself than to the sheriff. He shook his head while he pitted what the sheriff had just told him against some of what Leona herself had said two nights prior. "If that's how she feels, then what was all that righteous garbage she fed me the other night about the noble causes behind the Civil War? She even went as far as to try to convince me that her brother had fought and died for the truest and most honorable of reasons."

"That was probably because she thinks the federal government shouldn't have the right to be tellin' us all how to run our lives. She believes that some matters ought be left up to each individual state to decide—even if it is something not everybody in the state agrees on, like slavery. I reckon most folks around here feel that way about the North. A law that might seem just for one area of this country isn't always equally just for another. Just like with that slavery issue. The federal government just doesn't take everyone into consideration when they go to passing out laws. If they'd just be a little more considerate of *everyone's* rights, then there'd be no problem."

But what about the Negroes rights to freedom? Lathe wondered, believing the sheriff's way of thinking to be very narrow-minded; but he decided not to get into another pointless discussion about a war that had long since ended, so he changed the subject to something else that was bothering him.

"What do you know about this George Parkinson fellow who keeps spending so much of his time hanging around Leon—er, Miss Stegall's house."

"Not much. Just that he's a mountain trapper turned drifter and has taken a temporary liking to Little Mound," the sheriff answered then offered another grin. "Or maybe it's Miss Stegall he's taken a temporary liking to. But then it could be his liking isn't all that temporary."

For some reason that comment rubbed Lathe the wrong way. "Well, I think it would be wise on your part to keep a close eye on him. I don't know why, but there's something about that man that bothers me."

"Probably because he spends so much of his day visiting with your favorite patient," the sheriff commented, again studying Lathe's expression to see what might be revealed. Talk was, something out of the ordinary was going on between him and Miss Leona—something more than the usual doctor-patient relationship. But then, again, talk around Little Mound was never all that reliable.

"No, it has nothing to do with Miss Stegall," Lathe quickly assured him. "It's just that I have this eerie feeling I've seen him somewhere before and although I can't remember exactly where it was, I feel almost certain he was up to no good at the time."

"Well, if you do finally remember where you've

123

seen him, and it turns out he was up to no good, let me know. I like to keep an eye on any troublemakers that may be in town. But, to tell you the truth, he seemed like a pretty nice fellow to me. Just in need of a good shave and a haircut is all. Seems *real* concerned about Miss Stegall's health."

"Still, I think you should keep a close watch on him," Lathe repeated then stepped to the door and plucked his hat off the wall peg with an annoyed jerk. "I guess I'd better get back out there and see if I can find out anything more about where Zeb might have gone. I'll check back with you in the morning."

He slapped his hat back onto his head when he stepped back out onto the boardwalk, but it did little to protect him from the glare of the afternoon sun. He wrinkled the right side of his face to keep the slanting rays from blinding him while he started across the street to where he had left his horse tethered to one of the ornate hitching posts that bordered the courthouse lawn.

There were still a few hours before dark, time enough to ride out to the Sobey farm and see if John Sobey had uncovered anything yet that might indicate Zeb had been there.

Until he had viable proof Zeb had left the area, he planned to continue visiting the families of anyone who had been killed in the Civil War. He also planned to continue stopping in at the different places that sold medical supplies to see if anyone made any purchases that might indicate a gunshot wound.

One way or another, Lathe would find Zeb Turner and when he did, he would see to it justice was finally served.

Chapter Seven

"I'll see who's at the door," Ethan said, frowning that Leona would even consider getting up out of her chair for something so unimportant. "You just stay put."

"But, George, like I keep trying to tell you, I'm *not* helpless," Leona complained. "As long as I keep my right arm pressed close to my side, I don't have any pain and I'm not all that dizzy anymore. Why even the doctor has admitted I am doing a lot better. That's why he agreed that you could give me back my clothes and allowed me finally to get out of that bed." If only she could have convinced them to let her go back to work.

"Still, there's no need you exertin' yourself when you don't have to," Ethan pointed out. "I'll get the door. You just keep tallying up those books and receipts you made me go get for you."

Having discovered there was little point arguing with either George or Lathe when their minds were that set, Leona smiled to herself and settled back into her chair.

It was amazing how quickly she and George Parkinson had developed their natural, caring friendship. She felt as if she had known him forever, yet she had never even met him until three days ago.

She supposed the reason their friendship had budded so quickly had something to do with the fact he reminded her so much of Ethan. Although there were several definite differences between the two, there were also many similarities. In a way, having George there was like having a part of her brother back and she liked that. Even if it was only for the next few days.

When Leona reached for the pencil she had just set aside, her reflective smile faded into the concerned frown that had tugged at her face for the past several hours, since she had started trying to catch up on her bookwork.

The meager columns of figures in front of her looked pathetic. So pathetic, she knew she could not wait any longer to have her brother declared legally dead. She had to have that loan for her business to survive. No matter how badly she dreaded seeing Ethan's name printed across a death certificate, she had to find enough courage to have it done. Even Ethan would have thought it the sensible thing to do — anything that might save the Mercantile from further ruin.

Leona had worked it all out in her mind while lying awake in bed the night before. She knew she should have mentioned something about her decision to John earlier that day when he had stopped by to see how she felt.

He would have been by to see her sooner, but had been out of town most of the week and had just that morning learned about Tuesday night's incident. He hadn't stayed long, because he had fallen so far behind at work, but still she could have found the time to tell him how she had finally reached her decision so he could start on the paperwork. Problem was, she had been unable to force the words out of her mouth. Why did it have to be so painful?

"Who is it, George?" she called out, eager to get her thoughts off of the dreadful thing she had to do and onto something else.

"Don't know yet," he called back while he reached for the door latch. "I haven't opened it yet."

Still, he could tell by the shape of the shadowy figure through the ivory lace curtains that the visitor was a woman; but he could not yet make out who it might be. He just hoped it was not someone who might unexpectedly recognize him and then turn around and try to convince Leona he really was her brother and not just someone who looked amazingly like him. But then again, no one had recognized him yet, not decisively.

He stroked his heavy beard while he considered how very much he had changed during the past nine years—both physically *and emotionally.* It was little wonder no one had recognized him. At times he hardly recognized himself.

"Hello, may I—" he began even before he had the door completely open, but the greeting caught at the back of his throat when he saw who it was.

Sarah.

Sarah Martin.

The younger sister of the very man he had accidentally killed so many years ago. The sister of his very best friend.

He felt a cold, prickling knot form in the pit of his stomach and took a deep breath to steady himself before finishing his statement with as much calm as he could muster, "—help you?"

Sarah looked at him with an odd expression then blinked several times as if to push a questioning thought aside. Finally she smiled. "Hello. My name is Sarah Martin. I'm a friend of Leona's. I understand she's been badly hurt. Is she feeling up to visitors?"

"I'll say," Ethan said then forced a generous smile, altering the curve of it just enough, so it would not seem too familiar. His legs felt shaky when he stepped back to let her inside. "She's about to go insane with want of someone to talk to. Come on in and see for yourself."

He swallowed hard after she stepped past him, then paused to look at him again. She smelled of lavender soap and lemon verbena and her blonde hair shimmered bright gold. His nostrils flared slightly while he breathed deeply the sweet scent. "She's in that room off to your right. Got tired of sittin' in bed all day and decided to get some book work done."

"That certainly sounds like her," Sarah commented then laughed.

Ethan had forgotten how beautiful Sarah's laughter sounded. He felt his chest tighten with so many regrets. "Just go on in and make yourself to home. I'll be in as soon as I've checked the vegetable stew I've got cookin' for her supper."

Sarah took several steps then looked back at him again curiously. "Do I know you?"

Ethan shook his head adamantly then felt an unaccountable urge to cover the ugly scar that disfigured his right cheek with his hand—but didn't. "No, ma'am. You've never seen me before in your life. But your friend, Miss Stegall, seems to think I look something like her brother, Ethan. Maybe you knew him."

Sarah's eyes widened. "That's it. You do look a lot like Ethan. In fact you look very much like him. Especially around the eyes. But then again, I think Ethan was just a little taller than you are and not nearly as—," she hesitated, not wanting to make him feel awkward for being such a large man, "—*muscular* as you. Still, you do look a lot like him. How long have you known Leona?"

She narrowed her eyes while she wondered why Leona had never mentioned her handsome new friend who looked so much like Ethan.

"About three days," he answered, then decided to explain. "I was there the night she got hurt. I feel kind of responsible for what happened because I didn't do one single thing to help her. I guess I was just so stunned by what was happening that I didn't think to react in time. Fact is, I didn't react at all until it was all over, then it was too late."

"And exactly what did happen?" Sarah wanted to know. "I stopped by the Mercantile to visit with her for a little while and was told that she was having to stay home because someone had stabbed her in the back with a knife. I couldn't believe it. Why, I saw her just last Tuesday and she was fine. Was it a robbery?"

"Why don't you let Leona tell you all about it? Just be warned that each time she tells the story it gets a little more elaborate." He chuckled, thinking Leona should have been a novel writer. "I'll be in after I've checked on her supper. I'd hate for that stew to burn to the bottom of the pot after all the work I've put into it." Not only had he had to go into town to get most of the ingredients, he'd had a hard time remembering all the things that their mother used to put into her stew. But evidently he had lucked out because the last time he sampled it he was surprised to discover it actually tasted the way it was supposed to.

Sarah continued to watch with a curious expression when he then turned and strode toward the

129

back of the house. He was such an impressively large man. Although he wasn't particularly tall, nor was he what one would consider fat; he was massive. He virtually filled the hallway with his presence.

Having found herself immediately attracted to his eyes, she wondered what the rest of his face looked like. If only he didn't have that thick accumulation of hair covering it.

She continued to study his back and speculated what he might look like with a haircut and a clean shave, until finally he ducked out of sight. She then turned toward the front parlor, eager to find out everything that had happened since she had been by to visit with her early last Tuesday.

By the time Ethan had finished in the kitchen and returned to the front parlor, Leona had already told most of her tale and was answering Sarah's jumble of questions. He paused in the doorway to listen.

"What happened to the man who stabbed you? Did they ever find him? Did you get a look at him?" Sarah wanted to know, leaning forward in her seat, eagerly awaiting the answers. Like Tony, she found the incident as thrilling as it was frightening.

"Oh, yes, I got a good look at him and he was a terror to behold," Leona said, eager to watch Sarah's bright blue eyes stretch to their limits. "He was *huge,* probably six foot five, and had a knife as big as any I've ever seen. I am very lucky to be alive after such a ruthless attack." That was the only part of her tale that was completely true. She *was* lucky to be alive, because although the wound was not all that deep, it had bled terribly. Another few minutes of bleeding and she might not have been there to tell her riveting tale.

Ethan chuckled after hearing his sister's latest description of Zeb. "He's grown another inch has he?"

Unaware he had returned, Leona jerked her head to face him. She immediately lifted an eyebrow and thrust her chin out as if to warn him to keep any further comments to himself. "Who's telling this story? You or me?"

"Why you are of course," he relented then took several steps into the room and sank into a nearby chair, duly chastened. "Please, go on. Don't let me interrupt."

Leona heaved an annoyed sigh, then believing they had discussed the incident enough anyway, she glanced back at Sarah with an amused expression. "I guess you've already met my new, personal guardian angel, George Parkinson. I'm not really sure why, but George has decided it is his undeniable duty to take care of me for the next few days."

"George?" Sarah repeated the name, tilting her head to one side while she again studied Ethan's strong features. Something about his large round eyes attracted her attention. Though he was smiling, his eyes revealed an inner sadness. "I used to have a brother named George."

Ethan felt a sharp pain pierce his chest for it was the sort of statement he had not wanted to hear from her own sweet lips, not when he knew he was the one responsible for her brother's death.

"Used to?" he asked, knowing a response of some sort was expected. "What happened to him?" He steeled himself for her answer, knowing that whatever the captain had eventually decided to tell the family, it would hurt him to hear it.

"My brother was killed in the Civil War," she explained, her voice suddenly soft and tender. Her blue eyes took on an anguished, distant look when she went on to say, "But he was very brave. He was awarded a medal posthumously for having died a hero's death in battle. We were told he was killed trying to save an injured friend."

"Oh?" is all Ethan could say, knowing that was not at all the way it happened.

How it hurt to see the pain Sarah still felt when she spoke of her older brother. He could well imagine how the entire family had suffered, *still* suffered. And there was no one to blame but himself. How he despised himself for what he had done. How he wished he had died that day, too. Then he would not have been forced to live with the sickening realization of what he'd done.

"Yes," Sarah continued, her eyes glimmering with a fine sheen of tears while the memories tore painfully at her heart. "Papa had the medal mounted in a special glass frame. It hangs on the wall near the front door, right beside a picture George had taken when he and two of his friends went to Shreveport only a couple of years before he eventually went off to war. He was probably about sixteen then, but it's the only large picture we have of him."

"I imagine your family is very proud of him," Ethan said, feeling more wretched by the minute. He remembered that trip to Shreveport and all the fun the three of them had shared. They had called it their first real adventure and what an adventure it had been.

Ethan swallowed around the constriction swelling at the base of his throat. If only George *had* died the hero's death, then *all* the memories of his friend could be happy ones, like how the three of them had lost their innocence in a Shreveport brothel and how George had enjoyed it so well, he went back for seconds. If George had died by anyone's hand but his own, Ethan would not be so constantly tormented by the truth.

"Oh, they *are* proud of him," she agreed. "We all are. Very proud. Just as proud as Leona is of her brother, Ethan. Although Ethan's body was never found and a medal was never awarded, we know he also must have died bravely. You see, Ethan was George's best friend. It wouldn't surprise me if they didn't both die in the very same battle, fighting side by side."

And in a way they had, Ethan thought sadly but let the dismal feeling pass when Leona suddenly changed the focus of their conversation to him.

"Don't you think George looks a little like Ethan?"

"Yes, I do," Sarah agreed. Both women turned to face him squarely. "He looks a lot like Ethan. He may be a little shorter than Ethan would be by now and a little broader across the shoulder, and a *lot* hairier; but they do favor. They really do."

Leona laughed as she, too, studied Ethan's thick beard and his bushy shoulder-length brown hair. In truth, she had never seen so much hair on one man. "Sarah, you certainly have a way of putting your finger on the obvious. Also, Ethan would never have allowed himself to feel so guilty about an incident that had had absolutely nothing to do with him. Why George here was a good block and a half away when that horrible man suddenly grabbed me and put that knife to my throat. There was nothing George could have done to save me. Yet he still thinks it was somehow his fault I ended up with this large gash in my back. Ethan would have had the good sense to realize he was not to blame for something like that and wouldn't be feeling so guilty. If anything, he'd be shaking his head and asking me how I had managed to get myself into such a foolish situation."

"I don't know," Sarah said, in ready defense of

Leona's deceased brother. "You make Ethan sound so cold-hearted when I always thought of Ethan as having a pretty warm and generous heart."

"That's because you had such a terrible crush on him," Leona reminded her and smiled fondly at the memory. "But instead of noticing you, he was too wrapped up with his plans to go off to college and become a world renowned businessman."

Ethan's eyes widened when the brunt of Leona's words struck him. The most beautiful girl in school had had a crush on him? It couldn't be, and if it was, why hadn't Sarah let *him* know it? Why hadn't Leona? Knowing about it would have made all the difference in the world. As it was, he had been too afraid Sarah might laugh at him to ever tell her how violently she made his heart jump whenever she was around. Even now, she stirred his blood like no other woman could. He glanced at her left hand and was relieved to see no engagement ring nor wedding band.

"No," Sarah corrected her. "His lack of attention had nothing to do with college. Ethan and George were too excited about the possibility of going off to war to notice anyone or anything else."

Leona's smile faded and her eyes took on that sad, forlorn look again. "That's true." She paused for a long moment, then admitted. "Sarah, I'm thinking about having Ethan declared legally dead."

To Ethan, her words had struck like a sharp blow to the stomach. "Your brother isn't legally dead?" In all that time no one had bothered to have the legal papers drafted? Hadn't the captain's letter convinced them he was dead? It had certainly sounded convincing enough to him.

"No," she answered then explained. "The army never found his body, which of course isn't all that

134

uncommon. But because they had failed to locate any physical proof of Ethan's death, the army refused to have him declared dead. Instead, he was placed on a long list of missing men."

"Still, the war has been over for nearly five years," Ethan pointed out.

"That's true; but for some reason, I could never bring myself to having the matter settled. But now I don't have much choice. If I don't have Ethan declared legally dead, I can't get the loan I need to keep the Mercantile functioning until first harvest."

Aware first harvest always brought a great influx of customer payments, Ethan didn't question what that had to do with anything. Instead, he asked, "What does having your brother declared dead have to do with getting a loan?"

Leona explained it to him the way Bebber Davis had explained it to her last Tuesday morning. When she was finished telling about her humiliating visit to the bank, both Sarah and Ethan were so angry their hands balled into fists.

"What that foolish man won't do to try to coerce you into marrying John," Sarah muttered. "Why can't Bebber get it through his thick head that you do not love that self-centered son of his? Why can't he see that you and John are just friends, and barely that?"

"I don't know," Leona said with a weary shake of her head. "Although I do like John enough to attend a dance or go on a group picnic with him occasionally, you are right. I do not love him. But obviously, his father believes I'm the only woman in this town who can produce the grandson he so desperately wants."

"But what would be the point of having children if you don't love the man who gives them to you?"

135

Sarah wanted her know, her delicate brow knitted. "I know I'd never agree to marry a man I didn't love."

"Me either. Which is why you and I are both doomed to be spinsters for the rest of our natural lives. You lost the only man you ever loved and I have never found one worth loving."

Sarah shook her head and offered a sad smile. "It's hard to say I *lost* someone when I never really had him. If you remember, he never thought of me as anything more than his best friend's little sister."

Ethan blinked, stunned to hear her speak of him with such reverence. "You mean you loved Leona's brother so much that his death has prevented you from ever falling in love again?" He thought about that for a long moment, before asking, "And I remind you of him?"

Leona rolled her eyes toward the ceiling then grinned, glad to have momentary relief from the oppressive sadness that had again settled over them. "Don't go getting any ridiculous notions, George. You don't look *that* much like him."

Sarah laughed that golden laugh again and her blue eyes sparkled with renewed delight. "My, you certainly are bold for a guardian angel."

"Yeah, I suppose I am," he said, grinning, also glad to get away from such depressing subjects. "But then again, how do you know that all guardian angels are not this bold? How many have you ever actually met?"

"None that I can recall," she admitted readily, having taken to Leona's new friend immediately. "Not a single one." She then glanced at Leona and winked. "To think, he cooks, he cleans, he washes clothes and takes care of any little accidental knife injuries you might get. Why he has managed to do more around here in three days than you usually get done in a month," she said, then laughed. "What else could a woman possibly ask for in a man?"

"But I'm not the one who took care of Leona's injuries," Ethan was quick to supply, though why he thought he should clarify that point was beyond him. Maybe it was because he felt there were enough lies between them already. "I get squeamish when I see blood, especially if it's a woman's blood. The doctor is the one who took care of all her cuts and bruises."

"What doctor?" Sarah asked, puzzled. "Little Mound doesn't have a doctor." She then glanced at Leona. "I thought George was the one who has been taking care of you."

Leona looked at Ethan curiously, remembering that he had known about Doc Owen the night she was injured. She wondered how he had known such a thing when he supposedly had just arrived in town, but she decided not to question him about it while her friend was there. Instead she filed that curious bit of information away in the back of her head and returned her attention to Sarah while she explained about the doctor. "He has been taking care of me off and on since then. But another man took care of the wound itself. As it turns out the man I was telling you about, the one dressed in black and hiding in the alley with his pistol drawn ready to shoot was really a doctor."

"A doctor who tries to shoot people?"

"That's right," Leona said with an expression that showed she thought it peculiar, too.

"A *doctor?*"

"Yes. His name is Lathe Caldwell and even though he does wear a gun, it turns out it's his mouth he shoots off the most," she quipped, feeling perverse pleasure for having said it. She wished he had been there to hear it. "Lathe seems to think that

137

because he's an attractive young doctor who served as a surgeon in the Civil War, everyone is supposed to be in complete awe of him. He loves telling people what to do and gets very, *very* testy when his orders aren't followed to the letter."

"He's young?" Sarah asked, lifting a brow while she studied her friend's annoyed expression. The fact that Leona had called this *young* doctor by his given name had not escaped her. "And he's attractive, too?"

"In an undeniable sort of way," Leona admitted, then laughed and leaned closer. "Actually, if he wasn't so utterly conceited, and if he didn't have such foolish ideas about some things, he'd be downright handsome. But as it is, that insufferable, overly inflated male ego of his gets well in the way of his good looks. You know the type."

Sarah nodded that indeed she did. "Only too well."

Ethan wanted to laugh. He had never heard two women openly discuss the attributes and defects of a man before. It intrigued him that women obviously scrutinized men in much the same manner that men scrutinized women. He wondered what these two would say about him when they got together again after he had left. He hoped they would prove much kinder in their appraisal.

"Well, at least Lathe is out there still trying to capture the man who did that to you," Ethan said, not knowing why he felt so obliged to come to the man's defense. After all, he had been sent to capture him for the captain, not defend him to his own sister.

"Only because he wants the man for another reason," Leona explained, remembering it had something to do with a murder.

"The man who stabbed you wasn't captured?"

Sarah asked, clearly alarmed. She had not yet questioned Leona about that part of the story. She'd just assumed Sheriff Lindsey had brought him in. Sheriff Lindsey was usually very good at bringing any outlaws to justice.

"No, he got away," Leona admitted with an annoyed frown, then afraid that she might be frightening Sarah needlessly, she added, "But he's long gone from these parts by now. He lit out of Little Mound like a jackrabbit with his tail on fire. As fast as that horse of his was making tracks, he's probably three states away by now."

Ethan wasn't too sure of her assessment. He had heard a rumor that Zeb might have been shot, which surely would have slowed him down. Still, he did not want to frighten Sarah either. Besides, Zeb would have no reason to harm her. "Or he could be halfway to California, dependin' on which direction he headed after he lost the sheriff."

For the next hour, at Ethan's careful direction, the conversation followed a much lighter vein. The three talked about whatever trivial topics crossed their minds until eventually it was time for Sarah to leave.

Because Sarah had promised her father not to breathe a word about their unexpected house guest to anyone, she did not tell Leona about the injured man they had found lying in their pasture nor the fact that the man had served in the same troop with their brothers. Instead, she decided to save that story for a later day.

When she left Leona's house shortly after five, all she acknowledged was that she still had a few errands to run before heading home. She did not mention that those errands included buying a jar of sulphur salve to put on Zeb Turner's leg wound to help stop the infection that had already set in. Nor did she mention that she would have to purchase him another pair of trousers. There had not been one single change of clothing in his saddlebags. Whoever it was Zeb was running from had frightened him so terribly, he had ridden off and left all his clothing behind.

It was a shame that a war hero should end up being treated that way.

Although it was not what he had planned, Ethan was still at Leona's when Lathe stopped by to check on her, and to pick up the pistol and shirt he had left in the kitchen that morning.

Afraid Lathe might yet remember where it was he had seen him, Ethan had hoped to leave long before Lathe returned. Lathe was the most probable person to remember having seen him before. And if Lathe ever did remember exactly where he had seen him and when, he would immediately realize he could not be the trapper from the Ozarks he claimed to be.

"You still here?" Lathe asked, eyeing the husky man with obvious suspicion after stepping inside. Because the men were nearly the same height, their eyes met straight on. "Don't you think it looks a little improper for you to be over here *all* the time?"

"Not when she's been injured and needs someone to help her tend to her chores," he answered simply, though he was tempted to point out that it was probably less improper for him to be there helping her during the day when people were constantly coming and going than it was for Lathe to be there keeping an eye on her at night.

Lathe crossed his arms and wondered if Leona's chores were *all* this man was tending to, but kept the comment to himself.

"Besides I was just leaving," Ethan continued, though in truth, he had been headed for the kitchen to check the stew one last time when he had heard the knock. He reached out to catch the door before it closed at the same time he snatched his hat from the wall peg, as if to prove his intention to leave. "You'll find Leona in the parlor reading."

Lathe did not like the easy way Leona's name had rolled from his tongue but before he could comment, Ethan continued with what he had to say.

"And I have a big pot of stew already cooking on the stove. It's been simmering for several hours so it should be about done, but it is very hot. Be sure to take it off the fire and let it cool for at least ten minutes before you spoon her up a bowl. Oh, and some of the neighbors have brought a few desserts and things like that over. Those are sitting on the counter. After Leona finishes her stew, she can have her choice of lemon or blackberry pie or what's left of the chocolate cake."

Lathe narrowed his gaze. Although he had not intended to stay but a few minutes, he would much rather be the one to serve Leona her supper than give this man a reason to stay any longer. Something about this George Parkinson just didn't add up right. If only he could figure out what it was about the man that bothered him. "Anything else?"

"Not that I can think of," he answered then stepped on through the front door. "Just remind her I'll be back in the morning with that rented carriage like I promised."

"Why are you coming over in a carriage?" he asked, thinking it too soon for her to be accepting romantic drives through the country. True, her health had improved at an amazing rate, but her

141

shoulder was nowhere near healed enough for that sort of gallivanting.

"So she won't have to walk that two and a half blocks to the Mercantile," Ethan answered. "I know she claims to be as good as new and two and a half blocks isn't all that far, but I'd feel a lot better about her decision to go in and check on her store tomorrow if I knew she didn't have to walk."

"She's still determined to go to work in the morning?" Lathe asked, although he was not surprised.

"As far as I can tell, she is. She sent me into town earlier to fetch her ledgers for her and ever since I got back, that's all she's been talkin' about. Gettin' on back in to work. That and the fact she's also considering headin' over to some lawyer's office for awhile."

"On a Saturday?" Lathe sounded skeptical. "What lawyer is ever in his office on a Saturday?"

Ethan shrugged then plopped his hat on his head. "Evidently this one is. His name is John Davis and while he was by here earlier this morning visiting Leona, he mentioned something to her about expectin' to be in his office most of tomorrow. He said he needs to catch up on some of the work he missed while he was out of town this week."

Although it hurt to think of Leona having to do something so painful, Ethan felt it was probably for the best. Or was it? For some reason, the thought of his sister having him declared legally dead gave him the woollies.

"Truth is, John Davis is not a very likeable man," he went on to say. "But Leona seems to think a lot of him as a lawyer. So, I guess she'll want to stop by there sometime tomorrow so she can ask him to do whatever it is he has to do to have that brother of

142

hers declared dead."

"Why can't she wait and do that next week?" Lathe wanted to know. "She will be taxing her strength enough as it is, what with her foolish decision to go back to work this soon."

Ethan shrugged again. A part of him still wished she could put it off awhile longer while another part of him hoped she could get through it quickly. "Don't ask me. I just do what I'm told."

"And why is that?" Lathe wanted to know, narrowing his gaze while he tried to figure out again the reason this man seemed so familiar. "Why is it that you come here every day and do every little thing Miss Stegall asks of you?"

"Because she says I remind her of her brother," Ethan answered, thinking it a plausible answer. "I hadn't never had no sister before. I kinda like the idea of her thinkin' about me like that. Makes me feel kinda important."

"Then what you are telling me is that you mostly think of her as a sister?" Lathe studied his reaction, eager to know if he spoke the truth.

It made Ethan nervous to have Lathe stare at him so intently. "That's because I always wanted one," is all he was willing to say, then he headed for the steps. He paused just long enough to give Lathe a quick glance. He knew by the grim, distrustful expression on the man's face that Lathe did not like finding him there.

At first, he had believed Lathe's annoyance over having found him still there had been on account of all the talk it might cause; but now it occurred to Ethan that the real reason the good doctor seemed so bothered about his presence had little or nothing to do with his concern for Leona's reputation. Lathe was obviously jealous of all the time he was spending with Leona.

Ethan wanted to chuckle at the absurdity in that, aware that Lathe had no way to know that Leona really was his sister, much less that he had become so hungry for her company during the past several years that he would gladly grab any opportunity to see her. Lathe obviously thought he was hanging around because he, too, was interested in her as a woman.

But then it really didn't make much difference what Lathe thought. He would be out of the picture soon enough.

While wondering if his sister was well enough yet to do without Lathe's care, he continued, "Tell Leona I might be a little later than usual in coming by tomorrow. There are a few errands I need get done first. Also tell her I'll keep my eye out for that runaway dog of hers like I promised. If I find the mutt, I will personally drag him back home by the scruff of his little neck and put him on that chain myself."

Lathe waited until Ethan had closed the gate and was headed toward town before he bothered to close the door.

Aware he would be there awhile, he took off his hat and his holster and laid them on a nearby table then turned toward the front parlor where George had indicated he would find Leona. When he entered, he discovered Leona curled on a sofa, holding a small book in her left hand. Her right arm was pressed tightly against her body to keep her shoulder immobile. Lathe had to smile. She looked so beautiful and serene sitting there in the soft yellow lamp light, her skirts arranged in prim folds around her slippered feet.

At that moment, it was hard to imagine Leona as

anything but a proper and genteel lady, the type who would go to great lengths to do whatever was expected of her. But he knew the truth—too bad that her actual temperament was a far cry from the sweet, demure kitten she appeared to be. In fact, when angered, she displayed the rebellious behavior of a human wildcat.

Not wanting her to know he'd stood in the doorway appraising her for several minutes, for fear of what she might read into such odd behavior, he entered the room with long, slow, nonchalant strides.

"So, who was it this time?" she asked without bothering to glance up from her book. As close as it was to suppertime, she had expected it to be another neighbor leaving food.

"Me," he answered and grinned when she snapped her head up with such surprise that her mouth popped open and her book fell closed. "Why? Who were you expecting?"

She blinked and looked past him toward the hall. Her pulses vaulted into rapid action. "Where's George?"

"On his way back to the hotel, I suppose," he said with a careless shrug, though it bothered him that she had thought of the other man so quickly. Was it really a brother-sister kind of relationship that had developed between the two? Or did they share feelings a little more caring than that? "He did ask me to tell you that he would be by with a carriage in the morning, but also wanted me to warn you that he might be a little later than usual because he has a few things to do first."

"He's already gone?" She crossed her arms, feeling her skin prickle with sudden apprehension. Every time she and this man were alone, she found herself having to battle a wild mixture of emotions she

145

didn't care to fight. "He left just like that? Without bothering to say goodbye?"

Lathe did not like the concerned look on her face. George's leaving had upset her more than it should, that is if she truly thought of him as a mere brother. "Yes, he left just like that. He did seem in a hurry for some reason. Asked me to take care of serving your supper."

Leona's heart leaped frantically with the realization that they were again alone and would be for the remainder of the night. Why being alone with him should bother her at all was not all that clear; but the fact it did indeed bother her was undeniable. It bothered her in ways she did not fully understand.

"That really won't be necessary," she said a little too quickly. "I can serve myself. I'm not exactly helpless." She set her book aside and slowly eased her feet to the carpet. For some reason, it felt much safer to have both her feet firmly on the floor whenever Lathe was around.

"Maybe not, but I more or less promised him I'd take care of anything you needed before I left." He noticed how quickly she'd stiffened after his suggestion of helping her and he wondered why she should be so receptive to George's assistance yet so afraid of accepting his.

"Then you aren't staying the night?" Why she felt disappointed instead of relieved was a mystery to her. With Lathe out of the house, she might finally be able to get a good night's sleep.

"No, I'm not staying. I'll be leaving in just a little while."

Leaving? Already? she wondered, but tried not to let the explicit feeling of sadness show. "Where are you headed next?"

She had wanted to ask if she would ever see him

again, but decided he would misread her reasons for wanting to know.

"Back to the hotel," he answered, realizing that she must have thought he meant he was leaving Little Mound for good. "You have recuperated a lot faster than I ever expected, so you really don't need me here at night anymore. I feel like I have taken advantage of your hospitality long enough." He grinned after that last comment, aware her hospitality never been offered. He had stayed those past three nights entirely against her will.

When he sat on the sofa beside her, he leaned forward to touch her nose lightly with his finger. Although he knew the action would annoy her, for some strange reason he could not resist. "Sorry if my leaving disappoints you."

Leona's brown eyes grew very large and very round when a powerful current shot through her, making her feel both vibrantly alive yet oddly afraid. It was like that *whenever* he came into direct contact with her.

"Why would that disappoint me?" she asked then leaned casually against the arm of the sofa, hoping he could not tell how strongly his touch had affected her. "I never invited you to stay here in the first place."

"That's true," he admitted agreeably and continued to stare intently into the shimmering depths of her dark eyes. She had the most amazing brown eyes. They were large, expressive, and shaped like almonds; and they revealed a wealth of diverse emotions—even when she refused to look directly at him, like now. "But, as your doctor, I felt it was my duty to stay."

"That's another thing," she said. When she looked up to see what his expression might be, he caught

147

her hesitant glance with his eyes and held it captive for a brief moment. She swallowed back the rising sense of trepidation she always felt whenever she caught him looking at her and wondered if there was any way to ease her rapidly pounding heartbeat. "I never *asked* you to be my doctor."

"But then again, you never asked me not to," he reminded her and again touched the end of her nose with the tip of his finger. He loved the way the corners of her eyes crinkled whenever he did that.

"Only because I was unconscious at the time," she reminded him, wondering why he felt it perfectly all right to touch her whenever he liked. Even though they were not what one might consider intimate touches, they caused all manner of havoc inside her and she wished he would stop. She also wished he would find some other place to sit. Perhaps in another room. "Had I been fully conscious that night, you never would have been allowed to doctor me."

"Much less be allowed to rip your clothes off of you," he added, wondering why he felt such a perverse desire to provoke her. It was then that he realized he actually enjoyed watching her eyes shimmer with outrage. It was that unique combination of fire and vulnerability that had attracted him to her.

Leona gasped at the flagrant reminder of the bold liberties that had been taken. "You had no right to do something like that—especially without a woman present."

"You were there," he pointed out. "And as I recall, you proved to be very much a woman."

Leona's eyes widened while she wondered what that comment was supposed to mean. Exactly what liberties had he taken while she was unconscious? She felt the blood drain from her face. Her breaths came in short erratic gasps while she struggled to fill her lungs with much needed air. "If you were any sort of gentleman at all, you would not find such pleasure in reminding me about what happened."

"I guess I'm not a gentleman then," he admitted with a light shrug then promptly changed the subject, before she forced him to admit the truth, that he had been so concerned about losing her that night he *had* behaved like a perfect gentleman. He would rather she worried awhile longer about what might have happened that night. "Are you hungry?"

"No," she lied when the truth was she was famished. She had been inhaling the savory aroma of George's stew for the past several hours.

"But you will eat," he said, more as a comment than as a command. "If for no other reason than to be rid of me sooner."

"Well, if that's what it takes to get you out of my house then bring on the food," she said and met his probing gaze with a defiant lift of her chin. "I'll choke down whatever you put before me."

Another amused grin twitched at the corners of his mouth, causing two long, narrow dimples to form in either cheek when he rose from the sofa and headed from the room.

When he returned several minutes later, he carried a tray with a large, steaming bowl of stew, a tall glass of chilled water, and two slices of bread that either Ethan had baked earlier in the day or some concerned neighbor had brought by for Leona's meal.

"You didn't have to bring it to me in here," she protested, wishing he would stop that incessant grinning. It was hard to keep hating someone who displayed such a captivating smile. "I could have come to the dining room to eat."

She looked at him questioningly. If he thought she

was still that helpless, why was he planning to leave her alone that evening?

"It just so happens I enjoy indulging beautiful women," he explained, then wondered from where *that* statement had come. His intention had been to make another antagonizing remark to torment her further, but instead he had come out with what had sounded suspiciously like a compliment. Rather than allow that unexpected comment to hang in the air, he quickly asked, "Where do you want me to set this?"

As startled by the surprising statement as he had been, Leona stared at him several seconds before snapping awake, then quickly made room on the lamp table beside her. "Right here will be fine."

He moved to set the tray in the small space she had cleared.

"Is there anything else you think you might need?" he asked while taking the folded napkin off the tray and handing it to her as a waiter might have done.

Leona reached for the napkin hesitantly. When his hand then brushed lightly against hers, she felt as if a sudden bolt of lightning had shot from her fingers up through her arm. Startled, she yanked her hand away and placed it protectively in her lap. Her whole body trembled as a result of the unanticipated reaction to his touch. "No, I can't think of anything."

"Good," he said, still holding the napkin out for her. His arm also tingled as a result of their accidental touching but he had refused to let her see the powerful reaction. He continued to hold the napkin out for her until she finally accepted it. Then he stepped back and sank into a small armchair that faced the sofa at an angle. Suddenly he felt it unsafe to sit on the sofa beside her.

"Aren't you leaving now?" she asked, feeling very

awkward at the thought of him watching her while she ate.

"Not until I've had a look at your injury."

Wondering if he intended to remove the entire bandage again, leaving her entire upper body naked in his presence, Leona's eyes rounded with renewed alarm. She wished she had thought to slip a camisole on over the bandage. "But you looked at it just yesterday."

"And I plan to look at it again tomorrow and every day until either you are fully healed or it is finally time for me to leave this place."

Again the mention of his leaving made Leona feel strangely unhappy, although she should have felt deeply comforted. "And when are you planning to leave Little Mound?"

"As soon as I find out in which direction Zeb Turner headed. All I'm waiting for is some indication that someone has actually spotted him. Right now, he could be just about anywhere."

"Why is it so important to you that you and the sheriff catch him? I know you explained that he is a bad man and a murderer, but there are many men who fit that description. Why are you so obsessed with seeing this particular man arrested, and how is it that you came to be working so closely with Sheriff Lindsey on this matter when you claim to be a doctor? Is there a bounty of some sort on Zeb Turner?"

Lathe wondered what he should tell her. Although there was indeed a small bounty on Zeb's head, he did not plan to collect it. Just seeing him dead would be reward enough. "Let's just say I'll be well rewarded for his capture."

He considered explaining how, when suddenly he was distracted by a movement in the hallway. Although he had not glanced over in time to distinguish exactly what had caught his attention, there had definitely been a movement.

Afraid Zeb had somehow discovered where he was and had decided it was time to reverse roles, Lathe slowly stood. Zeb's smartest move would be to try to kill him, and thereby be rid of his worst problem once and for all. Lathe immediately reached for his pistol, only to be reminded that he had left it in the hallway — in the same hallway where he'd just detected a movement. The thought of being shot with his own pistol galled him.

With long, nimble strides, he moved away from the chair, toward the doorway. When he neared the rectangular opening, he reached for the small flower vase on a nearby table and quickly turned it upside down, dumping the flowers and water onto the floor.

"What do you think you're doing?" Leona asked, thinking his behavior very peculiar. "You are ruining my carpet."

Having forgotten to caution her, Lathe glanced back and held a finger against his lips. He then motioned toward the hallway with a slight jerk of his head, indicating trouble.

Before she could question him further, they heard a loud clattering crash. It sounded like it had come from the kitchen.

Leona's eyes widened to their very limits.

Someone was in the house.

Chapter Eight

Ethan headed straight for the freight office, eager to send a second telegram. Although he did not yet know the full extent of Leona's financial problems, he had already decided to help her as much as possible by asking Captain Potter to wire him more money.

He still had over a hundred dollars of that last batch of money Captain Potter had sent him, but he could tell by the way Leona had talked, she needed a lot more than that. He would ask for as much as he dared have sent at one time; then, as soon as the money was transferred, Ethan intended to hand it over to Leona. Knowing she would never accept it otherwise, he planned to tell her it was a personal loan, even though he did not intend to be around when the time came for her to repay.

As much as he enjoyed seeing Leona again, he did not dare stay in Little Mound any longer than was absolutely necessary. As soon as he had completed his current assignment and Lathe had been returned to Alabama to face the murder charges the captain was so determined to have him face, Ethan would leave Little Mound. He knew that if he stayed, someone would eventually recognize him and once that happened questions would be asked. Questions he would rather not have asked. And the townsfolk would not bear knowing the answers. Nor would George's family.

Because of the senselessness of the death he'd caused, Ethan knew he was no longer fit to live among these good people.

Not after having killed one of them. Not after having killed his own best friend. No, it was better for everyone concerned that the people of Little Mound continue to believe Ethan Stegall was dead than to discover what a worthless, vile excuse for a human being he really was.

To Ethan, it seemed perversely appropriate that he was being forced to work for someone like Captain Jeremiah C. Potter, a man willing to do *anything* to anyone to get what he wanted. If anyone deserved to have such a despicable man for his boss and to live such an intolerable life, he did.

Besides, by doing whatever the captain wanted him to do for however long the captain wanted him to do it, Ethan knew he was keeping George's family from learning the truth. As long as he continued to do the captain's bidding, George's family could go on believing their oldest son had died a hero's death. They would never have to know how utterly senseless their son's death had really been.

And Leona could go on believing that he, too, must have died a hero's death, fighting bravely for a cause he had at one time truly believed in. Yet now, looking back, he was not all that sure the South *had* been right to secede from the Union. Nor was he all that sure he and his friends had done the right thing by fighting for causes that he now knew would have done little more than help the rich get richer.

At the time, those causes may have seemed like things worth dying for; but later, after the reality of what they were doing had had time to soak in, it

154

did not seem like the right thing to do at all. Nor did it seem right for the newly formed Confederate Army to force them to continue fighting for those causes in which they no longer believed. But that was exactly what the army had done. It was why there had been so many deserters during that final year of war.

Why Ethan hadn't deserted along with some of the rest of those unhappy soldiers was a mystery to him. The war had left him both confused and bitter. He no longer felt strongly about much of anything — except for the very real feeling that he wanted to help Leona save the Mercantile.

Because the sky had already begun to turn a dark, murky grey, Ethan feared the freight office might already be closed. But when he turned from Cypress Street onto Market Street, he noticed the front doors still pushed back and the brightly painted sign still hung in the largest of its four windows, indicating that the office was "open for business."

Eager to get his telegram off, he entered the building with long determined strides, heading immediately for the area where the bulky telegraph equipment was kept. Hurriedly, he scrawled out his message, then handed the paper to the same man who had sent his first message days earlier.

"That's not how you spell *complications*," the wiry little man was quick to point out, but with a cheerful smile. "And that's not how you spell *a thousand*."

"Then correct it," Ethan snapped, annoyed by the unwanted reminder that during the nine years since his graduation from high school he had forgotten a good deal of what he had learned. He supposed it was because he spent so much of his time around men who had had very little schooling. "Just

155

be sure you send that message as soon as you can."

"I'd send it right now if you'd just hand me the money to pay for it," he said, looking at him with a suspiciously arched eyebrow, as if he thought Ethan's request for such an enormous amount of money meant he was dead broke.

Ethan mumbled to himself while he stuck his hand into his pocket and extracted the exact amount. If he had thought to bring his wallet with him, he would have paid with the twenty-dollar gold piece he had tucked away inside for emergencies and would have then waited for the man to count out all that change. "Just see to it that message gets out sometime tonight. I want that money transferred to the local bank by Monday morning."

Then without hanging around to watch, since he did not understand enough about Morse Code to know if the man was sending his message or some silly nursery rhyme, Ethan headed back out the door. After having sampled his stew all day, he was not hungry, but he was not ready to return to his hotel room either. He had too many matters to think about and no real desire to think about them — at least not yet. Instead, he walked across the street to a small saloon that also served food. He planned to eat and drink until he hurt.

Lathe gripped the neck of the porcelain vase firmly in his hand then slipped quietly into the dimly lit hallway.

Quickly, he scanned the shadows, searching for further movement. Certain no one was there, he moved soundlessly toward the front door where he had carelessly left his pistol in plain sight.

He was relieved to discover that the weapon was still there and he decided that if the intruder was in-

156

deed Zeb Turner, he must be half blind or else he had entered the house by another means.

While Lathe continued to scan his surroundings, watching for any indication of movement, he reached for the familiar ivory handle of his pistol and slowly eased it out of its holster. With the weapon now firmly in hand, he turned in the direction the sound had come.

After discovering that the dining room was empty, he carefully made his way around the large dining table and kept his gaze trained on the narrow, swinging door that opened into the kitchen.

While he was still several feet away, he heard another noise, this time from inside the kitchen. The muscles around his stomach tightened when he remembered he had left his other pistol on the counter near the stove earlier that morning. He could still end up being shot by his own gun.

Hoping to have the element of surprise on his side, Lathe decided not to put off the confrontation any longer. In one swift, lithe movement, he flung himself into the room, his pistol gripped in both hands, pointed in the general direction of the last sound he'd heard.

Every muscle inside his body felt limp with momentary relief then tensed again with immediate annoyance when he discovered the source of the strange sounds. The same dog that had escorted them the night of the incident had somehow gotten into the house and now stood in the middle of the kitchen with his big, hairy face shoved into a large metal pot.

Obviously, the meddlesome canine had knocked the stew off the counter where Lathe had left it cooling just minutes earlier and was helping himself to what remained.

"Scraps!" Leona shouted, startling both of them. "Look at the mess you've made! Just where have you been?"

Leona turned to Lathe, her delicate brows drawn together into a perplexed frown. "Did you let him in?"

Lathe shot her a look of pure annoyance. "Do you think I would have come bursting in here with my gun drawn and my heart racing a mile a minute if I had known the culprit was just a dog?"

"I guess not," she admitted, shaking her head. Then she glanced around, still puzzled. "I just don't understand how he gets in and out of this house like he does. All the outside doors are kept closed and all the downstairs windows have screens."

"Still he's been sneaking in and out of this house for months now." Her brown eyes narrowed. "I just wish I knew how he does it."

"I'd be pretty concerned about it, too," Lathe agreed. "Because if a mere dog can figure out how to get in and out of this house without you knowing it, I imagine most humans could easily figure out how to do the same thing." Still feeling weak from having gone through such a frightening experience, he set the pistol he held on the counter beside the one he had left that morning and rubbed his hands over his face, knowing that this time, when he left that house, he would take both weapons with him. He did not dare leave either gun behind now, not if it was that simple to enter Leona's house undetected.

"If it's that easy, why can't *I* figure it out?" she asked, then noticing she had left him the perfect opportunity for yet another of his bristly remarks, she glared at him with clear warning. "And don't you dare try to insinuate that perhaps I'm not all that

158

human."

When Lathe grinned, those two long, narrow creases formed on either side of his mouth and immediately captured Leona's attention. She drew in a quick breath, aware he had to have the most captivating smile she had ever seen, and her pulses pounded with as much force as they had when she had believed there was an intruder in the house.

"I hadn't really thought of it," he admitted, wishing he had. "But I *was* planning to point out that evidently you are not quite as smart as your dog here."

"I should have known," she muttered with thorough annoyance, then bent forward to grab Scraps by the metal loop attached to his collar, using only her left hand. "Come on, boy. It's time for you to go outside and get reacquainted with the loose end of that chain."

Still grinning, thinking how adorable she looked whenever she became that exasperated, Lathe bent forward to pick up the pot and followed while she awkwardly tugged the animal toward the back door. He considered offering his help, but knew it would be a pointless gesture. She had yet to accept any help from him at all—at least not *voluntarily.*

"He might as well have the rest of the stew," he commented—no one else would want to eat it after having seen that slobbering animal stick his entire face into the pot.

Remembering Scraps's tendency to growl and flash teeth whenever he got too close, Lathe waited until Leona had the animal securely fastened to the small chain before stepping close enough to dump the remaining stew into his supper dish. Although it had not been very long since sundown, it was extremely dark in the tree-shrouded side yard where the dog was kept chained. Still there was just enough moonlight filtering through to allow him to see what he was doing.

"There you go, boy. A feast fit for royalty."

Scraps sat on his haunches, eyeing him cautiously.

Leona huffed with annoyance. "The only thing royal about that mangy canine is the fact he can be a royal pain when he wants to be." She had sounded like she was still very annoyed with the disobedient dog, yet at the same moment had reached forward to rub his scraggly black head.

Scraps pulled his brown eyes off Lathe and looked up at her, thumping his tail against the grass appreciatively.

If Lathe had not known better, he would have sworn that goofy dog was grinning at her. But then, all things considered, he would grin, too, if Leona were ever to show him such easy affection. He watched with growing fascination while she gently stroked the dog's head, mesmerized by the delicate movements of her hands.

How he envied that animal.

"What am I going to do with you, Scraps?" she sighed then returned her hands to her hips while she righted herself.

Scraps tilted his head to one side as if giving that question serious consideration but then he immediately turned his attention to the food Lathe had poured into his dish.

Still shaking her head, though with less annoyance, Leona walked back toward the house, her hips gently swaying beneath the soft fabric of her light blue cotton dress. A mild night breeze tugged at her skirts and at the long tresses of her mahogany hair, which she wore in a loose twist at the back of her neck. Just before she reached the back steps, she glanced toward the three-quarter moon and sighed. "It is such a lovely night. Hard to believe we had such a warm, humid day."

Her natural inclination might have been to remain outside and spend a few minutes enjoying the glimmering moonlight splashing across her yard and the gentle evening breeze that pushed ever so softly against her skin. And if Lathe had not been there, she might have done just that. It had been days since she had been outside.

Shivering slightly at the sudden realization that she and Lathe stood alone in the moon-drenched back yard where no one could see them, she turned and headed toward the steps again. Just the thought of being alone with such a virile, attractive man in what most people would consider a romantic setting caused her heart to beat at twice the normal rate. Her whole body tingled with renewed awareness.

"Yes, it is a lovely night," Lathe agreed, having followed closely behind.

He paused long enough to notice their surroundings then looked again at Leona who now stood on the top step gazing down at him, as if she wanted to say something but couldn't quite find the words. Her satiny skin reflected a soft, ethereal glow, and the moonlight caused her dark hair to shimmer with silvery highlights.

She looked as enchanting as any fairy princess and at that moment an overwhelming desire to touch her flared to life inside him, making him immediately aware of the consequent danger.

Not only did he want to touch her, he wanted to kiss her; and although he knew it could result in his own emotional undoing, he was unable to resist temptation.

He stood but two feet away when he set the pot

161

aside to free his hands then reached out to pull her gently into his arms. Eager to feel the warmth of her soft body against his, he circled her with his arms and crushed her to him.

Feeling the warmth of her body against his only made his need to kiss her grow worse. But because she had remained on the top step and he stood on the next down, it had positioned her mouth awkwardly above his, just out of reach. Not about to let that hinder him, he slipped his right hand behind her head and pulled her parted mouth downward to meet his in what flared into an instantly passionate kiss.

Not having realized Lathe's attraction for her, Leona was too surprised and too pleased to offer an immediate protest.

Although she had thought him physically appealing right from the start, she had been too annoyed by his bold, domineering behavior and by the absurdity of his unrealistic opinions to allow herself to realize just how attracted she had become.

The fiery, jolting sensation that shot through her when he first pulled her body against his had let her know just how deeply she desired the man; yet at the same time this had been so unexpected, it left her temporarily stunned.

With her heart pounding at a frantic rate and her thoughts dazed from having been taken into his arms so suddenly, she felt breathless—and thoroughly confused. A strange, all-consuming heat invaded her bloodstream almost immediately after his lips had descended upon hers and now that heat spread languidly yet forcefully through all parts of her body, leaving her weak and wanting. And even though it made absolutely no sense, she liked being kissed by Lathe. Liked it very much.

But why should she like being kissed by a man who had behaved so atrociously toward her and whose opinions about the war had proved so intolerable?

She should be pushing him away. Chastising him for having dared be so bold. But by the time any real thought of protest finally occurred to Leona, it was too late. She was too enthralled by all that was happening inside her. The intensity of it was too bewildering. She became so overwhelmed by this rising torrent of unexpected emotions, that she had to lean against him just to keep her bearings. She could not remember ever having felt such a shattering response to anything or anyone in her life.

The strong physical need that now swept through her body circled and gathered until it became a stark, quivering ache that eventually settled at the very core of her being. The need she felt became so powerful and so basic, it startled her; but oddly enough, it did not frighten her. The strange mixture of feelings was like nothing she had ever experienced, but she sensed that it offered no real threat.

She was totally unprepared for such a staggering reaction to something as simple as a mere kiss, but still felt no desire to flee. Rather than pull away from his intense embrace and run for safety, she regarded these strange new sensations as matters well worth exploring. She wanted to know more about the peculiar new stirring of her heart, more about what made her legs ache and her toes tingle.

Slowly, she lifted her arms to encircle his neck — because the step was nearly level with her shoulders — and she shyly pressed her hands against the corded muscles. How strong that neck felt to the sensitive tips of her fingers — how very solid were his muscles, so unlike her own.

When Lathe then moved onto the top step beside her, the change in his height forced her to lift her arms even higher, causing her breasts to rise and press intimately against the hard planes of his chest. Startling shafts of sensual delight shot through her, sparking off another vibrant, exhilarating whirlwind of sensations that moved quickly through her, making her forget the pain she still felt in her right shoulder — making her forget everything but Lathe, and the magnificent passion he had so easily aroused.

Never had Leona known such a wondrous feeling of self-awareness. Her whole body felt suddenly alive, surging with an inflamed desire to explore these strange occurrences happening inside her.

Even so, somewhere in the back of her pleasure-enshrouded brain, an internal alarm sounded. The faint warning urged her to pull away, before it was too late, before these newly aroused desires encouraged her to do something she might later regret. But she was unable to concentrate on the silent message long enough to understand the true danger. She had become lost in a swirling sea of emotions so strong, so turbulent — they made it impossible for her to think — made her not *want* to think — made her want only to feel and know more.

While her thoughts continued to flounder helplessly in the obscured shadows of her mind, Lathe's strong, demanding hands pressed into the small of her back, crushing her pliant body more firmly against his. Slowly, his hands moved with deep, circular motions up and down the delicate curve of her spine, all the while careful to avoid the injury at the base of her shoulder.

The gentle massage stimulated Leona with yet

more penetrating shafts of explicit pleasure. She literally ached with a weakness so profound and so uncharacteristic that when one of his hands eventually strayed from its course along her back and slowly edged a path toward her ribcage, she trembled in response. The same hand then moved slowly upward, stopping every so often to caress and explore the different areas of her body, until he gently cupped the underside of her breast. Despite the several layers of bandage that covered her, his touch burned into her delicate skin, branding her with yet more heated desire.

Again the silent alarm sounded. It admonished her for having allowed Lathe to take such liberties. But once again there was an unexplainable breakdown in communications between her brain and the rest of her body. She chose to ignore the frantic message.

Instead of reprimanding him for his boldness, she responded to the intensified sensations by timidly sliding her palms across the hard, rounded contours of his back in what began as a shy yet, eager exploration.

Marveling at the feel of such a strong, muscular back and of the firm, powerful shoulders that lay just beneath the soft fabric of his shirt, she pressed her hands harder against him.

Lathe responded to her arousing touch with a faint growl and the kiss deepened.

Hungry for the taste of her, while he took the whole of her breast into his palm and marveled at the firmness, he slipped the tip of his tongue through the slight parting of her lips and gently urged her to open them further. Forgetting the breast temporarily, he glided across the velvety curves and contours of her mouth, dipping ever

165

deeper, eager to sample more and more of her.

To his delight, she responded in kind, though timidly at first. He could not remember having known such sweetness nor having craved a woman so intensely. The desire to take her pounded through him with such force that it made him want her more than he had ever wanted any woman. It was then he realized he would have to be extremely careful of his own budding emotions or chance losing his heart to this beautiful, alluring woman. And that might ruin everything he had fought so hard to accomplish.

Although Leona had hoped to be the one to find the strength to pull away from the passionate kiss when the time came, she had been unable to do so. Not because Lathe had physically overpowered her nor had he restrained her in any physical manner. She simply did not want to stop whatever madness this man had started.

She had fallen prey to that lunacy called passion and wanted more of whatever pleasures it had to offer.

Her common sense had abandoned her entirely and her womanly desires, now fully awakened, had moved in to take its place. Although she still did not particularly like this man, nor did she care for some of his more foolish opinions, she desired him with a passion she had never known existed. She wanted to pull him right into her soul and make him a part of her for now and evermore.

It was the realization that they were not in love and that one day he would leave her that brought a stab of sheer agony to her heart, but still it did not convince her to pull away.

To add to her ever-growing fears and confusion, Lathe was the one who finally broke the kiss.

"It's getting late," he said in a very gruff voice.

He was having as difficult a time catching his breath as she was hers. His chest heaved laboriously with each attempt to draw more air into his lungs. "It's been a long day. We both need to get some sleep. I'd better go."

Leona was never more bewildered nor more hurt than when he suddenly set her aside, then hurried into the house to gather his things. Barely a minute later, she heard the front door clatter shut and he was gone.

Standing alone in the darkness, she remembered his earlier intention to stay and check her wound and she wondered what she had done to make him want to leave in such a rush. She must have done something terrible to cause him to forget about her injury. Then, with an aching heart, she realized exactly what she had done to appall him.

She should have been the one to pull away, not him. She was the woman; she should have shown more restraint and when she didn't, he must have decided she was a loose woman. Because of that, he now wanted no part of her. He thought her tarnished, and who could blame him?

He had obviously been testing her with that wanton kiss to discover what kind of woman she was, and she had led him to believe she was the very worst sort possible.

Ashamed and confused by her own impetuous behavior, she turned toward the house. With her head bent and her shoulders slumped, she wondered how she would ever face him again.

Her misery was all-consuming. The ache in her chest grew until the pain became overwhelming, and for the first time since right after her injury, she felt faint. Quickly, she sank into a nearby wicker chair, all the while wondering if there was anything she

167

could to do to right the wrong she had just done. She realized that no matter what she did or what she said, he would always remember how willingly she had responded to his kiss and would continue to think the worst of her.

She decided the best thing to do would be to avoid him all together. It was the only way to save herself from facing further embarrassment.

Later that night, Lathe ate a quick meal at one of the few restaurants in town still open, then returned to his hotel room, but he soon discovered that he was too restless to sleep. The vast emotions that had sprung to life inside him while at Leona's earlier continued to plague him.

Finding an odd sort of comfort in the darkness that cloaked his hotel room, he sat cross-legged on his rumpled sheets, wearing only his nightshirt, his back propped against the wall. Vacantly, he stared through the second-floor window, watching a patch of black clouds move slowly across the bleak night sky.

He had been totally unprepared for the powerful feelings Leona had so suddenly aroused inside him. They were the exact sorts of feelings he did not want to experience. Not just yet. They were far too deep and far too restrictive, and had no place in his life.

It bothered him to know that his emotions had willfully reached beyond the natural urge a man felt whenever he was attracted to a beautiful woman. What he had felt tonight had far surpassed that, otherwise he never would have pulled away as he did. He simply would have allowed nature to take its course, enjoying whatever pleasures Leona had to offer. But the intensity and the sheer importance of what he had felt when he had held her in his arms had been too great, too all-consuming. He had realized immediately how dangerously close he had come to falling in love with her—and that worried him.

Although he had assumed he would enjoy kissing her, he had not expected the kiss to cause such profound feelings toward her—nor did he want them.

Right now he had no room in his life for any type of emotional commitment. These new feelings he felt toward Leona would just end up getting in the way, intruding on the task he had dedicated himself to do.

He could never keep his attention focused on bringing his brother's killer to justice if his thoughts constantly veered to someone else. The distraction would only hinder his quest for justice.

But what could he do about it? What he felt for Leona was already a very strong and viable part of him. There was no way he could change the feelings he already had.

Still, if he allowed these new emotions full reign, he might become so involved with what he felt for her that he would eventually lose sight of what was really important.

He must not allow that to happen. He must not allow his own foolish heart to get in the way of such an important mission. Jonathan deserved to have his killer brought to justice; and Lathe felt he deserved to be there to watch him hang.

For five years, he had tracked the man who had so ruthlessly slit his young brother's throat. Lathe had put aside his own plans, which had been to collect his half of the family treasure he and his brother had buried nine years earlier so he could establish a medical practice in some small, thriving town in need of a doctor.

It had always been Lathe's dream to be a country doctor; but it had always been a part of that dream to have his brother at his side. The way Lathe and his brother had it planned, Lathe was to open a successful medical practice in a small town somewhere in the South while Jonathan ran a flourishing cattle ranch nearby.

Although the two intended to have separate families and live in separate homes, they had vowed to share their lives forever. They both wanted their children to live in the same town and become as close as they were.

Two brothers could not have loved each other more.

While continuing to stare idly out the window, Lathe rubbed the inside of his right thigh with his thumb, absently tracing the ridge of the scar while his thoughts returned to the day he and Jonathan had first decided to sell all their land and most of their belongings then bury the proceeds until all threat of war had passed. Even back then, when secession had been little more than a lot of angry talk, he and Jonathan had realized war was inevitable. They had also known from the outset that the South could never win such a war, not if the fighting lasted any time at all.

Although most of their Southern neighbors had truly believed in the South's ability to win such a violent war — for no other reason than because they thought "right" was on their side — Lathe and his brother had recognized that there were too many other factors working against them. Lathe, especially, had formed some very serious doubts because he had been finishing his last year at Yale College during that time and he knew exactly where the country's true strengths lay.

Most of the nation's factories were located in the North, including the ammunition and weapons factories, and almost all the nation's important resources came from the Northern states. About all the South had at that time was an abundance of cotton, which could be traded abroad for weapons, if a viable market could be found.

Therefore, rather than risk losing their family fortunes to the North, and knowing that their home state of Alabama lay in a centrally located area where much of the fighting and destruction might occur, he and Jonathan had both shown enough foresight to free their slaves then sell their land and their livestock while the early talks of war were still going on.

It was that early foresight that allowed them to trade most of their family wealth for gold while there was still gold to be had. They had immediately buried that gold and several treasured family heirlooms deep in a dense patch of woods not too far from Mill Run, the small town where the sale of their land had become final.

Wanting to be certain they could recover that buried treasure after the war was over, and not lose it because of a lack of familiarity with the ever-changing terrain in that area, they decided to use a knife and scratch the coordinates of the exact location into the insides of their thighs, deep enough to leave prominent scars. As a special safeguard, they each scratched only one of the two coordinates into their thighs. Lathe had carved the longitude into his and Jonathan carved the latitude into his.

And even though they both planned to join the Confederate Army in non-combatant capacities — Lathe as a surgeon and Jonathan as a surveyor —

they knew they still stood a very real chance of being killed. Therefore they decided to mail a letter to their Aunt Carole Caldwell with those same numbers cleverly incorporated into the text and had asked their aunt to save the letter for them. It had proved to be a very wise precaution because Lathe could not remember the other coordinate and, after nine years, would have had an extremely hard time trying to find the exact location of the gold when the time finally came.

Lathe closed his eyes against the resulting pain when he remembered how enthusiastic his brother had been while they formulated their plans to come together again just as soon as the war had officially ended.

Because of the special nature of their military duties, they knew it was very unlikely they would remain in the same division for long. Therefore, they had made special plans to return to the same town where they had finalized the sale of their land. Each was to wait there until the other had arrived.

Because the town was only a few miles from where they had buried the gold, pictures, and jewelry, it would be easy for them to collect their buried treasure and begin their new lives together right away. They had planned to leave word of their exact whereabouts at the sheriff's office.

The sharp ache in Lathe's stomach swelled until he had to knot his hands into hard fists to hold back the frustration and anguish. If only he had gotten to Mill Run a few days earlier.

It was while Jonathan waited for Lathe to arrive that he was so brutally killed. Murdered in the livery stable barely a week after the war had ended and only four days before Lathe eventually arrived.

Lathe had one solace and that was that there had

been a witness. A teenage boy who had worked at the livery, but had fallen asleep in the loft, had awakened in time to see the scuffle below.

At the trial that followed, that boy had bravely identified Zeb Turner as the man who had attacked Jonathan from behind. He had also been able to describe the knife in great detail.

It was the same knife Zeb had pressed to Leona's throat just a few nights ago. The knife had an unusual ivory and leather handle and, at the time of the trial, the leather still carried the stains of his brother's blood.

Because of that boy's brave testimony, Zeb had been found guilty and sentenced to hang. But later that same night, someone helped Lathe's brother's murderer break out of jail and supplied him with a horse and enough money and food to get quickly and cleanly out of the state.

Knowing that the local sheriff had enough problems with all the confusion and violence that had followed the sudden end of the war, Lathe had taken off immediately, determined to track Zeb down himself.

All he had carried with him at the time he left was his pistol, most of the money from his last two pay packets plus what little cash Jonathan had carried at the time of his death, and the small photograph of Zeb Turner that the sheriff had taken from him shortly after his arrest. In the photograph, he wore a Confederate uniform.

Because money was usually in short supply and Lathe had not taken the time to return to Alabama to try to recover the family treasure, he had constantly been forced to stop and find work during that time. He usually worked only until he had just enough money to continue

173

in pursuit of his brother's killer.

But even with having to stop and work from time to time, Lathe had always managed to maintain Zeb's general location—until now. For the first time, Lathe had no idea where Zeb might be hiding.

But having an exact location really didn't matter. Zeb would surface again somewhere. He always did. And when he did, someone would recognize him. The jagged, L-shaped bullet scar across his left hand and the narrow set of his dark eyes gave him away. And when he did finally surface again, Lathe would be right behind him because no matter how long it took, he would eventually capture Zeb Turner and then haul him back to Mill Run to watch him hang as he originally had been sentenced.

This was the whole reason Lathe could not allow himself to become emotionally involved with anyone—not just yet. He *had* to keep his priorities straight.

As desperately as he wanted Leona Stegall, he wanted Zeb Turner more.

He must not lose sight of that fact.

Chapter Nine

When Ethan appeared at Leona's door late the following morning, she almost did not recognize him.

"What happened to you?" she asked with wide-eyed amazement when she stepped back to let him inside.

"Stopped by the barber shop for a haircut," Ethan explained, grinning at her stunned reaction. "That's why I figured I might be a little late this morning. It had been so long since my last trip to the barber, I wasn't too sure how long it would take to cut it and also trim my beard back some."

"If that's what kept you, I'm surprised to see you were able to make it at all today," she said, then returned his grin, unable to pull her gaze away from him. "I'd have thought it would take hours to cut through all that hair. My, what a difference it makes. Were you aware you had ears?"

"Yeah, I knew I had a pair of them in there somewhere," he chuckled then waited to see if she would think the haircut had made him look even more like her dearly departed brother. The main reason he had not ordered the entire beard shaved off for the summer was his fear that a clean shaven face might cause Leona to realize the truth. He *was* her long lost brother, not just someone who looked and occasionally acted very much like him.

If it had not been for the constant rise in temperatures and the fact that Sarah would probably prefer to see him a little less hairy, he would have left his hair and his beard exactly the way it had been. But with two such strong motivations to spur him on, he had decided to take the chance and have about eight inches of his hair and nearly three inches of his beard cut away. He just hoped he had not made a serious mistake.

"You don't look nearly as intimidating as you used to," Leona commented while further studying the overall impact of the unexpected haircut. With his dark hair now only a few inches long and brushed back away from his face, and his beard barely an inch thick and neatly combed, he looked far more civilized than she had ever thought he could. She wondered what Mrs. Haught would have to say about him now, remembering how the older woman had referred to George as that "abomination" sitting half-naked on her front porch the day she had brought the soup.

"Less intimidating?" he asked and frowned. "Is that good or bad?" He wasn't sure. There were times when his menacing looks had come in rather handy.

"Definitely good," Leona admitted, still unable to take her gaze off him. Although it had not yet occurred to her how much more like Ethan he now looked, she knew there was something about his changed appearance that fascinated her. "You look downright handsome."

"You ready to go?" Ethan asked, glad to hear she approved of the change but eager to focus her attention on something else. "I've got that carriage I promised."

"I'm almost ready. I was just looking through some of my parents' papers trying to find the letter my brother's captain had sent shortly before the end of the war. It explained the questionable nature behind Ethan's death and why he had been declared merely

176

missing instead of dead. I thought John might want to see it again, just in case there was some information in it he might need before he can have Ethan declared legally dead."

The sparkle left Leona's eyes at the reminder of what she had been trying to find and why. Her expression became so sad at the mere mention of what she must do, it tore Ethan's heart into a hundred ragged pieces, making him glad he had decided to send for the extra money. He might not be able to provide the amount she needed to save the Mercantile completely, but he hoped it would be enough make up for at least some of the pain he had caused her through the past several years.

"Before you go to any more trouble searching for that letter, I think you should know that I've arranged to have a thousand dollars transferred to the local bank on Monday morning."

She looked at him, puzzled, wondering what the money had to do with her having to look for the letter.

Aware she had not yet made the connection, he added, "The reason I am having that money sent here is so I can lend it to you. It probably isn't enough to get you completely out of all the financial trouble you are in right now, but I figure it's bound to be a good start."

Leona continued to stare at him with her pretty forehead drawn and dimpled and her mouth sagging, still too stunned by what he had said to fully believe it. She would never have imagined George as having that kind of money. He certainly did not dress like a man who had a thousand dollars stuck aside somewhere. Although his clothes were by no means ragged nor threadbare, they certainly were not of any real quality either. If he really did have that amount of money, it was probably every cent he had in the world. It would not be right to take so much money from a man who really could not afford to lend it.

"I appreciate the offer, but I can't take your money," she said and shook her head adamantly. "Why that's probably all the money you have.".

"I don't think you realize just how lucrative fur trapping can be," Ethan explained, determined to make her say yes. "I happen to have squirreled away quite a hefty sum over the past few years. How else could I afford to travel around like I do without having to stop and find work to help pay my way? Besides, didn't you claim you would be able to pay back that loan you'd hoped to get at the bank right after first harvest?"

She nodded that she had, still too surprised by his offer to believe it was true.

He smiled again and shrugged as if everything had been decided. "Then, it's not like you'd be keeping my money forever. I'll get it all back this fall." He bent his head forward, then looked up at her through his thick, dark lashes, the way a pleading little boy might have done. "You have been so kind to me these past few days. Please, let me do this one little favor for you."

Leona bit her lower lip while she considered the true generosity of his offer. If she accepted his money, she could put off having Ethan declared legally dead a little while longer—a thought that appealed to her greatly. "Are you sure loaning me that much money won't put you in a bind of some sort?"

"Not at all. I'll still have more than enough to live on. Please, just say you'll accept the money when it comes."

He had no doubt the captain would send the full amount he'd asked for. The man would do whatever it took to see that Lathe was finally captured. Or more accurately put, the captain would do whatever

178

it took to see Lathe *dead*. Although he had never come right out and actually stated the fact, Ethan knew his boss well enough to know he would never rest easy as long as Lathe remained alive.

Whether the captain intended Lathe to die by a legal hanging or by his own hand, Ethan was not sure; but the fact he wanted Lathe dead was clear — *very* clear. It wouldn't surprise Ethan if the captain allowed Zeb to have the honor of doing him in, especially after all the trouble Lathe had caused over the past few years.

Ethan was glad the captain had not asked him to do anything more than capture Lathe and hold him. Even though he had killed men before, it had always been accidentally. He did not think he could kill someone intentionally, no matter what the reward. He just did not have the heart for premeditated murder. And if that was indeed what the captain had in mind, the deed would have to be left up to someone else.

"I'll take the money, but only if you will agree to charge interest," Leona said with a determined nod, unaware her friend's thoughts had drifted to other equally important matters.

Aware she was serious about his charging the interest, Ethan shrugged. He knew it would prove pointless to argue.

"If that's the only way I can get you to take the money, then okay, I'll charge you interest. But I'll agree to only half the interest the bank would charge," he told her, determined to have some say in the matter, although he wasn't sure why he bothered. He had no intention of being around when the time came to pay back the loan. In actuality, it was his gift to her, to compensate for the pain his fabricated death had caused her.

Leona drew in a sharp breath, prepared to argue

179

that he deserved the full four percent, but before she could actually state so aloud, Ethan spoke again, his thick eyebrows drawn low over a pair of penetrating brown eyes.

"Take it or leave it," he said then crossed his arms to let her know that was his final offer.

Leona's mouth pressed into a flat, stubborn line but when she saw how truly determined he looked, her lips twitched at the corners until finally they lifted into an agreeable smile. "You leave me little choice. I'll take it. All one thousand of it — at two percent interest. But I want our agreement down in writing."

"Why, don't you trust me?" He looked hurt. "You think I'll up the interest behind you back?"

"No, I trust you. I just want to be sure you would still be able to get your money back should something happen to me."

"Nothing is going to happen to you," he said, thinking it a wasted effort to write out an agreement on a loan he never intended to collect, especially when it wasn't even his money. He tried not to think about what the captain would do if he ever found out the truth about what Ethan was doing.

"Still, I would feel better about it if we were to put it all down in writing," she said. "By the time your money arrives on Monday, I will have two copies of the agreement written out. All we'll have to do is sign them."

"Whatever you say," he said, not wanting to argue about something so unimportant. "Will you still need to get that letter?"

"No, I guess not," she said with a wider smile than she'd borne in quite some time. Although a thousand dollars was not enough to purchase everything the store needed, it would certainly help in getting a basic stock of goods. She could do without some of the fancier items for now.

Blinking back her tears of gratitude, she reached for her handbag. "Let's get going. I have a lot of work to do."

When they arrived at the Mercantile a few minutes later, there was only one customer inside, which proved how truly pathetic her business had become. Saturday mornings were normally her busiest because that's when so many of the local farmers and ranchers came in to see about a lot of their shopping needs.

While Mrs. Sanford continued to take care of the occasional customers, Leona and Ethan leafed through the different warehouse catalogs deciding exactly what she should purchase with that thousand dollars.

Aware that the sooner she received her goods, the sooner she could start to fill her customers' orders again, Leona decided to limit her purchases to the two warehouses in nearby Marshall, Texas. By doing so, she might end up with fewer goods to choose from, but knew she could have those new purchases within a couple of days. If she traveled to Shreveport to make her purchases, she would have more items to choose from but it would take well over a week before she could restock her shelves. And if she dared wait for the new goods to be freighted in, she knew it could take as long as two weeks. She was far too eager to restock her shelves to wait that long.

By four o'clock, Leona had the final order written and had tallied the amount it would cost, to the final penny.

"That will leave me with just enough left over to pay that forty dollars in taxes I owe and hire a man to drive over to Marshall and pick up the merchandise," she said, glancing over her figures one last time to make sure there were no mistakes. "If I can find someone willing to leave here on Monday, I should be able to start putting that new stock on my shelves sometime Wednesday afternoon." Her eyes sparkled at the thought. "By Thursday morning, I could finally be back in business. *Really* back in business."

"Why do you have to hire someone to drive?" he asked, thinking that a needless expense.

"Because I'm not up to making the trip myself," she confessed, aware of how very tired she felt just from what little she had done that day.

Although she hated to admit it, Lathe Caldwell had been right; she had not yet regained all her strength. Even though most of the pain had left her shoulder and she could move about with a lot more ease; she still became exhausted far too easily.

"It's at least a five-hour drive to Marshall," she went on to explain. "And there's no telling how long it will take the warehouses to fill those orders. I'd then be forced to stay the night and then wake up early the following morning to make the long trip back. As much as I'd like to, I just can't do it. Not as weak as I feel right now."

"But what about me?" he asked, looking insulted that she had not thought to ask him. Although he would be perfectly happy to stay right there in Little Mound where he could spend more time with his sister and Sarah Martin—*and* keep a close eye on Lathe—he would gladly do that one small favor for her.

Even if Lathe did suddenly decide to take out after Zeb again—that is if Zeb was still alive—Ethan was confident he would be able to find them both easily enough. Lathe always checked in with the local sheriff of whatever town he visited. "I don't have anything important to do next week. Why don't you let me go to Marshall for you?"

"Because you will have done enough by lending me the money," she said. "I can't ask you to transport the merchandise, too."

182

"Oh, yes, you can. And you just did," he said with a firm nod, warning her not to argue. "I plan to leave just as soon as that money has cleared the bank Monday morning."

There was still a tired sort of excitement glimmering in Leona's eyes later that afternoon when she and Ethan climbed back into the carriage to return to her house. Although she barely had the energy to sit erect, her heart continued to pound with continued excitement.

"You hungry?" Ethan asked after he had made himself as comfortable as possible on such a thinly padded seat. Suddenly, it had dawned on him that they had skipped lunch.

"Not especially," Leona admitted, adjusting her skirts then leaning back heavily against the carriage seat. She grimaced when the gentle pressure caused her shoulder to ache but she was too tired really to care. All she wanted to do was go home and take a long nap.

"What's wrong?" he asked, having seen the pained expression flitter across her face.

"Nothing really. It's just that my shoulder is hurting again."

"I hope you didn't do any new damage to it today." He studied her pale expression worriedly. She did not have the strength to hold her own head up. Instead she rested it against the back of the seat. "We will never hear the last of it from Dr. Caldwell if you did."

"I don't think you have to worry about that," she said and closed her eyes against the grim memory, aware of how shamefully she had behaved the evening before. "I think I already *have* heard the last of it from Dr. Caldwell."

"Why, what have you done now?"

She lifted her head just enough to cut a curious

glance his way. "What makes you think it's something I did?"

"Just a hunch," he said, then grinned. "You seem to have a real knack for saying or doing the exact wrong thing where that doctor is concerned. Tell you the truth, I'm surprised he's put up with you this long."

Leona offered a brief, ironic smile. George couldn't have hit that nail any more squarely on the head than he just did. "Let's just say he probably won't be putting up with me any longer. Fact is, it is very doubtful he will bother coming over to check on my progress at all anymore."

Ethan wondered what had happened to cause such a rift between the two and realized that if what Leona said was true, if the young doctor had indeed washed his hands of his new patient, there was no real reason to put off trying to capture him.

It was only because he felt Leona might still be in need of a doctor's care that he had put off the abduction. But if it was true she would no longer be receiving Lathe's care, he might as well get it over with. Even so, he would have to wait until after he had returned from Marshall with the merchandise because as soon as he had Lathe, he would have to haul him well away from Little Mound. It was the only way he knew to keep the captain from coming there and discovering the real reason he had wanted that thousand dollars.

"The doctor must have given you a clean bill of health, then," he said, looking at her questioningly.

"Not exactly," she muttered then glanced away. She did not want him to see her shame. "He hasn't even bothered to look at the injury since Thursday."

While Ethan wondered why she suddenly looked so hurt, the truth struck him and struck him hard. Despite the many scornful remarks she had made about

Lathe over the past few days, she had grown extremely fond of him.

Ethan thought back to some of the comments she had made to Sarah while describing Lathe to her. Although she had labeled him both arrogant and impossible, she had also admitted she found him very attractive. It bothered Ethan to know his sister had developed such strong feelings toward a man like that, especially when Lathe could never become a real, lasting part of her life.

Lathe was a dead man.

Pure and simple.

Which meant Leona was headed for yet another painful loss.

Ethan shifted uncomfortably in the seat while he started the horses at a slow walk.

"Maybe it is just as well that he won't be comin' around any more," Ethan said, hoping to lift her spirits. "There's just something about that man that isn't quite right."

"You feel that way, too?" she asked and turned to look at him questioningly. "Do you think that maybe he's really not a doctor? That perhaps he only pretends to be one?"

"No, I feel pretty certain he's a doctor," Ethan admitted, thinking it would be unfair to deny him that. "It's something else that bothers me." Because he did not want her asking a lot of questions that could end up reflecting badly on him, Ethan decided not to mention that Lathe was suspected of having committed a cold, brutal murder. Nor would he mention that the only witness to that horrible murder had been Zeb Turner, the man Lathe remained so determined to find.

Though Ethan himself had never put much stock in anything Zeb had to say, Captain Potter did. That explained one reason why the captain was so determined Lathe be captured. Zeb was the captain's good friend, but even more important than that was the fact that the man Lathe was supposed to have killed was the captain's younger brother.

While Ethan continued to mull the reasons he had been sent to capture Lathe, Leona sat despondently wondering what it was about Lathe that bothered her—besides the fact that he had found her kiss so offensive. But rather than continue speculating on the matter, she decided to pay the sheriff a visit first thing Monday morning. She wanted to find out how he and Lathe had come to be working together in their failed attempt to capture Zeb Turner.

She wanted to know how a man who claimed to be a doctor had become involved in something so dangerous.

It surprised both Leona and Ethan when they arrived in front of the house several minutes later and saw an unfamiliar carriage near the street, then spotted Lathe sitting on the front porch waiting for them.

When he stood, Leona noticed he was hatless and wore his thick brown hair brushed away from his handsome face. He had dressed in a pair of dark blue dress trousers and wore a matching lightweight dinner coat over a pale blue dress shirt. He also wore a black necktie and a pair of gleaming black congress boots.

He waited until they had climbed down from the carriage and entered the yard before coming forward to speak to them.

"I was beginning to think you two had gotten lost," he said, forcing a smile while he stared pointedly at Ethan, immediately aware of the significant change in his appearance. "It's after five o'clock. I thought you normally closed the store at four on Saturdays. That's what you have posted on the door."

Leona's heart was pounding too rapidly to allow

her to concentrate on anything more substantial than the surprising fact that Lathe was there. Rather than try to explain every little thing they had done since closing time, Leona simply nodded and kept her answer simple. "The store does close at four. But I had a lot to do today."

Because she still felt embarrassed over her shameful behavior of the evening before, she did not meet his gaze when she walked past him. Instead, she focused on the steps leading to her house while she continued to walk slowly toward the front veranda, unsure what she should do once she reached the house.

Should she turn and invite them both inside or explain how very tired she was and hint they should leave?

It occurred to her then that she did not feel nearly as tired as she had just a few minutes ago. Instead, she felt strangely invigorated. Or perhaps it was fear that caused her heart to pound so rapidly. But whatever the reason behind her quickened heartbeat, she no longer felt weary or sluggish. Instead, she felt very exhilarated — very much alive.

Because Lathe had mistaken Leona's refusal to look at him when she passed as an unspoken admission of guilt, his gaze hardened. He wondered just what these two had done to fill that missing hour. The thought of Leona in another man's arms caused his blood to run ice cold through his veins and made his chest constrict with an unexplainable rush of anger.

"Besides, I had no idea you would be here waiting," she went on to say. Pausing at the foot of the steps, she turned to face him, but was still unwilling to look directly at him. She was too afraid she would find contempt marring his handsome face, contempt for her deplorable behavior the evening before. "I really didn't expect you to come by today."

"Neither did I," he admitted, still not sure why he

had. When he first left the hotel, his plans had been to dine alone. But instead of crossing the street to the nearest restaurant, he had found himself hurrying toward the livery to hire a carriage so Leona would not have to walk.

Thinking this an odd response, Leona finally gathered the courage to look at him. When she did, it became her immediate undoing. He looked impossibly handsome in his dark, tailored dinner suit. The fitted lines accentuated the powerful build of his muscular body, reminding her of the strength she had found in his passionate embrace.

Her already rapid heartbeat quickened even more. Again she fought the intruding memory of what had happened the night before. "Then why are you here?"

"I had hoped you might feel up to going out for dinner," he said. He resisted the urge to look away and gazed deeply into her almond-shaped brown eyes while anticipating her reply.

He prayed she would not take what had happened between them the previous night as a reason to say no. He had not intended to take advantage of her like that. It just sort of happened. Just like his being there now had just sort of happened. Despite his earlier resolution to stay away from her for fear of what might happen between them, he wanted to spend that evening with her. He wanted it almost as much as he wanted to capture Zeb Turner.

"She's not hungry," Ethan put in when Leona did not immediately respond, thinking only to help.

"Why?" Lathe quickly turned his hard, accusing gaze on the man he considered his strongest rival, still annoyed over the fact he had gone to all the trouble of having his hair cut and his beard trimmed. Lathe could well imagine what had prompted such dramatic change. "Have you two already eaten?"

"No," Ethan admitted, then quickly added, "But

188

just when we were leaving the store, I asked her if she was hungry and she told me she was too tired to eat. All she wants to do is take a quick bath and go on to bed."

"Even so, it is essential for her to eat," Lathe reminded him. "Eating properly is the only way she will ever get the rest of her strength back."

"A lot you care," Ethan quickly pointed out all the while studying Lathe's angry expression, trying to decide just how deeply the doctor did care for his sister. "You haven't even bothered to look at that injury of hers since Thursday."

"There are reasons for that," he said, shifting beneath Ethan's accusing glare. "And as it turns out, that happens to be another reason I came by. I want to be sure she didn't cause any new damage while working today; but first I think she needs to eat something." He then turned to look again at Leona. "What do you say? Would you like to go get something to eat before I take a look at your back?"

Hoping to delay the inevitable, already fighting a strong flood of emotion that had arisen at the mere thought of having partially to disrobe for him again, she quickly responded, "I guess I really should eat something."

Ethan frowned, wondering what had brought about such a sudden change of heart. He hoped it wasn't because she actually *wanted* to spend her evening with Lathe, not when Lathe would soon be snatched right back out of her life again. Ethan felt he should do something to keep these two apart. "I think it would be a lot easier on her if I just heated up some of that stew I made yesterday."

Lathe quirked a grin, aware he had him there. "I'm afraid there's not any left. Leona had an intruder last night; one with a special hankering for stew."

Seeing a mixture of concern and confusion pulling

189

at Ethan's face, Leona quickly explained to him what Scraps had done. When she finished relating the story, she admitted to being glad she had the unwieldy canine back on his chain, but still wished she knew how he managed to get in and out of her house so easily. The only part of the incident she did not bother to tell her new friend was what had happened shortly after she had rechained the dog and had turned to go back inside. Her blood warmed at the memory of having suddenly found herself in Lathe's strong arms then chilled again when she remembered what his reaction had been to her shameful behavior.

Unable to think of another logical reason to keep Leona from having dinner with Lathe, Ethan finally conceded. "Well, if the stew is gone, I guess a restaurant is about the only other choice she has." There certainly wasn't any other food in that house. Clearly, his sister did not care to cook her own meals.

Not wanting to face Lathe alone, especially after her scandalous behavior the night before, Leona quickly injected, "You know, George, you haven't eaten all day either. Why don't you come along with us? We can make a threesome out of it. It will be fun."

When Lathe cut Ethan a gaze that indicated he was not exactly welcome, Ethan became just that much more determined to go. "Well, if you are sure you don't mind."

"Of course, we don't mind," Leona said, glancing at Lathe, glad she would not have to face him alone. She was surprised to see such a dark glower and realized that obviously he did mind. She then realized that he must have had a severe change of heart. He obviously wanted a second chance to be alone with her—wanted a second chance to make her swoon in his arms. She felt an acute rush of excitement while

190

she tried to decide if that was to her advantage or not.

The thought of being in his arms again terrified her. What if next time, *neither* of them pulled away? What would happen then?

She must not allow him the opportunity to find out. Again she looked eagerly at George. "There is so much we don't know about each other. By having dinner together, the three of us can get to know each other a lot better."

Those words struck Ethan hard. He did not want Lathe knowing him any better for fear the man might eventually remember where it was they had originally seen each other. Lathe had yet to remember the incident in the hotel, but how long could that last? "On second thought, maybe I'd better decline the offer. I have a lot I have to get done tonight."

Leona's heart plunged into her stomach then vaulted to her throat. She made one last desperate attempt to convince him to join them. "But even so, you have to eat."

"I can always grab a quick bite later," he insisted, then on impulse, bent forward to kiss her cheek as he had done that morning nine years ago when he had left for the war. While he was near her ear, he whispered softly so only she could hear, "You can handle him."

Leona's eyes widened, but she made no response while she watched her friend turn and walk slowly toward the street. By the time he had climbed into his carriage and had driven off, she realized she now had no other choice but to have dinner with Lathe. *Alone.*

Chapter Ten

When Sarah entered the bedroom, she was surprised to see Zeb sitting up in bed staring idly into the small fire her younger brother had started for him just moments earlier. Because the brisk March wind was coming in from the north, it looked as if they were in for an unusually cold night and their mother had ordered fires started in several hearths.

"How are you feeling?" Sarah asked when she stepped forward and reached for his empty food tray, pleased to see his appetite had returned.

"My leg still hurts a little, but I'm feeling a whole lot better today than I was yesterday about this same time." He grimaced when he remembered how severe his pain had become while she had gone into Little Mound to get the medicine.

"That means the sulphur salve is working," she explained, happy to hear it. "Mother thought that was what you needed to turn back the infection and bring the swelling down."

"She sure must have been right. By the way, I never did get a chance to thank you for going all the way into town to fetch that medicine for me," he said. "I was in way too much pain by the time you got back to think of anything nice to say."

"There's no need to thank me," she assured him then smiled to confirm her words. "I was glad to do

192

whatever I could to help." Besides, that particular trip into town had provided her the opportunity to meet Leona's new friend, *George Parkinson.*

She felt a perplexing leap of her senses whenever his image appeared before her unbidden. Such an intriguingly handsome man, despite the small facial scar and all that hair. Her smile widened when she remembered how self-conscious he had behaved whenever she caught him staring at her during her short visit with Leona. Apparently she interested him as much as he interested her.

Zeb watched the beautiful smile unfold across Sarah's face and felt an immediate stirring of his blood. How he yearned to pull her into that bed and strip her of all those needless layers of clothing.

"It's nice to know there are still people like you around, especially when you consider how lazy and cruel some folks can be." His eyebrows arched with concern when he suddenly realized how long it had taken her to return with the medicine and clothing. He remembered having drifted in and out of consciousness at least three times before she finally returned. "You didn't tell anyone about me while you were in town, did you?"

He studied her expression closely, searching for any indication she may have turned against him.

"No, of course not," she assured him. "I remembered what you told Father: that there is a man out there somewhere who wrongfully blames you for his brother's death. Why, you are no more to blame for that young soldier's death than the Yankee who shot George is to blame for his. When someone dies in battle like that, it is senseless to try to put the blame on any one person."

Zeb fought the urge to grin, glad she had remembered the story exactly the way he had told it. "And yet this man is so obsessed with his decision to put that blame on me, he's stayed hot on my trail for nearly five years."

Sarah shook her head, appalled that something like that could happen. "I still think you should go to the sheriff and ask him for protection rather than to continue running and hiding the way you do. It's not right that you should continue to be persecuted for something that is not really your fault."

"Problem is, I don't seem to have the same faith in the law that you have," Zeb said, hoping she would accept that excuse and stop questioning why he had refused to take some sort of stand against the man. "I just feel a whole lot safer keeping on the run."

"Well, for the time being you are safe enough here you don't have to run for awhile," she vowed. "Father is not about to let anything bad happen to you. Not after finding out you served under the very same commander that my brother George did."

"Your father is a good man. I just wish I could tell him more about your brother's death but I was too busy saving my own life that day to see exactly what was happening to those around me," he lied, knowing how upset they would be to learn the truth. "But you can be sure of one thing. If Captain Potter recommended that George be awarded a medal for bravery, then your brother definitely went down fighting a good fight."

Sarah swallowed back the lump forming in her throat as she picked up the tray and turned to leave. Although she wasn't too sure what to believe about George's death anymore, it felt good to hear someone who had been there say such kind things about him.

If only Zeb wouldn't look at her the way he did. She would love to know more about the battle that eventually took her brother's life. As it was, she chose to stay away from him as much as possible.

* * *

Of all people to be dining at the Silver Swan Restaurant that Saturday night—*Mrs. Haught,* Leona thought, casting her gaze ceilingward while Lathe pulled her chair back then helped seat her.

She sighed inaudibly as she settled into the small upholstered chair, fully aware of the gossip she would soon have to face.

According to Mrs. Sanford—who had kept her ears and eyes open while working at the Mercantile during the past few days—the talk concerning Leona's suspected involvement with Dr. Lathe Caldwell had already begun, probably because of all the time and attention he had shown her those first few days following her injury. But that was clearly speculation and most people paid very little attention to obvious speculations. But now that Mrs. Josephine Haught was about to bear personal witness to the two of them dining together at the Silver Swan, the stories would run rampant. Leona just hoped the gossip would not reach John Davis's ears anytime soon. She was not ready to have him come to her demanding an explanation.

Although Leona did not like the way John seemed to think he deserved an explanation whenever she did anything out of the ordinary, she knew she would have to give one to him anyway. If for no other reason than to help douse the outrageous stories that were soon to sweep Little Mound like wildfire.

And judging by the way Mrs. Haught kept staring at her with such open-mouthed astonishment, Leona knew that the worst of those stories would start circulating that very night. Why, by church services in the morning, half the town would believe she and Lathe Caldwell were seeing each other romantically. By that following afternoon, John would undoubtedly have heard at least portions of Mrs. Haught's tale and would probably decide to pay her a call.

She breathed another silent sigh. If only George had agreed to come with them. Then Josephine Haught would not know which of the two men to focus her gossip on, and the stories would become so confusing and so contradictory that no one would pay much attention to them.

"Are you comfortable?" Lathe asked as he stepped to the opposite side of the small table, bringing her disturbing thoughts back to him.

"Yes, quite comfortable," she answered, though in truth she could not have felt more *uncomfortable*. It was annoying enough to see so many familiar faces stealing quick glances at them and to know her friends were all wondering about the extent of her involvement with the handsome young doctor; but the realization that she and Lathe would eventually return to her house where he would want her to open her dress so he could remove the bandage and examine her injury made her stomach feel all knotted inside.

"Good," he responded and quickly sank into the richly upholstered chair across the table from her. "That's why I chose this place. I was told it was the nicest restaurant in town and I did want a place where you could be comfortable. I realize you've had a very tiring day."

He then reached for his crystal water goblet and took a long, leisurely sip while he studied how extraordinarily beautiful Leona looked in the soft candlelight that filled the elegantly furnished room.

The Silver Swan was indeed Little Mound's finest restaurant. It rivaled many of those found in the big cities. Although the building itself was not all that fancy, it was large enough to hold the ornate blue marble entry and a small, elaborately decorated parlor to receive those patrons who had to wait to be seated.

Thick, dark blue draperies hung over the windows in both the parlor and the main dining area, where plush carpets cushioned the floor. The hallway that led from the parlor to the largest of the two dining areas had a floor made of gleaming dark wood with a narrow blue carpet running up the center. The white and blue wallpaper and the various appointments accented the deep color of the carpets and draperies impeccably. Considering how small the town was, the restaurant was very luxurious and conducted a surprisingly brisk business.

It was where John usually escorted Leona whenever they went out together. She grimaced when she realized how irritated he would be when he learned she had gone there with someone else and wondered if she should make a special effort to be the one to tell him.

Although she had never felt romantic inclinations toward John, she did consider him a friend and knew he would feel betrayed enough just because she had agreed to come there with Lathe. But to find out about it from someone like Josephine Haught would upset him even more. She just hoped he never found out that she had allowed Lathe to kiss her in a way she had never let John kiss her. John would become furious beyond belief. She shuddered at the thought of what he might do.

"You look preoccupied," Lathe said for want of a better word to describe her troubled expression, then glanced down to smooth his napkin across his knee with easy masculine strokes. "What's wrong?"

"Nothing," she responded a little too quickly. "Nothing at all. Why would anything be wrong?"

"I don't know, you just looked a little concerned about something," he said, then reached for one of the two menus at their table. Aware of how ill-at-ease she

197

had become, he decided to change the subject to something else.

Casually, he studied the fancy printing on the menu before him then he pursed his mouth into a thoughtful frown. "I wonder if their steaks are any good."

During the next several minutes, the conversation between Leona and Lathe continued to sound stilted and forced, but as the evening wore on and they both began to relax, they spoke with far more ease. By the time their meals arrived, they were joking and teasing each other about the silliest of things. Leona was delightfully surprised to find out that beneath his cold, harsh exterior, Lathe had a natural sense of humor and that he offered such quick, candid responses to her endless flow of questions.

For the first time since their argument concerning the importance of Civil War, they were actually getting along. They laughed and teased and laughed some more—until she made the mistake of mentioning Zeb Turner's name.

At her utterance of Zeb's name, it was as if a black cloud descended over Lathe. His expression hardened and he became suddenly introspective as he pulled his gaze off her and turned his attention instead to the food on his plate.

Leona wondered what it was about Zeb Turner that provoked such a grim reaction. There was something about that situation Lathe was not telling.

With the conversation now slowed to a mere trickle, Leona also turned her attention to the food on her plate. Having received much smaller portions, she finished long before Lathe and in the awkward moments that followed, she watched him intently from across the table.

The soft candlelight accentuated the strong lines that composed his face, making Lathe look even

198

more handsome. Her heart hammered like a school-girl's when his remarkably blue eyes then rose again to meet hers. But he looked at her for only a few seconds before returning his gaze to his plate.

In that instant, during those fleeting seconds their eyes had met, Leona sensed that Lathe was actually a very vulnerable man. He was not at all the cold, imperious man he pretended to be. Instead, he was someone who could be easily hurt, or perhaps he already *was* hurting from something—and hurting deeply.

At that moment, while she studied his quick, forced movements, Lathe was no longer the demanding, arrogant young doctor who expected his every word to be accepted as law. Tonight, something had changed; he was completely different.

Before, his harsh exterior had seemed solid, impossible to penetrate; yet now she sensed a yielding aura of compassion. Suddenly she realized what a profoundly caring person he really was, which was reflected by his chosen profession. Caring yet deeply tormented. But by what? And why was a man like that traveling around the country trying to help capture some common criminal when he could be putting his medical training to better use? It just didn't make any sense.

"Looks like somewhere along the way you overcame that ailing appetite of yours," he commented, aware she had again become lost in thought.

The unexpected comment brought Leona's straying thoughts back to her present surroundings with a jolt. She had noticed when he first glanced up from his plate again. Still, she had not really expected him to speak.

"Yes, I suppose I did," she replied when what he had said finally registered and she realized he expected an answer. "But I don't see where you have much room to talk. Not considering how much food you managed to put away." She nodded toward his empty plate then watched, fascinated, when he brought his hand up and placed the last bite of steak into his mouth. There was something distracting in the way his lips came together and virtually caressed his food while he chewed.

Aware Leona was watching him closely, Lathe waited until his mouth was again clear before justifying his comment. "Ah, but your getting your appetite back is a good sign. It means your body has finally realized it needs the nutrition to get better." He smiled with approval while he set his fork across his plate. When he then leaned forward to brace his chin with his hands, the candlelight shaped deep shadows along the strong, masculine curves in his cheeks, making Leona even more aware of how profoundly attractive he was. Her body became all warm and tingly in response, causing her brown eyes to sparkle with a deep, radiant glow that seemed to please Lathe.

Dazedly, she wondered why Lathe didn't smile more often.

"So," he commented, then sat back again, aware he finally had her full attention yet not all that sure what they should talk about. Wanting to keep that glittering sparkle in her beautiful, almond-shaped eyes, he immediately decided not to discuss either his continued involvement with Zeb Turner or her incredibly unrealistic views about the war. He did not want to renew any of their past arguments, especially tonight.

"Did you find time to stop off at your lawyer's today?" he asked, having decided that should be a safe enough topic and wanting desperately to keep their conversation alive. Although they had both finished eating, he was not yet ready to return to her house, knowing that after he had examined her wound and replaced her bandage, he would have no other excuse to linger in her company.

"No, I saw no real reason to," she admitted with a slow smile that indicated the gratitude she now felt toward George. "I have decided not to have my brother declared legally dead just yet."

"But I thought that was something you were told you had to do before you could get that big bank loan you so desperately need to salvage your business." It seemed peculiar to him that a woman, who had just a few days earlier been quite willing to risk her own health just so her store could remain open, would choose not to do the one thing that could save her business. "How can you get the loan without it?"

"I really don't need that bank loan anymore. Or at least I won't be needing one for awhile." Her brown eyes glinted with childlike excitement when she leaned forward in her chair as if about to reveal a secret. "George Parkinson has offered to lend me one thousand dollars to help me get back on my feet."

"Parkinson has volunteered to do *what?*" Lathe asked, clearly surprised. His blue eyes narrowed with immediate suspicion. "Where did someone like George Parkinson get that kind of money?"

"He's been saving most of his money for years because he's always wanted to be able to travel around and see the country at his leisure. That's why he doesn't have to stop and take on odd jobs to help pay for his food and lodgings. He already has all he needs."

"And he's decided to lend it to you," Lathe commented, not at all pleased by George's unexpected show of generosity. It meant Leona might end up feeling obligated to him. Just the thought of that made the muscles in his chest tighten with immediate resentment. Again, he wondered where George had come up with that kind of money. Most trappers barely made enough to live on.

"Yes, and it was all his idea. He really is such a dear, sweet person," she said, her voice warm with true fondness. "He didn't even want to charge me interest."

"Imagine that," Lathe muttered, wishing he had been the one to come up with the money instead of George. If only he had had enough time to return to Alabama, get the information he needed from his aunt to recover his family's money, then find the exact location where it had actually been buried, he would have plenty of money to lend her. But as it was, he barely had enough cash to last him another two or three weeks. If Zeb didn't show his ugly face soon, Lathe would be forced to take on yet another boring job just to earn some more money. "Who would have thought old George would turn out to be so generous?"

"I know," she agreed, then went on to explain. "That's what kept us so long today. It took a lot of pencil work to figure out the smartest way to spend that much money. Why, by the time I finished putting everything down on paper, I had a six-page order. I just hope George can get it all into one wagon. I'd hate for him to have to make two trips."

"George is going after the merchandise, too?" *Where did the man's generosity end?* he wondered bitterly. And just what did he hope to gain by being so nauseatingly helpful?

Lathe's mouth compressed into a narrow, flat line when he realized exactly what George did hope to gain from having made such a generous offer. George not only hoped to win Leona's deepest affection, he hoped to earn her eternal gratitude. A hard, painful knot formed in the very core of his stomach and it occurred to him then that, for some reason, he was

202

jealous. Jealous of a man he barely knew and over a woman he had originally hoped to ignore.

"He asked to go," Leona explained, her face animated with excitement. "He intends to leave sometime Monday morning, just as soon as his money has been transferred to this bank and released to us. By Wednesday night, he should be back with most or maybe even all of the merchandise and I can start filling my shelves with the new stock."

Leona was so thrilled over the prospect of being able to save her business without having to have Ethan declared legally dead, she did not notice who had entered the main dining room until he was already bearing down on their table.

Her eyes rounded with immediate concern when she recognized the newcomer's angry face.

"John," she breathed, then cut her gaze to Lathe, who had heard her startled gasp but had yet to realize the reason.

"Don't tell me," John stated in a deep, grating voice, not waiting for Lathe to turn around. "This is the notorious *doctor* who has been taking such wonderful care of you." The harsh lines that distorted his otherwise handsome face made him look as if he had bitten into something bitter.

"Yes," she responded then swallowed hard, wondering if he intended to cause a ruckus. Even though Mrs. Haught and her husband had left several minutes earlier, there were still several others in the room who knew them and would be quick to spread various accounts of their encounter. She tried to appear extremely composed when she nodded to verify Lathe's identity. "This is Dr. Caldwell."

She glanced at Lathe, who had turned in his chair to look questioningly at John. Without really meaning to, she introduced the two men as she had come to know them, by their first names. "Lathe, this

203

is John — John Davis — my attorney."

Lathe's expression changed from cautiously curious to just plain annoyed when the name first registered in his mind, but John did not give him an opportunity to respond to the introduction.

"Lathe is it?" he went on, his tone extremely harsh. Having removed his bowler when he first entered as a courtesy to those around him, he now shook the small, rounded hat in Lathe's direction, and glared accusingly at him. "And since when is it appropriate for a young female patient to refer to her doctor using his first name?"

Although Lathe had taken an immediate disliking to John Davis, he decided not to do anything to cause Leona any further embarrassment. Instead of offering an appropriate quip, he stood and immediately held out his hand. "When the patient and doctor are also good friends, I think it is quite appropriate," he explained in the most civil tone he could summon at that particular moment. But when John responded by thrusting his pompous chin forward while refusing to accept the proffered hand, Lathe could not resist adding one small jab, "Especially if the doctor and patient have become as *close* as Leona and I have during the past few days."

Leona's eyes widened at such a startlingly bold remark and quickly glanced about to see who might have overheard such a scandalous comment. Fortunately, because of the late hour, the main dining area had emptied somewhat, and there were only a few diners scattered about the surrounding tables — none within immediate earshot.

"Close are you?" John asked, then looked at Leona as if he planned to hold her accountable for everything Lathe said. "That's not what I was told when I stopped by to visit with her yesterday. The impression she gave me was that she could barely tolerate you."

Lathe had no reason to doubt that, therefore did not offer a quick response.

"John, I never said anything like that," Leona quickly scolded while cutting her gaze nervously from Lathe to John. "The truth is, the doctor and I *are* friends, but we are *just* friends," Leona explained in a very real attempt to cool John's rising temper before it flared into something he could no longer control. "Nothing more."

Wanting to make sure Lathe did not say something to dispute her, she shot him a quick, meaningful glare. Her eyebrows lifted with immediate suspicion when she noticed a look of pure innocence cross his face.

When John also turned his attention back to Lathe, his mouth curled into a dark scowl and his narrowed eyes glinted to display the depth of his scorn. Although his next words were clearly directed to Leona, his gaze remained fastened to Lathe's while he raked his fingers impatiently through his stylishly cut brown hair. "Just friends, is it? Well just you see that it stays that way. I'd hate for my future wife to sully her reputation over the likes of this crass-looking gigolo."

"*John!*" Her voice offered a sharp warning when she pushed her chair back and stood, wanting her height to be more equal with that of the two men. "You know as well as I do that I have never in my life agreed to marry you."

"Ah, but you will," he said as if it were inevitable then turned to offer her a caustic look before repeating those words to emphasize his meaning. "You *will*. And that's why you are to stay away from this man in the future. If for some reason you feel you still need a doctor's care, I'll send for Doc Edison in Karnack."

Then just as abruptly as he had appeared, he spun about on his boot heel and left, marching straight out of the restaurant, without bothering to acknowledge anyone else in the room.

"Nice fellow," Lathe commented, his face void of any expression when he finally turned to look at Leona again. "Quite a charmer."

As upset as the confrontation had left her, Leona had to chuckle. "Yes, I thought you'd like him."

Embarrassed by John's behavior and knowing it had been witnessed by many of the people around them, she kept her gaze on the napkin she still clutched in her hand. They may not have been close enough to overhear everything said, but they had definitely been close enough to have noticed the anger on John's face.

"I guess we should go," she said, already setting the napkin aside, eager to be away from the others.

"Yes," Lathe agreed, remembering his earlier plans. "I'm ready to have another look at that wound of yours. Unless of course you would rather John sent for that other doctor."

"I have no intention of sending for another doctor," Leona said, scowling at the thought.

"Good, then I'll continue to be your doctor. Let's go. I'm eager to have a look at that cut. A lot can go wrong with an injury if it's not properly tended, and we certainly don't want to take any chances."

A shivering wave of awareness washed over Leona when Lathe quickly tossed enough money to pay for their meals onto the table then reached out to cup her right elbow with the warm curve of his left hand. While being gently directed toward the door, her thoughts alternated between what was about to happen and what had already happened.

With his hand still at her elbow, subtly guiding her down the narrow hall, and the frightening prospect of having to partially undress for him looming just moments ahead, her insides spun with such a wild, dizzying rush, it left her feeling weak and wobbly yet vivaciously alive.

By the time they had stepped out onto the boardwalk, Leona's heart pounded with such an alarming force and her breathing had become so labored, that she felt as if she had just run a long race.

If only she could be certain of what lay ahead.

Seconds later, when she and Lathe stepped away from the lighted area in front of the building, she noticed how very dark it had become during the short time they had been inside. The outside temperatures had dropped several degrees, causing the north wind to blow cold and brisk against her face; yet a strange sense of inner warmth continued to radiate from the one spot where Lathe still touched her.

It was not until he had helped her into the carriage he'd rented and had finally removed his hand from her elbow, that the first real effects of the cold temperature settled over her.

Without Lathe's touch to warm her, her blood chilled quickly. In an effort to hold onto some of her own body's warmth, she crossed her arms and pressed them close to her while she watched Lathe hurry around to the opposite side of the carriage. She wished she had thought to grab her shawl before leaving the house, but had not expected the temperature to drop quite that rapidly. At least she had thought to change into her dark blue dress, which had much heavier sleeves than the pale blue she had worn earlier that day.

"Would you like my coat?" he asked after climbing onto the seat beside her, having noticed her huddled form. Without waiting for a response, knowing she was just stubborn enough to refuse his offer, he quickly shrugged out of his dark blue dinner coat and draped it over her shoulders.

The gesture alone was enough to cause an unexpected wave of exhilaration to sweep through her, but when she noticed how his body's warmth and his spicy male scent still clung to the inner lining of his coat, it caused her to feel downright giddy inside.

For the next few minutes, while Lathe sent the carriage rolling along the graveled streets toward her house, all she wanted to do was close her eyes and bask in the gentle warmth that had taken over her body. It was several minutes before she gathered enough of her sensibilities to say anything.

When she did finally speak, it was to voice aloud the question that had been plaguing her the most: "Lathe, why did you tell John that we had become very close during the few days we have known each other?"

"I don't know," he answered. When he turned to look at her, his gaze lingered on her soft, inviting lips. His breath caught when he remembered how exhilarating it felt to kiss those lips. "Perhaps I did it because I wanted him to know he isn't the only one interested in you. I guess I wanted to make sure he understood that I care for you, too."

Leona blinked, unable to believe she had heard right. It was not at all the sort of answer she had expected to receive.

Nor was it the sort of answer Lathe had expected to give.

"Even after last night?" she ventured to ask. Her heart beat wildly at the thought he may have already forgiven her for her shameful behavior.

"*Especially* after last night." Though the road deserved his attention, he continued to stare at her, his pale blue eyes glittering with more than simple affection, his heart thudding like a young schoolboy's. How he yearned to pull her into his arms again and kiss her until she was again weak with her own raging desires.

"But I don't understand," she said, looking truly perplexed. "I thought you were angry with me about last night."

"Angry with you? Hardly!" His eyebrows arched, the absurdity of her remark temporarily cooling his ardor. "If I gave you the impression I was angry with you, I'm sorry. The truth is, I was angry with myself."

"With yourself?" Her eyebrows dipped lower still. "But why?"

His mouth flattened into a harsh line when he looked again at the street. "Because I never meant for anything like that to happen."

"Oh, I see," she commented, though she really didn't see. Didn't see at all. If he really cared for her like he had just implied, then why was he so opposed to kissing her? Was she that unappealing to him as a woman? Obviously so. She frowned when she realized none of her previous suitors had thought so. Just Lathe.

Suddenly, the implication behind her thoughts registered and she glanced questioningly at Lathe.

Could he possibly be considered a suitor? Just because he had kissed her and had invited her to have dinner with him? Her brow furrowed then lifted into an incredulous expression when she realized what a ridiculous notion that was. He had just admitted that he had never even wanted to kiss her.

No, what he felt for her was exactly what he had told John he felt, a very close friendship. Nothing more.

For the next few minutes, while Lathe and Leona rode together in companionable silence, each became deeply engrossed in his or her own thoughts. Neither seemed aware of the gentle jostling of the carriage as it clattered and creaked along the graveled street nor of the continuous clopping of the horse's hooves as the animal slowly shortened the distance to her house.

Although his actual words had made Leona feel somewhat less than desirable, there was one very real consolation to Lathe's earlier pronouncement. If he was *that* opposed to kissing her, she would not have to worry about any recurrence of what had happened the previous night.

Aching with a sense of disappointment she had no reason to feel, she decided it was time to change the general direction of their conversation — before he took it upon himself to explain why he found her so unappealing. "I wonder if it is going to get cold enough tonight to warrant building a fire," she said, thinking the weather a safe enough topic to discuss.

"Probably so," Lathe responded then glanced at her briefly before slowing the carriage for the final turn. "But don't worry about the cold, I'll be sure to start a fire for you before I leave."

But nothing like the fire you started for me last night, she mused grimly then leaned back and pulled his coat tighter around her shoulders, wondering why she suddenly felt so gloomy.

Chapter Eleven

Scraps barked excitedly when he spotted the small, single-horse carriage pull to a slow stop in front of the house.

"That dog of yours certainly does derive great pleasure from announcing my arrivals," Lathe pointed out as he climbed down on the street side of the carriage. He hurried to secure the tether strap to one of the three ornate hitching posts in front of Leona's house. "Earlier, when I came by here to see if you would like to have supper with me, that animal of yours started barking and jumping around in such a wild frenzy, I thought he was going absolutely berserk."

"He already *is* absolutely berserk," Leona corrected him then glanced off toward the back yard where she could barely make out the animal's dark, bouncing shape in the night shadows. "He barks only at the people he knows. He usually ignores strangers. He'll stop all that after we've gone inside," she said with an air of confidence she did not quite feel, never really certain what that mule-headed mutt might do. "He won't have anyone to bark at then."

Even after they had climbed the front steps and crossed the veranda to the front door, Scraps continued to bark. Fortunately, as Leona had predicted, the moment they stepped inside and closed the door with a clattering jolt, he stopped his loud, incessant barking . . . and started whimpering instead.

"I have to admit, you certainly do know your dog," Lathe said, trying not to laugh out loud, aware Leona was trying unsuccessfully to ignore the deep, mournful sounds coming from outside. "He stopped barking the minute we closed that door."

Leona flattened her eyebrows, annoyed that he found the situation so amusing, and she continued to scowl while she slipped his coat off her shoulders. "I don't know what that animal's problem could be. He normally doesn't whine and carry on like that unless it is very, very cold outside."

By the time Leona had draped Lathe's coat over a nearby chair and began brushing the resulting wrinkles from her sleeves, Scraps had slowly worked himself into a sharp, woeful howl.

"I guess I had better let him in," she finally said, when it became apparent his complaining would only grow louder. "Apparently he thinks it is cold enough to want to come inside."

"It is pretty chilly, even in the house," Lathe admitted as he reached for the buckle of his holster, then remembering his earlier scare, decided to leave it be. "While you let the dog inside, I'll get started building that fire I promised. Where do you keep the firewood?"

Leona reached for one of the shawls from the hall tree and quickly flung it around her shoulders. "Since it is nearly the middle of March and most of our cold weather should have been behind us by now, I've already cleaned out the woodboxes in most of the house but there is usually plenty in the kitchen. If not, there's a big stack of it out near the carriage house."

Preferring not to use the wood she had already brought inside to use for cooking, Lathe followed her to the back door, where there was just enough light falling through the windows to allow them to see. While Leona crossed the yard in one direction to let Scraps off his chain, he hurried to the woodpile to collect an armful of logs.

After gathering as many as he could safely carry in one load, he turned back toward the house, unable to see much over the tall stack of logs.

When he lifted his boot with the intention of taking his first step toward the house, a deep growl penetrated the darkness. The sound came from only a few feet away, yet when he set his foot back down, the growling stopped.

Perplexed, thinking Leona hadn't yet had enough time to release Scraps, and unable to think of another animal that could make such a low, menacing noise, he decided it must have been his imagination. Again, he lifted his boot with the intention of taking a step. And again he heard a resulting growl.

Unable to see the area directly around him because of all the logs, he still could not locate the exact source of the deep, threatening sound. When he finally lowered the boot forward to take that first step, he heard a quick movement then felt a sharp series of jerking tugs on his leather holster. It took all his agility not to loose his balance and allow the logs to roll and topple to the ground.

"Scraps, leave him alone," Leona ordered, hurrying across the yard to intervene. "What is the matter with you? That man is our friend," she explained sharply, though she remembered a time when she, too, had considered him the enemy. But that was before she had made an effort to get to know him. "Let go!"

Moving closer, she grabbed the growling dog by the collar and tugged hard. Because he refused to let go of the holster even by force, she became so annoyed, she popped him soundly on the head with the flat of her palm. When he opened his mouth to

213

yelp aloud his complaint, she quickly jerked him away.

Aware of his defeat, the animal became immediately docile, glancing up at her with those huge, sad brown eyes as if to ask why she felt it necessary to actually clobber him. Yet, despite his look of animal innocence, she continued to hold him firmly by his collar, aware of how quickly that disposition of his might change.

When she then glanced at Lathe, her cheeks flamed bright red. There was just enough moonlight tumbling through the newly leafed trees to let him see how embarrassed she felt.

"I'm sorry," she said, shaking her head. "I don't know what got into him. He's hardly ever that aggressive, not even with the people he dislikes."

"Perhaps he has some unknown aversion to firearms," Lathe suggested, wondering how much damage the animal had done to his holster.

Although Leona continued to keep a firm hold on the dog's collar, Lathe turned so he could watch the animal carefully before taking another step toward the house. If the dog made another lunge for him, he wanted to be ready to drop that full load of logs right on top of his mangy head.

Minutes later, after the three had entered the kitchen and the door was again closed, Leona flung her shawl aside then knelt in front of the dog and tried again to explain that Lathe was a friend.

"Don't you remember? He was here just last night," she said, hoping to persuade the animal to leave their guest alone. "He's the one who gave you the rest of that stew."

Scraps studied her sincere expression then looked at Lathe, tilted his head to one side, and curled his lips back but did not actually growl.

"Stop that!" Leona admonished. "He also happens

214

to have saved my life. He deserves a little more respect than that."

Lathe thought that an odd comment to come from her, considering how little respect she had shown him thus far. "Well, while you two try to determine whether I'm friend or foe, I think I'll go get that fire started in your bedroom," he said. His arms ached under the strain of all that weight.

"In my bedroom?" Leona's heart jumped with immediate alarm. It had never occurred to her that he planned to build the fire there. Was that also where he intended to conduct his examination of her wound. "Why my bedroom? Why not the front parlor?"

"Do you plan to sleep in the front parlor?" he asked, looking at her with a peculiar expression.

"Well, no, but—"

"Then why bother building a fire in there? Why not build the fire where it will do the most overall good? Unless of course you intended for me to build two fires, but why waste firewood on two separate fires when one will do?"

Leona's mouth pursed into a short, flat line. It was hard to argue against such clear logic.

It was also hard to argue against an empty room, which is exactly what she was left with when Lathe then turned and carried the wood out of the kitchen.

Thinking perhaps hunger had caused Scraps to behave so strangely, she hurried to get some leftover food and fill the large, dented bread pan she kept for him in the back room. Several minutes later, after she felt certain the animal was calm enough to cause no further harm to her guest, she left him in the storage room to finish his meal. Quickly, she washed her hands of any splattered food or loose dog hair, then stopped by the hall mirror long enough to check her general appearance before proceeding toward the bed-room.

When she entered the room, she found that Lathe already had a small fire blazing in the hearth and now stood, leaning forward against the mantel, braced by one strong, muscular arm. His other arm hung relaxed by his side. The flickering glow of the small fire danced warmly across the deep planes of his face. There was a fascinating contrast of strength and vulnerability about him while he stared down into that fire, lost to his own thoughts.

He heard the slight rustle of her skirts when she came closer and he snapped out of his reflective mood and then turned to face her. "There. That should have this room feeling all cozy and warm in no time."

"Thank you," she said and took another step toward him, holding her hands out to the fire's warmth for lack of anything else to do. She knew she no longer felt chilled, and wondered if that was due more to the fire or to Lathe's presence. Both had a definite warming effect on her, only the sort of warmth Lathe offered seemed to be generated somewhere inside her.

"We'll wait until the room becomes a little warmer before I check that wound," Lathe said, eager to put off ever having to leave.

Although he continued to lean with one arm propped against the mantel, he turned to face her. The dancing lights from below continued to reach up and caress the deep, masculine lines of his face, making him appear somehow more accessible than ever before.

Aware of how very close they stood to one another, Leona's breath swelled inside her chest, unable to push its way past the sudden constriction that had formed at the base of her throat.

A strange light reflected from the depth of his blue eyes, a light that had nothing to do with the flickering flames of the fire below. When she realized how terribly drawn she felt to that tiny glimmering light, her heart raced with such an unanticipated burst of energy, she felt her pulses throb at various points along her body.

Startled by such an overwhelming reaction, she quickly glanced away. She focused first on her hands, which were still held out to the fire, then on the flames themselves while they reached out to quell the darkness that surrounded them.

It was while she continued to study the strange, hypnotic effect of the splashing yellow flames that she realized Lathe had not bothered to light a lamp. The only illumination in that entire room came from that one fire . . . and from the fascinating sparkle still reflected in Lathe's eyes.

Unable to resist a second look, Leona again lifted her gaze to his and felt a strong, vibrant current pass between them. Her whole body tingled with unexpected awareness when she watched him slip his hand off the mantel and stand upright before her.

When he bent his head to gaze at the perfect sculpture of her upturned face, he felt his desire for her swell to unbearable proportions. He cursed himself for wanting to touch the supple texture of her skin and for again wanting to sample the honeyed sweetness that clung to the outward curve of her lips.

How he yearned to pull the pins from her mass of dark hair, eager to run his hands through her long silken tresses.

"Why do you have to be so incredibly beautiful?" he asked, his voice filled with torment, making it sound as if her beauty were more an affliction than an attribute. While he continued to stare past her thick, dark lashes into a pair of brown eyes that seemed to swallow him whole, he dampened his lips with the tip of his tongue, preparing for the kiss to come.

That had been a question Leona would have found impossible to answer even if her thoughts hadn't been fastened on the erotic movement of his tongue. As it was, she was having such a hard time getting her labored breath back under control, she gave up on rational thought altogether.

While Leona continued to struggle with what seemed like an extremely limited amount of oxygen, Lathe's gaze again traveled over her beautiful face then eventually returned to its original location, eager to become lost in the shimmering depths of her huge, brown eyes once more.

Dazed by her nearness, he could not remember why he had ever sworn not to touch her again. It was hard to concentrate on anything beyond the tantalizing memory of her kiss. Feeling very much like a doomed man, he caught her in his arms and pulled her quickly into his powerful embrace, his head already bent to claim her mouth in the long, violently sweet kiss that followed.

Although Leona feared what he might think should she again surrender to the burning passion that engulfed her whenever their lips touched, she was unable to resist his intimate embrace. She had so wanted to prove to him that normally she was not that sort of woman, but there was something about him that set her mind to reeling and made doing the right thing impossible.

Instead of pulling away as she'd planned, she did just the opposite and pressed her body harder against his. That same strange, shimmering warmth swept through her as before, quickly melting any last traces of resistance. The heat flooded her senses with such exhilarating force, that it made her feel vigorously alive, strangely light-headed, and even a little weak in the knees.

Yielding to the unfamiliar sensations, she lifted her arms and pressed against the strong muscles rippling along his back and lower neck with her open palms. He responded to her shy touch by tightening his embrace, bringing their bodies ever closer.

Although still a little frightened about where their passions might lead, Leona felt just as eager to explore the sensations this man had so easily brought to life within her—eager as she was frightened to find out where these strange new sensations might lead.

Her thoughts, muddled though they were, focused first on the intense longing his hungry kiss had awakened inside her then slowly ventured to thoughts beyond. Daringly, she wondered what it would be like to appease these strange, new desires burning inside her. She wondered what it would be like to have a man like Lathe make love to her—a man so very gentle, yet so truly commanding.

While the desire that had blazed within them continued to grow more and more intense, the kiss deepened.

Just as eager to feel the pressure of her soft curves against the harder planes of his own body, Lathe pressed his hands more forcefully against the base of her spine, but when that did little to quell his appetite for her, he slowly brought his hands around to her slender waist then edged them upward across her ribcage, toward her breasts—knowing the right one was still bound with bandages but the left one would be free for exploration.

Aware of his destination and the extreme danger that loomed only moments ahead, Leona's brain sent out its first clear warning; but as before, the frantic message went unheeded. Although in her heart she knew what they were doing was wrong, she could not bring herself to stop him. She felt so helpless when she allowed him to continue pressing her body intimately against his with one hand while the other worked its way slowly upward.

The fire blazing inside her gathered even more force when it neared the very core of her being, making her want Lathe more than she had ever wanted a man. She responded to this strange, raging need by pressing her body harder against his, wanting somehow to bring him closer.

Within seconds, the roaming hand finally reached its destination, and when his fingers brushed lightly against the rigid tip, Leona gasped with pleasure. Even through the dress and the camisole beneath, his touch set her on fire. She arched her shoulders to give him easier access to his find, oblivious to any pain caused by the added stress to her wound.

The pleasure of Lathe's touch had slowly drugged her and the fire still raging inside her shot quickly through her, until it affected every part of her body. She knew if she did not do something to free herself at that exact moment there would be no stopping him. Yet somehow she still could not gather the strength needed to pull away from his masterful touch.

She had already passed the point of no return, as had Lathe. There would be no stopping the wildfire that raged inside her. It no longer mattered whether she was being driven into madness by desire or by love, though she suspected the driving force inside her to be a combination of both. She was lost.

Amazingly, the sensations inside her continued to grow until they became almost more than one woman could bear. Even so, she continued to lean against him, eager for more. While allowing his hand and mouth to continue working their extraordinary magic, shaft after jolting shaft of pure, unadulterated pleasure shot through her body, leaving her ever more pliant to his touch.

Breathlessly, she focused so intently on what the one hand was doing to bring her further pleasure; she was unaware that the other hand had deliberately worked its way to the many buttons along the back of her dress.

One by one, Lathe released the tiny fasteners, until he had the upper half of her dress undone.

Parting the garment to allow himself access, he slipped his hand inside and gently cupped the unbandaged breast. He ached with a need that became so strong it shook him. He closed his eyes and gently explored the softness of the treasured find, caressing its fullness with the inner curve of his hand while his thumb stroked the tip until it grew rigid with desire.

Unable to wait any longer, he pushed the upper part of her dress down over her shoulders, letting it hang loosely from her waist. Hurriedly, he moved to untie the silken straps of her camisole, anxious to see and taste that which had brought his hand such pleasure.

While he continued to work with a particularly stubborn tie, he lifted his gaze to her flushed face and could tell by the high color of her cheeks and by the way her mouth remained parted yet her eyes had drifted shut that she was just as anxious for what was about to happen as he was. He also sensed that this would be her first time and although he knew by the rapid rise and fall of her chest, he could take her then and know complete fulfillment, he decided to proceed slowly.

When he finally had the stubborn tie unknotted and was able to tug the sheer cotton garment down to her waist and expose her full, round breast to his view, Scraps started to bark again. Lathe tensed then moaned with relief when Leona did not seem to notice; but seconds later, he groaned from utter frustration when there came a demanding knock at the door. The sharp sound snatched them both from the dizzying state of passion and dropped them sharply into the startling realm of reality.

While Leona struggled with trembling hands to refasten her dress, Lathe smoothed his hair with one agile swipe of his hand then walked out with such easy, masculine grace, it left her feeling unaccountably annoyed. How could something that had left her feeling so weak and quivering have had so little effect on him? It hurt to realize he had not felt the same impact she had. There she was, so completely shaken by what had happened she could hardly function, yet Lathe had been able to walk calmly out of the room as if nothing had happened.

Seconds later, as soon as she had finished rebuttoning the dress and had taken the time to glance in a mirror to make sure her hair was still in place, she hurried toward the front of the house, as curious to find out who her late-night visitor might be as she was eager to make it appear as if nothing out of the ordinary had happened.

When she entered the main hallway, she noticed Lathe and Tony Newland talking near the front door, Tony's eyes stretched to their very limits. Leona thought he looked extremely pale then noticed his clothes were torn and his shirt was streaked with dirt.

"You've just got to come, Doc," he said, his voice shrill with youthful desperation. "She ain't movin' at all. And you can see the bone stickin' right out the side of her leg. Please, Doc, you are the only one around here I know who really knows what to do to help her."

When Leona stepped closer she realized that the streaks on the boy's shirt were not dirt, they were splatterings of blood.

"How bad is she bleeding?" Lathe asked, already grabbing his coat. When he glanced over his shoulder and noticed Leona's curious expression, he shrugged apologetically. "His mother has been in an accident. I have to go."

Aware that he might need help, Leona hurried toward the hall tree and reached for a shawl. "I'm going, too."

Not about to refuse her assistance, Lathe opened the door and waited for Tony and Leona to pass ahead of him.

"Where is she now?" he asked as soon as he had pulled the door closed and followed closely behind them.

"Over on Main Street, right at the far edge of town," Tony said, glancing over his shoulder while he continued toward the street at a pace so brisk it was hard for the others to keep up. "We was on our way back from visitin' out to Aunt Deborah's house. My little cousin, Nicholas, has been real sick. Ma wanted to go out and spell my aunt for awhile so she could get some sleep. Something in the dark musta spooked the horse 'cause all of a sudden he took off runnin' toward town. I tried to make him slow down, but he wouldn't do it. He just kept runnin'. Hard as he could. Then suddenly I heard somethin' crack. The next thing I knew, the whole buggy had flipped over on its side, with the horse still a draggin' it. I had already fell out, but Ma was still inside."

As soon as Tony stepped through the gate he'd left open, he turned toward town.

Lathe knew the boy must have run all the way there and planned to run all the way back, so he called out, then motioned toward the carriage. Tony climbed in obligingly. Leona followed.

"Which direction?" Lathe asked, as soon as he had snatched the tether strap loose and leaped up into the

223

carriage to join the other two. Even before he was fully settled into the seat, he had already snapped the reins hard, setting the horse into quick motion.

"Three blocks up and one block over," Tony told him, pointing toward the exact direction with his hand. "Hurry, Doc. She's bleedin' bad." He looked away then added in an emotionally strained voice, "I don't want my Ma to die, Doc. Please, don't let her die."

While Lathe concentrated on arriving at the scene of the accident as quickly as possible, Leona put her arm around the boy to comfort him. A sharp pain pierced her heart when she felt his whole body tremble beneath her touch.

"Over there," Tony said when they rounded the last curve and had a large part of Main Street in sight.

Leona glanced in the direction he pointed and in the dim street light saw a dozen or so people either standing or kneeling around a large piece of twisted wreckage. She felt her stomach twist into a cold, sickened knot of dread when they drew close enough to see the pale faces. Several of the women had turned away, unable to bear the sight, while a few of the others continued to look on in stunned horror. One woman had become so ill by what she had seen, she had sat down in the street to avoid fainting.

"Make room for the doctor," Tony said, leaping from the carriage even before it came to a complete stop. Within seconds he had fought his way into the center of the crowd and knelt helplessly at his mother's side.

Knowing Lathe would be just as eager to follow, Leona took the reins from him then secured them to the tether bar and set the brake before climbing down herself. Her heart was pumping as she elbowed her way into the small crowd. Terrified of what she might see, she waited until she was near Lathe before glanc-

MORE PASSION AND ADVENTURE AWAIT... YOUR TRIP TO A BIG ADVENTUROUS WORLD BEGINS WHEN YOU ACCEPT YOUR FIRST 4 NOVELS ABSOLUTELY *FREE*
(AN $18.00 VALUE)

Accept your Free gift and start to experience more of the passion and adventure you like in a historical romance novel. Each Zebra novel is filled with proud men, spirited women and tempestuous love that you'll remember long after you turn the last page.

Zebra Historical Romances are the finest novels of their kind. They are written by authors who really know how to weave tales of romance and adventure in the historical settings you love. You'll feel like you've actually gone back in time with the thrilling stories that each Zebra novel offers.

GET YOUR FREE GIFT WITH THE START OF YOUR HOME SUBSCRIPTION

Our readers tell us that these books sell out very fast in book stores and often they miss the newest titles. So Zebra has made arrangements for you to receive the four newest novels published each month.

You'll be guaranteed that you'll never miss a title, and home delivery is so convenient. And to show you just how easy it is to get Zebra Historical Romances, we'll send you your first 4 books absolutely FREE! Our gift to you just for trying our home subscription service.

BIG SAVINGS AND FREE HOME DELIVERY

Each month, you'll receive the four newest titles as soon as they are published. You'll probably receive them even before the bookstores do. What's more, you may preview these exciting novels free for 10 days. If you like them as much as we think you will, just pay the low preferred subscriber's price of just $3.75 each. *You'll save $3.00 each month off the publisher's price.* AND, your savings are even greater because there are never any shipping, handling or other hidden charges—FREE Home Delivery. Of course you can return any shipment within 10 days for full credit, no questions asked. There is no minimum number of books you must buy.

ing toward the splintered carriage. An immediate constriction pulled at her chest when she glimpsed Darlene Newland's body still tangled in the wreckage, her left leg bent awkwardly into the wreckage behind her.

"We didn't move her, Doctor," one man said after Lathe had knelt beside the mangled carriage and leaned forward to find out exactly what he was up against.

His forehead knitted when he saw how severely twisted her left leg looked. Then he noticed a large, bloody piece of broken bone poking through a thick, jagged tear in the skin. He recognized the bone to be the tibia and realized the fibula was probably broken, too, but had not pierced the skin. He decided the smaller bone was probably lodged in her muscle somewhere. He just hoped the other break proved as smooth as this one appeared to be. Nothing was harder to set than a splintered bone.

"We decided to wait until you got here first," another man explained. "We didn't want to do the wrong thing."

Nodding that he understood their precaution, Lathe reached into the wreckage, inches below where the largest portion of the woman's head protruded. He wanted to see if she still had a pulse and if she did, how strong.

"I'm glad you didn't move her," he commented while studying the woman's poor color. If anyone fit the description, pale as a ghost, this one did. His eyebrows notched into a troubled frown while he pressed two of his fingers against the base of her throat. The pulse was so weak, he had to move his hand twice before finally locating a shallow movement.

As soon as he was certain what he'd felt was a pulsebeat, he turned to meet Tony's fearful gaze and nodded reassuringly.

225

His mother was still alive. Though barely.

"First thing we need to do is take her somewhere where I can examine her. I sure can't take care of that leg out here on the street." He glanced at the men closest to him. "Will some of you help me free her from the wreckage then help me get her to my buggy?"

"Where you gonna take her?" one man asked, already helping to break away several of the jagged pieces of wreckage that held her prisoner. "You ain't got an office around here, do you?"

"You know he doesn't," someone else admonished. Lathe never bothered to see who spoke.

"That means he's got no choice but to take her on out to her house."

"But that's nearly a mile out. She'll never make the trip, not with all the blood she's lost."

"Looks like he'll have to take care of her right here then."

Aware they nearly had the woman freed, Lathe glanced up to locate Leona's face among those in the crowd. He found her standing only a few feet away.

Seeing the questioning look in his eyes, she nodded. "He's taking her to my house. It's only a few blocks away. That way, I can act as Dr. Caldwell's nurse."

Everyone sighed with collective relief, glad Leona had proven so generous, aware there were not many people who would allow a bleeding woman to be brought into their homes and chance ruining their carpets and furniture forever. But not many people were like Leona. Darlene Newland's life might be saved yet.

But first they had to get her there.

Because a large portion of her body was still trapped between a bent wheel and the main part of what was left of the buggy, one set of men pried a

226

larger opening with a long lever while another set helped Lathe pull her free. As soon as they had her safely freed from the wreckage, Lathe gripped the front of his shirt and pulled hard, popping his buttons in several directions.

Several of the women gasped and hurried away, while others stood mesmerized by it all.

Lathe quickly pulled the shirt off his back then held it in both hands and immediately ripped it in half. He used part of the torn shirt to place a tourniquet around the lower part of her thigh, about a foot above the damaged area where several inches of bone still protruded through her leg. After he managed to slow the bleeding to a trickle, he used the other part of his shirt to bind the wound itself, hoping to prevent the opening from becoming further caked with dirt.

Quickly, he worked his fingers over the rest of her body to see what else might be broken. While he worked, he was careful not to expose any more of her body to view than was absolutely necessary.

"We'll need a stretcher of some sort," he commented after discovering that she had at least two more broken bones. He glanced around, hoping to see something in the wreckage they could use. "Break the splintered pieces off that floorboard," he ordered, and within seconds several men had hurried over to do just that.

While Lathe braced several areas of the unconscious woman's body by using pieces from the wreckage for splints, the men quickly broke away the jagged pieces from a large section of the buggy's flooring with the brute strength of their bare hands.

Leona was surprised at how readily everyone had accepted Lathe's authority. Within minutes, the remaining women stepped back to give the men more room, allowing them to place the large piece of flooring on the ground next to Darlene's motionless body.

At Lathe's command, they gently slipped her over onto it. Several men then grabbed the edges of the planking and helped carry her to Lathe's carriage.

Tony had become so pale by then, he looked as if he was about to faint. Still, he followed closely behind them — his gaze focused on his mother's blood-splattered face. "She ain't gonna die, is she, Doc? You ain't gonna let her die, are you?"

"Not if I can help it," Lathe said with more assurance than he actually felt. He also kept his gaze on the woman's pallid face, aware that she had not as much as twitched an eyelid when they moved her. Nor had her body jerked with any of the expected reflexes. "But we do need to hurry and get her to Leona's."

No one seemed to notice how easily Leona's given name had rolled past his lips. For once, no one seemed to care.

While following alongside the others, Lathe held Darlene's arms pressed against her body so they would not dangle. He glanced ahead to the carriage.

"Lift her high so we can ease her in without bumping her against anything," he cautioned, giving orders as if he thought he were back in the army again: a first lieutenant in charge of an entire medical unit. "Keep her feet higher than her head. I want what blood she has left going to her brain. Watch that left arm. It's broken. I don't want it bumped against anything. If she doesn't fit in there flat, cock the board at an angle, just make sure her feet stay above her head."

The men never questioned his authority. They did exactly as told.

Because Darlene and the huge board she lay on took up most of the floor space in Lathe's carriage, he was forced to sit with one leg curled under him after he climbed in. He turned to look at Tony and Leona, then frowned, aware he had room for only one other person and then only if that person knelt entirely in the seat. But he needed both of them there.

Frantically, he glanced around to see if there was any other transportation nearby. He noticed several horses but only one other carriage. It was parked at an awkward angle on the opposite side of the street as if it had been vacated in a hurry. "Whose buggy is that?"

"Mine," answered one of the few women who remained. She was already headed toward it. "Come on, Leona, let's let Tony ride with his mother. You go with me."

Because Lathe felt it better for his patient to travel the bumpy streets at a slow but steady pace, Leona and Iris Rutledge reached the house several minutes ahead of them. Leona was not too surprised to find Scraps outside, waiting for her on the front porch even though she remembered Lathe had closed the front door before they left; but she was too concerned about Darlene to worry about that now.

Wanting to be ready when Lathe arrived, Leona shooed the dog aside then hurried through the front door to light several lamps in the dining room. As soon as she felt there was sufficient lighting for what Lathe would have to do, she cleared the table of everything, including the table cloth, then replaced it with a white sheet.

By the time she finished with the room and returned to the front door, Lathe and Tony had arrived, followed by several men on horseback.

Chapter Twelve

With Leona, Iris, and Tony at his side, helping however they could, Lathe worked throughout the night setting bones, digging out tiny fragments of wood, and cleansing and stitching cuts.

One of the onlookers had thought to ride out to the Newland farm and tell the family about the accident. Duane Newland was there within the hour but because the burly six-footer had nearly fainted when he saw so much of his wife's blood splattered about, he had been asked to wait in another room. Leona and Iris took turns advising him of the progress being made.

By midnight, several of Duane and Darlene's friends had heard about the accident and came to be with him while he waited, all wishing Doc Owen were still alive, certain he would have the skill required to see Darlene through her current dilemma. Unaware of the many crises Lathe had faced during the Civil War, they were worried that such a young surgeon would not have the experience needed to save their friend.

Shortly after daybreak, when Leona went into the parlor with an updated report, she found Duane hunched forward in a chair, his forearms hanging limp over his knees, staring bleakly into an empty fireplace.

Everyone except Duane stood the moment she entered and quickly rushed forward to hear the latest news. They all asked their questions at the same time.

"How is she?"

"What does the doctor say?"

"Is she going to live?"

"What about that leg, will she be able to keep it?"

Leona waited until Duane had turned to face her with wide hopeful eyes before answering any of the questions. "The doctor told me there's a very strong possibility Darlene will live because even after all the blood she's lost and all the terrible suffering she's been through these past few hours, she continues to have a weak but steady heartbeat."

"That sounds like a good sign," Shirley Lindsey, the sheriff's mother, stated. Then she reached out to pat Duane reassuringly on the shoulder. "What's he doing now?"

"For now, he's just waiting to see what happens. He has already done all he can do to help her. He says it is in God's hands now."

"Then we should pray," Duane suggested, glancing at his friends with teary eyes. "We should pray long and hard." He pressed his eyes shut, causing a tear to drop down his cheek while he clasped his trembling hands beneath his chin and silently began moving his lips. Touched by his unyielding devotion to his wife, everyone else in the room did the same.

It was not until after Darlene had been made comfortable in Leona's bedroom and Tony and Duane had fallen asleep in nearby chairs that Lathe finally left his patient long enough to go outside and get a breath of fresh air while he washed the last of the blood from his skin.

When Leona noticed him leave the room, she followed, wishing she could offer him something to eat. He looked so tired.

"You've had a long, rough night," she commented while she watched him scrub away the last of the dried blood, using water he'd drawn directly from the well. She had glanced at the clock on the way out and saw that it was already nearly eleven. "You really should go into town, change clothes, then go get yourself something to eat."

"It's Sunday morning. None of the restaurants will be open for at least another hour," he pointed out, then rubbed his still wet hands over his tired face in hopes to revitalize himself. He was reminded he needed a shave. "Besides, I can't leave here until Tony's mother has regained consciousness. I have to know that she's going to be all right."

When Leona looked at Lathe then, she saw him in a different light. Having watched him work so diligently through the night, performing medical miracles with the crudest of instruments, she now understood why George had been so quick to accept the fact Lathe really was a doctor. After having seen his work, there was no doubting his profession.

"Lathe, why is it that a doctor as talented as you obviously are doesn't have a practice somewhere?"

Lathe's tired expression hardened, causing the muscles in his jaw to pump spasmodically while he dried his hands on a towel Leona kept near the well. "Because there are other matters in my life more important than being a doctor."

"There are matters more important than saving lives?" she asked, unable to conceive anything more important than saving a person's life. "How can that be?"

When he turned to look at her then, she saw a deep, woeful torment dimming his pale blue eyes, re-

232

placing his earlier anger with a look of total anguish. Not knowing how he would respond, she fought a very strong urge to take him into her arms and comfort him.

"Yes," he admitted. He turned his face skyward, allowing the sun to dapple his face through the thick branches of a nearby oak. Had it not been for the large, spreading tree, the whole back porch would have been bathed in sunlight at that moment. "There is one thing more important than saving lives. At least it is to me." Then eager to change the subject before his weakened state brought him to tears, he took a deep breath, then glanced curiously toward the kitchen. "Either I'm so hungry I've started to hallucinate or I smell food cooking."

Leona also drew in a deep breath then blinked with surprise. "You are not hallucinating. I smell it, too. But it must be coming from one of the neighbor's houses. I'm afraid there's not much food in my house."

When they entered the house through the door that opened into the hallway, the aroma became stronger. Glancing curiously at each other, they followed the rich aroma as far as the dining room where they were both delightfully surprised to discover not only that the room had been thoroughly scrubbed and swept, but a large tablecloth had been draped over the table and several places were set.

They next heard a clatter from inside the kitchen followed by someone's cheerful humming. Looking at each other with questioning expressions, Lathe and Leona then headed together toward the sound to see what other surprises lay ahead.

Inside the kitchen, they found Iris Rutledge and Sheila Sanford hard at work preparing an amazing amount of food.

"Seems like just about everybody in town has heard

about what happened," Iris explained with a wide grin when she glanced up and saw that they had entered. "There was a steady stream of people stopping in on their way to church to leave off food and offer their best wishes."

She then looked at Lathe and beamed. "They were all so relieved and somewhat amazed to hear that Darlene is not only still alive after such an accident but that she is now resting peacefully, and they decided to show the new doctor their appreciation in the only way they know how." She waved toward the countertops filled with different offerings. "You can't imagine how excited everyone was to find out we have such a reliable doctor. Most of them were just like me and didn't even know we'd had one come to town."

Leona looked at her curiously. Obviously she had not run into Josephine Haught during the past few days.

Iris shook her head and looked truly perplexed. "We were sure surprised when Tony suddenly took off claiming he was going to go get a doctor. At first we thought the poor boy had gone absolutely mad, but then a few of the people admitted to having heard something about a new doctor in town, so we waited to see if you'd really come."

Lathe frowned, aware Iris thought he was there to set up a new practice. "I don't want you to get the wrong idea about me. I'm not here to stay. I'm just passing through."

Leona's heart twisted at the painful reminder that Lathe would never become a permanent part of their lives. But rather than let anyone see how deeply his announcement had affected her, she turned away and pretended to be taking a quick inventory of all the food.

Meanwhile Iris's happy expression changed to one of true concern. "But we need a good doctor like you

234

around here. Been needing one for quite some time."

"And it shouldn't be too difficult for you to find one," Lathe admitted, aware this was just the sort of town most doctors wanted, himself included.

Grimly, he met the older woman's gaze to let her know he could not be swayed. "But it won't be me. I have too many other matters to take care of before I can consider starting a practice."

He could tell Iris was curious to know what those matters might be, but she was too polite to ask. Rather than allow the awkward silence to linger between them indefinitely, he nodded toward the many pies displayed along the far end of the counter and asked, "Would one of those happen to be apple?"

"Three of them are apple," Iris offered, aware that it had been his way of letting her know she had touched upon a topic he did not care to discuss. She turned to reach for the largest of the three. "How big a piece do you want?"

Before Lathe was through, he had eaten more than half the pie, but claimed he still had plenty of room for the lunch Iris and Sheila were so busily preparing.

Although the subject of Lathe's intention to leave Little Mound was never mentioned again, it continued to haunt Leona's thoughts for the rest of the day. She believed as Iris did that Little Mound needed a good doctor and wished they could find some way to make him stay.

Later that afternoon, after Darlene had finally awakened and proved she could keep her pain medications down, Duane decided they had taken advantage of Leona's hospitality long enough. With Lathe's approval, he had a wagon rigged with a mattress and special bedding and had Darlene moved to their own home just before it turned dark.

Lathe stayed behind long enough to examine Leona's wound before heading to the Newlands' to make sure his patient did not suffer any new injuries during the move.

While he examined Leona's cut, he behaved very professionally, acting as if nothing out of the ordinary had happened between them, as if the passionate kiss they'd shared just moments before Tony's knock had never happened.

Keeping a calmly reserved expression that revealed nothing of the turmoil twisting inside him, he removed her old bandage, cleansed the area around the cut with a special aseptic cleanser he had bought for her but had used mostly on Darlene, then rewrapped the shoulder with fresh bandages.

"There now, that should do it," he said after having tied the bandage in place, his tone very indifferent, as if he had spoken to someone he hardly knew.

"It's a good thing you bought all those bandages when you did," she commented, her tone light. Although she was deeply annoyed and hurt that he continued to treat her so coolly, she did not want him knowing how truly affected she was. "It sure saved on my sheets."

"I really should have thought to buy them earlier," he admitted while he placed the remaining bandages back in the package they had come in and set them aside. "It is far more sanitary to use boiled bandages than use someone's bedsheets."

"It might be a good idea for you to buy several different kinds of bandages and keep them in a small bag like most doctors," she suggested, eager to again broach the possibility of his staying.

"But then I'm not like most doctors," he reminded her. Instead of pursuing that subject again, he reached for his holster, which he had laid on a table nearby, then for his hat. "Even so, I think I'd better ride on over to the Newlands' and check to make sure Mrs. Newland is doing all right." Then, as soon as he had done that, he planned to go by Sheriff Lindsey's office to find out if anyone had seen Zeb yet. It had been almost twenty-four hours since he had heard anything.

"I'll be back by tomorrow night to check on you," he said. He just hoped he could continue to keep his desire for her under control. After last night, he was far too close to losing his heart to her and there was not yet any room in his life for someone like Leona.

After having observed the real Dr. Lathe Caldwell in action, Leona was more baffled than ever. The fact that Lathe would rather pursue the Zeb Turners of this world than open a doctor's office and perform the special work he was trained so well to do, simply did not make sense.

Having seen how truly committed he could be to saving a life, she found his unwavering desire to hunt down bad men to be totally illogical. It made her more determined than ever to have a little talk with the sheriff about him. She wanted to know how they had come to be working together on that failed attempt to capture Zeb. She was also curious to know how long Lathe had been a bounty hunter and what had prompted him to become one in the first place.

Rather than head straight for the bank, where she and George intended to meet shortly after nine o'clock, Leona left the house a little early and headed in the opposite direction, toward Jefferson Street.

Because it was a typical early Monday morning, the streets and sidewalks were already crowded, especially in the area around the courthouse. Rather than continue at the same slow speed as the rest, Leona took a shortcut across the courtyard lawn, not caring that her hemline would become soaked from the morning dew. She was too eager to have her talk with

237

the sheriff, then get on to the bank where she and George could collect that money and be on their way. She wanted that wagon on the road before noon.

It was a few minutes after eight when Leona stepped back onto the sidewalk that circled the courthouse. When she glanced across the street toward her destination, she was surprised to see Lathe come through the front door. He paused long enough to check first his watch then his pistol before heading for his horse with long determined strides.

Instead of the evening clothes she had become accustomed to seeing him wear, he was again dressed mostly in black. He had his black holster strapped around a pair of close-fitted black riding trousers and he wore a dark grey cotton shirt, open at the collar.

A cold, foreboding chill tumbled down Leona's spine when she realized he looked far more like a gunfighter than a doctor and she again wondered what had prompted a man like that into becoming a bounty hunter.

Not wanting him to see her, she turned her face to one side and waited until he had ridden off toward the south before crossing the street and heading for the sheriff's door. When she entered, she found Sheriff Lindsey seated at his desk, sipping a steaming cup of black coffee while shuffling casually through his mail.

"Sheriff?" she said, glimpsing around to make sure no one else was in the room to overhear their discussion.

"Yes?" he responded automatically. When he glanced up and saw Leona Stegall standing in the center of his office glancing nervously about, his eyes widened. He quickly set his coffee aside and stood. "What can I do for you, Miss Stegall?"

"You can answer a few questions," Leona said, getting right to the point, never one to mince words.

238

"Questions? What sort of questions?"

"They have to do with a mutual friend of ours, Lathe Caldwell." She hesitated, trying to decide the best way to ask them. "To be truthful about it, I am *very* curious to know more about him."

"But I don't understand. If you want to know more about Lathe Caldwell, why have you come to me?" the sheriff asked, one eyebrow arched as if trying to figure out her reasoning. "After all, I only met the man last Tuesday and only briefly then. Why I haven't even known him a full week yet."

"But you must know something about him or you never would have asked him to help you try to capture Zeb Turner," she pointed out.

"Me ask him? Afraid you got that all wrong. *He* came to *me*. Showed me a wanted poster on the man he was after and asked for my help. When I looked at that poster and saw that Zeb Turner was a convicted killer sentenced to hang in Alabama, I figured I'd better help the man in any way I could."

"Even though you didn't know anything about him?"

"Didn't need to know anything about Caldwell. All I needed to see was that he had a wanted poster showing a five-hundred dollar reward on a man he claimed was right here in our town. At that point, I didn't see any reason to go asking a lot of questions. Everything I needed to know was right there on that wanted poster. They just don't go around puttin' five hundred dollars on a man's head unless they are convinced he's guilty."

"But surely you must know something about Lathe."

"Just that he's dead set on taking that Zeb Turner fellow back to Alabama," he answered, aware she had just referred to Caldwell by his first name—very friendly. "That and the fact he's supposed to be a doctor of some sort. I heard he's already saved two lives in this town." When he looked at her then, there was a knowing sparkle in his eye but he tried to sound as if he didn't know what to believe. "Heard one of those lives he saved was yours."

Leona frowned, wondering why the sheriff had phrased it like that when he had known from the beginning that Lathe had saved her life.

"Well, you certainly heard right," she admitted, willing to give him that much. "He did save my life. And he also saved Darlene Newland's life."

"That's what I thought. Want to know what else I heard?" Sheriff Lindsey asked, not about to let the matter drop. Clearly he wanted to see her reaction to the latest gossip first hand.

"Does it have anything to do with why Dr. Caldwell is so determined to capture a convicted killer from Alabama?" she asked, looking him directly in the eye as if daring him to repeat anything else he had heard.

The sheriff's mouth twitched as if fighting the urge to grin. "No, ma'am. Doesn't have to do with nothing like that," he admitted.

"Then I'm sure I'm not interested," she said, narrowing her gaze as if to warn him of his place before turning and flouncing determinedly out of his office.

The sheriff waited until the door had clattered shut behind her before chuckling out loud, very pleased by her display. "That's not the way I heard it."

The wide grin he had fought so hard to contain stretched full width across his face while he watched her work her way along the busy street. "That's not the way I heard it *a tall*."

Having been told that Lathe was the one who had gone to the sheriff for help instead of the vice-versa, Leona was more confused than ever. The harder she

tried to make sense of it all, the more baffled she became — and the more determined she was to find out
why a man trained to be a doctor had chosen to become a bounty hunter instead.

By the time she arrived at the bank, she was so lost
between thoughts of Lathe and of finally getting the
money she needed from George, she did not notice
Sarah Martin coming out as she was headed in.

"Leona," Sarah said, surprised to see her there.
When Leona did not immediately respond, she
grabbed her by the arm and pulled her off to one
side.

Leona's look of startled surprise quickly smoothed
into a happy smile when she recognized her friend.
"Sarah, what are you doing here? Why aren't you out
at the farm?"

"I'm running errands for Father," she explained,
then pulled her further away from the main flow of
pedestrian traffic. Her cheeks were flushed and her
eyes wide with wonder when she glanced at the bank's
windows as if trying to decide if they could be seen
from inside. "Your friend George is in there," she said
in a voice barely above a whisper. "And you should
see him. He's had his hair cut and his beard
trimmed. He hardly looks like the same man."

"I know. I saw him Saturday, right after he'd already been to the barber."

"Oh?" Sarah asked, her pretty eyes darkening with
immediate caution. "And did you already know he
was inside?"

"Yes, he told me to meet him here."

"Oh? Are you two becoming close?"

Leona blinked with surprise at the resentment she
had detected in Sarah's voice. "Yes, we are; but not
in the way you may think."

Sarah's right eyebrow lifted cautiously while she
carefully studied Leona's face. Clearly, she wanted to

believe her friend spoke the truth. "Then why did he ask you to meet him here?"

"Because he plans to lend me a thousand dollars."

Sarah's eyes widened with surprise then narrowed again with renewed suspicion. "And just where does George Parkinson plan to get hold of a thousand dollars?"

"Why right here," Leona said with a quick wave of her hand as if that should have been a foregone conclusion, after all, it *was* a bank. Then, aware Sarah was prone to believe anything she said, she bent forward and spoke in low tones as if she intended to tell her something confidential. "He plans to rob the place. After hearing how terribly Bebber Davis treated me last week, he decided this bank deserved to be robbed."

Taken in completely by Leona's story, Sarah's hands flew to her mouth then her gaze cut to the front door. "He could go to jail for something like that." She cut her fearful gaze toward the door then looked at Leona beseechingly. "He could even be killed. You have to stop him."

"*Stop* him?" Leona asked, knitting her eyebrows as if finding the suggestion ludicrous. "Why should I want to stop him when I plan to *help* him." She held up her oversized handbag as if to offer proof. "Why do you think I brought this? We have to have something to carry all that money home in."

Sarah gasped with alarm then reached out to grab Leona by the arm. "Leona, no. You can't."

"Oh, but you are wrong. I most certainly *can*. And I most definitely will *not*." She waited until the illogic in that had time to sink in before laughing. "Oh, Sarah, you are always so gullible. Your whole family is. You always believe anything anyone ever tells you."

Sarah took a quick breath, unsure now what to

think. "Then you and George are not planning to rob the bank?"

"Not without a gun, no." She then held her palms out to reveal the obvious. She was unarmed.

"Then why you here?" Again, Sarah looked at her, suspicious.

Aware Sarah was back to worrying that something more than a friendship had developed between them, Leona took her by the hands and answered truthfully. "The first part of what I told you is true. George really is planning to lend me a thousand dollars. Last Friday, after hearing what Bebber Davis had said to me, he sent a wire to the bank he uses back home asking for that amount of money to be transferred here by this morning."

Leona sighed aloud to show just how relieved she felt. "It might not be quite enough to solve *all* my financial problems, but it should buy me enough time to try to figure out how to go about raising the rest of what I need. At least for now I should have enough money to keep an adequate supply of stock on my shelves, and without having to have Ethan declared legally dead."

Sarah's eyes widened when she realized Leona was telling her the truth. "Then George is wealthy, *too?*"

Leona wondered what she meant by the word *too*. In addition to what? Being so helpful?

"Wealthy enough to lend me a thousand dollars until first harvest," she answered. Then finally it dawned on her. Sarah was interested in George. Her brown eyes brightened when she realized *how* interested. "Why don't you come with us? We are planning to stop off at Mattie's for breakfast after we finish here." That was a complete fabrication, but she knew Sarah would never figure that out. Besides, it was such a *teeny* white lie.

"I don't know." Sarah bit the inner edge of her lower

243

lip while she considered what she should do. "I still have several errands to take care of for Father and I promised Mother I'd be home by noon."

"But it's not even nine o'clock yet," Leona pointed out. "Surely your errands won't take that long."

Again Sarah glanced at the bright reflections splashed across the bank's windows, as if wishing she could see inside.

"Well, I haven't had breakfast yet," she admitted.

"Good. Then it's decided," Leona said, grasping her arm and practically dragging her toward the door, not wanting her to have time to back out.

When they stepped inside a few seconds later, they found George only a few feet away with his hands shoved in his pockets. His face was turned toward the ceiling as if he had become fascinated by the fan slowly turning overhead. Leona tried not to grin when she realized he must have been watching them through the window but did not want them to know.

When Leona looked from George to Sarah, she shook her head, wondering why she had not noticed it before: George was just as attracted to Sarah as Sarah was to George. Suddenly the matchmaker inside her crept forward and she decided that before the morning was over, she would have those two making plans together.

With that thought tucked neatly at the back of her mind, she looped her arm through Sarah's and led her to where George stood, still pretending he had no idea they were there. Eagerly, she tugged at his coat sleeve.

"Did you get the money?" she asked, eyeing his coat pockets, hoping to see a telltale bulge. When she did not, she worried there had been problems.

"Not yet. I wanted to wait until you got here." Although the words he spoke were in response to Leona's question, it was Sarah who held his attention.

He could not drag his gaze away from her beautiful face. "I figured it would give them more time to verify the request. You can bet they'll want to double check a transaction of that size before handing the cash over to us."

Leona glanced at the tellers' cages across the room, then back at George. "What if there's a problem? What if your bank hasn't sent the transfer notice yet?"

"Then we'll have to wait until they do," Ethan conceded while he, too, looked at the three men behind the bars, all busily helping those customers already in line. "But don't start thinkin' such negative thoughts. That money has got to be here by now. Most banks have been open since eight and the telegraph office has been open since seven. Come on. Let's go get it so I can finally be on my way."

"You mean so *we* can finally be on *our* way. We haven't had that breakfast you promised yet," she said as if to remind him of a promise he had made. Then before he could say something to ruin her plan, she quickly added, "By the way, I've invited Sarah to come with us. She hasn't had breakfast either."

Ethan blinked twice while his mind quickly put together the fact that somehow Leona had worked it out so he and Sarah could have breakfast together. Although he did not remember having said anything about stopping off for breakfast before leaving town, he was not about to argue the point. Nor would he mention the fact that he had already eaten once.

"Then let's get that money so we can go eat," Ethan corrected, grinning broadly as he stepped toward the teller cage.

Sarah and Leona followed, standing beside him, waiting patiently for the man in front of them to finish his business.

"May I help you?" the teller behind the center window asked after only a few minutes. He glanced from

245

one to the other as if trying to decide which of the three was really next.

"Yes," Ethan said, taking a small step forward to let the man know he was the one doing business with him. "My name is George E. Parkinson and I believe you have some money for me. The arrangements should have been made by wire either sometime Saturday or first thing this morning."

"Just a minute, please," the teller said, pausing long enough to scribble the name on a small sheet of paper.

While the teller hurried off to discuss the matter with his supervisor, Ethan glanced at the clock. Nine-thirty. Surely the money was there by now. He had stressed that it was urgent the captain get it there as quick as he possibly could.

When the teller returned a few seconds later, he looked at Ethan with more respect than he had before. "Why, yes, Mr. Parkinson. We do have some money here for you. In fact we have been assigned to pay you a thousand dollars."

Ethan split a wide grin when he glanced over his shoulder at Leona. "See, I told you it would be here."

Leona smiled, too, but her gaze remained on the teller. Her heart pounded with vigorous force while she waited for the man to begin counting out the money.

"Now, sir," the teller went on to say, already pulling out his cash drawer where five different denominations of currency stood in nice neat stacks and six different sized coins filled small metal boxes. "If you will just show me your identification, then I will be happy to give you the entire amount."

"Identification?" Ethan said, a sickly feeling pulling at his gut. "Why do I need identification? I just told you who I am."

"That may be, but it just happens to be one of the

246

bank's rules," the teller said. "None of the tellers can hand out that kind of money without having seen some form of identification first. Unless, of course, we happen to know you personally. But I'm afraid I've never seen you before, sir. So, if you don't mind. I need to see some identification — anything that might have your name on it."

When Leona looked at Ethan and saw how ill he looked, she knew something was wrong. "Don't tell me you forgot to bring some form of identification."

"I'm not even sure I have any," he said, looking at her with a perplexed, little-boy expression. "Most people usually take me at my word that I am who I say I am." Besides, he hadn't been George Parkinson long enough to have even a letter with his name on it.

"What are we going to do?" Leona asked, then, aware she was about to lose her one real chance to restock her store without having to have her brother declared dead, she turned to the teller and pleaded. "Can't you make an exception just this once? The man is from out of town and didn't think to bring any identification with him."

"I'm sorry, but I have to have verification that this man is indeed George E. Parkinson."

"What if someone else were willing to identify him? What if I were to agree to sign a sworn statement that he really is who he says he is?"

The teller looked at her with a queer expression. "I don't want to appear rude, ma'am, but I don't know you either. Do *you* have any identification?"

"No, but I'm Leona Stegall. I've lived here all my life. Ask some of these other people." She gestured to the other patrons milling about the lobby. "Most of them know me."

"But do any of them know Mr. Parkinson?"

"No," she answered, clearly exasperated. "But they know me, and I know him."

"But what if they don't have any identification with them?" the teller asked, starting to look flustered, aware several people were now staring at them. His small face tightened into a pensive frown then suddenly relaxed when he finally came up with what he felt a workable solution. "I know. If you really are from around here then surely you know Mr. Davis, the bank's president. If you can get him to come out here and personally tell me it is okay to give this man all that money without any reliable identification, then I will gladly hand it over to him."

Leona felt her heart sink to the pit of her stomach. Bebber had already proven how uncooperative he could be where she was concerned and he was probably still angry with her for everything she'd said last Tuesday. He might very well decide to get even with her by refusing to release George's money to him.

"Are you sure there's no other way?" she asked, dreading the confrontation.

"I'm very sure," the teller said in a decisive tone, looking a little annoyed that she had not thought his idea a good one. "Mr. Davis is in his office like he is every Monday morning. All you have to do is tell his secretary you want to speak with him, then ask him to give me permission to release this man's money without the proper identification. Meanwhile, I have other customers to take care of." He looked past them to the next person in line, eager to be done with the problem at hand. "May I help you, sir?"

"Well?" Sarah asked when it was clear the teller did not intend to discuss the matter further. "What are you going to do now?"

When Leona glanced at her, her expression was bleak but the tone in her voice remained coolly unaffected. "I'll do what the man told me to do. I'll go have a talk with Bebber. Wait here. I'll be right back."

Chapter Thirteen

"Leona!" Bebber said with a combination of surprise and delight when he looked up to find her standing beside his secretary just outside his door. "I was just thinking about you."

"Sir, Miss Stegall would like a word with you," the secretary said, eager to fulfill her duties so she could get back to her desk.

"Of course, send her right in," he said, rising from his seat to make Leona feel welcome. He waited until the secretary had left the room before indicating the chairs facing his desk. "Please, have a seat."

Leona found his friendly greeting a little unnerving, considering how angry he had been with her last Tuesday. While she accepted the offer of a chair, she tried to figure out what had happened to change his behavior so drastically. Unable to believe he'd had such a complete change of heart, she studied his expression carefully.

"Leona, dear, I am so pleased to see that you have finally come to your senses," Bebber hurried on to explain, also sitting. He rested his elbows on the arms of his chair and folded his hands over the slight paunch of his stomach then looked across at her much as a proud father would survey his own offspring. "I knew that if we just left you alone for a few days so you could give the matter some serious thought you would finally come to realize that it's the only way."

Leona blinked, confused. Nothing about that entire conversation had made any sense. "The only way to what?"

"To get that loan you need," he said. Although he kept a smile in place, the delighted expression diminished and he looked at her cautiously. "Isn't that why you are here? Haven't you decided to go ahead and have Ethan declared dead so you can finally have enough collateral to borrow the money you need to save your business?"

"No," she answered with a firm shake of her head, wondering why he thought that. "I'm here on behalf of a friend."

What was left of Bebber's cheerful expression fell into a harsh, flat line. His hazel eyes narrowed beneath a set of heavy eyebrows when he leaned forward in his chair. "And who might that be?"

"His name is George Parkinson. George *E*. Parkinson," she embellished, having heard the teller call out the complete name—although she had no idea what the initial might stand for, if anything.

"George Parkinson?" he repeated. One eyebrow lifted with obvious contempt. "That wouldn't happen to be your new doctor friend, would it? I thought John asked you to stay away from him."

Leona's eyes widened in a combination of surprise and anger: surprise that Bebber had even mentioned Lathe, and anger that John had not merely *asked* her to stay away from him, he had *ordered* her to, as if he had some unspoken right to tell her what to do.

But rather than get into a discussion that could distract them from her real reason for being there, she responded only to the question and left the following comment alone. "No, George Parkinson is not the doctor you've obviously heard about. But George did

250

have a large part in saving my life. Not only did he help the doctor carry me back to my house where I could be properly cared for, George also handed him whatever the doctor needed to repair my injuries and helped him hold me down when I tried to fight against the pain."

"Then George Parkinson is not the man you were seen with at the restaurant Saturday night?"

"No, that man's name is Lathe Caldwell," she explained, then immediately changed the subject. "If George had been seen with anyone Saturday night, it would have been Sarah Martin." She leaned forward and spoke in a soft voice as if about to reveal something confidential. "Fact is, he's been sweet on Sarah ever since he got to town."

"Then you are not here to get your loan?" He looked so disappointed, Leona almost felt sorry for him.

"No."

"Can I take that to mean that you've finally decided to marry John so he can help you save your business from ruin."

Leona realized the man would never give up in his quest for a grandson, eager to carry on the family name. "No, I have no plans to marry your son. And I am not here about that loan." Feeling a little guilty, she glanced at her folded hands. In a way, she *had* come to the bank to get a loan, but not from Bebber. "I still haven't been able to bring myself to have Ethan declared dead."

"But you can't keep putting it off," Bebber insisted, wanting to convince her to take one action or the other, believing his son would benefit from either. "I don't think you truly understand how quickly time is running out for you. You need either to have that brother of yours declared dead so I can give you that loan you need, or you need to climb down from

251

that high horse of yours and agree to marry John so he'll feel obligated to help you out."

When Leona did not immediately comment, he proceeded in a completely different tone of voice, "Dear child, unless you restock your shelves soon, you will lose every customer you ever had. Plus, I understand you still have not paid the forty dollars in back taxes you still owe on that place. Not only could you lose your business, you could lose the building, too." He sighed heavily, tired of waiting for her to come to her senses. It was in her own best interest to marry his son. Why couldn't she see that?

"You don't have to remind me of how truly serious my dilemma is," Leona said, her tone flat. They had discussed all that before. She now had less than a month to come up with her back taxes. "I am well aware I could lose the building if I don't pay the full forty dollars by next month."

"Obviously, I do need to remind you. You have to do something to save the situation—and soon."

"And I plan to," she assured him. "But for now, all I want from you is one small favor."

"Oh?" He tilted his head back so that he was looking at her through the bottom half of his eyeglasses. "And what might that favor be?"

Ready to get on with it, Leona explained the problem George had had with the teller and was surprised when instead of questioning her further, Bebber immediately rose from his seat. He rubbed his hands together when he stepped away from his desk, obviously intending to help.

"That's Schulz," he said as if that alone should explain everything. "He's new here." As soon as he had circled to the desk, he motioned toward the door with a quick flick of his hand. "Come. I'll introduce you."

"And will you also instruct him to let George have his money?"

"Of course," he said, smiling jovially. "You know I'll do anything for a future part of the family."

Normally, Leona would have stopped to remind him yet again that she and John were not now and never had been engaged, but decided under the circumstances to let the remark slide.

Within minutes after Bebber and Ethan were introduced, Ethan was asked to sign the name George Parkinson at the bottom of a printed receipt. He then stepped back to wait while the teller slowly and meticulously counted out the correct amount. Ethan did not glance away until he heard Bebber speak to him.

"I understand you and Sarah Martin here have been seeing a lot of each other lately," Bebber commented in an obvious attempt to be sociable, clearly impressed with Ethan's money.

Ethan blinked with surprise, not knowing what to answer. If he agreed, he would probably embarrass Sarah, but if he disagreed he just might be refuting something Leona had said.

"And I hope to see a lot more of her," he finally responded, proud of himself for having come up with such an appropriate answer. He glanced at Sarah to see if she had heard the comment and discovered she was still watching the teller count the money. The only indication she might have overheard his response was in the almost imperceptible way her eyes had widened.

Thinking it was the perfect opportunity to let her know exactly how he felt, Ethan took a quick breath and continued, "Fact is, I dread having to be out of town during the next few days because it means I won't be able to see her again until I get back. I'm sure gonna miss lookin' at that pretty face of hers while I'm gone."

"George! You are making Sarah blush," Leona admonished playfully. Her eyes sparkled while she allowed the matchmaker in her to play havoc. Turning away from the teller, she reached out to touch Sarah's flushed cheeks. "I don't think she realized just how very much you have come to care for her."

"That's 'cause I'm not very good at tellin' people how I feel," Ethan admitted. "Never have been."

Bravely, Sarah brought her gaze to meet Ethan's. Everyone waited to hear what her response would be, but before she could comment, the teller quietly interrupted.

"Mr. Parkinson, sir. Here is your money. All one thousand. I've counted it twice myself, but you might want to count it a third time just to be certain."

Ethan held out his hand and watched while the teller laid the inch-thick pile of bills into his hand. A slow grin split his beard when he turned to hand it to Leona. "Since it is to be your money, you might as well be the one to count it."

"Her money?" Bebber asked. His back stiffened with immediate alarm. "What do you mean, it's *her* money?"

"Just what I said," Ethan responded, looking at Bebber as if unaware he had created a problem, all the while revelling in the shocked expression on the older man's face. "I'm loaning it to her."

"But you can't do that," Bebber sputtered, blinking rapidly while his gaze shot back and forth between the two.

"Why not? It's my money," Ethan pointed out, then extended both arms for his two escorts. "Come ladies, lets go have that breakfast I promised you."

Panicked, Bebber grabbed Leona's arm before she could slide it in around Ethan's, forcing her to turn and face him. "Why didn't you tell me that money was for you?" he demanded.

"I guess because you didn't ask," she replied, glaring pointedly at the area where his fingers dug painfully into her upper arm. "But I did warn you that I planned to do something soon and I now have." She nodded curtly toward the money still in her hand. "With this money, I can finally pay off my taxes and refill my shelves. You were right about one thing. Time *is* running out for me—or at least it *was*."

Aware he had no right to detain her physically and that several bank patrons were staring at them curiously, Bebber let go of her arm, but held her in place with his angry glare. "And do you honestly believe you can save that Mercantile with a mere thousand dollars?"

"No, but it's a start."

"And that's *all* it is. A start. That thousand dollars is only a short-term solution to a long-term problem. In a couple of months you'll be right back where you are now. Dead broke with nothing to sell and months yet before your customers can start paying you what they owe. All that money will do is put off the inevitable for a month or two."

Leona lifted her chin and met his icy glare straight on. She was tired of the way the Davis men were always trying to tell her how to run her life. "That may be true; but obviously that is exactly what I have chosen to do, and it *was* my decision to make. Good day to you, Mr. Davis." Without further comment, she slipped her arm into Ethan's and walked with him and Sarah toward the door.

Too angry to respond, Bebber spun about on his heel and marched directly into his office, leaving a lobby full of gaping patrons behind.

Between his failed attempts to track down Zeb Turner and the obligation he felt toward Darlene Newland, Lathe had very little time to spend with Leona, which suited him just fine. After a considerable amount of soul-searching, he had finally gotten his priorities back on track. Saturday, he had found out just how distracting Leona could be. She was a very *beautiful* distraction, granted; but an alluring, unwanted distraction nonetheless.

He had traveled too many miles and suffered far too much pain and heartache to allow anything or anyone into his life that could in any way jeopardize his plans.

After several hours of deep soul-searching, he had finally returned to his senses. Now, because of the danger she represented, whenever he stopped by to see her, he stayed only long enough to check her wound, make sure no infection had set in, and quickly replace her bandage. He refused to allow the strong feelings she still aroused to regain control of his common sense. He would continue to be her doctor, but nothing else.

By Tuesday, the cut along her back had healed enough for him to be able to remove the stitches that had held it together. He then reduced the size of her bandage to a small patch of cotton gauze for two reasons. It would allow him to examine the wound without actually having to remove any of her clothing, which would help him in his efforts to remain aloof; and it was quicker to tape a small patch into place than wrap and tie a full bandage. From then on, all he would have to do would be to unbutton the back of whatever garment she wore, peel off the old bandage, tend the wound, then quickly tape on a fresh bandage. He could be in and out of her house within a few minutes, which would make those daily visits with her a lot easier to bear.

Later that same night, several hours after Lathe had removed her stitches and left, Leona lay in bed trying to figure out what she might have done to cause such a dramatic change in his behavior toward her. She wondered what had become of that kind, attentive man from Saturday night—the man who had held her so tenderly yet had kissed her with such hungry passion? Why was that same man suddenly treating her as if nothing like that had ever happened? He acted as if she were just another patient he felt obligated to see.

For the dozenth time since she had gone to bed, Leona carefully recalled the events of that previous Saturday night, trying to figure out what had happened to cause such a significant change. She no longer believed that these sudden bouts of coolness had anything to do with repulsion.

By having kissed her that second time, and with such obvious passion, he had proved he obviously enjoyed kissing her. So why was he now treating her like a stranger? And where did he go all day? She rarely saw him in town during the daytime and when she did, he was usually headed into or coming out of the sheriff's office. The *same* sheriff who had tried so very hard to convince her that he and Lathe barely knew each other—yet they saw each other several times every day.

From the conversations she'd had with Duane and Tony Newland, she knew that Lathe was still stopping by their house twice daily to check on Darlene's progress, but he stayed just long enough to make sure she had taken her medicine and to check and treat her injuries. Then he was gone again.

Something else was taking up most of his time. But what? Or who? Was he still searching for Zeb Turner? Did he honestly believe the man had stayed in the area? Or was he now after someone else?

Groaning wearily while she sat up in bed, she jerked at her twisted covers in a futile attempt to straighten them, then wondered why she couldn't simply put Lathe out of her mind and get the sleep she so desperately needed. Sometime that following afternoon, George would return with a wagon full of merchandise that would need to be unloaded, checked one item at a time, then placed on her shelves and tables to sell. She would need to be well rested for that.

Twisting sideways to slam her fist into her pillow in an effort to make it a little more comfortable, she wondered what time it was. Although a bright streak of moonlight fell across the clock on the far side of the room, she could not see the hands well enough to make out the time but she knew it was probably midnight by now.

Or later.

She groaned again. Why couldn't she just lay her head back down and fall immediately asleep?

Eager to give it one last try, she again pulled the bedcovers to her chin then squeezed her eyes shut and plopped her head backward onto the pillow she had just severely trounced.

To force her thoughts from Lathe, she tried focusing on happier subjects, such as the delightful prospect of finally being able to restock her shelves. She wondered how long it would take for word to spread that she was back in business, and she considered spending part of what little money she had left to place a small advertisement in the *Little Mound Tribune*. She opened her eyes and smiled perversely when she realized the advertisement would serve two purposes. Not only would it announce the fact that she had finally restocked, but it would drive Bebber Davis completely berserk to know she had followed through with her plan.

While trying to decide the best way to word such an advertisement, Leona noticed what sounded like a

258

buggy or a wagon traveling along the narrow street that passed in front of her house.

She wondered who would be out that late and decided it must be a night traveler just coming into town. Vaguely, she wondered if the traveler was headed for the hotel and if so, wondered how much trouble he would have rousing Mr. Stickrod from his sleep in an attempt to get a room. She knew how hard it was to wait on the man when he didn't have his ear horn and she could imagine what it would be like to have to rouse him from his sleep. Her thoughts then drifted to the day that ear horn had arrived at her store and she had delivered it to him in person.

It wasn't until she heard Scraps bark that her thoughts returned to what was happening around her and she realized the buggy had stopped somewhere nearby. Curious to see why anyone would have stopped on their street so late at night, she went to the window and glanced toward the street but saw nothing unusual from that angle. The buggy had either stopped a little further down the street or else it was directly in front of her house.

By the time Leona had slipped on her dressing robe and was headed toward the front of the house, Scraps had stopped barking. Still she went on into the parlor to have a look.

With all the curtains drawn, she headed for the closest window. When she reached out to pull the curtain back so she could have a peek, there came a loud knock at her door. Startled, she jerked her hand back as if it had been burned then turned toward the sound, her heart hammering vigorously within her chest.

She took a deep breath to calm her thudding heart but it pounded even harder when she realized it could be Lathe. Perhaps he had also been unable to fall asleep and had decided to come over and explain his odd behavior to her. Perhaps he would apologize for having behaved so coolly toward her and want to kiss her again.

Although deep down she knew none of that would really happen, she could come up with no other reason why anyone would be knocking so late at night. She headed immediately for the door.

Reaching up to rake her fingers through her tousled hair while she made her way through the darkened hallway, she called out, "I'm coming."

When she heard no response to her announcement, she became fearful again. If it were someone she knew, that person would have responded. Her skin prickled and for once she wished Scraps had broken loose from his chain and chased whoever it was away, as he had so many times in the past.

Cautiously, she parted the lace curtains just enough to peer at the sagging silhouette that stood outside her door and stared with utter disbelief when she realized that tired but brawny shape could only belong to George Parkinson.

Too concerned for his welfare to worry with the fact she was in her dressing robe, she opened the door to let him inside. "George? What's wrong? What happened?" She turned to light a nearby lamp so she could see his face.

"Nothin's wrong," he said when he stepped inside, straightening his shoulders as if he had suddenly found renewed energy; yet he did not bother so much as to close the door.

"If nothing is wrong, then why are you here?" she asked while she fumbled with the lamp. "Why aren't you in Marshall?"

"I'm here because I didn't have anywhere else to go. The livery is closed and there's no other safe place for me to park that wagon full of merchandise I got outside. You may claim that Little Mound is mainly full of good, honest people, but I didn't feel right about leaving everything out on the street overnight."

"You already have the merchandise?" she asked, hurrying back to the door before getting the lamp lit. When she saw the heavily loaded wagon sitting directly in front of her carriage gate, she squealed with delight. "How'd you ever get there and back so fast? I wasn't expecting you until sometime tomorrow afternoon."

"I decided not to stay over to get any sleep. I wanted to surprise you," he admitted with a grin.

"Well you've certainly done that." She stepped out onto the front veranda to get a better look. When she saw how impossibly high the merchandise was stacked, she shook her head with amazement. "How did you ever manage to get everything in one load?"

"I didn't."

"You mean there's *more?*" she asked, laughing with delight. Never having had to place such a large order, she had not realized just how bulky the shipment would be. With all the merchandise she saw before her, she could fill her shelves to the brim. And with yet more merchandise to come, she might even be able to put several items away in overstock.

"There was still about half of the load sitting on the dock when I left. But I decided to go ahead and have it shipped over by public freight rather than make a second trip. Don't worry, I paid the shipping charges out of my own pocket so you wouldn't have to spend any of that money you got left. I should be able to pick up the rest of your things right here at the local freight office sometime Thursday afternoon."

"But you shouldn't have to pay for something like that," she argued. "That should be my expense not yours."

"But I was the one who decided to have the merchandise shipped — and strictly due to personal reasons." His grin widened. Although he knew he could never become a permanent part of Sarah's life, he did want to share part of what time he had left with her.

He knew that their seeing each other would make it just that much harder on him when it came time to leave; but he also believed that whatever time they spent together would be well worth the heartache he would eventually suffer. He had never enjoyed a woman's company as much as he did Sarah's.

"By not having to make a return trip, I can spend a little more time trying to get to know Sarah Martin," he confided. "That is if she don't object."

Leona laughed at such an absurd remark. "I hardly think she'll object. The truth is, you are all she has talked about since last Saturday when you suddenly declared your feelings for her right there in front of the entire bank."

"Then that didn't make her mad?" he asked, thinking it might have.

"Not in the least. Truth is, after she found out you had agreed to help me, she volunteered to come by sometime tomorrow afternoon," she paused when she realized the time. "I mean sometime *this* afternoon and help us put away some of the new stock. Although she's one of my dearest and most helpful friends, Sarah has never volunteered to do that sort of work for me before."

"You think maybe she likes me?"

Leona shook her head, unable to believe he could be so blind, then nodded. "Yes, I think maybe she does. But there is one little problem with her having agreed to come by this afternoon to help."

"What's that?"

"I don't intend to wait around until then to start putting out this stock. I was having a hard enough time trying to fall asleep before, there's no possibility

I could get any sleep now. I'm far too excited for that."

When she looked at him then, her brown eyes sparkled with such delight it brought a burning sheen of tears to Ethan's eyes. He loved seeing her happy. "So, what do you plan to do?"

"As soon as I change into my street clothes, I intend to take that wagon to the store and start unloading what I can. Since you've already promised to help me with the heaviest work, I'll expect you first thing in the morning to help unload any items I find I can't lift."

"What do you mean first thing in the morning? I'm not going nowhere," Ethan said with a resolute wave of his head. "I'd much rather help you get everything there now. I can wait to catch some sleep later."

"But you can't have had any sleep since Sunday night," she protested. "Not and have made it back this soon."

"Didn't need none," he assured her, though he had dozed from time to time during the ride back. Fortunately the horse knew enough to stay on the road and didn't stray into a ditch. "And I don't need no sleep now. But if you are really all that concerned about me, then hurry up and get dressed. The sooner we get started unloading, the sooner we'll be finished."

Lathe awoke in a cold sweat. His whole body trembled and his heart pounded with a force so fierce that he felt it throb in every fiber of his being. Paralyzed by his own fear, he stared into the darkness overhead and listened to his own rapid gulps for air.

He'd had that dream again.

Ever since Zeb's fateful escape, Lathe had been plagued by the same recurring nightmare. In it, he was always surrounded by a strange dull blue, a moving haze. Because of the thickness of the swirling mist, he could never actually see Jonathan, but he could hear his brother's panic-stricken voice calling out to him, begging someone to save him. Whenever Lathe called back to ask where he was and what he wanted him to do, Jonathan's response was always, "I'm over here, surrounded by darkness. Send Zeb to me. It's the only way you can save me. Do it, Lathe. Do it."

After having that same dream several times, Lathe had plunged headlong into the thick haze—determined to find Jonathan, and explain to him how very hard he was trying—when he had heard a blood-curdling yell. It was Jonathan's death cry. And it had brought Lathe awake with a start.

Afraid to go back to sleep for fear the same dream would be waiting to torment him, Lathe decided to take a walk to clear his thoughts.

He knew that until he finally did catch up with Zeb Turner, he would continue to have that same dream. And the more time that passed with no indication of where Zeb had gone, the worse the dream would become, and more helpless he would feel.

Even though he thoroughly understood the reason he had the dream, he was unable to stop it from haunting him. It frustrated him to know that he had failed his brother so completely. In five years of trying, he had not yet brought Zeb to justice and at the moment didn't even know where he was.

With no real direction to take, Lathe had reached a dead end. Until Zeb surfaced again, all he could do was sit around and wait—and continue to ask questions of people who were getting awfully tired of having him come around. And who could blame them? Talking to the people Zeb might eventually try to contact was the only thing he could do.

If only the man would show his ugly face somewhere or leave some other little clue that would let him know where he had gone. *Something.* Anything that would put him back on the right track.

Yet until that happened, until Lathe finally brought his brother's killer to justice, he knew he would continue to be plagued by that same, horrifying dream.

Pulling his shirt collar up to ward off the late night chill, Lathe walked the same path he had walked several times during the past few nights. Only tonight he noticed an unusual light coming from just down the street. Curious, he headed toward it, aware as he neared the bright glow that it came from the windows of Stegall's Mercantile.

Thinking it odd, he stepped closer and peered into the larger windows facing Main Street. What he saw inside made his blood turn ice cold. Leona Stegall was in George Parkinson's arms, laughing happily and looking up at him in that coy way only a woman could.

Lathe's gut clenched into a hard knot when he realized that George had intentionally lied to him. Leona *was* in love with him. Theirs was not at all the brother-sister kind of relationship George had made it out to be.

So many emotions washed over him. Anger, disbelief, and a deep sense of betrayal circled him at a dizzying speed, then slowly amassed into one painful knot that settled in the pit of his stomach. He felt like such a fool for having believed nothing special had developed between Leona and George.

The anger he felt while he watched George bend to kiss Leona on the forehead became so intense, so overwhelming, that he turned and walked quickly away.

And for the first time in days, someone new took Zeb Turner's place in his thoughts.

* * *

It was nearly five o'clock in the morning and Ethan was so tired by the time they had unloaded the wagon and Leona had checked everything off the packing slip, he could hardly think straight. But because she had remained as determined as ever to finish the job as soon as she could, he refused to leave—even when she came right out and insisted he go get some rest.

"But if you don't go on back to the hotel and get at least a few hours of sleep, you will look just awful when Sarah comes by to help us this afternoon," she pointed out, thinking that might help change his mind. He looked exhausted.

"But if I left you here alone, then you would be far more likely to try to pick up something you shouldn't and reinjure that shoulder of yours," Ethan replied, unable to believe his sister's stamina. She had just worked an entire night, without any sleep at all, and was still full of vigor.

"I promise. I won't lift anything heavy," she vowed, then crossed her heart as she had done so many times as a child, whenever she wanted to convince someone she spoke the truth. "I will leave all the heaviest items for you. I'll admit I do want to get as much of this merchandise on the shelves as possible before I open those doors later this morning, but not so much I'd risk hurting myself."

"But then you really should consider leavin' something for Sarah to do," he pointed out. "Remember, she's comin' by this afternoon expectin' to help in some way."

"Oh, I'm sure she'll find something to do," Leona responded with a knowing smile. "That is if you're still here. But I guess that's only if you are still *awake*. Won't be much fun for either of you if you suddenly doze off about the time she gets here."

266

"All right, all right. I get the idea," Ethan said, holding up his hands as if to admit defeat, all the while laughing.

When he did that, Leona's smile fell and her eyes filled with remembered pain. She tried to swallow back the constriction that had clamped around her throat but couldn't.

"What's wrong?" he asked, aware of the sudden change in her expression. He stepped forward, wanting to do something to bring that happy smile back but not knowing how.

She stared into his bewildered expression a long moment, then shook her head and turned away. "Nothing. It's just that when you did that—when you raised your hands like that, as if to give up—you reminded me of my brother again. He used to do that very same thing whenever he wanted me to stop my teasing."

She blinked back the resulting tears but refused to turn around and face him. "And earlier, that sad way you looked while I was telling you about my parents' death was just exactly how Ethan had looked the day we found out our Grandmother Ruby had died."

Ethan felt a hard, fast pulse throbbing near the base of his throat. Did Leona suspect the truth? What would he do if she suddenly decided to ask him straight out? Could he continue lying to her even then?

Confused and shaken, he reached out to touch her, still wanting to reassure her, but afraid to do so. He paused with his hand only inches away from her then let it drop again to his side. "I'm sorry, Leona. I didn't mean to do nothin' to upset you."

Leona forced a smile and turned to look at him again. "There's no reason for you to feel sorry. It's not your fault you look so much like my brother. Now, go on and get out of here so you can get some sleep and

267

I can get back to work."

Aware he had allowed himself to revert back to some of his old habits because he was so very tired—too tired to concentrate on being someone he was not—Ethan decided it might be better if he did leave. "Okay, I'll go, but only because I want to be wide awake when Sarah gets here." He headed for the door, but paused just seconds before placing his hand on the latch. "I'll be back in a few hours. I just hope I don't find *you* asleep on the floor when I get here." He then laughed again, only this time in a way she would not recognize. "Just remember your promise to leave the heaviest items for me."

By the time Ethan had walked the short distance to the hotel, he was grateful to Leona for having forced him to leave. His feet refused to move as quickly as he wanted and his arms hung like lead weights at his sides. He could not remember ever having felt so tired—nor so happy. It felt wonderful to see his sister's spirits soar again.

Having planned all along not to be gone more than one night, he had not bothered to check out of the hotel, so he shoved his hand into his pants pocket to find his room key. The morning clerk, who was already at the desk, glanced up when he heard Ethan's heavy footsteps in the lobby.

"Mr. Parkinson. You're back. Good, I have a message here for you. It came late Monday morning." He glanced around, then smiled before holding a small piece of paper out to him. "Ah, here it is."

Ethan felt a sharp, sinking sensation in the lower portion of his stomach when he stepped forward to take the folded paper from the young clerk. Most of the people who knew him as George Parkinson knew he planned to be gone several days and would have waited to leave a message. He stared at the paper as if it had the power to catch fire and burn him.

"Who left the message? Do you know?"

"It's from the telegraph office," the clerk explained. "Andy Edwards brought it by here Monday morning on his way over to Mattie's for a late breakfast." He wrinkled his forehead while he tried to remember. "I guess it was about ten-thirty or eleven when he stopped in, but you'd already left for Marshall."

When Ethan glimpsed the name George *Ethan* Parkinson on the outside, he knew who had to have sent the message but he quickly opened the page and glimpsed the signature to verify the fact. His stomach coiled into an even harder knot when he saw the name he feared most penned in the telegraph operator's neat script; but he did not read the actual message until he reached his room.

Worried that something had either already gone wrong or was *about* to go wrong, he waited until he was in his room and seated on the bed before unfolding the page again. With trembling hands he read the words within: "For that much money, your plan had sure better be a good one. I will arrive there as soon as I finish my business here. I want to help however I can."

At the bottom was scrawled the name, Captain Jeremiah Clayburn Potter—as if he were still in the army. The document was dated Monday, March 14, 1870. Although the telegraph operator had neglected to write down the exact time, Ethan knew that if it had been delivered around ten-thirty, then the captain had probably sent it around nine o'clock. *Two days ago*.

Aware of how radically the captain's telegram had changed matters, Ethan crumpled the page in his hand.

Even though Leona was now free of any real medical danger, he was not quite ready to abduct Lathe. Not when it meant having to leave Little Mound.

269

Although he wasn't exactly sure why, Ethan wanted more time to make his move. He *had* to have more time. And oddly enough, he wanted Lathe to have more time, too. After all, the man had saved his sister's life; he deserved *some* compensation for that.

Knowing that at least forty hours had passed since that telegram had been sent, possibly more, Ethan grabbed his hat and headed back out the door. He wanted to be waiting outside that telegraph office when it opened. He wanted to get a return message off as quick as was humanly possible. He had to convince the captain that his help was not needed—at least not yet.

Ethan shuddered at the thought that his boss might suddenly show up and take over.

He *had* to persuade the captain not to come—if he wasn't already on his way.

The frightening realization that the captain might already have finished whatever business he had in Alabama and could already be on his way to Little Mound made Ethan walk all the faster. He had to keep the captain away from there. He had to try to keep him from catching up with Lathe, especially there in Little Mound.

For Leona's sake.

He knew from the way she looked whenever anyone as much as mentioned Lathe's name that she had come to care for him deeply. Maybe *too* deeply.

Chapter Fourteen

Ethan knew that it would take nearly an hour for the telegram to reach Alabama, but there was little else he could do but go back to the hotel and pray for a response to come — anything that would indicate the message had arrived in time to stop the captain from catching the next train to East Texas.

Wanting to know as quick as he could whether he had succeeded in postponing a very volatile situation, he handed the operator two extra nickels and requested that any response be delivered to him right away. Then he went back to the hotel.

Tired, but no longer sleepy, Ethan glanced up at the dreary sky while he retraced his steps along the gusty street. Another late-winter storm was rumbling in from the north, though it seemed to be several hours away. Smiling perversely, he decided the bleak weather matched his dismal mood perfectly, and he continued to walk with his face turned toward the chilling wind.

With no way to know what was about to happen to Lathe or himself, his stomach churned with the same cold, twisting motion as the dreary, storm-filled sky.

Now that he had gotten to know Lathe personally, Ethan found it hard to believe that the man could ever have murdered anyone. Truth was, Ethan had never seen any real, tangible evidence that proved

271

Lathe to be a dangerous killer. He had only the captain's word for that. But he *had* seen the stark determination in the older man's eyes and knew that he desperately wanted Lathe. It was obvious the captain believed Lathe was his brother's killer and there had to be a good reason for that.

Still, the prospect of having to hand Lathe over to a man as vindictive as Captain Potter made Ethan feel physically ill.

Even so, Ethan was deeply afraid of the retribution he himself would face if he allowed Lathe to get away from him yet again—especially after having requested all that money to make sure he got the job done right.

Still, he was no longer all that certain he could go through with it. He did not feel right about handing Lathe Caldwell over to a man who so desperately wanted to see him hang—whether by his own hand or by that of the sheriff back in Alabama. But what other choice did he have?

If he did not do exactly what the captain wanted, not only would his horrifying secret be revealed to everyone concerned, but there was the very real likelihood that the captain would be angry enough to have *him* killed instead. After all, it had been nearly five years since this all started and the captain's patience was running extremely thin—and besides, that was just the way the captain was. If he didn't eventually get his hands on Lathe, he would seek retribution in any way he could and on anyone he felt responsible.

Twisting his whiskered face into a deep frown, Ethan wondered if there were some way to get around his orders to turn Lathe over to the captain. There had to be some way to appease the captain's prolonged desire for revenge and yet allow Lathe to live. But how?

Pressing his lips together until they virtually disappeared beneath the thickness of his beard, he considered simply bushwhacking the man somewhere, then stealing something from him that would prove his identity, like that fancy gold ring engraved with the letter *C* he always wore. If he could get his hands on that ring, he could then take it to the captain and claim it to be proof that he had been forced to kill him.

If only Ethan knew for certain that Zeb Turner was dead, he just might try it. But the way his luck normally ran, Zeb would still be alive, and as soon as Lathe found that out, he'd take out after him again. Zeb would then relay that fact to the captain, asking for more protection.

Ethan shuddered at the thought of what would happen then. The captain did not take too kindly to being betrayed for *any* reason. No, Ethan knew his only option at this point was to capture Lathe, then hand him over as planned—and have yet another death on his conscience.

"I thought you told me she would be having to close her doors by now," Roy Porterfield said as soon as John Davis had closed the door to assure their privacy. "I was just by Stegall's and saw Leona putting fresh stock on her shelves—and a mighty lot of it. What happened to our deal? Did you go soft on me or something?"

"Nothing has happened to our deal," John said then took a cautious step back, not certain what the tall, angry man might do. "And I really did think she would be closed down by now. Just like I thought we'd be married by now."

"And that's another thing. A couple of weeks ago, you were so damned sure that stubborn woman

273

would finally give in and marry you. What happened to that? Did she finally find out what a horse's rump you really are?"

John narrowed his eyes and glared at Roy, willing to take only so much verbal abuse. "She found a way to get some of the money she needed. But don't worry, she didn't get nearly enough to put herself back in business for long. Our private agreement still stands. You'll just have to wait a little longer is all."

Roy shoved his hat to the back of his head and ran his burly hands through his curling hair, clearly frustrated by the unexpected turn of events. "But if she found a way to get that much money once, what makes you think she can't do it again?"

"Because my father and I happen to know the source of her sudden windfall and we feel confident we can convince that same source not to be so generous with his money in the future," John said. The muscles in his jaw hardened while he considered just how far he would be willing to go to convince Leona's new friend, George Parkinson, to keep his money to himself. "Leona may have found a way around her problem for now, but I know her too well. In a few months, she will have let most of her new merchandise go on credit and will be right back in the very same shape she was in last week. Only this time, she will have to come to *me* for help."

"But what if she doesn't? And what if she doesn't end up marrying you like you want? What if after all your plans and promises, you don't get control of that Mercantile after all?"

Angry that Roy had such sudden doubts, John thrust his chin forward and narrowed his eyes until the hazel color was barely detectable through his thick eyelashes. "The simple fact is that if Leona doesn't agree to marry me, she won't have a chance in hell of getting the money she needs to stay in business," John explained, even though he had no intention of giving it to her.

"Are you sure your father won't break down and loan it to her?" Roy asked, trying to view the situation from all angles.

"Of course, I'm sure. Father will continue using the promise of a loan to try to convince her to have her brother declared legally dead so when I do marry her there won't be any problem with my selling the business; but he has no intention of ever letting her have any actual money. This time she will have to marry me to get what she wants—or even what she *thinks* she wants. Truth is, after I finally do get her to settle down and have children, she will be glad I forced her to sell that business."

"You sure must love that woman an awful lot to be willing to go to such lengths to trick her into marrying you," Roy commented with a chuckle. "Either that or you are so used to having your way that you can't stand the thought that someone actually refused you something. And the way I hear it, she's refused you plenty."

"Roy, you are treading on thin ice," John warned in a low, threatening voice. "If you've changed your mind about wanting that building for your own mercantile agency, just say so. Otherwise, I'd advise you to keep such comments to yourself, especially where Leona is concerned."

"As long as the deal is still on," Roy said, smiling agreeably. "Because not only do I still want the larger building that looks right out on the square, but I want her out of business. As long as she's willing to sell her products so ridiculously cheap, I don't dare hike my prices to where I want them."

"Then just consider this a temporary setback," John assured him. "Within a month or two, Leona will be broke again and this time she will have to come to me

275

for help. When that finally does happen, you and I will both end up winning. You will finally have the sort of location you've wanted for so long and I will finally have the sort of wife I've wanted—one who will stay home and take care of the house and the children rather than spend her every daylight hour working in that blasted store."

John smiled for the first time since Roy had entered his office when he added, "After all, once Leona has married me and I then work my way around the loose wording of her parents' wills by getting her to have her brother declared legally dead, she will no longer have a store to bother with. She can then concentrate solely on what it takes to make me happy."

Ethan could hardly believe he had fallen asleep. As upset as he had been over the captain's telegram and the very real possibility that he could already be on his way to Little Mound, he had thought sleep impossible. But evidently he was far more exhausted than he first realized. Instead of merely lying on the bed resting while he sorted through his thoughts, he had at some point drifted off to sleep and had then slept for several hours. It was already noon.

He had slept a lot longer than he had intended, so he hurried to change shirts, then washed his face and arms with a cool, wet washcloth, as much in an attempt to wake himself as to clean away the road dust still clinging to his skin from the night before.

Originally, he had planned to catch only a few hours of rest before heading on back to the Mercantile to help Leona finish putting away her new stock. He wanted to be there, looking very busy and very helpful whenever Sarah arrived early that afternoon.

He also wanted to see if there might be a message waiting for him at the desk.

Even though he had asked that any messages be sent on up to his room, he knew from experience that often it was next to impossible for him to be roused from a sound sleep. It was possible that someone had tried to wake him by knocking on the door but had failed. Or at least he hoped that would be the case. It had been nearly six hours since he had sent that last telegram. The captain should have had plenty of time to send a response by now — *if he were still in Alabama.* As eager as the captain was to get his hands on Lathe, it was very possible he had already left for Texas. He could be arriving at any minute.

With that same sickly feeling crawling through his stomach causing his heart to race with mounting apprehension, Ethan hurried out the door and down the narrow staircase. He went immediately to the front desk. There he found an older man seated on a tall stool, bent over a small ledger, immersed in thought.

Ethan glanced around for the usual clerk but when he did not find him, he tapped on the upper portion of the split-level desk with his knuckle, eager to get the older man's attention. When that failed to do the trick, he tapped harder on the wooden surface. And when that didn't work, he leaned forward and waved one hand near the ledger while rapping as hard as he could with the other. His heart continued to hammer with fearful anticipation while he waited for the older man to notice him.

"May I help you?" he finally asked before reaching into a shelf below for an ear horn, and then placing it to his ear. For some reason, he crinkled the side of his face to which he held the huge wooden instrument.

Well, no wonder, thought Ethan with a sharp sigh, unaware he had held his breath until it came down either to releasing it or turning colors. "My name is George Ethan Parkinson. I'm up in room twelve. Are there any messages for me?" He wet his lips with growing anticipation while he watched the man slowly search through a small stack of folded papers.

Sorting them out one at a time, the man meticulously unfolded each page then held it very near his face, mumbling while he carefully searched the page for the name Parkinson, then set each off to one side.

"No," he finally said, then started back through the papers a second time as if to double-check. "No, there doesn't seem to be anything here for a George Ethan Parkinson. Nothing at all."

Ethan's stomach hardened with dread. Evidently, the captain had already left for Little Mound. "Are you sure? Are you absolutely sure there isn't a message there from the telegraph office for me?"

"Doesn't seem to be. But then, I haven't been here very long. It could be that Daniel took the message then put it in his pocket. He does that from time to time, though I keep telling him it is a bad habit."

"And where is Daniel?" He asked, again hopeful.

"Gone home to eat a bite of lunch." The man glanced at a huge, decorative clock that stood against the far wall. "But he should be back here in about fifteen or twenty minutes, this being Wednesday and all. We are usually short-handed on Wednesdays."

Ethan, too, glanced at the clock and wondered what he should do. It was now after twelve-thirty. He had so wanted to get on over to the Mercantile before Sarah arrived; but if it turned out the other desk clerk did have a message for him, he would want to know about it right away. He would ask to have the message delivered to him at Leona's, but he was afraid she might question him about it. Yet waiting around for the other clerk to return might cause him to miss seeing Sarah, especially if she decided to come early.

While Ethan leaned heavily against the desk, stroking his whiskers as if that might help him decide what to do, he heard footsteps just overhead and glanced up in time to see Lathe headed down the stairs. Feeling guilty, aware that the man who wanted Lathe dead could very well already be on his way to Little Mound, Ethan looked away and hoped Lathe would not notice him.

"Well, well, well," Lathe said in a deep, sarcastic tone just seconds before his boot connected with the main floor. "If it isn't Leona's dear *brother.*"

Ethan's next breath lodged at the base of his throat, making it hard for him to speak when he turned back toward Lathe. *How did he ever find out the truth?*

"What do you mean?" he asked, in a voice so strained, he'd sounded choked, already wondering what would be the best way to handle the situation. Although he had thought to bring his rifle with him, he had leaned it against the desk to set it out of his way while he stopped to see if there had been a message. Lathe, on the other hand, had his sidearm strapped directly to his thigh, ready to draw and fire. It was not a very promising situation.

With his right hand hovering very near his firearm, Lathe's eyes narrowed into two steely blue slits, revealing the depth of his anger. "Don't play games with me, Parkinson. It just so happens I saw you with Leona last night. I now know that it's not a brother-sister relationship you're after."

Having heard him use the name Parkinson, Ethan expelled such a slow, deep sigh of relief, that he felt as if his whole chest had caved in. Lathe didn't know who he was after all. But realizing that he should be insulted by what Lathe had just said, he thrust his jaw forward and spoke in a low, angry voice. "Just what is it you are trying to say?"

When Lathe noticed the man with the ear horn leaning ever so slightly toward them, he pulled George away from the desk so the remainder of their conversation could be held in private. "I'm not *trying* to say anything. I'd coming right out and *saying* it. I know only too well what you are trying to do. It just so happens I *saw* you holding Leona in your arms last night, or should I say very *early* this morning, at a time when you two obviously thought no one else would be around."

"You saw me holding Leona?" he asked, wondering when that was.

"I also saw you bend down to kiss her. And don't go trying to convince me that it was just a *brotherly* hug and a *brotherly* kiss. I saw the adoring way you had her looking up at you. You don't have me fooled one bit."

Although Ethan's first inclination had been to try to convince Lathe of the truth—that it was indeed a brotherly hug and kiss he'd witnessed—he quickly changed his mind. Remembering that the captain could very well be on his way, he decided it would be best for everyone concerned if he were to put as much distance as possible between Lathe and Leona. Therefore, rather than say something that might soothe Lathe's anger, he decided to try to drive a permanent wedge between the two.

Even if it meant telling another lie.

"So, what if I am trying to make her feel grateful to me?" he asked, tossing his head back. "It's not like you've laid any claim on her."

Lathe swallowed in an attempt to control his mounting anger, aware he would dearly love to be able to lay a claim on Leona's heart but didn't dare. He owed it to Jonathan not to become committed to anyone or *anything*, other than the capture of his killer. "So you admit it," he said, his heart ripping into tiny pieces at the thought of Leona falling in love with George. "You admit that you are trying to win her heart."

"I admit nothing," he said with a clear, distinct tone, not wanting Lathe to go to Leona with any of this foolishness. "But if it ever turns out she wants me, then at least I'll be there for her. Can you say the same?" He didn't wait for an answer. "You know you can't because just as soon as you find out where your evil Mr. Turner went you'll be off and running again, without a thought to what your leaving might do to her."

Ethan watched Lathe's facial expressions, hoping he would see something that might indicate the reverse. If only Lathe *would* give up his pursuit of Zeb for Leona, then he could carry through with the plan of pretending to have killed him and not worry that the captain might find out.

That was if he could get the captain to return to Alabama immediately.

Lathe stared at Ethan a long moment, wishing that what he had just said had not been the truth. But it was. He was obligated to bring Jonathan's killer to justice. But rather than give George the grim satisfaction of hearing him admit the truth—that he would indeed have to leave whenever he finally found out where Zeb had gone—he spun about on his heel and marched out of the hotel lobby.

Just as he stepped out into the wide gravel street, it started to rain. Rather than run for the cover of a nearby walkway, he continued right down the middle of the street toward the Mercantile. Although he had no idea what he would say when he finally got there, he planned to let Leona know exactly what he thought of her foolish behavior.

"Now I don't know whether to go or stay," Captain Potter said, glaring down at the telegram the messenger had just handed him. After closing the front door, he turned back to face his younger brother, Richard. "This says that Ethan won't be needing anyone's help for several days and for me not to come until I'm sent for."

"I guess all that money must have been for some sort of elaborate setup," Richard concluded, his expression pensive, not knowing how Jeremiah might react. "I wonder what Ethan has up his sleeve."

"Well, whatever it is, it had sure better work this time." He narrowed his demonic green eyes until they became two penetrating slits of anger, causing Richard to take a tentative step back. "It's been nearly five years now and I'm getting sick and damned tired of having to send him and Zeb money every few months."

"Still, if what you told me is true, it will be money well spent." Richard cautiously reminded him, then offered a timid smile, hoping to keep his brother's anger at a minimum. "Didn't you tell me that the Caldwell treasure is supposed to be worth nearly a million dollars?"

"It's really hard to say what it's worth for sure. Could be it's worth even more than that. That young brother, Jonathan, never did quote any real amount to me. But by figuring in what he claimed they sold and what he planned to buy just as soon as the war was over, I figure it has to be worth at least that much."

Glad to see the captain calming somewhat, Richard continued to keep the conversation focused on the money. "But what I don't understand is how you ever got him to tell you about that buried gold in the first place. You never have told about that."

"That's because you don't need to know," Captain Potter snapped then tilted his head to one side as if debating whether he should let his brother in on the whole story or leave him only partially informed.

"But why not?" Richard asked, his heart hammering excitedly, aware by his brother's expression that he was actually considering telling him. "Are you afraid I'll try to get to the money before you do?"

"No, you would never be that foolish." He laughed at the thought.

"Then why won't you tell me how it is you came to know so much about the Caldwells?"

Captain Potter glanced at the two half-filled valises he had hurried to pack, still undecided about what he should do next. Should he go through with his original plan to join Ethan in Little Mound early that following day or wait until he was actually needed? Would his being there jeopardize Ethan's plan in any way, or would he actually be of some help?

Unable to decide, he rubbed his tired face then sank into a nearby upholstered chair and pressed his eyes closed. Ever since he had gotten Ethan's last two telegrams, he had been too excited to eat or sleep because after all these years, it looked like they were finally closing in on Lathe.

"Why are you so curious about the Caldwell treasure?" he asked as he tipped his head against the scrolled back of the elegantly carved rococo chair, not bothering to open his eyes.

"I don't know why—I just am," Richard admitted, also sitting. But rather than lean back, he pressed his hands together and leaned forward, longing to hear whatever his brother might say.

The captain opened his eyes just enough to look at Richard's eager expression and realized how little harm it would cause to tell him what had happened, especially now that it looked like he was just a few days away from getting his hands on the Caldwell fortune.

Sighing wearily, he closed his eyes again and while he considered just how much he should tell his younger brother, he let his thoughts drift slowly back — to a chilly autumn afternoon nearly six years ago.

It was near the end of the war, though he and his men had had no way of knowing that, at the time. The way it had looked to them then, that war could have continued on for an eternity. Both sides appeared to be losing far more than they could ever hope to win, yet neither side seemed to be faring any better than the other.

Having already been told by his three scouts that there were no Yankees in the vicinity, he and several of his men had decided to play a few hands of poker to help pass the time. Because they had four decks of cards among them, there were four different games being played in various areas of the camp. The captain remembered having sat at the table nearest the campfire and asking to be dealt in.

With no threat of an immediate battle hovering over them, several bottles of whiskey were produced. Because it was the only way they had to keep their minds off the endless atrocities of a war most of them hated, many of the men began to drink and drink heavily.

As usual, the more he and his little group drank, the louder and more talkative they became, until finally one of the men at his table — a surveyor who had been assigned to his command only weeks earlier, named Jonathan Caldwell — began to spout off about something Potter had found very interesting.

Although the captain had yet to reveal any of his rambling thoughts to his eagerly awaiting brother, he smiled and opened his eyes to stare idly at the ceiling. How vividly he recalled what had happened back in the fall of 1864 — events that were to change his life forever.

Because Caldwell had started winning heavily that day, he had puffed himself up like a young cock and had begun muttering something about how very rich he would be after he'd added his new winnings to all that gold he already had.

At the captain's encouragement, Caldwell eventually leaned forward as if about to tell the men seated around him a well-kept secret, and then he revealed his plans to buy a big piece of land, miles wide, and build a big, fancy house right in the middle of it. His plans at that time were to buy that land and build that house somewhere in northwest Louisiana where the war had caused very little destruction, and settle down to raise cattle or cotton.

Aware that he must have stumbled upon something well worth knowing, Captain Potter had pretended not to believe that Caldwell could ever get his hands on that much money and by doing so, managed to trick the drunken fool into telling him more about "all that gold."

By asking just the right questions while continuing to ply him with liquor, the captain eventually learned all about how Private Caldwell and his older brother, Lathe, had buried a veritable fortune somewhere in the northern half of Alabama. Having foreseen the war as inevitable and realizing the amount of destruction that could be caused by such a war, the two brothers had sold everything they owned, then used the money to buy as much pure gold as possible. They then buried that gold where no one else could find it and to be sure they could locate it when the time came, each brother had proceeded to carve the information they would need right into their own flesh. But as an added precaution, each had carved only part of the information they would need.

Although young Caldwell had declared repeatedly that he was not supposed to tell anyone about their gold, it had not stopped him from revealing most of the information the captain had wanted to hear.

Caldwell had even gone as far as to mention that there was a town somewhere in Alabama where he and his brother planned to meet when the war was finally over so they could collect the gold right away; but by then the young private had become so drunk he could not remember the name of it.

Caldwell was so inebriated by that time — as the captain knew — the lad would probably not even remember having let his valuable secret slip; but the captain was also aware that the other two men sitting in on the poker game were not quite so far gone and might very well remember everything.

Aware that the information he had managed to extract from the drunken young private could one day be worth hundreds of thousands of dollars, or possibly even millions, depending on the value of gold after the war, the captain had decided not to risk sharing that new knowledge with the other two men. He did not want either of them coming up with the same sort of disreputable idea he had and then beating him to the fortune. The only way for him to be sure he was the only one to try to cash in on what Caldwell had told them was simple: he would have to find some way to eliminate the competition.

Captain Potter's smile widened when he remembered just how easy that had been.

"So, are you going to tell me or not?" Richard asked, tired of waiting for his brother to say something.

The captain's smile faded just as quickly as it had formed, when he glanced down at the telegram still in his hands and then turned to Richard. With a slight grunt, he slowly pushed himself forward then forced himself up out of the chair. "I'll tell you about it on the way."

Richard's eyes widened with excitement. "Are you going to let me go to Little Mound with you?"

"No, of course not," the captain snapped, clearly annoyed by such an absurd question. "I can't let you go to Little Mound. You are supposed to be dead, remember? Lathe is supposed to have killed you, or so Ethan thinks. You will have to stay here and wait for me to return."

Having expected as much, Richard nodded while he followed his brother to the door then glanced back at the still open valises and frowned. "Aren't you forgetting your clothes?"

"No, I'm not headed for the train station just yet. I'm headed to the telegraph office. I want to send another message to Ethan. I want him to know when to expect me."

Chapter Fifteen

Still hoping for a response to his earlier telegram, Ethan waited in the hotel lobby until the younger desk clerk had returned. Ethan was disappointed yet a second time.

There had been no messages for him at all that morning.

Unwilling to believe the captain was indeed already on his way to Little Mound, Ethan headed back to the telegraph office, hoping that perhaps a message had arrived at a time when there had been no messenger to carry it to him.

It was already after one o'clock and Ethan knew Sarah would be arriving at the Mercantile any time, so he hurriedly made his way around the slower pedestrians thronging the boardwalk. Just the thought of being with her again thrilled him as nothing else in his life ever had. His anticipation was such that he could hardly breathe.

Although by then the rain had slowed to a thick, grey drizzle, there was just enough moisture still falling from the sky to keep most people on the covered boardwalks. Had it not been for the fact that he wanted to look his very best when he saw Sarah, Ethan would have lost patience with having to move about so slowly and would have taken to the street where he could travel at his own brisk pace.

Even so, within a very few minutes after he had left the hotel, he turned onto Market Street and could see the brightly painted sign that hung in front of the telegraph and freight office only two blocks away. Still, it seemed to take him forever to reach the front door.

When he finally did enter the small planked building, the telegraph operator glanced up, then frowned with annoyance. "Mr. Parkinson, what are you doing here? You told me you would be at the hotel. I just sent a messenger over there with that response you were waiting for. I gave him instructions to have the desk send it right on up to your room."

"Was it from Captain Potter?" Ethan asked, holding his breath, afraid to hope.

The operator nodded. "I don't really recall what the message was, something about wanting to hear from you. But I do remember it was from that same captain you've been sending your messages to. If you want to know exactly what it said, you will probably find it waiting for you at the front desk. I told Andy to leave it with strict orders that you receive it just as soon as possible. Since you're not in your room at the moment, they'll probably be watching the front door for you."

Ethan sighed happily, relieved there had been a response. It meant the captain was still in Alabama. He had gotten the message off in time.

Grinning wide, Ethan reached into his pocket and pulled out several coins. "Give these to the messenger for his trouble. And tell him if there are any other messages to make sure they are also delivered to the hotel right away."

"Will do," the operator said, taking the money and putting it into his vest pocket. "I'll send any messages on just as soon as they come across the wire. You can count on it."

Although the rain had stopped and the sun had started to peek through the clouds by the time Ethan left the telegraph office, the street had become so muddy during the past few hours, that most people

289

continued to keep to the boardwalks. Knowing it was now nearly one-thirty and afraid Sarah might grow tired of waiting and leave before he ever arrived, he again hurried as best he could through the slower, less motivated pedestrians.

By the time he reached Main Street, his pulse was racing, as much from the aggravation of having had to fight such an impossible crowd as from the thought of seeing Sarah again. With visions of her timid smile dancing in the back of his mind, he paused in front of *The Tribune,* which was across the street, to double-check his reflection in the tinted window.

After assuring himself that his hat and jacket were on straight and that his beard was still neatly combed, he hurried across to the side door of the Mercantile.

When he did not immediately find Sarah working in the main part of the store helping Leona arrange the merchandise, he went into the storage room at the back. When he returned to the front, his face drooped with disappointment. There had been no one in the storage room either.

"Where's Sarah?"

Leona looked up from the silverware she had been arranging across the top of a wide strip of black velvet just long enough to answer. "Sarah hasn't arrived yet. I imagine the weather delayed her. But now that it has finally quit raining, she should be right along." She then glanced out the nearest window in time to watch a bright patch of sunlight turn to shadow. "Did the rain bring colder weather?"

Ethan stared at her with a blank expression for several seconds. Now that she had asked, his skin did feel a bit chilled but he could not tell if that was due to the weather or to his disappointment. "I really didn't notice how cold it is. I suppose it's probably down to about the fifties by now."

"Doesn't seem right." She frowned when she returned her attention to the silverware display, adjusting a fork that looked to be a little too far to the left. "Not for it to be in the fifties one day, then up to about eighty degrees the next and down in the fifties again a few days later. I wish Mother Nature would make up her mind."

Ethan frowned when he realized how stiff Leona's movements had become and how tired and deeply tormented she looked. Dark, curving shadows had formed beneath her eyes. Her whole body looked weighted and weary. She had skipped one night of sleep and it had finally begun to take its toll.

"You certainly have been workin' awful hard. Looks to me like you're about to be through with puttin' up the stock," he commented, walking around and surveying all she had done in the past few hours. "I guess it wouldn't hurt for you to go on home for awhile and catch yourself a little nap. I can handle everything here for you."

Besides, it would give him a chance to be alone with Sarah.

"There's really nothing much to handle," she commented, glancing around at her freshly stocked shelves and tables with a forlorn expression. "One of the reasons I've been able to get so much work done, is that I decided to keep the store closed until I have everything in its place." She shrugged, then breathed a silent sigh. "Besides, I'm not all that tired."

Ethan looked at her, puzzled. If that were true, then why did she look so unhappy when just hours ago, she had been so full of energy and excitement. "If you are not all that tired, then why the long face?"

"Lathe was by here earlier," she said. Her lower lip trembled at the painful memory.

"Oh?" Ethan responded, then glanced away as if not interested in what she had to say. "And did he say

291

anything about me?"

Leona's eyebrows notched, thinking that an odd question. "No. Why would he say anything about you?"

"No reason. It's just that you are actin' like you might be a little annoyed with me about something. I thought maybe it was because of something Lathe said."

"Truth is, he didn't say anything."

When Ethan turned to look at her he saw tears in her eyes. Her voice was strained with emotion.

"I don't know what I did to make him so angry with me, but he came bursting in here a little while ago, back when it had first started to rain. Then, without saying anything at all, he stormed right up to me, his arms stiff at his sides, and then just glared at me. You could *see* the hatred in his eyes. I was so baffled by his behavior, I didn't know what to say, so I just stood there staring back at him."

Her face tightened with further confusion and anguish while she continued, "After a few seconds, he narrowed his eyes and opened his mouth like he was about to say something, but then he turned and stalked out of here without ever having spoken a word."

Ethan felt a sharp, stabbing pain when he saw just how deeply Lathe's anger had hurt her. He knew Leona had taken a special liking to Lathe, but he had had no idea that she cared so strongly for him.

Because he felt partially if not completely to blame for Lathe's sudden outrage, Ethan considered telling her the truth. He wanted her to understand that Lathe's anger was not her fault. But he knew she would demand to know why he had tricked Lathe into believing the worst and he didn't have any alternative explanations for that.

"What could I have done to make him so angry?"

she repeated in a emotionally strangled voice, her gaze again distant while she tried to figure out why Lathe had behaved so strangely.

"Maybe it wasn't nothing you did. Maybe it was something someone else did." His brown eyes lit with a sudden idea. "Maybe it had to do with that man he's been chasing after. Maybe Lathe had just found out that Zeb had gotten clean away and it made him so angry, he couldn't even talk about it."

Leona shook her head. "I don't think so. I feel pretty certain it had to do with me. And it wasn't just anger I saw in his eyes. There was something else. Something I can't quite identify, but I'm sure was directed at me."

"I think you are imagining things. You are probably reading more into his strange behavior than you should," Ethan said, then put his arm around her shoulders in a comforting manner. "But whatever might be troubling him, I don't think you should let it bother you like this. At least not now. You've got too much work to do. I noticed there were still a dozen or so crates and nearly as many barrels in the back yet to unpack."

"Most of them are already empty," she admitted, then forced a smile. "I'm keeping some of the sturdier cartons for my customers to use to hold their larger purchases. About all I really have left to unpack are a few sets of dishes and several dozen glasses."

"If that's so, then what'll be left for me and Sarah to do?"

"There's still plenty to be done around here. One thing I want Sarah to do is paint a large sign for my front window announcing that I have just received a fresh shipment of goods. Sarah is much more talented with a lettering brush than I could ever hope to be."

A slow smile spread across Ethan's face. Leona had just brought up his favorite subject. "I'll bet she *is* good at painting. I'll bet she can do just about any-thing she sets her mind to."

Leona rolled her eyes heavenward, aware he was far too awestruck to do anything but find ways to compliment his lady fair. "Well, not quite," she admit-ted, remembering that her friend had absolutely no talent when it came to stitching a straight seam. "But she *is* the kind to give whatever it is her best try."

In an effort to help George pass the time until Sarah arrived, Leona showed him where she wanted him to place several of the heavier items she had been unable to lift earlier.

Wanting to be free to watch Sarah paint when the time came, he hurriedly placed the two plows and three wheelbarrows she had ordered in the front win-dow at just the angle she wanted. He then stacked the new laundry tubs in the far corner, where they could be easily seen from either of two directions. He next hurried to set up the new St. Louis washer machine in the special spot Leona had reserved near the front door.

It was not until he had everything in place and had stopped to mop his brow with his handkerchief that Sarah finally walked in.

"Why is the front door locked?" she asked, her gaze darting about the room until it came to rest on Ethan's startled face. Quickly he straightened, then brushed his clothing with several short swipes of his hand.

"Because I don't want my customers coming in here until I have everything ready," Leona explained, though she knew Sarah had not bothered to listen. Her friend was already on her way across the room to where Ethan stood gawking down at her like some love-struck schoolboy.

Thinking the two would welcome any opportunity to be alone, and knowing she would not be very good company in her present mood anyway, Leona hurried to tell Sarah about the sign she wanted her to paint. She showed her where she'd left the paints, canvas, and brushes, then went on into the storage room to finish polishing the silver rims of the special glasses and plates she had ordered. When she finished that, she decided the regular plates and glasses could use polishing, too. Anything to keep herself busy for the next hour or so.

Although Ethan knew he could probably be more helpful in the back with Leona, he could not bear the thought of leaving Sarah's smiling presence. He tried to make himself look useful by holding whatever brushes she was not using, then handing them back to her whenever she decided she needed them again.

The next couple of hours were two of the happiest in Ethan's life. He and Sarah found so many things to laugh about, so many little secrets to share with each other. Even though he knew his time around her would be short—knowing that within a few days he would either have to satisfy the captain's orders by capturing Lathe or risk the man's violent anger— Ethan decided to enjoy thoroughly whatever time he *did* have.

The only real setback to his happiness that day came from the fact that while he and Sarah found so many reasons to laugh and tease each other, Leona continued to mope about the back room, so preoccupied with her dreary thoughts that she rarely even noticed when they spoke to her.

He felt like kicking himself for not having realized just how much Lathe had meant to his little sister and he felt guilty knowing he was one of the main reasons she was now so miserable. Finally, he had had his fill of watching her suffer, and he decided that if he deserved to have a few fleeting moments of happiness, then she did too.

Despite the fact that Lathe could never become a permanent part of her life, any more than he could hope to become a permanent part of Sarah's life, Ethan now believed that his little sister deserved whatever degree of happiness Lathe could bring to her in the short time they could be together. The fact she would undoubtedly be hurt when he left no longer mattered much. What really mattered was the fact that she was hurting now.

He decided the best thing for him to do would be to tell Lathe the truth about what he'd done, and simply allow nature to take its course from there. If Leona were meant to share a tiny portion of her life with Lathe, then so be it. At least she would know what it was like to have loved.

Having finally made up his mind to do the right thing by Leona made Ethan feel even happier than he already felt — so much so that when Sarah later invited him to her parents' house for supper that coming Saturday, he accepted without giving the matter a second thought. It was not until later, after she had left, that he realized the grave mistake he had made.

By the time Ethan returned to the hotel, he was busily trying to figure a way to avoid having dinner at her parents' house. It would be too painful to have to sit at the same table with George's family — especially his mother. He had been such close friends with George through their younger years that Mrs. Martin had become a second mother to him. He could not bear to face her, knowing what he had done. Not even as someone else.

Ethan had become so immersed in his apprehensive thoughts that he forgot all about that telegram from the captain, and instead of stopping at the front desk as he had earlier planned, he headed straight for the stairs, out of habit.

"Mr. Parkinson," the desk clerk called to him, dipping his eyebrows with annoyance when that did not catch the burly man's attention. He raised his voice then tried again. "Mr. Parkinson, I have a message here for you."

Ethan continued toward the stairs, still trying to determine some way out of his predicament, too engrossed to allow the name he had been using for more than a week to register in his mind.

"Mr. Parkinson, *sir!*" the clerk tried again, this time shouting so loudly that Ethan finally noticed him, as did several other guests milling about the lobby.

"Who me?" He blinked, trying to focus his thoughts on what the clerk had to say.

"You *are* the only Mr. Parkinson residing in this hotel," he responded tersely, still annoyed that Ethan had not responded to his first call. With a pinched scowl, he held up a folded piece of paper. "I have a message for you. I was told to give it to you the very next time I saw you."

Embarrassed to have forgotten, Ethan stepped over and accepted the message.

"Sorry, I had my mind on something else," he admitted sheepishly, then tucked the note into his front pocket before turning and hurrying back toward the stairs.

He waited until he had closed the door to his room and had tugged off his wet boots and stockings before bothering to sit down to read the actual message. When he did, a cold chill shot down his spine, causing his skin to break out in gooseflesh. It was not at all what he had hoped to read.

George E. Parkinson:
    I am packed and ready to leave. I will give you only a few more days to try to fulfill your duties alone. If I haven't heard from you within a week, I will come anyway. I'm running thin on

patience. It is time to finish this thing.

The message was signed simply "Captain Potter" and dated March 16, 1870, but this time, the hour the message had arrived was noted at the bottom. He wondered what had taken the captain so long to respond. The message had not come in until 12:15 P.M.

Judging by the date, if Ethan did not find some other reason to keep the captain from leaving Alabama, he could expect the man to arrive in Little Mound on about the twenty-third or twenty-fourth.

Since his time in Little Mound was about to be even shorter than before, he decided to go ahead and have that supper with Sarah and her family on Saturday. With the captain pressing him like that, there would not be too many more moments they could share together; therefore he should try to take advantage of any and every opportunity to see her.

Meanwhile, he needed to do what he could to patch things up between Lathe and Leona. They now had less than a week.

Every moment was precious.

"What do you want?" Lathe asked after he'd opened the door and found George standing in the hallway, hat in hand. Because they were very close to the same height, he met his adversary's gaze with a determined scowl.

"To talk to you for a moment," Ethan answered. He saw no reason to pretend otherwise and placed his hand against the door to prevent him from slamming it in his face. "Can I come in?"

Lathe stared at him a long moment before finally stepping back to let him inside. "And just what is it you think we have to talk about?"

"Leona," he said, eager to get right to the point.

His eyebrows arched when he noticed all the clutter around him. The room looked like a cyclone had struck. The bed was a twisted mass of sheets and covers, and clothing hung across every post and chair. Funny, he had always thought Lathe would be much neater than that; but then it was possible that he was simply too upset at the moment to care what his room looked like.

"I think we've already said all there is to say about Leona," Lathe responded, his tone deep and bitter. He was still hurting from having found out she cared for someone else, and he felt angry to know she and George had both lied about the relationship that had developed between the two. *Brother and sister, indeed!* "I can't think of anything else we could have to say to each other."

"How about the truth?" Ethan asked—then quietly closed the door when it became apparent Lathe had no intention of doing so. "I purposely led you to believe that something very special had developed between me and Leona when it has not. At least not in the way you seem to think."

"Don't give me that," Lathe said. He stepped back and cocked his head at an angle, wondering why George was so eager to fill him with more of his lies. "Don't forget. I saw her in your arms with my own eyes."

"That may be true, but you didn't really understand what you saw." He scowled when he realized how confusing that sounded. "What you saw at the Mercantile this morning was a quick hug of gratitude, nothing more. We had just unloaded the last couple of crates out of the wagon and she had gotten her first good look at just how much merchandise there really was. She was so thrilled by it all, she hugged me—out of sheer excitement, not because she had started to care for me in some special way."

"And what about the kiss?" Lathe reminded him, his voice still filled with skepticism. "Was that just your way of reacting to all that excitement?"

"The only kiss I can remember giving her was one on the forehead, and it was the same sort of kiss I would give to a sister if I had one. You have to believe me. There is nothing more than friendship between us."

Lathe arched one eyebrow while he studied the sincerity evident in Ethan's expression. "*Why* should I believe you?"

"Because I'm telling you the truth. And because I feel bad about having led you to believe the worst. And because Leona looks so miserable and confused knowing you are angry with her but not having any idea why. You should see the way she's mopin' about. It's like you took the heart right out of her. Don't ask me why, but that fool woman has fallen in love with you."

"She told you that?" Lathe's heart soared at the thought but then took a slow, spiraling plunge downward. He did not want her to be in love with him. She would end up being hurt.

"She didn't have to tell me," Ethan explained, not about to put words into Leona's mouth. "I can see it in her eyes whenever she talks about you. There's just this certain sparkle. And to tell you the truth, Lathe, I've seen that same twinkle in your eyes when you look at her."

Lathe could not deny that he had fallen in love with Leona. "But I don't understand why you are telling me all this. What's in it for you?"

"Nothing. I'm tellin' you because I'm hopin' it will make you want to patch things up with Leona. It breaks my heart to see her so unhappy. I guess I thought that maybe if you were told the truth about what you saw, then you'd realize your mistake and go

300

on over there to make amends. Besides, it's not fair to let her go on thinkin' you are angry with her for something she did when the truth is you aren't angry at all. Just jealous. And over something she never even did. It was just something you *thought* she did."

When Lathe did not attempt to deny his feelings, Ethan quietly added, "I'm sorry I let you believe there was something special goin' on between us. I had no right to do that. I should have told you the truth right when you first confronted me at the hotel."

"But then again, part of what you said *was* the truth," Lathe admitted sadly then shoved his jumbled covers aside so he could sit on the bed. When he spoke again, he could not bring himself to look at Ethan. "When I finally do find out where that man I've been following has gone, I'll be gone, too. Probably within that same hour. It is very important I find him."

"Why is all that so important? Because he hurt Leona?" Ethan asked, though he knew that was not the reason.

"No. Because he murdered someone very special to me," Lathe explained, choosing to remain vague rather than reveal any of the painful details. "And because of that, I have to find him and take him back east to hang."

"But it's been over a week now since he got away, and nobody has seen him," Ethan reminded him. "What if he's already dead?"

"That snake has hidden out for longer periods of time than this before surfacing again," Lathe said, his jaw flexing to reveal just how deeply his hatred ran. "I have no choice but to believe he's still alive. Considering how long I've been tracking that man and how badly I want to see him hang, it is impossible for me to think of him as dead. Even if someone claimed to have seen his body, I still wouldn't believe it. I'd

301

have to see that body for myself. And even then, I'd want to touch it, to make sure it was as cold as the man's body he murdered."

Lathe looked so angry and so sincere about what he had just said that Ethan frowned with confusion. None of it fit the story the captain had told him. The way the captain had told it, Lathe was out chasing after Zeb because Zeb was the only living witness to a murder Lathe had committed—the murder of the captain's only brother. "Who is it your man was supposed to have killed?"

"There's no supposed to about it," Lathe corrected. His facial muscles contracted with so much repressed anger it caused Ethan to take a step back. "He has already been tried, found guilty, and sentenced to hang."

"He has?"

"Yes, but as it turned out, someone broke him out of jail the night before they were to slip that rope around his little neck. He got away just hours before having to pay for his crime—which is why I plan to leave Little Mound the very second I find out where he's gone. I have to capture him and take him back to Alabama so they can finally do what it was they were supposed to do five years ago."

Ethan was more confused than ever. "You say he was actually convicted?"

"I've got the papers to prove it. There was a witness who saw him do it. And that's why I'm so reluctant to patch things up with Leona. I don't want to end up hurting her." *Any more than he wanted to end up hurting himself.* "I think maybe it would be better in the long run if I just stayed away from her."

"But you can't. You're her doctor. What about that big cut on her back?"

"It's almost healed."

"But it isn't healed all the way and won't be for

302

weeks yet. She could still get an infection."

"Not if she continues to keep the wound clean."

Ethan let out frustrated breath, then decided the only way to get through to him was to be frank. "Look, Lathe, I know you're not plannin' to be around here forever. So does Leona. But if she's willing to share that time with you, then why not continue to see her? To tell you the truth, you could do a lot worse than spend your time with Leona. She's quite a lady."

"You don't have to tell me that," Lathe snapped, no longer certain what he should do. Ethan had slowly worn down his resistance. "I'm not a fool, you know."

"Then why aren't you with Leona right now?"

Lathe looked at him for several seconds, trying to think of a fitting response, only to realize there was none. Perhaps he *was* a fool for not wanting to take full advantage of what little time he could spend with Leona.

"Well?" Ethan prompted, not about to let it slide. He wanted a response.

"Okay, I'll go see her," Lathe finally said, as relieved as he was apprehensive for having agreed to it. "I'll get cleaned up and go on over there tonight."

"And will you apologize for your recent behavior toward her?"

Lathe breathed a loud sigh of exasperation. "What's with you? Why do you feel you have to go around acting like everybody's big brother?"

Ethan just laughed. "Try to remember, most apologies tend to start off with the words 'I'm sorry.' Once you get past those two little words, the rest of it comes pretty easy.

Chapter Sixteen

The sun had begun to set, leaving Ethan's hotel room cloaked in grey. Oblivious to the settling darkness, Ethan sat forward on the edge of his bed with his face clutched between his hands, trying to decide what to believe.

Lathe had sounded so straightforward and had looked so sincere when he'd explained his reasons for wanting to capture Zeb, it was hard not to believe him. But then, it was just as hard not to believe the captain, who had been equally as intent about wanting Lathe captured. It was impossible to decide which of them was telling him the truth.

But figuring out which man was telling the truth wasn't Ethan's most perplexing problem. The most perplexing problem had come about due to his own change of attitude toward Lathe.

If only he hadn't met him. The more Ethan got to know Lathe, the better he liked him — and the less he wanted to see any real harm come to him. Even if the original story were true and Lathe had murdered the captain's brother, Ethan now believed he had to have had just cause. Lathe was not the cold-blooded type. He could never have done something like that out of spite nor could he have done it for money. Ethan was certain of that much.

But then again, knowing that Lathe was not the cold-blooded killer the captain had claimed him to be did not alleviate his problem. It did not really matter what Ethan now thought of Lathe, he was still duty-bound to find some way to capture him and turn him over to the captain. He knew if he didn't follow through on that, and soon, the captain would eventually decide to take his anger and frustration out on *him*. The captain was not a very tolerant man.

Ethan shuddered at the thought of what would happen if the captain suddenly decided to do his worst. So many people would be hurt, including Sarah, and this time the injuries would leave scars far worse than the one on his face. He shook his head in his misery. If only he, and Jason, and George had not been in such a hurry to join the Confederate Army, they would never have wound up in the command of an unscrupulous man like Captain Potter.

But at the time it had seemed like just the sort of adventure to see them off to college. They joined only a few weeks after the fighting had begun, thinking it a grand way to spend that coming summer.

If only they had known.

Ethan moaned and then fell back onto the bed, oblivious to its complaining squawk while his thoughts wandered back to the first of those four long, bitter years. When the three first left Texas, they were excited and extremely idealistic, believing they were out to help right all the wrongs in the world. But it had not taken long for those youthful feelings of enthusiasm and invulnerability to wear off.

After the conflict, which was supposed to last only a few months, had dragged into years—and after they had watched their close friend, Jason Seguin, die in battle—the war slowly generated into a very real nightmare from which there was no honorable escape.

Because of the many horrors they were forced to endure daily, he and George had both cultivated serious drinking problems — a common failing among many of the soldiers during the latter part of the war.

Whenever there was no whiskey to help dull their daily torment, George and Ethan had each come to depend on the other to keep his spirits up. They soon had become as close as any brothers might, if not closer.

It seemed odd now that they had not sat in on the same card game the day all hell broke loose. They'd spent so much of their time together.

Ethan closed his eyes against the painful memories. The images of what happened during the earlier part of that afternoon were still so vivid. It made it seem as if it had happened just months ago instead of years.

After the company scouts had returned to assure them there wasn't a Yankee soldier within at least three miles of camp, Ethan and George had become involved in the different card games scattered throughout the main yard just outside the tents.

Since they thought they were temporarily safe from any threat of battle, most of the soldiers in camp began to drink pretty heavily early in the afternoon. Shortly before it was to turn dark, after several hours of continuous drinking and card playing, their outfit was suddenly attacked by a band of Yankee soldiers.

With no warning, a volley of bullets had peppered them from both the north and the west.

Because so many of the men under Captain Potter's command had been drinking all day, they panicked.

There was a lot of shouting and confusion in the melee that followed.

Ethan could barely recall his scramble for cover. He couldn't remember if he or one of the other men had thought to topple their table onto its side so they could use it for protection; but it turned out to be the very act that had saved his life.

If only one of the first men shot had not fallen into one of the cook fires, causing an unusual amount of smoke and giving off a putrid stench that only added to the confusion and chaos . . .

It was during that smoky battle that Ethan thought he noticed men in Yankee uniforms slipping into the main part of the camp from a small patch of woods along the north side. Aware the enemy was then only a few hundred yards away and advancing quickly, he had immediately raised his rifle and fired several times through the billows of smoke at the thin, dark shadows that moved quickly into the camp.

Seconds later, while he had paused to reload for the fifth or sixth time, he heard his captain cry out those blood chilling words: "Damn it! Stegall! Turner! Cease firing. You are shooting at our own men!"

Unable to believe their mistake, Ethan froze and didn't fire again. Neither did Zeb.

Shortly after the shooting had finally stopped and Ethan felt it was finally safe to crawl out from behind the table, he hurried to the general area where he remembered having fired his rifle and found George's body, lying face down in the dirt, the back of his shirt soaked with blood.

The captain quickly covered the body with the sheet they had been using for a tablecloth, but not before angrily chastising Ethan for having just killed one of their own men — *his own best friend*.

Later that same night, Captain Potter called Ethan into his tent, anxious to strike a bargain with him. After professing to know exactly how devastated Ethan must be, he had explained how, for certain *favors,* he would be willing to keep his mouth shut about the whole unfortunate incident. To Ethan it was a godsend.

Not only would the captain's agreement to keep silent prevent Ethan from having to face an immediate court martial, it also would keep George's family from ever having to learn the truth. And after having examined the body, the captain had explained that the truth was explicitly clear. George had died almost instantly from Ethan's bullet and it had happened while he had been running from the enemy, which the captain felt was probably why Ethan had mistaken him for an advancing soldier. Rather than stay put and face the enemy like a man, George had taken off running in Ethan's direction.

The captain agreed that as long as Ethan was willing to cooperate with him in *every* way, he would even go as far as to have George declared a wartime hero and would even be willing to carry that proclamation to the point of having his family awarded a medal in George's name.

All he wanted Ethan to do in order to make it all happen was to "loan" the captain most of the savings he knew he had stashed away in his gear, which were considerable, and the fancy gold locket his mother had given him for luck just before he had left for war. As long as Ethan agreed to hand all that over to the captain and continued to lend him at least half of whatever pay he earned during what was left of the war, no one else would ever have to know the truth.

Because Ethan had been unable to bear the thought of George's family ever finding out that *he* was the one who had accidentally killed their eldest son, he agreed to everything. He had promptly turned over all his money and the locket, and promised also to lend him half his pay for the remainder of the war — even though he knew the captain meant any and all such "loans" to be permanent gifts.

It was not until the war had finally ended and Ethan was preparing to return to Little Mound that it became clear: Captain Potter had no intention of letting the incident die. Although Potter could no longer threaten him with the humiliation of a court martial, because the Confederate Army no longer existed and all crimes of war were rumored already forgiven, he could still

308

threaten him with the prospect of telling George's family the truth about the questionable nature of their son's death. It was not too late for them to find out their son had died a coward and at the hands of his own best friend.

Because Ethan still could not bear the thought that the Martins might find out the truth, he had allowed himself to be manipulated into working full time for the captain.

The way he saw it, he had no choice but to agree to do whatever the captain asked of him—*short of killing*. He had stood his ground on that issue. He would work for the captain, doing whatever grisly job there was to do; but he would never kill again.

Believing himself to be about as worthless as a human being could get after having murdered his own best friend out of sheer carelessness, Ethan felt it was downright appropriate that he should be forced to spend the rest of his life laboring for someone like Jeremiah. It seemed like just punishment for the terrible thing he had done.

To prevent his own family from ever finding out just how vile he had become, he vowed that very same day never to return home. He thought it would be better to let his family think he had died a soldier's death. The following morning the captain wrote a letter to Ethan's family, proclaiming him dead. It had also explained why there had been no body to be shipped home. Ethan had then mailed the letter himself.

"John, I really am too tired right now to discuss it," Leona said when she turned to lock the side door. Now that she was finished restocking her shelves, all she wanted to do was go home, take a long, soapy bath, then crawl into bed and get a full night's sleep.

It was unusually cold for March and already the day

had grown dark; and Leona was in no mood to hear John tell her what she should or should not do about Ethan. "Besides, now that I'm restocked, I really don't have to worry about having my brother declared dead for several months."

"But what's to be gained by waiting?" John asked, grasping her by the shoulder, forcing her to turn around and look at him. Because of the darkness, she could barely make out the angry lines on his face. "Either your brother is dead or he isn't."

Leona felt too drained both physically and emotionally to argue with him. "Which would remain true whether I have him declared so or not, therefore I really don't see why it is so important that I do it right away, especially when I no longer need that loan."

"But eventually you will need it," John said, bending forward in his effort to convince her. His eyebrows dipped low and his expression hardened with something beyond his normal concern. "A thousand dollars worth of merchandise isn't enough to keep you going two months, much less all the way into the middle of the summer, which happens to be about the earliest you can hope to get any money out of all those customers who still owe you from last year."

While he continued to hold her imprisoned with one hand, he gently stroked her cheek with the other, using the outer curve of his index finger, thinking that might coax her into doing what he wanted. "It's either go ahead and have Ethan declared dead so you will be able to get that loan when you need it or finally come to your senses and agree to marry me." While continuing to stroke her cheek, he bent even closer, as if the proximity of his face to hers might affect her decision. "Just think, Leona, if you would just climb down off that high horse of yours and agree to marry me, you could have just about anything your heart desired. I happen to be a very wealthy man."

Leona frowned, aware her skin did not respond to John's touch in the same way it had responded to Lathe's. She felt no response to John's touch at all, only an annoying sense of boredom. And a strong desire to be set free. "I told you. I don't want to talk about this right now. I haven't had any sleep in well over thirty hours. I am extremely tired."

Thinking that it might be to his advantage, John continued to hold her with one hand while stroking first her cheek then her hair with the other. "All you have to do is agree to marry me and not only will I let you go home and get some sleep, I will have you there in less than five minutes." He gestured toward the familiar bradded Simpson carriage that stood directly in front of her store.

Leona clenched her teeth, angry over his refusal to let go of her arm. "I don't want a ride. I just want to be left alone." When she tried to free her shoulder by jerking back, he tightened his grasp more. If it had not been for the thickness of her shawl, the grip might have been painful. "John, let go of me."

"Not until you have agreed to marry me," he stated firmly. "I'm tired of having to ask."

"And I'm tired of *hearing* you ask," she said with a defiant toss of her head. Having finally reached the breaking point, she narrowed her brown eyes and glared at him, aware of how dramatically he had changed during the past few weeks. Or perhaps she was the one who had changed. Either way, she had grown tired of his constant attempts to dominate her. "How many times do I have to tell you *no* before you finally catch on to the fact I will never, *ever* marry you? At one time, I may have considered you a good friend, but all that has changed. You are *not* the sort of man I would ever want to spend the rest of my life with."

"Oh? And *who* is?" John asked, his teeth gritted in a poor attempt to hide his temper. "Hasn't it ever oc-

311

curred to you that if you decide to wait around for the perfect man to appear, you will never get married. There just aren't any such animals." He let out a sharp breath, then spoke in a slightly milder tone. "At least with me you would be guaranteed a good life. You would want for very little."

Leona bit into the sensitive lining of her lower lip while she tried not to let the unexpected images of Lathe interfere with what she had to say. "Truth is, John, I'd want for quite a lot. And because of that, I'd rather die destitute and alone than spend even one day married to someone like you."

"You don't mean that," he admonished. The muscles in his jaw flexed rhythmically while he glared down into her defiant gaze.

"Don't I?" She again tried to wrench herself free of his grasp only to find herself suddenly locked in his arms.

"Leona, please, I love you. I always have and I always will," he then attempted to force a kiss on her, thinking to bend her to his will by arousing her innermost passions.

Appalled by his behavior, Leona twisted with all her might to avoid the unwanted contact of his mouth against hers and she screamed for him to let go. When that did not discourage his attempt to kiss her, she stepped as hard as she could on his foot, planning to break free when he jumped back in surprise.

But when all her forceful action did was make him try even harder, she felt a constricting sense of panic grip her throat. She did not often find herself in situations she could not handle and it terrified her to realize John's conduct was beyond her control. Because it was so late, there were very few people left on the street in that part of town; and of those still milling about, none would be willing to go against a powerful man like John Davis.

312

Or so she thought.

"Let go of her!" she heard, just a split second before she saw Lathe's furious face coming toward them.

When his harsh command did not bring the appropriate response, Lathe tried again, this time grabbing John by the shoulder and jerking him around to face him. "I said let go of her!"

"Oh? And just who are you to tell me what to do?" John asked, finally letting go of Leona, but foolishly taking a swing at Lathe. He missed by several inches.

"I already told you who I am. I am a friend of Leona's," he said just seconds before delivering a hard, sound blow to John's chin. "A very *close* friend."

The force of the blow sent John sprawling onto the planked walk. After a stunned second, he pushed himself back to his feet then raised his hand as if prepared to try once again to deliver a blow of his own. But after glimpsing the pistol strapped to Lathe's side, he quickly lowered the hand and used it to brush the dirt from his clothing instead.

"That was a very foolish mistake," John snapped, so angry over what had happened, his hands shook. He reached up to touch the reddened area along his chin then grimaced at the resulting pain. "I can now have you arrested for assault."

Lathe shifted his weight to one leg and cocked his head at a haughty angle to indicate how very little that bothered him. After having seen what John was trying to do to Leona, he was too angry to care whether he ended up in jail or not.

Leona had taken the opportunity to move away from John and now spoke from a safe distance away. "You try to, and I'll have *you* arrested for the exact same reason."

John's eyes narrowed as if unable to believe Leona would do such a thing. "But I didn't do anything to you I haven't done before."

"Then I'll have you arrested for *multiple* assaults," she

313

responded defiantly. "Because unless they've changed the laws that protect a lady from a man's unwanted advances, you happen to be every bit as guilty of criminal assault as Lathe. Probably more so since he was merely defending my honor."

"What honor?" John ground out bitterly, then rather than continue the argument out in the open where someone might overhear, he stalked furiously toward his carriage. He paused just long enough to cast another angry glance over his shoulder. "Leona, you have made a very serious mistake tonight by not agreeing to marry me."

"That may be so, but it is definitely a mistake I can live with," she retorted, her heart hammering at such a savage rate, she could barely breathe. The fact that John was leaving without causing any further trouble was reason enough to set her heart racing but it was the realization that Lathe was the one who had come to her rescue that sent her pulses soaring.

"You'll regret having said that," John warned, then climbed on into his carriage. "Before summer is here, you will come crawling back to me on your hands and knees begging for my forgiveness."

"Don't hold your breath," she said, for no other reason than she wanted the last word, then she slowly smiled. "On second thought, do hold your breath. Blue is one of my favorite colors."

John glared at her for a long moment before turning his attention back to Lathe. "I'd advise you to get out of Little Mound while you still can. You've caused nothing but trouble since you got here and I've had just about enough."

"Is that a threat?" Lathe asked, grinning to show how little the words had bothered him.

"Consider it a bit of friendly advice," John said then snapped his reins hard, sending the carriage forward with a clattering jolt.

Lathe watched while the dark shape jangled quickly out of sight. When he spoke again, he sounded more amused than angry. "You know the more I get to know that fellow, the less I like him." But when he then turned to look at Leona, all trace of humor left his face. Several locks of hair had pulled loose during the struggle and her shawl was twisted about her shoulders in a rumpled heap. "He didn't hurt you did he?"

"Thanks to you, he never got much of a chance," she said, and smiled to show her gratitude, aware that whatever anger he had felt toward her earlier was now gone. "It was lucky for me that you passed by when you did."

"I wasn't exactly passing by," he admitted. "I was on my way here to see you. I wanted to explain why I have been acting so strangely toward you these past few days—and to apologize." He linked his arm with hers then turned and started along the boardwalk in the direction of her house.

Leona's insides spun in a crazed rush of giddiness, for she realized that he was finally ready to tear down whatever barriers he had set up between them. "And why have you been acting so strangely?"

Lathe continued to walk, but turned his head to look at her so she could see that he meant what he was about to say.

When he had first decided to take George's advice and apologize, he had not realized just how far he intended to take that apology. But now he knew he had to be as open as possible with her, if he wanted her fully to understand his behavior. "The truth is, I think I am falling in love with you and I don't want to do that."

Leona's eyebrows arched at such a confusing statement. She didn't know whether to be overjoyed because he had the same as admitted to having fallen in love with her, or feel insulted because he didn't *want* to have

315

those sort of feelings for her. "I don't understand. Why would you say that?"

"Why would I admit that I'm falling in love with you?" Lathe asked, although he knew it was the other comment she questioned. "I guess because you happen to be one of the most beautiful, captivating women I've ever had the misfortune to meet."

One of Leona's eyebrows dropped but the other remained sharply arched. She was still not sure what to make of this odd conversation. "No, I meant why is it you don't want to fall in love with me? Are you afraid of me?"

Aware that what he was about to say was very serious and not wanting her to take his next comments lightly, he stopped, then turned to face her. Because of the shadows created by the store awning and the fact that they stood half a block from the nearest street lamp, there was barely enough light to see her expression. How beautiful she looked — even with her hair all askew and her clothing rumpled.

Impulsively, he reached out to smooth an errant lock of her hair into place, pleased when she closed her eyes in response to his gentle touch.

"It has nothing to do with being afraid, little one," he admitted, thinking she deserved as much of the truth as he dared give her. "I don't want to fall in love with you, because I can't stay and make you a permanent part of my life. As soon as I find out where Zeb Turner has gone, I'll be leaving."

"But you could always come back here after you've finished," she suggested, wondering why he hadn't thought of that himself. "After you catch the man and finally do whatever it is you think you have to do to him, you could return."

"But that might be years from now," he explained, wanting her to see that it was not quite as simple as she had made it sound. "I have already spent nearly five

316

years trying to hunt down Zeb Turner, and it might be five more before I finally do catch up with him. I can't ask you to wait that long."

"But what if I don't mind waiting—however many years it takes?" she asked. Her huge brown eyes glimmered with hope. "What if I'm willing to wait for however long it does take?"

Lathe felt a wide range of emotions while he gazed at that hopeful expression, unable to believe she might already care for him. "Are you trying to tell me that you already do love me?"

Feeling a moment of uncharacteristic shyness, Leona looked away for a second but brought her gaze back to meet his before responding. "That depends on what it is you've been trying to tell me. Do you really love me or is it just that you *think* you do?"

A tiny grin twitched at the outer corner of Lathe's mouth, causing a tiny dimple to quiver in his cheek while he considered what he should say.

Although what he longed to do was take her into his arms and confess the truth—that he *was* already deeply and devoutly in love with her—he was still not all that sure it was the *right* thing to do. She might be perfectly willing to wait for as long it took him to fulfill his promise to his brother, but was *he* willing to put her through that? Did he have the *right* to put her through such a long wait?

"Let me just say I have developed strong, definite feelings toward you and leave it at that," he finally responded, avoiding a direct answer all together. "After all, I really don't know too much about you and you don't really know all that much about me either."

"That's a very good point," she said with a brisk nod, though she already knew enough about him to recognize how she felt whenever he was near. His touch alone sent her heart racing at astonishing speeds. "It seems to me that every time I have ever bothered to ask

317

you anything about your past, you have always managed to change the subject."

"There's an art to that," he admitted and let his grin grow full width before resuming his walk with her.

Despite the unseasonably cold temperature, Leona felt oddly warm and contented walking beside Lathe and did not really mind that he had yet to tell her what she wanted to know.

For the next several minutes, they continued together in silence, each immersed temporarily in his or her own thoughts. It was not until they turned onto Maple Street that Leona finally broke the companionable silence.

"Am I to gather that you are no longer angry with me?" she asked, then closed her eyes briefly to enjoy the gentle pressure of his arm against hers. She opened them just in time to notice it was time to step down and cross yet another street.

"I was never really angry with you," Lathe admitted, his eyes instinctively drawn to hers. While continuing their stroll, he studied every intricate detail of her beauty. Even with the night shadows moving slowly across her face there was a delicate glow about her. "I just thought I was angry, but that was before George so kindly pointed out that what I was feeling wasn't anger but jealousy."

"Jealousy? Because of John?" Leona shook her head at such a preposterous notion. Although John was reasonably handsome and extremely wealthy, he paled in comparison to Lathe.

"No, not because of John. It is easy to see that John is little more than an annoyance to you. I was more jealous of George." He still felt a tiny pain clutch his chest when he thought of the two of them in each other's arms.

"Because of George?" Her face twisted into a peculiar expression, finding it hard to believe anyone could be

318

jealous of the sort of feelings she had for George. "But why?"

Lathe hesitated, feeling awkward about having jumped to such an unfair conclusion, especially now that he had been told the truth. "Because of all the time you've been spending with him lately and because I also saw you in his arms. I guess I just presumed the worst. I decided you cared for him a lot more than you were willing to let on."

"When was I in George's arms?" she asked, having forgotten the earlier incident.

"Early this morning, long before the sun ever came up."

Leona's forehead wrinkled while she tried to remember having been in George's arms, then smoothed again when it finally dawned on her. "But that was just a hug between friends."

"I know that now."

Her forehead wrinkled again when she realized just how odd a situation that had been. "What on earth were you doing out at that hour?"

"I was out taking a walk when I happened to pass near the store and notice the light," he looked away, feeling awkward about what he had done. "When I, ah, happened to glance in through the front window, I saw you two holding each other and laughing. I stood there just long enough to see him bend down and kiss you."

"But why would anyone be out taking a walk at that hour?" she asked, thinking it peculiar behavior.

"I had some serious thinking to do and I can think better when I'm out walking," he admitted. "You can imagine my surprise when I found you and George out at that time of night."

"We weren't exactly out," she corrected, wondering if he yet understood the innocence of the situation. "We were busy putting up the merchandise he had just brought back from Marshall."

319

"That's what George later told me," Lathe admitted then leaned forward to open the gate in front of her house. He waited until he had closed it again before he continued. "But at the time, I had no idea why you two would be there—just that you were there and in his arms, and that he felt it was perfectly all right to bend down and kiss you."

"But it wasn't that sort of kiss," she insisted, thinking he was still not convinced.

"I realize that now. It wasn't like the ones we've shared."

Caught off guard by the sultry tone in his voice, Leona glanced away, her whole body tingling from the vivid memories of his kiss. "As long as you understand that George and I are just friends."

"And what about us? What are we?" He glanced around to make sure no one was coming up the street or peeking out a nearby window, then he pulled her gently into his arms. "Are we just friends?"

"I don't know what we are," she answered honestly, finding it suddenly hard to take a needed breath. When Lathe then bent slowly forward, clearly intent on kissing her again, her heart hammered with such strong, concentrated force, it felt as if it might burst right through the walls of her chest. "I just know how I feel about you."

Lathe paused with his mouth so close to hers she could feel his breath warm against her cheek.

"And I know how I feel about you. Somehow you have managed to keep me sane and yet make me crazy all at the same time," he admitted in a low husky voice just seconds before his lips descended over hers in what turned out to be an amazingly tender kiss.

Chapter Seventeen

It was not until Lathe had pulled away to gaze longingly into her eyes that Leona realized just how strongly she had yearned for him to kiss her—and how desperately she wanted this moment to last. When he dropped his hands from her sides and stepped back, a wintery chill swept over her, making her wish he'd take her into his arms again and keep her warm forever.

"Would you like to come inside for a cup of coffee?" she asked, not ready for him to leave. "It won't take but a few minutes to prepare a fresh pot." Had she thought to bring home any food that day, she would have offered to make him an entire supper. She blushed at the thought of wanting to please him in such a way. It was not like her to have such domestic thoughts.

"I couldn't ask you to do that," he said, not wanting to put her out but at the same time not wanting to say *no* either. He could tell by looking at her that she needed some sleep, yet he still did not want to leave.

"But you didn't ask," she pointed out, her eyes sparkling with anticipation. "I volunteered. Besides, I could use a cup or two of the magic brew myself."

"But aren't you planning to go on to bed?" he asked, thinking it odd. "According to George, you were up all night, working like a madwoman. Aren't you exhausted?"

"No," she answered honestly. For some reason, all feeling of exhaustion had left her hours ago. "Besides, you haven't had a chance to examine my injury since early yesterday morning." After having pointed that out, she immediately started toward the house, hoping he would follow.

"That's true," he said and eagerly fell into step beside her. "And I should be ashamed for having neglected you. I've been by the Newlands' house twice today to check on Darlene's progress yet I haven't been by to check on yours since yesterday."

She paused halfway then turned to look at him. "So, you'll stay and have coffee with me?"

"I'd be delighted."

Linking his arm through hers, he walked with her up the stairs and to the front door. He waited for her to unlock the door before bending forward to open it for her. Together they entered the darkened hallway.

"It'll take just a second to light a lamp," Leona said, hurrying further into the familiar room. "Go ahead and make yourself comfortable. Take off your coat. Loosen your tie."

Rather than follow her into the darkness, Lathe remained by the door while he quickly shrugged out of his coat.

"I guess your dog has finally decided to accept me," he said, wanting to keep a conversation alive, feeling oddly distanced from her even though he knew she was only a few yards away. "He didn't bark at me tonight."

Having located the lamp, Leona felt for the compartment beneath that held the matches. "Either that or he's gotten loose again and is out roaming the streets looking for something to steal," she responded with a chuckle, for once not caring what harm the dog might cause. She was too happy to allow anything so trivial to bother her.

While she singled out a match from the six or so in

the tiny drawer, she heard a noise behind her and gasped. A scant second later, both heard a deep, coarse growl in the darkness. "But then again," she said, having recognized Scrap's familiar growl, "it could be that he has found his way into the house again and is right here with us."

She struck the match just in time to watch Scraps make a lunge toward Lathe, knocking him to the floor with the force of his front paws. "Scraps, no! Scraps get off of him!"

But Scraps had little intention of letting his prisoner free. While continuing to stand over his prey, with his snarling face hovering barely inches above Lathe's startled expression, the animal continued to growl with a deep, menacing tone.

"Scraps, I said get off him!" Leona shouted again, quickly lighting the lamp so she could see to rescue Lathe. When she arrived at their side, she bent over the growling dog intending to drag him away by his collar only to discover the collar completely gone. She tried circling her arms around his neck to pull him off, but Scraps managed to wriggle free of her grasp each time, determined to intimidate their visitor.

"Perhaps if you offered to feed him," Lathe suggested, his eyes wide while he continued to stare up into the dog's snarling face.

Afraid to take his eyes off the animal, he felt for his coat, which he'd been holding just a few seconds ago, eager to find it and toss it over the dog's head, but his fingers did not brush against any fabric. Evidently the coat had flown in a different direction.

He next considered reaching down and pulling his pistol out of his holster to have it ready in case the animal decided to bite him, but then he remembered the animal's obvious aversion to sidearms and decided that such a move might provoke him into an even worse frenzy. He decided his best course of action at that particular moment was to take no action at all. He waited for Leona to do something.

"Feed him? Good idea," Leona said, knowing Scraps was always ready to eat. Hurriedly, she turned toward the kitchen. "Scraps, come on, boy. Food, Scraps, *food!*"

Scraps lifted his head just long enough to glance in Leona's general direction, then looked back down at Lathe, who still lay motionless beneath him. He tilted his hairy head to the side as if trying to decide which he considered more important — eating or terrorizing — then suddenly he leaped from Lathe's chest and trotted happily down the hall toward the kitchen.

Lathe let out a relieved breath while he pushed himself to his feet. He spotted his coat nearby and when he bent to pick it up, wondered if he shouldn't just put it back on and leave. But then he thought of Leona and the kiss they had just shared outside and tossed the coat haphazardly across a nearby table. He then brushed the dust off his trousers and shirt while glancing down the hall toward the kitchen.

He had to do something about that dog.

But rather than provoke the animal, he decided he'd do that something later. For now, he felt it best to stay away from the kitchen and wait near the front door for Leona's return. After several minutes, he heard the back door slam and then heard several muffled, but decidedly feminine maledictions coming from the side yard.

When Leona returned minutes later, her hair was even more mussed than before — and she looked even more beautiful. Her cheeks had acquired the same high color of pink as adorned her dress and her eyes were huge, and round, and sparkling from the lamplight.

"He's back on his chain," she said after reentering the room, not knowing whether to apologize or laugh. Now that the crisis was over, the image of the huge dog pinning Lathe to the floor struck her as funny. Finally, her desire to laugh won over, but she tried to hide her laughter behind a delicately raised hand.

Lathe cleared his throat and tried to look genuinely insulted when all he felt at that moment was a deep-seated desire to take her into his arms again.

"I gather that you think it is amusing for a visitor in your home to be knocked to the floor by a deranged animal," he said, advancing toward her, his blue eyes narrowed into a playful, yet menacing expression. "What sort of person are you?"

Leona couldn't help it. She tried to look dutifully chastised, but a bubble of laughter slipped past her trembling lips. "If you could have seen your face!"

"Funny was it?" he asked, continuing slowly toward her, stalking her much as a lion would its intended prey.

Aware of his sinister expression, Leona kept her gaze locked with his while she took several steps backward.

"No, of course it wasn't funny," she lied, laughter still bubbling inside her while she continued to back away — thinking she was headed toward the nearest door, where she could flee to safety.

"Then why are you laughing?" He arched his eyebrows accusingly and continued slowly forward, his body motionless except for the agile movement of his long, muscular legs.

"Who me? Laughing?" she asked. She tried to sound perplexed by such an accusation but could not stop chuckling long enough to make it believable. It was not until she felt her back bump against the wall and she realized she had totally misjudged her direction, that her laughter came to an abrupt halt.

Startled, she turned her head just long enough to find out where that door had gone and she frowned when she noticed she had missed the thing by several yards. With her brown eyes stretched to their limits, she returned her gaze to Lathe's and found that he was already upon her. With a fathomless expression, he braced his sturdy arms against the wall, one beside either shoulder to prevent her escape, then bent forward until their eyes were but inches apart.

"Do you know what I do to people who make the mistake of laughing at my misfortunes?"

"No, what?" she asked in a tiny voice, not really afraid of what he might do, but wishing she knew exactly what to expect. With a wavering smile, she lifted her hand to brush some dirt from his shirt, as if her only desire were to be of some help.

"I usually try to show them how it feels."

He slowly inched his hands inward until his wrists were pressed firmly against her shoulders, sending a flood of warmth through her body.

"How what feels?" she asked, finding it hard to concentrate on his words when his mouth was so very close to hers.

He then tucked his hands between her back and the wall, bringing her forward slightly. "I think it is only fair you discover how it feels to be pinned to the floor by some deranged animal."

With his determined gaze holding her prisoner, he slipped his arms on around her and pulled her further away from the wall. Then ever so gently, he lowered her onto a nearby braided rug.

"I hope you aren't planning to do something you will regret," Leona said, swallowing hard, but not out of fear. She knew he would not hurt her.

"No, I don't think it is anything I will ever regret," he stated and continued to gaze deeply into her eyes while he positioned himself directly above her by bracing his arms on either side of her.

"Well, then I hope you aren't planning to do something *I* will regret," she said, already running her tongue over her lips in anticipation of the kiss she knew was to come. Her whole body tingled with awareness while she considered how exciting it was to find herself suddenly in such a compromising position.

"I don't think it is anything you will regret either," he vowed just seconds before his lips descended to hers, offering a generous kiss that sent her senses scattering.

Overwhelmed by the staggering desire she felt for Lathe, and by the deep hunger he had so easily brought to life inside her, Leona closed her eyes to immerse herself in the wondrous feelings that had accompanied this sudden outburst of passion. For once, she was glad Scraps had chosen to make his home there, for it was the animal's impetuous behavior that had led to such a deeply sensuous kiss. Never had she known such rapture.

Lathe groaned, overwhelmed by his own flaming desire. Although the kiss had started out to be little more than a playful sampling of her sweetness—a tender exploration of the woman who had slowly but surely been driving him insane with her bold beauty and her headstrong opinions—it quickly exploded something far more demanding.

With the passion of a man who had long denied himself something he had not even been fully aware he wanted until now, he bent his elbows, which lowered his body to a more intimate closeness, while he continued to devour her with yet more deeply demanding kisses.

Leona's eyes flew open when she felt the gentle weight of his body pressed against hers; but rather than react with some show of resistance, she let her eyelids drift slowly shut again. As of yet, she saw no real reason to make him stop. She had become far too captivated by the swirling tide of delightful sensations that spilled languidly through her body.

Even when his hand slipped beneath her head and lifted her mouth, she did nothing to try to stop or even slow his ardor. She was too caught up in the spinning vortex of pleasure Lathe had created inside her, unable

327

to believe the strength of her tempestuous desire, unable to cope with its explosive force.

Instead of offering a proper protest or making any real effort to free herself from his impassioned embrace, she lifted her arms to encircle his strong neck and shyly allowed her fingers to slip into the soft thickness of his curling brown hair.

Leona had yet to show any indication of stopping him, and Lathe's kisses became hungrier still. He teased the sensitive curve of her slightly parted lips with the tip of his tongue until they divided further—parting far enough to allow him to slip inside and touch the moist warmth of her mouth.

Eagerly, hungrily, he sampled her sweetness, but a sampling proved not enough.

Never had he wanted to possess a woman more than he wanted to possess Leona. Although he knew he could not commit himself to a lifetime of such pleasure, he yearned to know what it was like to make love to her.

The kiss became instantly more demanding.

Leona gasped in response to the increased level of passion. Suddenly the room did not have enough air. She took in what oxygen she could with short, rapid breaths.

The warm feel of his lips while they fiercely caressed hers, along with the gentle teasing of his tongue inside her mouth was slowly driving her to a fine point of madness—and beyond. Wave after fiery wave of pure liquid desire poured from her heart and into her bloodstream, possessing her body quickly and completely.

That strange inner occurrence, coupled with the feel of her breasts pressed intimately against the smooth plane of his hard, muscular chest made her cry out with an internal need she had never known existed. Suddenly she wanted him to know how gloriously he had affected her and she pressed her mouth harder against his, hoping that by doing so she could share with him some of the passion she felt.

Leona had never experienced such a startling response to anyone or anything in her life. A fire raged inside her — a fire so intense so all-consuming it threatened to envelope her entire being. The magnitude of what she felt then was as frightening as it was thrilling. Her heart soared as if it had taken wing.

Still, she sensed a very real danger lurking nearby and knew she should try to push him away before the kiss progressed any further. But it was as if he held some sort of mysterious power over her, a power so strong that it made her body refuse her own inner commands. She felt utterly helpless but at the same time wondrously alive, more alive than she had ever felt in her life. Soon the feeling of danger ebbed and she was slowly lured into an even higher state of madness.

It was not until Lathe shifted his weight to one side so he could move his hand to the tiny buttons at the back of her dress that the nagging sense of danger again returned. Then seconds later, when he opened the dress enough to slip his hand inside, gently pushing the soft material downward until he'd exposed the camisole beneath, Leona finally managed to locate the sense of mind and the inner strength she needed to break her mouth free from his deep, hungry kisses.

"Lathe, I don't think —" she tried to say, but the gasping words of reason became lost when he again covered her mouth with his and resumed working his special magic. This time, when he lowered his weight, she had a strange, uncanny sense of belonging. Suddenly she felt she *belonged* in Lathe's strong arms, *belonged* to his rapturous kiss.

Because of this strange new sense of belonging, any lingering desire she felt to stop him slowly faded into nothing, until she lacked any desire to stop him at all. When he eventually slipped his hand beneath the thin fabric of her camisole and claimed the breast he had so

329

eagerly sought, all she could do was moan softly in response.

Her whole body trembled from the effect of his gentle touch on her naked skin while she arched instinctively toward that touch. She was lost in a churning sea of emotions so strong, so turbulent, she could no longer concentrate. She could only respond, respond to the gentle ministrations of the man she loved. Respond to the only person who had ever made her feel like a woman.

While Lathe continued to explore the full roundness of Leona's breast, more of the deliciously warm, starkly tantalizing sensations rippled through her, until she became delirious with some unknown need. She closed her eyes and fought for each breath, reveling in the heated sensations that now burned brilliantly inside her.

Filled with a longing every bit as potent as Leona's, Lathe pulled away just long enough to gaze down into her drowsy expression and he knew by the eager way she strained her breast against his palm that her passions had become fully ignited, burning deep within her. He knew that he could take her within the time required to remove any necessary clothing, and she would let him; but he chose to move more slowly. The startling realization that he loved her made him want this undertaking to be as pleasurable for her as he knew it would be for him.

Gently, he tugged on one of the satin sashes holding her camisole until it easily gave way. Leona trembled when he swept the thin fabric aside, giving himself full view of the thrusting, round breast beneath.

Eager for more, he quickly rose on one knee and turned his attention to the rest of her clothing. Piece by piece, he removed every garment, until her entire body was open to his view. He felt his breath lodge in his throat when she finally lay naked before him. How gloriously beautiful she was.

For a brief moment, he knelt beside her and gazed longingly at her, then he slowly removed his own clothing. His eyes were dark with a consuming desire when he lay down beside her again and slipped back into the warm circle of her arms. Slowly, and deliberately, before returning to the sweetness of her mouth, he traced tiny kisses along her cheek and jaw until she bent her head back to accommodate him better.

Unable to resist the slender column of her ivory neck, he trailed the feathery kisses ever downward, across the pulsating hollow of her throat, until he eventually reached one of her ripened breasts.

When his mouth finally claimed the hardened peak, Leona's fingers curled compulsively, digging into the firm muscles of his back. His tongue gently pulled at the sensitive tip, causing her to moan aloud in response to the startling heat that had shot through her like summer lightning. The pain was as exquisite as it was unbearable.

Delirious from the onslaught of such sweet torment, she offered no protest when he moved to place more of his weight on top of her. His mouth returned to hers for another magnificent kiss while his hands continued to roam freely over each splendid curve of her body. His fingertips gently teased and taunted while coming ever closer to the sensitive peaks of her breasts with light, circular motions.

Leona arched her back, wanting him to hurry and reach his obvious destination while her own hands roamed eagerly over the manly shape of his body. She explored first the firm muscles along his back then the rippling muscles along his arms. His body's warmth intensified the already sensitive tips of her fingers when she felt the rounded surface of his shoulders, then the gentle contours along his back.

She strained her arms to feel the taut, lean muscles

that were a part of his hips and upper thighs. His skin felt good to her touch and she marveled at the many differences in his body as compared to hers.

While Lathe proceeded to sample the sweetness of Leona's mouth, he continued his exploration of her body until he was finally forced to give in to his desperate need and grasp the straining breast. When he again teased the tip with the side of his thumb while cupping the rest with his fingers, Leona brought her shoulders off the floor, another result of her newly awakened passion.

Writhing in sweet ecstasy, she was not certain how long she could bear the tender torment and she clutched at his shoulders while the startling sensations continued their rapturous assault. She tossed her head restlessly against the deeply demanding ache that filled her. She longed for him to stop, before the powerful sensations became too much to endure, but found herself arching ever higher, eager to give him easy access to whatever pleased him. She shuddered with the delectable sensations building inside her, higher and higher, degree by degree, until she felt she might burst.

A strange, throbbing pain had centered itself somewhere low inside her and had reached such a magnitude she could no longer endure it. Her body craved release from the sensual onslaught raging within her, although she did not yet understand what might bring her that release.

"Lathe, please," she moaned aloud, so lost to the glorious haze that surrounded her, she was unaware she had spoken at all.

Drawing in first one breast, then the other one last time, Lathe finally moved to fulfill her, gently and lovingly, until the barrier inside her was broken. He then moved with gradual force, until he drove their wildest longings, their deepest desires to an ultimate height.

When release came for Leona only moments before

it came for Lathe, it was both wondrous and shattering. She bit into the soft flesh of her lip to keep from crying aloud her pleasure. Her fingers dug deep into his skin while she rose to meet him time and time again. Suddenly she knew what it meant to be a woman. Never had she felt so fulfilled. So deeply satisfied. So gloriously alive.

If only such feelings could be hers forever. If only the man she loved wasn't so obsessed with finding Zeb Turner.

Slowly, Leona's happiness plummeted until she was overcome with a morose feeling of sadness. If only he could learn to love her in the same way she loved him — then maybe he would be willing give up his search for Zeb Turner and be hers forever. It was all she could think about for the remainder of the evening, even after Lathe had left.

She went on to bed but was too restless to sleep, even after having spent so many hours awake. It amazed her to realize how important Lathe had become in her life. She could not stop thinking about him nor what the future would be like without him.

What she had to do became clear. She had to find a way to make Lathe forget his strange quest to capture Zeb Turner and she had to make him stay right there in Little Mound with her.

Sarah knelt in front of her father's chair, her blue eyes round with concern. "But, Papa, I have already invited him," she said, her tone as pleading as a young child's. "You have to let him come."

"No I don't have to. And you can just *uninvite* him," her father replied sternly, so angry with what his daughter had done that he refused to look at her and stared out the window instead. "I told you I don't want nobody but family in this house as long as we have Zeb here. There's a man still out there somewhere who wants to kill him, just for having done his duty the way he saw it in a time of war. I can't help it. I promised Zeb he would be safe while he's here."

"But he's doing so much better," Sarah pointed out. She leaned forward to cover one of her father's work-worn hands with hers, hoping a gentle touch might help bend his will. "He's able to get around with the use of that cane you made him. And if he continues to mend at that rate, he should be ready to leave here in a week or two."

Or at least she hoped so. She did not like the way the man looked at her whenever they were alone, which was another reason she wanted George to come. She hoped that once Zeb got a good look at how strong and solid her George was, he would give up any foolish notions he might have concerning the two of them.

"Then invite your new gentleman friend a week or two after he's gone," Bradford Martin suggested, interrupting his daughter before she had a chance to finish.

"I don't want to have to wait that long. Please, Papa. I want you and Mama to meet him now." She pressed his hand to her cheek to emphasize how important it was to her. George was a wanderer. She had to get him interested in her right away or chance losing him forever. "And I want him to meet you. Besides, what harm could it do for one person outside the family to know about Mr. Turner?"

"Plenty of harm if that one person happened to go back into town and mention the fact that we are hiding an injured man out here," he said, finally weakening enough to look at her.

"But we aren't *hiding* him," she pointed out, aware by the way his foot had started to tap that his resistance was slowly wearing away. "We are simply offering him a safe refuge. Besides, George wouldn't tell anyone about Zeb. Not if I explain to him why it is so important for

334

him to keep quiet."

"How can you be so sure? You yourself admitted you've only known the man for a week."

When his foot quit tapping and his shoulders sagged, she knew she nearly had him. Aware of how very hard it was for him to resist her dimples, she sank them deep in her cheeks and looked up at him through her lowered blonde eyelashes.

"Oh, but Leona has known him for nearly *two* weeks."

Bradford Martin shook his head, unable to keep his stern face. "For two whole weeks? Why he must seem like part of the family by now."

"So, he can come?"

Bradford stared down at his beautiful, golden-haired daughter for quite some time, then lifted his free hand to stroke her fair cheek. His blue eyes brimmed with a father's adoration when he finally relented. "I guess. But I'll give in only if you get his word that he won't tell anyone about Zeb before he ever sets foot in this house."

"I promise," Sarah said, her smile deepened as she pressed his roughened hand to her cheek again. "I love you, Papa."

"And I love you, too, Sarah," he conceded wearily then bent forward to kiss her shining hair. "Only heaven knows why, but I love you dearly. And if you believe your young man is the type that won't tell, then I have to believe it, too." Then his voice took on a teasing tone. "And who knows? Maybe I'll be able to get you married off to this one. After all, you *are* twenty-four years old. It's time I had grandchildren."

"Oh, Papa," she admonished even though the thought of marrying George and having children made her feel all giddy inside. "You never do give up on anything do you?"

Bradford stroked his face thoughtfully, then shrugged. "Seems to me I just did."

"Until Caldwell suddenly showed up here in Little Mound, everything was working out just fine between Leona and me. That's why I want you to find out why he's still in Little Mound and what it would take to make him leave," John said, slamming his fist hard across the top of his desk. His hazel eyes darkened with malicious intent. "I also want to know who that man is he's been following and why catching him is so very important to him. The sheriff told me there was a wanted poster out on the man he's after, so it shouldn't be too hard to find out more about him. I imagine the sheriff who arrested him did a thorough investigation. I want to know every little thing you can find out about either one of them. And I want to know yesterday."

"But what about George Parkinson? I thought you wanted me to find out about him."

"Well, it's been a week and you haven't managed to come up with squat on Parkinson," John pointed out. His expression hardened with anger. "All you know is that the money was wired to him by someone named Potter who refuses to respond to any of your inquiries and who the local sheriff has never even heard of. I just hope you manage to do a better job of finding out about this Dr. Caldwell."

The detective arched his shoulders at the intended insult, but kept any anger out of his voice. "If he really is a doctor and is in his early thirties, then I should be able to find out something about him pretty quick. There aren't that many schools that teach medicine in this country. It's just a matter of sending telegraph messages to each one."

"Then do it. I am eager to know exactly what it will take to get him out of my life," he paused, then corrected. "Or at least out of Leona's life. Look, Simpson, if you can't find anything I can use against him personally, then try to come up with something that will make her see that drifter for what he really is."

"I'll do what I can, sir," Simpson said with a decisive nod, then stood. "And I'll keep trying to find out more about Parkinson, too."

"As long as you remember that Caldwell is more important," John cautioned. His nostrils flared with contempt when he lifted his hand to touch his bruised jaw. "Do *whatever* it takes to get the information I need."

Chapter Eighteen

"On your way to open the store?" Lathe called out just before he reined his horse to a slower pace and turned him in closer to the sidewalk where Leona walked with her attention seemingly focused on the ground just a few feet in front of her. His pulses raced at the mere sight of her.

Having been unaware of his presence, Leona's hand flew to her throat when she turned to look at him. It startled her to find the object of her thoughts only a few yards away. She had not heard his approach. "What are you doing here?"

"I was on my way out of town and thought I'd stop by your house to see if you might like to have dinner with me tonight," Lathe said, studying every detail of her beautiful face in the bright morning sunshine. "You've put me off for these past two nights by telling me how tired you are. Surely by now you have had the opportunity to get some rest."

The leather squeaked when he bent forward in the saddle to get a better view of her in the dazzling sunlight. How lovely she looked in the azure blue dress she had selected, with her dark hair piled high into a thick arrangement of tiny ringlet curls. Her brown eyes sparkled brightly, making him think she was pleased to see him, and he noticed that her cheeks glowed with a rosier shade of pink than usual. "Please say yes. I miss being with you."

"To tell you the truth, after what happened to us while we were dining at the Silver Swan last Saturday, I think it would be wiser on our part to stay completely away from the local restaurants." She did not want either of them to suffer the embarrassment of another public confrontation.

"I find it hard to believe that you are that afraid of as insignificant a person as John Davis," he teased, his blue eyes bright with merriment until suddenly another, more sobering thought occurred to him. Perhaps the real reason she kept putting him off was that she'd had second thoughts about him. "Or am *I* the one who frightens you?"

Leona suppressed a grin while she studied the strong lines of his handsome features, glad he had chosen to hook his wide-brimmed hat over his saddle horn instead of keeping it on his head, where it would leave an unwanted shadow across his face. She liked being able to see every curve and contour of his face.

"You do not frighten me, Dr. Caldwell," she said, though it was not entirely the truth. The feelings he had aroused within her frightened her so much that she had been unable to sleep soundly for the past three nights. "You intrigue me."

"Then, I don't understand. Why have you turned down my last two dinner invitations and why are you about to turn down yet another? This is Saturday, you deserve a chance to rest and relax after a long week of work. Surely you are not *that* afraid of what John Davis might do."

"John Davis doesn't frighten me any more than you do. He merely annoys me. No, the reason I plan to turn down your very nice dinner invitation is that I plan to extend one of my own. I want you to come to my house for supper tonight."

Lathe pretended to look shocked by her suggestion and glanced around as if afraid someone might have overheard. "But what will people think when they find out?"

"Probably that I have some overwhelming desire to poison you," she said and chuckled at his exaggerated reaction, not really caring what was said. There was already ample gossip circulating about the two of them that would undoubtedly continue to grow, whether they fed it or not. "You are my doctor and I feel I owe you something for having saved my life. And since you've refused to take my money, you can at least partake of my food."

When he did not readily respond, she added, hoping to tempt him, "The reason I am out this early is that I intend to stop off at the farmer's market before opening the store, so I can get all the makings for my specialty."

"Which is?" he asked, raising a questioning eyebrow as if still concerned about her earlier reference to poison.

"Pot roast," she answered, her mouth pursed with playful annoyance, aware of his playful distrust.

"*Yankee* pot roast?" he ventured to ask, grinning again, reminded of just how strongly her opinions ran in that area.

"Hardly!" She tapped her foot with warning as she narrowed her eyes. "This will definitely be *Southern* pot roast. With all the trimmings."

"And what about dessert?" he asked, then dampened his lower lip by running the tip of his tongue across the inner edge. His eyes dipped down to take in the fitted lines of her dress before returning to meet her questioning gaze. "Is there any chance of having fresh apple pie?"

She had thought that he would make an entirely different sort of suggestion concerning their dessert, and

340

Leona wanted to laugh, but she managed to keep a straight face.

"If I have time," she conceded, trying to pretend the *other* thought had never crossed her mind by keeping her somber expression. "Problem is, now that I finally have some merchandise to sell, I am unable to close as promptly as I used to. As it is, supper probably won't be ready to serve until about eight. A good pot roast takes a few hours to prepare. Can you wait that long?" If not, she could always change the menu to her second specialty, braised chicken and rice, which could be ready in less than two hours.

"What if I volunteered to come by early and help?" he asked, eager to spend as much of the evening as possible with her.

"What help could you be in the kitchen?" she questioned as if thinking it an absurd idea, though in truth she was thoroughly delighted. After two days of deep soul-searching, she had come to the stark realization that she loved Lathe dearly and desperately wanted to be with him—no matter what risks were involved.

"I peel a magnificent potato," he said with a haughty wave of his head. "And I can grind black pepper or slice an onion without shedding a single tear."

"Very well," she said, trying to sound reluctant when what she actually felt was thrilled. "Come by about five and I'll put you to work." She decided that would give her just enough time after closing to return home, bathe, and change into a much prettier dress. "But not before five."

Lathe plucked his hat off the saddle horn then flipped it around and set it on his head. "Five it is."

Leona watched while he spurred his horse into a fast trot and headed out of town. She wondered where he could possibly be headed at such an early hour and if it had anything to do with Zeb Turner.

Sadly, she waited until he had turned down a neighboring street and was out of sight before starting toward the market again. After only a few steps, the reason why she suddenly felt so gloomy struck her like a bolt from the sky. She was jealous. Jealous of all the time and effort Lathe had spent trying to find out where that insignificant man might be.

Ethan stopped by the Mercantile on his way out to the Martin farm. He had left his hotel room early because he wanted someone's opinion on the fancy new summer suit he had just bought, complete with a black string necktie and a black silk handkerchief. Because he and Lathe were now on such friendly terms, he had stopped by his room first to see what his thoughts were concerning his new outfit, but discovered that he had already gone. That left Leona as the only one he could ask.

Although the coat felt a little snug through the shoulders and the trousers pulled a little around his upper thighs when he walked, it was the largest ready-made outfit he had been able to find on such short notice, so he'd bought it. But now he wasn't so sure he had done the right thing and wanted someone to reassure him.

Because George had become such a dear friend in the short time she had known him, Leona took time away from her customers to offer a quick appraisal of his outfit, which might have looked quite dapper on a man two sizes smaller.

"To tell you the truth, that coat looks a little tight across the back," she said, being as tactful as possible. With a speculative frown, she reached out to give the material a sharp tug, hoping to stretch the fabric a bit, only to discover no give whatsoever. "Perhaps if you didn't button it."

Ethan quickly unbuttoned the two front buttons, which did give him more room to flex his muscles but

342

also allowed the coat to gape open, revealing three inches of his shirt front.

Leona shook her head at how little improvement that had made. He looked like a lumbering schoolboy trying to get an extra season's wear out of clothes he had long since outgrown. "I think perhaps it would be better if you didn't wear the coat." She held out her hand to indicate he should take it off and give it to her.

Ethan quickly obliged, looking almost relieved to have been ordered out of it.

"What about these trousers?"

He glanced down at them with a doubtful frown.

"Well, the legs are long enough but they do look a little tight at the thigh," she said, tilting her head to judge the snug fit. "Try squatting down to see if the material will stretch any."

Again, Ethan readily obliged. He reached out to balance against a nearby building support while he hurriedly bent his knees. His brown eyes widened with mortification when his efforts were followed by a loud ripping sound. When he stood again, his cheeks flamed bright red—even through the thickness of his dark beard.

Leona put her hand to her mouth and tried not to laugh at his predicament. "I, ah, think it would be better if you didn't wear those trousers either." It took all the personal restraint she had to keep her expression sober when she held his coat out for him. "But I think it would be wise to put this back on, at least for now."

"But what am I goin' to wear to Sarah's?" His mouth drooped with boyish disappointment when he shoved his massive arms back into the straining arms of the coat.

"Just wear what you would usually wear on a Saturday afternoon," she suggested. "The Martins won't expect anything more than that."

"But I was hopin' to make a big impression on her parents."

And you certainly would have done that, she thought, but she decided he had already suffered enough and kept the comment to herself. "Impress them with who you are, not what you have on," she said, then smiled encouragingly. "I don't see why you should be so worried about meeting them."

"What they think is important to me," Ethan admitted while reaching around and feeling his coat tail to make sure it covered the rip in his trousers. "I want them to like me."

"They can't help but do that," she assured him, then noticed one of her customers waiting near the register, ready to make her purchases. "That is, if you prove reliable enough to arrive on time. I think I'd be more worried about being punctual."

She nodded toward the clock behind the far counter in an effort to hurry him. "Look what time it is. You'd better hurry back to the hotel and change. You have less than an hour, and the Martin farm is a good thirty-minute ride from here."

Ethan's eyes widened as he, too, glanced around for a clock. "What time is it?"

"Past eleven. You'd better get a move on."

"You're right about that, Little Bit. I'd better get right on out of here," he said, without realizing he had just used her nickname from when they were kids. With his hand still holding the hem of his coat so that it covered the tear in his trousers, he hurried out of the building and across the street to his horse, unaware that Leona was staring after him, too startled to speak.

Thinking only of the time and how it would look if he were late, he glanced around to make certain no one was behind him before he let go of the coat long enough to grasp the saddle and swing himself onto his horse.

He had to hurry. He had promised Sarah he would be there by noon.

Not wanting to disappoint her, he hurried back to the hotel and put on the only clean pair of trousers he had and selected one of his two clean shirts. Feeling much better in the blue plaid shirt and black trousers than he had in that confounded white suit, he put his hat back in place and headed back out the door. When he passed through the main lobby, he heard the single chime that denoted half past the hour.

It was eleven-thirty.

If he ran his horse part of the way and trotted him the rest, he could still be at Sarah's on time.

Relieved that he would not be late, Ethan turned his attention to what he should say when he again found himself face to face with George's parents.

His main fear, now that he knew he would be on time, was that George's mother might recognize him right away. Because of all the time he and George had spent together during their boyhood, Sherry Martin had become like a second mother to him. Could he fool her as he had fooled everyone else? Or would she immediately recognize him? What if he managed to get by her at first, but then accidentally said or did something that gave himself away?

He prayed that would not happen.

Although he hated the thought of having to lie to them about who he was and why he was in Little Mound, he hated even worse the thought of ever having to tell them the truth. He wanted George's parents to go to their graves believing their son had died a hero.

It was a few minutes before noon when Ethan turned onto the Martin property. Suddenly he was surrounded by familiar landmarks. A sickly feeling shot through him while he glanced around at the familiar trees and the small creek where they had spent many an hour catching tadpoles and crawfish. Although he was truly looking forward to seeing Sarah again, he was not at all sure that coming here to have lunch with her family was such a good idea.

Filled with renewed doubts, he pulled his horse to a stop several hundred yards from the house and frowned while he debated whether to go forward with his plans or simply turn around and head back to town. He was just about to choose the latter course when he spotted Sarah waiting for him in the yard. He could tell by her expression that she had already noticed him.

He now had no choice but to go through with it.

"Hello," he called to her and at the same time spurred his horse toward the house. "Did I make it on time?"

Although he had forgotten his watch, he felt certain he had arrived with several minutes to spare.

"Just barely," she admitted with a smile that looked a little too apprehensive to suit Ethan.

Her lack of enthusiasm worried him. Did she already suspect the truth?

"What's wrong?" he asked as he climbed down from the horse. "Did your folks decide against me eatin' lunch with you?"

"No, of course not," she said, although it had almost come to that. "It's just that I have something to ask of you before we go inside. There's something you have to promise me."

Ethan's skin prickled at the serious tone in her voice. He waited until he had tied the reins to the nearest hitching rail and had turned back around to face her before asking, "And what is it you want me to promise?"

"That you won't tell anyone about our secret house guest."

Ethan's eyebrows rose, intrigued that the Martins had a *secret* anything. They were usually such open, honest people. "What sort of secret house guest?"

Sarah glanced nervously toward the house then back

at Ethan. "First promise me you won't tell anyone. Not even Leona."

"I won't if it means so much to you." His expression changed from one of natural curiosity to one of growing concern.

"It really doesn't mean all that much to me, but it means a lot to my father. He gave him his word that no one will find out that he's here."

Ethan looked more bewildered than ever. "That *who's* here?"

"His name is Zeb Turner," Sarah began then again glanced nervously toward the house.

Sarah's words struck Ethan like a blow to the stomach. He struggled to catch his next breath while she continued with her explanation.

"About two weeks ago, we found him out in our pasture with a bullet hole through his leg. He was bleeding badly so we immediately took him in. Whoever it is that shot him is still out there hoping to kill him, so my father doesn't want anyone to know that he's here."

Zeb? Zeb, here? Ethan swallowed back the rapid rise of fear. He had to find a reason to leave. Zeb had no way to know about the recent lies Ethan had told. Zeb might unwittingly reveal who he really was.

"Who is it that wants to kill him?" Ethan asked, when he was finally able to catch his breath enough to keep a steady voice. He wanted to know if the reason she did not want Leona to know was that Zeb had already told them about Lathe.

"That's another problem. We don't know who the man is. Zeb won't tell us. He says he wants to handle the situation himself after he gets better."

"Well, if secrecy means that much to your father, then maybe I'd better just go on back to town and act like I never even came out here to begin with," he said, already reaching for the reins.

Sarah laid a restraining hand on his arm. "There's no

347

reason for you to leave. All I needed was your promise not to say anything and I already have that." Her voice sounded almost pleading in tone. "Come on inside. I want you to meet my parents. You'll love my mother."

Ethan chewed the inside of his lower lip, desperately searching for a reason to leave. "But it might make your house guest a little nervous to have a stranger around."

"He's already been told you are coming. Besides, he's not going to be our house guest much longer," Sarah responded through tightly compressed lips, clearly eager for him to go. "As soon as that leg wound of his has healed enough, he will be leaving."

Ethan wondered what Zeb had done to provoke such a hostile response on Sarah's part. Ethan decided it might be in Sarah's best interest to find out, even if it meant taking the very real risk of having his identity revealed. If Zeb was bothering Sarah in any way, he not only wanted to know about it, but he wanted to put a stop to it before it got out of hand.

"Okay, I'll come inside. But only to please you," he said, then drew in a sharp breath, aware that everything he had been trying to evade could very well come crashing down over him in the next few minutes. His only hopes were that Sherry Martin would not recognize him and that Zeb would catch on to what had happened and not mention his real name.

Leona was too stunned by what Ethan had said to concentrate on anything else, even the customers lining up at the register. Although she had been aware of several similarities between George and her brother, right from the very beginning, it was not until she had heard him call her Little Bit that she seriously suspected the truth.

As preposterous as it might seem, she now believed

that George Parkinson was not really George Parkinson after all. He was really her brother.

Or was he?

If George was really Ethan, then why would he try so hard to convince her he was someone else? Why would he lie about his identity, especially to her? And if he really was her brother, why would he let her go on believing he was dead when he was so very much alive?

None of it made any sense.

And yet if he really was her brother, there had to be a good reason for his having lied about such a thing. But what could that reason be?

The only way she could ever know for certain would be to confront him with her suspicions, so she decided to do just that. She would search for him as soon as she closed the store.

The tight knot that had formed in Ethan's chest made it that much harder for him to breathe. His heart drummed with a frenzied force, causing his whole chest to throb while he followed Sarah through the front door into the Martin house.

Although he had yet to see Zeb—or anyone else for that matter—he had a growing feeling that everything he had fought so hard to keep secret was about to be hurled out into the open. What would Sarah think of him then? He would be forever ruined in her eyes. As well he should be. After all, he was a liar and a murderer. He really didn't deserve to be in the same room with her. Still, he couldn't find the strength he needed to stay away.

By the time Sarah had stepped back to close the front door behind them, Ethan was so confused and worried about what was about to happen, that he could no longer think clearly. His blood pounded with such painful force, that the sound of it completely drowned out that of the door latch.

"This way," Sarah prompted with a slight wave of her hand when Ethan did not immediately follow her down the narrow hall dividing the house. "Come on. They don't bite."

With the enthusiasm of a condemned man headed for the gallows, Ethan followed, knowing she was headed for the dining room. He prayed Zeb would not be there.

"Mother, Father," Sarah began as soon as they had entered the room. She seemed as apprehensive about the meeting as Ethan, though for an entirely different reason. "This is George. George Parkinson."

With a proud smile she then turned to face Ethan. "George, these are my parents." She gestured to her mother first. "This is my mama, Sheralyn Martin. And this is my papa, Bradford Martin."

Ethan met Zeb's surprised expression with a deep, penetrating glare before turning to greet Sarah's parents with a tentative smile.

Aware he had forgotten to remove his hat when he first entered, he quickly snatched it off his head with his left hand at the same time he extended his right to her father. "Pleased to meet you, sir." He then turned to her mother and nodded. "Pleased to meet you, too, ma'am."

Sherry Martin's face brightened with a smile so familiar to Ethan, it made him ache.

"So you are George Parkinson. My, but we've heard a lot about you these past few days." She looked at Sarah with a teasing glimmer.

"Mama," Sarah warned, then, as a way to change the subject, hurried to finish the introductions.

"I also want you to meet my little brother, Sam, who will undoubtedly ply you with questions, and a friend of ours who is visiting for a few days, Zeb Turner."

Zeb struggled to his feet, using the cane the Martins

had given him. There was a glimmer of amusement and a look of relief in his dark eyes. "Did Sarah say your name is George?"

Ethan glared at him with stern expression, letting him know he needed to be very careful with whatever he had to say. "That's right. George *Parkinson*."

"Isn't that interesting," Zeb continued, then stroked his clean-shaven jaw with his hand. He looked downright pleased about having Ethan there. "I knew a Parkinson back during the war. Real nice fellow. You wouldn't happen to be any kin, would you?"

"That depends," Ethan said, glancing cautiously at Sarah then back at Zeb. "What was his first name?"

"Let me see. I think his name was Ethan; but then I could be mistaken. It's been five years since I last seen him."

Ethan narrowed his eyes then drew in a deep breath and responded. "No, can't say that I know anyone by that name. But it seems odd to me that people around here keep comin' up with that name. Sarah, here, seems to think I look like some local boy with that same given name."

Sherry shook her head with amazement. *"That's* who you look like. You look a lot like Ethan Stegall."

"See?" Sarah said, smiling triumphantly. "Leona was right. You do look a lot like her brother."

"Well, all I can say is that he must have been one gosh-ugly fellow," Ethan responded with a forced smile then immediately sought to divert the conversation. "My, but something sure does smell good."

"That's Mama's fried chicken," Sarah announced proudly. "It just so happens my mama makes about the best fried chicken in all East Texas."

"That's true enough," Bradford quickly put in, then gestured toward one of two empty chairs. "The only person I know who can even come close to matching her is Sarah." He then glanced at his daughter with a

351

teasing expression. "Yes, sir. One of these days my Sarah is going to make some lucky fellow a mighty fine wife."

Mortified, Sarah hurried past him to take her seat, and for the rest of the meal, managed to keep the conversation on a far less personal level. It was not until they had finished eating and Sarah had gone into the kitchen to help her mother and her little brother with the dishes that Ethan again found himself the center of conversation.

"You know, my daughter seems mighty taken with you," Bradford said as he shoved his chair away from the table. "And I must say, I am rather taken with you myself. You seem like a very nice young man."

Ethan knew Bradford to be direct, but he was still caught off guard by such an unexpected comment. "Why thank you, sir."

"No need to thank me. I was just stating facts," Bradford said, already pushing himself out of his chair. "Why don't we menfolk retire to the front porch while the womenfolk finish clearing off the table. It should be a lot cooler out there."

When he turned to head for the door, Zeb and Ethan's gazes met briefly. Zeb's eyes widened when he noticed Ethan's harsh expression.

"I think I'd better pass on going outside," Zeb said while he reached for his cane. "I'm starting to feel a little weak after havin' been up so long. I think I'd do better to get on back to bed for awhile."

"Do you need any help?" Bradford asked, having turned to face him again.

"No, I can make it that far. I just don't care much for the thought of going all the way out to the porch," he said, then waved them on. "You two get on out of here. I'll be all right."

Ethan tried to think of a reason to remain behind. He had not had a chance to let Zeb know that Sarah was not to be bothered in any way. "You sure you don't want some help?"

"Very sure," Zeb answered then paused just as he was about to hobble past them. "Just in case I don't get the chance to talk with you again, Mr. Parkinson, it was real nice meeting you."

"Oh, but I feel like you'll be seeing me again," Ethan said. "As I'm sure Mr. Martin has guessed by now, I've taken quite a liking to Sarah, too."

Zeb smiled briefly but made no further comment before continuing on out of the room. Several seconds later, Bradford signalled that Ethan should follow him out into the hall.

"I gather Sarah explained to you the need for secrecy as far as Zeb is concerned," he said, his voice low so Zeb would not overhear.

"She mentioned something about it, yes, sir."

"Good, then you understand how important it is that no one knows he's out here."

"No one will hear about it from me," he assured him, wondering who he would tell. Certainly not Lathe. That would be the same as killing Zeb himself. It wasn't that he particularly liked Zeb, because he could barely tolerate the sight of him — even cleaned up like he was. The simple truth was, Ethan could not live with another death on his conscience.

"Glad to hear it. I appreciate your cooperation," Bradford said, then reached out to pat Ethan soundly on the shoulder while both turned toward the front of the house. "By the way, did Sarah ever tell you she used to have a brother with the same first name as yours?"

Ethan swallowed hard, then answered, "Why, yes, sir, she did." His gut wrenched painfully at the thought of having to discuss his dead friend with his dead friend's own father. He immediately forgot all about trying to find some way to let Zeb know Sarah was off limits and started working instead on coming up with some shrewd way to change the subject without Bradford noticing.

"Did she also mention that he was killed in the war? Right near the end of it. Come, I'll show you the medal. He died a hero, you know."

"That's what she told me," he admitted. Aware Zeb knew the truth about what really happened to George, Ethan glanced back to make sure he had not changed his mind and followed, glad to find the hallway empty. "She said something about him being shot in battle."

"Odd thing about that," Bradford said and knitted his eyebrows when he came to a stop in front of a small, framed glass case that held both the medal of valor and a yellowed photograph of George. Ethan could imagine how many hours Bradford had spent carving the delicate woodwork that fitted around the glass front.

"That medal proves my son died a hero, and I truly believe that he did; but the fact that he was shot in the back still bothers me something fierce."

Ethan had felt a pain so sharp when he first glimpsed the image of his friend's smiling face that he did not at first realize the implication behind what Bradford had said. It was several seconds before the significance of the words soaked into his brain.

"What did you say, sir?" he asked, turning to look at him, bewildered that anyone would think George had been shot in the back.

"I said that it bothers me to know that George was shot in the back," Bradford repeated, his expression filled with a father's pain while he, too, stared longingly at the smiling image of his son.

"But what makes you think your son was shot in the back?" Ethan asked, deciding that an odd thing for the captain to have told him. What could he have been thinking?

"I don't *think* he was, I *know* he was. Saw it for myself. As soon as we got the letter telling us that George had

354

been killed, I went to the place where we were told he'd been buried and had his body dug up." Bradford's mouth quivered with remembered pain. "His mother and I didn't want him buried in some shallow soldier's grave. We wanted him to have a proper burial here in the family cemetery. We wanted him to lie out there beneath the same trees he'd climbed as a child, beside our other son, who had died shortly after childbirth several years earlier."

"And after you dug him up, you found out he'd been shot through the back?" Ethan asked, knowing that it did not make any sense. George had been headed toward him when he fired that fatal shot, not away from him. If it really was his bullet that had brought him down, it would have entered through his chest.

"Not only was he shot through the back, it was at a very close range." Bradford took a deep breath then looked away from the photograph to regain his composure. "Best I can figure is that some Yankee soldier must have slipped up behind him while he was fighting and shot him almost point blank in the back. It's the only explanation I can come up with that makes any sense." He closed his eyes to show how profound his misery was. "Poor George, I imagine he never even saw the man who shot him. He never had a chance."

Ethan stared at Bradford in horror. "But how can you be so sure the bullet didn't enter his body through the front?"

When Bradford blinked his eyes back open, there was a fine sheen of tears; but he managed to keep the pain out of his voice. "Because there wasn't a hole in the front. I got there within two weeks after he'd been shot and because of all the lime they'd used and the unusually cold temperatures, his body hadn't decomposed hardly at all. And after seeing that he'd been shot in the back, I found the courage to examine his injury a little closer. The bullet was still in his body—lodged in the back of his shattered spine. Other than that, he didn't have a scratch on him. The only injury was the one in his back."

Ethan felt for his collar. The whole room had grown unbearably hot, making him wish he could sit down somewhere. He remembered having seen that wound in George's back just seconds before the captain had tossed a sheet over the body; but he had always assumed that the back wound had been caused by a bullet as it *left* his body not entered it. "And what makes you so sure he was shot at close range?"

That also did not make sense. George had been quite some distance away from both him and the enemy when he suddenly took off running.

"I've been hunting enough to know my gunshot wounds. The man who killed my son couldn't have been more than four or five feet away. Cowardly way to kill a man, I'd say."

Ethan blinked while he tried to figure out what had really happened that day.

Who could have killed George? It had to have been someone in his immediate vicinity, yet the only two men Ethan could remember having been in that same area at that time were that young surveyor who had just hooked up with their group a few days before and the captain himself.

It couldn't have been the surveyor. He'd also been shot, almost immediately after the attack had begun.

It had to have been the captain. But why? And why had he lied about it? To cover up his own mistake? Surely it had been an accident. Or had it?

Ethan reached out to press his hand against the wall. He was so overwhelmed by everything he had just learned, that he could hardly stand and he needed something to steady himself while he thought through the newer developments.

What else did the captain lie about?

Suddenly, Ethan had doubts about everything. He could not even be sure Lathe was guilty of having killed the captain's brother because he had only the captain's word it ever happened. Fact was, he wasn't even sure the captain had even *had* a brother. But then why would Lathe be trying to track Zeb down, if not to eliminate the only witness to his crime?

Ethan wished there was some way to find out the truth about everything that had happened. After hearing what George's father had to say, he didn't know what to believe.

Chapter Nineteen

"Look, Caldwell, why don't you just give it up?" the sheriff asked, dropping his feet off his desk one at a time and looking very annoyed at Lathe. "You come in here every day, sometimes three and four times a day, asking if I've heard anything, and each time I end up havin' to explain all over again that if I do ever hear anything about your man, Turner, I'll send word to you right away."

He sighed heavily then leaned forward, resting his elbows wearily on his desk, knowing even as he spoke that Lathe was not about to give up. Lathe had invested far too much time and had gone through far too much trouble to turn his back on Zeb just yet. "The answer as usual is *no*, I haven't received any information about the man. Not a word. Like I keep tryin' to tell you; it has been nearly two weeks. That man you want has either managed to get clean away and is in another state by now or else he is out there dead as a rock somewhere."

Lathe did not want his own annoyance to show but he had to talk a little louder than he normally would to be heard above the rain splattering against the metal roof. "Look, until I see a body or I hear that someone fitting Zeb's description has actually been seen somewhere else, I have to assume he's still very much alive and hiding out around here somewhere. And because it has been nearly two weeks without even one report of someone having seen him, I have to believe that not only is he still alive and hiding out, but that he's somehow found someone who is either compassionate enough or just plain foolish enough to take care of him."

"And what makes you so sure someone is takin' care of him at all?"

"Because Zeb didn't have enough food with him to last this long without someone's help and judging by how much blood we saw on the ground that next morning, I don't think he was in any shape to go hunting for food on his own. No, Zeb has conned someone into taking him in. I just wish I could figure out who it is."

"Well, until you do find out, or until someone actually sees the man and reports back to me, why don't you give this search of yours a rest? It's pointless for you to keep ridin' around the countryside askin' total strangers if they've seen the man. If he really is holed up somewhere around here, it's because he *has* found someone willin' to protect him and if that person is all that intent on helpin', he isn't about to tell anyone about it — especially not you."

That was true enough. Lathe was fighting a losing battle and he knew it. He just didn't like having that fact pointed out to him. "Well, if you do hear anything, be sure to let me know immediately," he said through teeth so tightly clenched it caused a hardened ridge to form in his cheeks.

"I told you I would," the sheriff reminded him, waving his hands for emphasis. "I am not one to work against you on this."

"I know. It's just that sometimes it feels like *everyone* is working against me," Lathe admitted, then he reached for his hat. He shook some of the excess water onto the floor then shoved it back onto his head. "If you hear anything during the next few hours, I'll be at Leona Stegall's house having supper."

The sheriff fought the sudden urge to grin. Wait until everyone heard about *that* at church tomorrow. Speculation was already running rampant about those two.

"You'll be at Miss Stegall's," he repeated, somehow managing to keep his expression calmly composed. "I'll try to remember."

As disappointed as he was frustrated, Lathe slipped his rain poncho back on as he headed back outside. If only there hadn't been any truth in what the sheriff had said, then he could at least feel angry about what all had happened—or rather by what all had *not* happened. As it was, all he could feel was foolish and incompetent. He had been outwitted by his own brother's murderer—*again*.

He sighed aloud, in his mounting frustration. Zeb had never before managed to stay hidden quite that long. It simply was not in his nature to stay in one place for very long—but then Zeb had never been injured before either. It could be he wouldn't surface again until his injury was nearly healed, which could take weeks, or even months, depending on whether a bone had been shattered, or infection had been allowed to set in.

Or it could be the sheriff was right and Zeb was already dead, his body hidden away where it could not be easily found. It would be just like Zeb to crawl off into a small cave or some deep cavern to die, knowing it would make his body nearly impossible to find.

But until Lathe had absolute proof Zeb was dead, he had to presume he was still alive.

With his mood as gloomy as the weather, Lathe climbed onto his horse and started toward the hotel. It was after four-thirty. He had just enough time for a quick bath before changing his clothes and heading back out.

He washed off with cold water and dressed in the fitted black trousers, the loose-cut blue dinner shirt that accentuated his wide shoulders and the muscular curves of his arms. Then he put on his best black suspenders, and a lightweight black jacket. By that time the rain had stopped. The clouds had thinned until the sun had begun to peep through in places.

Wearing dry clothes and having had a quick bath, he felt much better, and knowing he would soon be with Leona again lifted his spirits even more.

The closer he came to Leona's house, the happier he felt and the easier it was to put most of his troubles behind him. It was while he hurried to be with her again, that he realized just how much she meant to him.

The past three nights were the first since his arrival in Little Mound that he had managed to sleep through the entire night. No nightmares had waked him in the wee hours of the morning. No cold sweat had soaked his bed.

All because of Leona.

He smiled when he remembered what it had been like to make love to her and then lie in her arms afterward. She had been warm and responsive—everything a man could want in a woman, *and more*. It was clear now that what he felt for her bordered on being love—if it wasn't *already* love.

If only he were free to explore his feelings for her more thoroughly, to allow their relationship a chance to flower into something even more vital, more lasting. But until the situation with Zeb had been settled, he didn't dare make any commitments to anyone.

Or did he?

His face wrinkled into a perplexed frown. Perhaps he could make one small commitment to himself without causing much harm to his principles.

If for some reason Zeb never reappeared, and never left any substantial clues as to where he'd gone, Lathe decided he would stay right there in Little Mound and give his budding relationship with Leona a real chance.

Then, if things worked out accordingly, and if she came to care for him despite his many obvious flaws, he might even find the courage to ask her to marry him.

Marry?

Lathe blinked rapidly at the peculiar thought. Although he'd often dreamed of living in a town about the size of Little Mound, he had never considered doing so with a wife and family at his side. Yet now it was all he could think about.

He liked the thought of making his home in Little Mound. He liked the people and liked the idea of opening a family practice there. It would be his dream come true, and to do so while married to a woman like Leona would make life about as perfect as it could possibly get.

Lathe smiled again at the thought of what his days would be like if he could only practice medicine again on a regular basis and at the same time be able to love Leona openly and completely — without that nagging fear of one day having to leave her.

His elated smile dissolved into a flat, grim line when he remembered that when Zeb did surface again, even months from now, he would have to give up whatever he had started there and go after him. He would have no choice. His priorities still lay with his brother.

His dream of marrying Leona and starting a small practice of his own would have to remain just that — a dream. Until he knew for certain that Zeb had paid his debt, one way or another, and was completely and permanently out of his life, he did not dare try to make either of those dreams a reality. It would hurt too much to have them and then have to give them up.

It would be better to leave things the way they were.

Leona hurried to get dressed.

It seemed absurd that the side trip to the hotel and

362

then to two of the more popular restaurants had taken over thirty minutes; but she had so wanted to find George — *or Ethan* — or whoever he claimed to be — that she had been willing to spend whatever time it took. Still, it had put her way behind.

Because of the unforeseen delay, she had been forced to trade in the leisurely rose-scented bath she had hoped to have for a quick rinsing with a wet cloth and a splash of lavender verbena and now she was searching frantically through her drawers for a pair of matched stockings.

Finally, after scrambling through all her drawers but one, she located a pair of black stockings close enough to call a match, though one had grey stitching in the toe and the other did not. With very little time left, she hurried to select the rest of her clothing. Quickly, she secured both of the stockings to her long, slender legs and had just slipped into her prettiest white ruffled underskirt and covered it with a petal-pink layered dress, but had yet to tie the wide burgundy sash or fasten the dozen or so pearl shaped buttons along the back when she heard Scraps bark. She knew by his sudden raucous enthusiasm that Lathe had arrived.

Hurriedly, she fumbled with the tiny buttons, but had only the bottommost two fastened when Lathe knocked seconds later.

Afraid he might think she had changed her mind about having invited him, she hastily tugged a stiff brush through her hair then without taking the time to draw the long shimmering tresses back into the usual loose, curling twist near the nape of her neck, she slipped her feet into her shoes and rushed to the door. Because her dress was still open in the back, she crossed her arms and clutched the top of the garment to her so it would not slip off her shoulders and embarrass her.

Careful not to present her back to him for fear he would glimpse her undergarments, she opened the door then stepped back to let him inside. Without mentioning why she was running so late, remembering how just days ago he had admitted to being jealous of whatever relationship she and George shared, she explained her predicament as best she could then began backing away, eager to return to her bedroom and finish dressing.

"Turn around," he commanded after she had gone but a few steps. He had waited too long to be with her again and did not want to spend even the next few minutes away from her.

When Leona's eyebrows dipped with sudden concern, his blue eyes sparkled. He was amused that she should behave so modestly after what had happened between them late Wednesday. She no longer had anything to hide from him. He had already seen it all.

Lathe's blood stirred at the memory of how truly perfect she had looked that night — and how truly perfect she had *felt*. How he ached to take her into his arms again.

"But I have not had time to fasten my dress or tie my sash," she reminded him, wondering why that fact had not yet sunk into his head. Couldn't he tell the garment was loose?

"I know," he admitted, smiling. "But it just so happens I can fasten a dress almost as well as I can unfasten one," he explained, further delighted by the high color that rose immediately to her cheeks. The pink color of her dress paled in comparison.

Rather than argue about something she would rather not discuss just yet, Leona reluctantly obeyed. She gathered her hair into one hand and held it out of the way while she slowly turned and presented her back to him.

If Lathe had thought he could glimpse the ivory curve of her back and the creamy roundness of her lower neck and shoulders and not react in much the same way he had three nights prior, he was greatly mistaken. Unable to stop himself, he reached forward to trail his fingertips across her exposed skin, delighted in the softness he found there.

Tiny chills skittered first up then down Leona's spine, creating sensitive layers of gooseflesh along her neck and upper arms. She shivered in response to the delectable sensations that had sent her heart racing at an alarming rate—all too aware he had yet to touch a single button.

"What's keeping you?" She clasped her teeth and drew several deep, steadying breaths while her pulses continued to race wildly and uncontrolled throughout her body. Thinking it might help to calm her jumbled nerves, she tried to swallow but couldn't.

"*You* are keeping me," he answered. He dampened the outer edges of his parted lips with a quick swipe of his tongue then drew part of the lower lip between his teeth in an effort to still his mounting desire while he reached for the lower buttons first. He knew there his fingers would be somewhat protected from the enticing warmth of her skin by the thin fabric of her camisole. "You are very beautiful and very tempting."

Certain Lathe could not see her expression from where he stood, Leona smiled. It thrilled her to know she "tempted" him. Yet at the same time, it frightened her. She knew only too well where that kind of temptation could lead and was not yet ready to try to cope with such overpowering emotions.

Rather than allow their conversation to continue along that same dangerous direction, she did what she could to alter its course. "I am also very hungry. I wish you would hurry and finish with those buttons so we can start our supper."

If only it weren't supper you were hungry for, Lathe mused while he gathered what willpower he needed to finish closing her dress. It felt as if he were working against himself when he finished the task by tying the burgundy sash into a perfectly shaped bow.

"So, what do you want me to do first?" he asked when at last he stepped away, as much an effort to settle his frazzled nerves as to indicate that he had finally finished fastening her dress. Aware his holster would only get in the way of any apron she might provide, he quickly unbuckled it and placed it on a nearby table, then shrugged out of his coat and laid it over the gun to hide it.

"I want you to do exactly what you volunteered to do," she answered quickly. Although her heart still raced with astonishing speed, she amazed herself by how casually she turned and headed toward the kitchen. "First, I want you to peel and cube the potatoes. Then scrape and slice the carrots and onions. I even have celery for you to chop. Meanwhile, I'll season the roast and get it started simmering."

It surprised Leona that her voice had revealed none of the confusion she felt, and by the time they had entered the kitchen her heart rate had calmed considerably.

The next hour and a half proved maddening for Lathe. Whether intentionally or not, Leona moved about the kitchen in what he felt was an extremely provocative manner, brushing her skirts against the backs of his legs repeatedly.

By the time they had the roast on to simmer and the vegetables soaking in chilled water ready to add later, he was consumed with a growing desire to take her into his arms and again seduce her into eager submission. But he decided it would be to his own advantage to wait—at least until after they had eaten and settled comfortably for the evening.

He did not want Leona to think that his desire to make love to her was the only reason he had come to see her again. He truly enjoyed being with her and he especially enjoyed hearing her varied opinions, though they did not always coincide with his own. He liked a woman who could think for herself.

It was just that as much as he enjoyed talking with her and discovering all about her, he enjoyed touching and kissing her even more. His blood stirred hotly at the tempting thought of what it would be like to sweep her into his arms and ravish her right there in the kitchen.

Unaware that Leona was struggling against similar thoughts, Lathe continued to battle his most basic impulse to seduce her. While the pot roast simmered over a low flame, awaiting the exact moment when the vegetables could be added, Lathe joined Leona in the front parlor, intent on sharing nothing more than a few minutes of polite conversation. Yet when he sat on the couch beside her and caught a simple whiff of her sweet floral scent, he could hold back his turbulent desire no longer. With the hunger of a man who had starved himself to the point of madness, he pulled her suddenly into his arms.

"Lathe!" she gasped, clearly surprised by his abrupt embrace. Her pulses leaped with elation when he responded to her exclamation by pulling her even closer. He then brought his mouth down upon hers with all the warmth and intensity of a man in love.

A simmering wave of wonder and contentment washed over her when she realized that to be the truth. Although Lathe had yet to speak the actual words, she could tell by the desperate way he held her and by the sheer adoration in his touch that Lathe loved her every bit as much as she loved him. If it had not been for that relentless determination of his to do whatever it took to capture Zeb Turner, she thought he might even consider making her a permanent part of his life. If he weren't so blinded by his desire to take Zeb prisoner, he would know that his place was there with her.

367

Believing that to be true, Leona lifted her arms to him and eagerly pressed her body harder against his, hoping that by doing so, she would make him want her so badly that he would forget his foolish undertaking and stay there with her instead.

With the longing of someone who now knew exactly what to expect from the wondrous act of making love, Leona gave of herself freely, passionately. She wanted Lathe to understand how very much she loved him, how very much she longed to become a permanent part of his life. As startling as it seemed, Leona wanted to become someone's wife — *Lathe's* wife. For the first time since her childhood, she needed someone — and needed him desperately.

While Lathe pressed his fingers into the gentle curve of her lower back, he, too, wished he could find some way to make what they shared last forever. He was pained by the knowledge that he might never be able to claim her for his own. If only Zeb would show his loathsome face and then let his guard down just long enough to be captured. Then it could all be over. He would no longer have to suffer that bitter torment of knowing his brother's killer was still out there somewhere, running free, mocking his brother's death.

But until that day, until he could finally fulfill that promise he'd made while kneeling at his brother's graveside, he could do little more than hope the day would eventually come when he could ask Leona to be his.

With the passion of a man who understood the likelihood that he would one day have to deny himself the person he loved the most, Lathe crushed his eyes closed and immersed himself in the overwhelming sensations created by their kiss. His desire to become a part of her, if only for the night, consumed him until he frantically fought to release the very same buttons he had so reluctantly fastened earlier.

Leona trembled with expectation when seconds later Lathe slipped the loosened garment off her shoulders. She closed her eyes and gasped with a sudden shortness of breath while she reveled in the many magnificent sensations flaming brilliantly inside her. Soon, the top portion of her dress lay at her waist and her camisole was quickly removed. She shuddered when he paused, reverently, to cup one of her breasts with his warm hand, flicking the tip with the side of his thumb until it grew rigid with the same rampant desire that consumed the rest of her.

Tiny bumps of tingling anticipation sprang to life beneath her skin when she felt his other hand tug her arm gently, encouraging her to stand so he could more easily discard the last of her clothing.

Within a very few seconds, she stood naked before the man she loved and met his adoring gaze proudly.

"You are exquisite," he murmured then bent forward to taste the slender curve at the base of her neck with the tip of his tongue. When he did, his warm breath gently caressed her ivory skin, which sent a whole new flood of tumultuous sensations skittering through her.

Leona moaned with pleasure and slowly brought her hands upward from his waist and began working with the many buttons that bound his shirt to him. In his impatience to be rid of all clothing, he slid out of his suspenders himself then reached for the top fastener of his trousers. Soon, he too was just as gloriously naked as she.

With no physical barriers left in their way, Leona embraced him with a love so overpowering and so pure it brought a rush of tears to her glimmering brown eyes.

Aware of her acceptance, Lathe's mouth sought hers in yet another overpowering kiss as he gently moved her onto the couch. Leona trembled in response. Her trembling came not from any fear but from the desperate need she had to show Lathe just how much she loved him. When he lay down beside her, cradling her gently in his arms while he continued to devour her with his wondrous kiss, a fire burst to life inside Leona so intense and so hot, that it raged immediately out of control. Helplessly and hungrily, she returned Lathe's kiss, aware that he alone had the power to stop this new ache burning inside her.

Consumed by a desire of equal intensity, Lathe tightened his embrace, pressing her body closer. Still, he could never seem to draw her quite close enough. Unable to hold back any longer, he rose above her then moved again to become a part of her. Leona responded fully, working with him until together they again reached that euphoric ecstasy that can only come to people who truly love each other.

Once fulfilled, Lathe fell back against the crumpled pillows he had not thought to remove from the couch, his energy spent, and for a long moment, they lay there in each other's arms, unmoving, basking in the aftermath of their love. They did not allow their happiness to be disturbed by the thought that such moments might not be theirs forever.

It was a dull thud near the doorway that brought them both out of their contented haze with a start. Leona screamed when she glanced toward the darkened hall and caught a quick glimpse of the pistol pointed in their direction.

John stepped around a large puddle in the alley then turned to glance back at the man following him. Although the sun had been down for nearly half an hour, he could still see well enough to make out the other man's questioning expression.

"The reason I sent for you is that I have already decided what it is I want you to do," he said. He kept his voice low though he was certain no one else was around to hear him. "Come on in and I'll get you the money you'll need." He bent forward to feel for the keyhole then quietly slipped the key inside. "It'll just take a minute."

"What exactly do you have in mind?" Simpson asked then turned to close the door while John fumbled to light a nearby lamp.

"Well, if everything you told me is true, then there's only one person who can make Caldwell finally leave Little Mound and that's this Zeb Turner fellow the sheriff told you about," John said while he crossed the room with long, hurried strides.

"That's true enough," Simpson said, nodding speculatively, already trying to second-guess John's strategy. "According to what the sheriff told me, Lathe Caldwell is obsessed with his crusade to capture that man and haul him back to Alabama to see him hang. It was because the sheriff wasn't really sure why Caldwell seems so determined to carry the pursuit through that I did a little investigating of my own. I was curious to find out exactly what it was old Turner did to earn himself a hanging. Imagine how surprised I was to find out he had killed Caldwell's younger brother in cold blood. I reckon that's why Caldwell would do just about anything to finally see that justice is done."

"Even leave Little Mound," John said, smiling for the first time since the two had encountered each other out on the street. Looking down, he reached into his vest pocket and pulled out a small key. "You certainly have done a good job for me thus far. I just hope you prove as competent with the rest of what I want you to do."

"You know me. I can do anything for money," Simpson said. The outer corners of his mouth curled into an envious smile while he watched John bend over and unlock the bottom drawer of his desk. From prior experience he knew that was where John kept most of his money — not in the elaborate wall safe behind his desk.

"Good," John said, still kneeling behind the desk. when he straightened again, he held two small stacks of currency bound with strips of paper. He offered them to Simpson one at a time. "Here's the two hundred I promised you for finding out the very information I need. And here's a hundred more to help you carry out the plan I'm about to propose." He waited until Simpson had taken the money then motioned toward the open drawer. "And there will be plenty more after you have finished."

"How much more?" Simpson asked. He peeked into the stacks to see what denominations had been included but he did not actually count to determine if the exact amount was there. Instead, he returned his gaze to John while he quietly folded the money then tucked it into his shirt pocket.

John studied his friend's expression in the dim lamplight for a moment, trying to decide what he should offer. "How does a thousand sound?"

"Like music to my ears." Simpson's eyes widened with surprise for that was five times what he had expected. "What do I have to do, kill the man?"

"Eventually, yes," John admitted, carefully gauging Simpson's reaction. If the man did not have the courage it would take to carry through with his murderous scheme, he needed to know at the onset. "But for now, all I want you to do is get him out of town. Out of town? Hell, I want you to get him clean out of this state."

"And just how do I go about doing that?" Simpson wanted to know. His expression indicated interest, rather than apprehension.

"By giving him a false trail. Sometime during the early part of next week, I want you to go to some rather sizable town about a day's ride north of here, say Daingerfield or Pittsburg, and report that your wallet

372

was stolen by someone fitting Zeb Turner's description. Be sure to mention those scars Sheriff Lindsey told you about, especially that one on his hand."

"Why north? Why Daingerfield or Pittsburg?" he asked, trying to understand the concept behind the idea.

"Because I want you headed out of state, and the town you choose has to be a place with a reliable sheriff and it has to be one that's near enough to have gotten one of Lindsey's telegraphs. But at the same time, it needs to be far enough away that you will have plenty of time to move on before Lathe gets there."

"And just where do I move on to?"

"Somewhere likely to get a report about that first robbery. After you get to that second town, I think you should wait a day or two then give another robbery report, only use a different name so no one realizes that both reports were made by the same man."

"And of course Lathe will get wind of the second robbery and head out immediately."

John crossed his arms and beamed, obviously very proud of his scheme. "Now you're starting to catch on."

"And how long will I have to keep that up?"

"Until you are well away from here, either deep into the Oklahoma Territory or up into Arkansas. I don't want news of Caldwell's death ever working its way back here. Meanwhile, I will see to it that Leona is reminded daily that Caldwell left her of his own free will. I also will make sure she believes his failure to return is because of that same free will. That way she won't turn into some foolish, grieving woman who refuses to put her lover's memory behind her. She'll be so hurt and so angry by what he's done, she won't care what happens to him. Fact is, she might even end up so angry over what he's done that she'll fall willingly and eagerly into my comforting arms."

He smiled when he realized just how perfect his plan

373

was. "Of course, I'll be prepared to say all the right things to fuel that anger and eventually I will win her over completely." He chuckled at his own cleverness. "And Leona is just stubborn enough to agree to marry me out of sheer spite."

"And you'd have her even under those circumstances?"

John's malevolent smile faded while he continued to stare at Simpson, this time without really seeing him.

"I'd be willing to have that woman under *any* circumstances." He then looked away, his hands clenching with determination. "And I will have her. Even if I have to drag her to the altar kicking and screaming, I *will* have her."

Chapter Twenty

Aware of the very real danger in the absurd situation, Lathe slowly eased off the couch and headed toward the door. He was too concerned with the fact that the gun could go off at any minute to care that he was stark naked and facing an enemy that had a penchant for latching on to various parts of his body and not letting go.

"Good, boy," he said in a strangely calm voice while he continued to approach the animal slowly, aware that every time the dog turned his head to the left, which was often, the pistol he held clamped between his jaws pointed directly into the room. His worst fear was that Leona would be accidentally shot, and with her only a few dozen feet away, the resulting wound could easily be fatal.

"I don't know how you got in this house or how you managed to find my gun, but I think it would be a very good idea for you to set the thing down on the floor — *gently,*" he said in a low, coaxing tone, his gaze frozen on the weapon clamped so awkwardly in the animal's mouth. Slowly, he held his hand out, palm up, to indicate he meant the animal no harm. "Either set the gun on the floor or let me take it."

"Lathe, be careful," Leona cried, equally aware that every time the dog cocked his head to the left, the pistol pointed into the room. She knew Lathe was the closest target. She could read the headlines now: *Naked Doctor Shot To Death By Deranged Dog.* "Don't make any sudden moves. If he dropped it, it could go off."

"Don't worry," Lathe muttered while he continued to slowly approach the watchful canine with his open hand still extended, palm out. Though he appeared outwardly calm, his blood pumped through his chest with such velocity, it felt as if he very well could explode. "I have no desire to have any valuable parts of my anatomy shot off by this animal."

For some reason that comment struck Leona as ludicrous and despite the seriousness of the situation, she started to laugh. When Scraps took his gaze off Lathe long enough to see what had made his mistress react so strangely, it gave Lathe the opportunity he needed. He made a quick dive for the pistol and managed to snatch it out of the dog's mouth with very little struggle.

Feeling weak with relief, he leaned heavily against the door jamb and watched while Scraps trotted over to Leona, his tail wagging as if he were eager to be let in on the joke.

"Good dog," Leona said, reaching out to pet him roughly on the head, relieved the gun had not fired.

"Good dog?" Lathe asked, thinking it an absurd statement. "After what he just did?" When he finally found the strength, he shoved away from the door frame and headed toward them, still holding the wet gun, all the while wondering which of the two he should shoot first. "I've heard of keeping a dog around for protection, but that was ridiculous. If you think it is about time for a guest to leave, all you really have to do is tell him."

Although Leona had managed to stop laughing, her brown eyes continued to sparkle with merriment when she slowly pushed the animal away and stood. Aware that her laughter might have hurt his feelings, she held out her arms to him. "I'm sorry I laughed."

"As well you should be," he retorted, already so overcome by the sight of her splendid body welcoming him into its warm embrace that he could no longer sound terribly insulted. "It was a very serious situation. I could have been shot while wresting that gun away from that mutt."

"What can I do to make it up to you?" she asked, lowering her chin to look suitably chastised while he headed toward her waiting arms.

When Scraps suddenly moved to block his path, Lathe glowered at the animal and held the gun out to Leona, butt first. "If you really want to prove you are sorry, you'll shoot that animal. Now. Before he can cause me any further aggravation."

"Why don't I lock him in the back room instead?" she offered, ignoring the proffered gun and stooping to grab Scraps by the scruff of the neck.

Unaware of what a truly provocative picture she made, Leona bent over the stubborn canine and began tugging sharply on his collar, her body reacting sensually to every abrupt movement. But despite her efforts, the animal would not budge.

Lathe could stand it no longer. With no thought of what the dog might do in reprisal, he stepped forward and scooped the surprised canine into his arms then carried him, kicking and yelping, into the back room. There, he promptly deposited him into darkness and, without giving the animal a second thought, closed the door. After sliding a heavy bolt into place, he stalked over to the kitchen table, turned it on its side, then as an added precaution, blockaded the entrance with it.

"Now where were we?" he asked, ignoring the fact that she was laughing again as he moved obediently into her arms.

"Leona? What are you doing here?" Ethan asked, peering at her curiously, then, realizing that he had yet

377

to button his shirt, he quickly jerked the front together with both hands. "Why aren't you in church?"

"Because I wanted to come here and have a talk with you instead," she answered honestly, lowering her eyelids while studying him in an entirely new perspective. There were so very many similarities. "It's important."

Seeing her serious expression, Ethan hurriedly buttoned the front of his shirt with clumsy fingers. "What is it you want to talk to me about? Did somethin' happen to Sarah?"

"No, it has nothing to do with Sarah. It has to do with you." When his only response to the comment was to stare at her with gape-mouthed concern, she flicked her tongue across her lips to fortify her determination, then asked, "May I come in?"

"Into my hotel room?" His dark eyebrows notched as if he thought it a scandalous idea.

"Yes. I have something I want to ask you and I really think it is something that would be better asked in private."

Ethan's gut clenched with a sudden, gnawing apprehension. "Why? What's happened?"

"Like I told you, it is something that should be discussed in private." She crossed her arms to let him know she intended to have her way on the matter.

Swallowing hard, he stuck his head out into the dimly lit corridor and looked both ways to make sure no one was around, then he quickly stepped back. "Okay, you can come in, but hurry 'fore someone sees you here."

Eager to speak with him, Leona did step quickly into the room. She refused his offer of the only chair in the room, then waited until he had closed the door and had turned to face her again before asking her first question. "How is it you knew about Dr. Owen that night I was hurt?"

The muscles in Ethan's chest pulled painfully taut

while he quickly tried to concoct a believable answer. Not ready to tell her the truth and yet not wanting to face her with a direct lie, he glanced down at the stained green carpet beneath his bare feet.

Because she had caught him still asleep, he had not yet had time to dress. All he had on were his trousers and a haphazardly buttoned shirt. His next thought was that because he and Lathe had taken to having a late breakfast together most mornings, his new friend could arrive at any moment.

What would Lathe think when he found the two of them alone in his hotel room, and him with so few clothes on? Ethan swallowed hard when he realized exactly what Lathe would think. He ran his hand over his beard while he tried to figure out some way to satisfy her questions without alerting her to the truth. Then he could hustle her on out of there.

"When I first got into town—" he began, frowning while he thought through what he planned to say, "—I—uh—my horse accidentally stepped on the side of my foot and crushed my littlest toe. It hurt somethin' awful so I asked a man I saw walkin' along the street if there was a doctor in town. He told me all about how your local doctor had died and not too long ago."

Leona tilted her head, doubting his every word. "Then why is it you didn't seem to *know* he was dead and, besides, how did you know right where his office used to be?"

Ethan curled his toes while he continued to stare down at the matted carpet then straightened them again when an answer eventually came to him. "That's simple to explain. I was in front of the hotel when I asked and the man pointed to a building across the street and told me that was where the doctor's office used to be. He also told me how the town council had bought all the doctor's supplies from his family and was tryin' to find a new doctor to come in and take over that office," he added, having learned why all the doctor's things were still inside the building just a few days ago.

That was something Ethan would not have known, and Leona might have actually believed him had he looked at her when he answered. As it was, she did not believe a word he said.

"I have another question and this time I want you to look at me when you answer." She waited until Ethan had slowly brought his gaze to meet hers before continuing, "Why did you call me Little Bit yesterday?"

Ethan's dark eyes widened with instant alarm just before he took a tiny step back, obviously wanting to place more distance between them.

"Did I do that?" Again he turned his gaze to the floor, refusing to look at her.

Leona noticed how rapidly his chest rose and fell, and knew she had struck a definite chord. "Yes, you did. And I want to know why."

He cut his gaze at her only briefly before he stepped over to the dresser and reached for his comb. In a pitiful attempt to appear largely uninterested, he stood in front of the mirror and began to work the stout comb first through his thick hair, then through his curling beard. "I really don't remember calling you that, but if I did—uh—I guess it was because I thought the name suited you."

"Ethan, don't lie to me. I won't stand for it," she stated staunchly, certain now that he was her brother.

Upon hearing his name fall from his sister's lips, a pain pierced Ethan's heart so sharp, tears sprang immediately to his eyes. He still refused to look at her. "How long have you known?"

"Since yesterday afternoon when you suddenly called me Little Bit. Until then, I honestly believed that you were just someone who looked amazingly like my brother. You have changed a lot, you know."

Because he had yet to turn and face her, she took the

380

few steps necessary to place herself in front of him, effectively blocking his view of the mirror. "But when I heard you call me Little Bit in such an affectionate tone, it all suddenly came together in my mind and I knew you were Ethan. What I don't know is why you bothered to lie about it in the first place."

Clasping his hands tightly around the comb in a futile effort to stop them from trembling, Ethan finally lifted his gaze to meet hers. "I had to."

"But why?" she asked, clearly not understanding.

"Because I didn't want you to find out I was still alive. I wanted you to continue thinkin' I'd died in battle like the captain's letter said."

"But *why?* Why would you want to hurt me like that? Why would you want to hurt our parents like that? What did they ever do to make you want to turn against them that way?"

"It would have hurt them worse to know the truth," Ethan admitted sadly, then gestured again to the only chair in the room. "Sit down and I'll try to explain it to you."

Thinking it might help her to concentrate better on what he had to say, she accepted the offer. She slowly sank into the chair and watched with perplexed apprehension while he lowered his weight onto the bed several feet away. When he looked at her then, it was with such a troubled expression, she knew that whatever he was about to tell her would be the truth.

There was a long, heavy silence before he shook his head and turned his tearful eyes toward the ceiling. "I really don't know where to start." He pressed his lips together to try to keep them from trembling like his hands.

"Start at the beginning," she said, so overwhelmed by her brother's outward emotion, she quickly moved to the bed beside him and took his hand. "Whatever it is, Ethan, I will understand," she vowed. Remembering

381

that he had failed to return after a particularly bloody battle, she believed he was about to admit to being a deserter. "Above all else, I am your sister. I love you."

"You might not after you hear the truth about what I did." He took a deep breath then blurted it out in a rush. "I killed George Martin. It was an accident. I didn't mean to. But I killed him just the same. It's why I can never tell Sarah or anyone else around here who I really am. It's why I didn't want you to find out either."

Leona stared at Ethan, too dumbfounded to speak; but the fact that she had not let go of his hand—had not dropped it as if he were some diseased leper—encouraged him to tell the rest. With tears of shame streaming wet trails into his beard and gathering at the roots, he told her first about the accident itself then told her everything that had resulted from the mishap.

"Until yesterday, I felt I owed it to the captain to work for him, especially after he kept his mouth shut about that whole, horrible incident," he explained. "Because of his willingness to keep quiet about everything, the Martins have never had to know the truth."

"What do you mean, until yesterday?" Leona asked. "What happened yesterday?"

Ethan's face twisted with confusion. He still had not come to terms with what George's father had told him. "Yesterday, while I was out at Sarah's, I found out that it might not have been my bullet that brought George down. Fact is, if what Sarah's father told me is true, it is very possible that the captain was the one who accidentally shot him and then decided to make it look like I was to blame in order to take any suspicion off himself. But what I don't understand is why he would be making me work for him if he's really the one who killed him. It just doesn't make sense."

"And what sort of work do you do for this captain?"

Aware of what she was about to think of him, he pulled his hands away from hers and placed them awkwardly in his lap. "Just about anything he asks me to do. The whole reason I'm here in Little Mound is because of the captain's orders. He's sent me to kidnap Lathe and wants me to hold him prisoner somewhere until he and some of his men can arrive and take him off my hands. He's promised me that if I do this one last thing for him, he will finally consider my debt paid in full. I can then be free of him forever." He looked at her, hoping to find a flicker of understanding, though deep down he knew he would find none.

"Kidnap Lathe?" Leona gasped. Her heart constricted with sudden fear. "Why would he want you to kidnap Lathe?"

"Because he says Lathe killed his little brother. That's also why Lathe is so dead set on catching up with Zeb Turner, because Zeb was the only witness to that murder. The captain says that if Lathe ever finds a way to get rid of Zeb, then he won't have to worry about hangin' for no murder."

"That's preposterous! Lathe's no murderer. He could never kill anyone."

"That's what I'm starting to believe, too. And even if it did turn out to be true and Lathe really did kill the captain's brother, it had to have been a provoked attack, not the act of cold-blooded murder the captain described to me. Lathe is no killer. If he was, he would never have given up the opportunity to catch up with Zeb in order to stay behind and take care of you. If he had any killer instincts, he would have left you behind to bleed to death. I guess that's why I keep puttin' it off. I just can't bear the thought of handin' someone like Lathe over to a mean, unscrupulous man like the captain."

"Then don't."

"I got no choice," Ethan said, looking down at his hands and shaking his head sadly. "If I don't follow through with the captain's orders, I could very easily end up the dead man in this." He paused, then brought his gaze to meet Leona's again. "But then maybe it would be better all around if I was the one killed instead of Lathe. The world's got no real use for me anyway."

"That's ridiculous," Leona scolded, trying hard to make sense of everything she had just learned. "The world has good use for both of you and you know it." She paused while she tried to find a workable solution. "Isn't there some way to get around all this without *anyone* being killed?"

"Well, I did come up with one idea," Ethan said, lowering his eyebrows with thought. "But then it probably wouldn't work anyway, especially when it turns out Zeb is still alive."

"Why? What was your idea?" she asked, suddenly hopeful, not caring that he had sounded as if he knew where Zeb might be. She could only worry about one problem at a time and right now Ethan's problem with his captain came first.

"It has to do with findin' some way to convince the captain that Lathe is already dead—that maybe because he somehow caught on to who I am and what I was up to, he tried to jump me and I had to kill him on the spot."

"But how could you convince him of something like that?"

"I don't know. I guess by sending him somethin' that would make him believe it was true. I was thinkin' maybe that ring Lathe always wears. The captain knows about the ring. In fact, that's one of the things he told me to watch for when I first went lookin' for him. He told me to look for a big gold ring with a fancy letter *C* etched into it. If only there was some way to get hold of that ring without actually hurting Lathe, then I could take it to the captain as proof the man is dead. I could tell him I plucked it off his hand right after I killed him." He paused to think about it more. "I wonder if Lathe ever takes it off."

"Do you really think it would work?" Leona asked, her mind already working on possible ways to get the ring.

"If Zeb was dead, I'm sure it would work. I can't see the captain makin' a trip all the way to East Texas just to see if there's really a grave, not after I presented him with that ring," he said, then his shoulders sagged. "But as long as Zeb is still alive, it wouldn't work anyway."

"I don't understand, what has Zeb got to do with any of this."

"Zeb also works for the captain and is in regular contact with him. And with him out there still alive, Lathe will eventually find out and start right in after him again—a fact Zeb is certain to relay back to the captain."

"But no one has seen Zeb since the night he was shot. Maybe he *is* dead."

Remembering his promise not to tell anyone about the Martin's house guest, he kept his answer evasive. "But then again, maybe he's not dead. I know Zeb. He's a pretty tough character. It would take more than a bullet hole in the leg to kill the likes of him."

Ethan closed his eyes, hating himself for his next thought: *but what if he were to tell Lathe where to find Zeb and let Lathe go ahead and finish him off? Then Zeb wouldn't be around to tell anyone anything.*

But he realized that would make Lathe a true murderer, which was not what he wanted. His next thought was to wonder whether Zeb could be bought off. Perhaps if they were to offer him enough money, he would be willing to keep quiet about Lathe still being alive. It would help if they could somehow assure him that Lathe would quit his chasing after him. But how could they convince Lathe to give up such a pursuit? Maybe if Zeb promised not to testify against him.

"Leona, I don't want to appear rude, but I need time

to think," he said, wanting to mull matters over. There had to be a way to get Zeb and Lathe to cooperate.

"I understand. Meanwhile, I will see what I can do about getting you that ring," she promised. She would do anything to save Lathe from whatever horrible fate awaited him at the hands of Ethan's ruthless captain.

"How?"

"I don't know how just yet, but I will find a way to get that ring." She then hurried to the door, eager to give Ethan the solitude he wanted. When she opened the door and found Lathe standing barely a foot away with his hand raised as if about to knock, she let out a startled scream.

"Leona? What are you doing here?" he asked, clearly confused, then glanced past her to where Ethan still sat on the bed, wearing a wrongly buttoned shirt and a rumpled pair of trousers. Without waiting for an answer, he turned and stalked angrily back to his room, shutting his door behind him with a resounding slam.

Chapter Twenty-one

"Lathe, it's me," Leona said in a voice loud enough to be heard inside after he failed to answer her knock. "Open the door. I want to explain."

She waited several more seconds, then knocked again. "Lathe, please, open the door." When he still did not respond, she sighed wearily then braced her cheek against the cold surface. "Lathe, it's not what you think. We were just talking." She waited half a minute more then finally gave up, aware he would not talk to her until he was ready. "When you're finally prepared to hear what I have to say, I'll be at my house."

She stayed a few more seconds then stood erect and, feeling annoyed and frustrated, headed toward the stairs. She wondered how she would ever manage to get that ring from him when she could not even get him to come out of his room long enough to talk to her. She hoped he would get over this initial burst of anger and then come to her house as she had suggested. Until he did, all she could do was wait.

"Do you have everything you think you'll need?" John asked, standing off to one side while Simpson made a quick check of his gear.

"As far as I can tell," he admitted then closed the flap

on the saddlebag and quickly tied it shut. "I should reach Daingerfield by tomorrow morning. I'll report the robbery as soon as I arrive. It'll probably take the local sheriff a few hours to decide that Zeb got clean away, so don't expect Sheriff Lindsey to get his notice until sometime late tomorrow afternoon. That means Caldwell will probably find out shortly after that, because, if I know Sheriff Lindsey, he'll go straight to him with the news, if for no other reason than to get him off his back."

"Good," John said with a curt nod. "That means Lathe should be out of my hair forever by tomorrow night."

"At the latest," Simpson added with a grin then hoisted himself into the saddle. "Keep in mind, I should be back here within a few weeks. Have my money ready."

"You just have proof that Caldwell is really dead," John said, then stepped away before someone could pass by the alley and spot them together. "I'll have the money."

Lathe paced the floor for several hours before finally calming down enough to think rationally about what had happened. With his anger abated, he again tried to recall the exact details of what he had seen.

He had seen Leona coming out of George Parkinson's room, fully dressed and with every hair in place. George was the only one who looked as if he might have dressed in a hurry, but then Leona could have come by unexpectedly. It was possible she had told the truth when, seconds later, she had proclaimed her innocence, saying they had done nothing but talk.

Lathe ran his hand through his thick hair. Why was he always so quick to think the worst? Surely she could not have willingly given herself to him if she was also in love with another. Or could she? Some women found it quite easy to go from one lover to another.

But not Leona. She was not the type to become intimate with a man unless she truly loved him and had become thoroughly committed to that love. She had said that her being in George's room was not what he thought. That could very well be true. And if it *was* true, there was only one real way to find out and that was to go have that talk with her.

When Lathe glanced at his watch, he noticed it was already after seven. By the time he arrived at her house, it would be nearly eight — a little late to be paying a social call. Still, he could not wait until morning to see her. Hurriedly, he straightened his clothes and combed his hair, then headed out the door.

Even though he no longer believed that anything shameful had happened in George's room, he was curious to know why she had been there and what they had talked about. He considered stopping by George's room and asking him, but decided he would rather hear it from Leona. Besides, it had been far too long since he had held her in his arms. A man could go only so long without quenching certain thirsts.

When Ethan heard the knock, he fully expected it to be Lathe demanding an explanation for what he had seen that morning. Knowing how hard it might be to convince him of the truth, especially when he was not yet prepared to reveal to him that he actually was Leona's brother, he was slow in answering.

"Ge-orge?" the small Mexican man asked, pronouncing the name awkwardly while staring up at him expectantly. "You Ge-orge Ethan Parkinson?"

Since that was the name Ethan had used for the captain, his skin crawled with sickening anticipation. "Yes. That's me."

The Mexican smiled, revealing a mouth filled with large, crooked teeth. "My name is Carlito. I was told to deliver this message to you. I was told it is of great importance."

Ethan gritted his teeth then held his hand out and accepted the folded piece of white paper. Holding it, it did not feel like the inexpensive paper the telegraph office used. It felt more like expensive stationery. "Who sent you?"

"I cannot say. I was paid extra *dinero* to keep silent. It is important I do."

That also sounded like something Captain Potter would do, and if the message was not a telegraph, that meant the captain was in town. He swallowed back the constriction clutching his throat. "Can you at least tell me where I can find the man who sent this?"

Carlito frowned, looked gravely insulted, then shook his head. "No, I can say nothing. Not to nobody." He then lifted his chin proudly. "I gave of my word. The man's life is at stake."

Ethan studied the short, little man with a raised brow. "What if I were to offer you five dollars to tell me?"

Carlito's chin lifted higher. "I am a man of honor, *señor*. I do not go against my word."

Ethan sighed, aware the man meant what he said. "Can you at least wait until I have read the message? I may have one to send in return."

Carlito nodded then let out a short breath, obviously relieved that Ethan did not plan to force him to tell. "Yes, I can do that."

Stepping back to get away from the shadows hovering near the door, Ethan quickly unfolded the paper and read the message that had been hastily scrawled inside: "Meet me between midnight and sunup at the abandoned house shown on the map below. I have a plan but I need your help."

Ethan's expression arched with surprise when he glanced down at the small hand-drawn map and noticed the signature below. The note was not from Captain Potter. It was from Zeb.

"Do you have a message to send back in return?" Carlito asked, tired of waiting while Ethan stared at the paper with an open mouth.

Ethan lifted his gaze and looked at the little man for several seconds before he finally replied, "Nothing that needs to be written down. Just tell him I plan to leave right away."

He glanced at the map a second time and felt pretty certain the house indicated was the Conway place, but he had not been there in well over ten years and wanted plenty of time to find his way in the dark. "Tell him I'll wait inside the barn."

Even though it was after eight o'clock when Lathe finally knocked on Leona's front door, she had yet to get ready for bed. She had not given up hope that Lathe would eventually calm down enough to want to have that talk with her.

"Lathe, why are you out so late?" she asked, wanting him to admit that, although it had taken him awhile, he was finally ready to hear the truth about what happened. Why else would he be there?

"Is it late?" Lathe asked, looking as if he had no idea what time it might be. "I hadn't noticed."

"Well, perhaps you should check your watch from time to time, then you would know that it is now well after eight o'clock," she said, trying to sound smartly aloof, when what she wanted to do was throw her arms around him and welcome him with a big hug. "You do still have your watch don't you?"

Rather than continue with such inane banter, Lathe decided to get right to the point. "Leona, I've come to apologize for my earlier behavior. When I saw you leaving George's room, I immediately thought the worst thing I possibly could and I shouldn't have. It's just that the mere thought that you may have ever been in someone else's arms drives me insane."

"Come inside," she said, aware the front porch was no place for the intimate talk that was sure to follow.

After Lathe followed her inside, she held out her hand for his coat and noticed that for the first time in all the weeks she had known him, Lathe had come there unarmed. She wondered if there was some significance in the fact he had left his pistol behind.

"Let's go into the parlor so we can talk," she said, but when she turned to lead the way, she felt a restraining hand on her arm. When she turned back to see why he had stopped her, she knew that talking in the parlor was not what he had in mind. She smiled when instead of politely following her, he slowly pulled her into his arms and bent to kiss her passionately. The kiss was his way of showing her he no longer believed she had done anything wrong. He accepted her innocence.

It pleased her to know he had overcome his doubts on his own, with no explanation from her. That meant he trusted her, as well he should, because she loved him more than life itself. There was nothing she would not do for him, nothing she would not do to keep him.

Her heart raced with wondrous anticipation when his fingers moved to undo the first of her many buttons then dipped inside to touch her delicate skin as soon as the opening had grown large enough to allow it. She knew intuitively that his were not the hands of a killer. They were the hands of a healer and the hands of a lover. Never could such gentle hands be those of a killer.

She moaned softly while he continued to unfasten the back of her dress. When he slipped the fabric from her shoulders, to reveal the lacy camisole beneath, she pulled away just enough to speak.

"Could you take off the ring? It's cold against my skin," she said, then held her breath while she waited to see if he would comply.

Without hesitating he tugged at the ring until it finally came off then quickly set it on a nearby table and returned to untie the satin straps that held the top of her camisole together. When all her clothing finally lay in a rumpled pile at their feet, he bent to gather her into his arms and carried her not into the parlor, but down the hall and into her bedroom.

The room was dark except for a silvery island of moonlight that fell across the bed. Reverently, he set her into that delicate glow and stared longingly at her for several seconds before removing his own clothing.

When he joined her on the bed, he was as naked as she. Lovingly, she opened her arms and pulled him gently to her. When they closed their arms around each other she had a distinct sense of belonging, though there had yet to be any verbal commitments exchanged between them.

The warmth of his body spread quickly through her, bringing her a deep, languid pleasure while their mouths came together once again, eager to explore by first sampling then devouring. Slowly, the warmth she felt was transformed into molten desire as Lathe's mouth left hers to trail tiny, nibbling kisses down her throat, across her collarbone, then down to her aching breast. She cried aloud with ecstasy while she savored the fiery sensations that stirred deep within her when his lips descended over the tip. The torrent that blazed to life inside her seemed unbearable when he began to draw lightly on the breast, causing the tip to become taut with desire. She clutched helplessly at his back, letting him know that her passions had flared instantly.

Hoping to let him know of the searing urgency she felt, she bent forward to kiss the top of his head then tried to bring his mouth back to hers when she lay back down, hoping somehow to slow the madness raging inside her.

But instead of complying with her silent plea, Lathe endeavored to drive her into further ecstasy. While his mouth continued to arouse the one breast with tiny sucks and nips, his hand gently teased the other, sending shocks of pure rapture through her, until finally she cried aloud her need. "Now, Lathe, please, now."

Finally, he returned his hungry kisses to her mouth, but at the same time moved to fulfill the needs he had so quickly aroused within her. While their tongues eagerly sought the sweet depths of each other's mouths, they worked together to complete the enchanted journey, soaring ever higher, higher, until they crested the top. Having again experienced the ultimate in lovemaking, they floated gently down again, bound together in each other's arms, their energies spent.

It was several minutes before Leona moved to light the lamp on her bedside table.

When she turned around to look at him, her long, glimmering hair was tumbling down around her shoulders, and Lathe could hold back no longer. He had to tell her how he felt. "Leona, I realize I have no right to tell you this, but I think you should know that I have somehow fallen in love with you."

Those were the very words Leona had longed to hear. Her heart soared with intense joy. Blinking back her tears, she lay back beside him. Propped on one elbow, she gazed at him adoringly. "And I love you. I never thought I'd ever hear myself say this to anyone, ever, but I do so love you, and I *need* you."

Lathe grimaced at the pain her words caused and looked away. "Please don't say that."

Leona's heart plunged as easily as it had taken flight, aware that whatever Lathe was about to say, it was something she did not want to hear. Still, she had to hear it. "Why? Why are you so afraid of hearing how I feel?"

"Because it will make leaving that much harder," he admitted, staring at the ceiling with hopelessness. "I never should have told you how I feel. I'm sorry for having done that."

"But why? Why do you have to leave? Why can't you forget about Zeb Turner and stay here in Little Mound with me instead? Why can't you let your love for me grow until it outweighs your hatred for him?" While he continued to stare at the ceiling, as if deciding how to answer that, she held her breath, wondering if he intended to tell her the truth — that Zeb had witnessed the murder.

"It's more than mere hatred that forces me to follow him," Lathe admitted, then sat up to face her with one leg bent, wondering just how much he should tell her.

It was then Leona noticed the unusual scar on the inside of his thigh but she knew their present discussion was far too important for her to question him about it just then. She knew that he was very close to telling her everything, so she prompted him with yet another question. "Then what is it that makes you so determined to find him?"

Lathe raked his hand through his hair. If he told her the truth, he would probably end up in tears in front of her, and he did not want her to think him emotionally weak. Still, he felt she had a right to know why he might have to leave. "Zeb Turner murdered my brother."

Leona blinked several times while allowing that surprising revelation to register. "He *what?*"

"He murdered my brother. Right after the war was over," Lathe said, tears of anger and frustration already burning his eyes. "In cold blood."

"But I thought you were the one who —" she began, but then stopped to think more about it.

"I was the one who what?" Lathe asked, thinking it an odd beginning to a sentence.

"The one who killed someone else's brother," she answered honestly, eager to get to the bottom of everything.

"*What?*" Lathe's eyes widened then narrowed then widened again. "What are you talking about? Whose brother?"

Leona decided to tell him at least some of what Ethan had told her. "There is an ex-Confederate Army captain out there somewhere who claims that you killed his brother. He also claims that the real reason you are so determined to catch up with Zeb Turner is because you want to kill him. The way it was explained to Ethan, Zeb is the only witness to that murder and if you ever do manage to catch up with him and kill him, then there would be no one left who could make sure you hang."

"Ethan?" Lathe asked, trying to make the tiniest sense of what she had said thus far. "Who is Ethan?"

"George is Ethan," she said, then noticing his expression become even more confused, she explained. "That's why I was in George's room this morning. I was confronting him with the truth."

"Which is . . ." Lathe prompted, already starting to piece it together but wanting to hear it from her just the same.

"Which is that he really is my brother, Ethan; but he couldn't tell me because he wanted me to go on believing he was dead."

"And why would he want you to think he's dead? And what does he have to do with this captain who claims I killed his brother?"

Leona explained it in the same way Ethan had explained it to her. Lathe did not interrupt her once. He waited until she had finished before asking any further questions. "And do you believe this captain? Do you

396

believe that I may have murdered his brother?"

"No, of course not, not any more than I believe that Ethan could kill his friend, George. To tell you the truth, I think this Confederate captain, whoever he is, is to blame for both deaths."

"You don't know the captain's name?"

"No, I can't recall that Ethan ever mentioned it. He just kept referring to him as 'the captain.' "

"Well, I want a name," Lathe said, already grabbing for his clothes. "And I want it now."

Leona, too, hurried to get dressed, just as eager as Lathe to put the final pieces together.

Because Lathe was dressed again long before Leona, he helped her with her buttons then held her hairpins for her while she quickly restyled her hair. It was nearly eleven o'clock when they finally hurried out the door. Rather than waste precious time by walking to the hotel, and knowing that the streets were virtually deserted at that time of night, especially on a Sunday, Leona hiked her skirts to her knees and climbed onto Lathe's horse.

While she was waiting for Lathe to climb onto the horse behind her, she glimpsed something moving on her roof and she finally realized how Scraps had been getting out of her house. Somehow he was opening the door to the one bedroom that had no screens and hopping out the windows whenever they were left open, which was most of the time during the spring and summer.

But how was he getting down from the roof without breaking his fool neck? To her amazement, about the time Lathe flicked the reins to start his horse in a fast trot, the dog made a downward leap toward a tree and slowed his fall by ricocheting off the trunk. If she hadn't been so worried about Lathe's situation, she would have laughed aloud at the dog's ingenuity. As it was, she barely gave his feat a second thought, other than to make a mental note to have those windows screened the first chance she got.

A few minutes later, when she and Lathe arrived at the hotel, he hopped down first then held his arms out for her. Within seconds, she had smoothed her skirts and they were on their way into the empty lobby, headed for the main stairs.

Eager to know why he had been falsely accused and by whom, Lathe hurried ahead and knocked on the door several seconds before Leona arrived at his side. When there was no answer, he tried again—louder.

"He must be out somewhere," he muttered in a voice deep with frustration. The muscles in his jaw tensed visibly when he realized he had no choice but to wait.

"Not necessarily," Leona explained. "If he's anything like he used to be, he's a very sound sleeper. Try again, but louder."

Lathe did, knocking so hard it sent a shooting pain through his knuckles. "I don't think he's here."

Leona frowned then jiggled the doorknob, hoping the clattering noise might catch Ethan's attention. Her eyes widened when she discovered the door unlocked. Curiously, she opened it just wide enough to stick her head inside. "Ethan?"

Because the lamps were out, she opened the door all the way to cast more light into the room. When she did, she noticed the empty bed. The covers were rumpled but had not yet been pulled back. "You're right. He's not here."

"I wonder where he could have gone?" Lathe asked, aware the saloons were closed on Sundays and it was far too late for any of the restaurants still to be open.

"Perhaps he went out to see Sarah again," Leona suggested.

"This late?"

"Well then maybe he decided to take a ride or a long walk so he could have some time to think. Believe me, he has a lot to think about." She had not yet told Lathe about Ethan's plan to take the ring to the captain in his stead. She was afraid Lathe would demand to face his accuser rather than let him believe he was dead. Nor did she mention that Ethan had hinted he might know where Zeb had gone. She felt it was enough for Lathe to know he had been accused of a murder — at least for now.

"I guess we'll have to wait until morning to talk with him," she said, hoping to be there when they talked. "Maybe we should plan to discuss everything over breakfast. We could go right next door to the Silver Swan."

"No, this is a talk I want held in private," Lathe stated. "Why don't I bring him to your house first thing in the morning. Better yet, why don't we all meet at the Mercantile about a half an hour before you'd normally open. It would be closer for us, and you wouldn't have to worry about being late to open the door should our talk last very long."

Leona agreed, then turned to walk with him back down the hall. When they arrived at her house, she did not invite him inside. She knew it was already after midnight and they would get little enough sleep that night.

Chapter Twenty-two

When Ethan arrived at the Conway place, he was appalled by its run-down condition. Evidently old Tom had either died or moved out years ago and let the place go to ruin. The small holly bushes Ethan remembered being neatly kept across the front had grown until the house was engulfed by dark leaves. The dooryard was strewn with broken limbs from the huge oak trees, and covered with ragged patches of both dead and freshly sprouted uncropped grass. The foliage was nearly three feet high in places and concealed most of what remained of the small wooden fence and part of a trough where the water had turned a deep, murky green. The left side of the barn door had come loose and it dangled by one hinge.

He shivered when he led his horse through the missing gate and into the main yard. With so many shadows to add to the gloom, the place looked downright spooky.

Remembering his promise to wait for Zeb inside the barn, he climbed down from the saddle and carefully pulled the crooked door out far enough to open the adjoining door. He led his horse inside and tied him to a small post. To get a better look at his surroundings, he struck one of the half-dozen matches he had thought to put in his pocket just before he left.

400

As expected, the barn was empty except for a few broken implements propped against the back wall and a thick haze of spider webs trailing from the rafters and loft. It could be hours yet before Zeb showed, so Ethan slipped his rifle out of its holster and headed back outside to have another look around.

Curious to see the house where he had played so often as a young boy, he climbed the front steps and peeked into the black chamber the overgrown bushes had formed around the porch. Again, he struck a match and noticed the boards covering one of the front windows had been pulled loose.

Drawn by a sentimental desire to see the inside, he stepped closer to the unboarded window. He carefully lifted the glass, then stuck his head inside and lit yet another match. When he did, he saw a single table and chair, and a small camp lantern. The table and chair were crusted with dirt and looked as if they had been there for quite a while, but the lantern looked new.

"Zeb?" he called out, thinking he may have come early. When there was no response, he slipped one leg inside, then the other. "Zeb, you here?"

When there was still no answer, he blew out what remained of the match and slipped inside the house, aware he would be much more comfortable seated in a chair for the next few hours than crouching on the steps outside. With just enough light to make out shapes, he set his rifle across the table and considered lighting the lantern, but saw no real need to waste another match and left it alone.

Instead, he sat back in the chair and let his thoughts wander to the days when his mother used to come out to the Conway place to pay her weekly visit on Mrs. Conway. Because his mother and Doris Conway had attended the same church and had been about the same age, with children about the same ages, they had stayed very good friends right up until Doris died about fifteen years back. But that all seemed so far away — so very far removed from what his life was now.

Barely an hour after Ethan had settled into the chair, just when he began to get sleepy from having nothing to do, he heard a horse approach. Glad Zeb had not made him wait any longer, he hurried outside to let him know he was in the house instead of the barn.

When he stepped outside he saw the rider headed through the missing gate, several hundred feet away. Although he could not make out Zeb's face because of the shadows, there was just enough light for him to see the markings on the horse and he knew it had to be Zeb.

He tramped through the tall grass toward where the rider had brought the horse to a stop. "Glad you came so early," he said, wanting to make Zeb speak. He felt a little uneasy about the fact that he had yet to see the rider's face, but then he saw the man pull a cane down from the saddle before he turned, to limp awkwardly in his direction.

"Glad you came early, too," Zeb agreed, hurrying as fast as he dared on a game leg in such tall grass. "I need your help."

"So your letter said." Ethan followed Zeb directly to the open window and decided Zeb must have been the one to pull the boards away in the first place.

Zeb fumbled his way to the table and quickly lit the lantern. He waited until Ethan had come over beside him then reached into his jacket and pulled out a rolled piece of paper. "Glad to see you brought your rifle," he commented, indicating the weapon still on the table. "I feel better knowin' we have more than one rifle."

Ethan felt a dark foreboding creep into his stomach. "Why? What's this plan you have in mind?"

"Killing Lathe and gettin' him off my back once and for all," Zeb said, quickly backrolling the paper so it would lay flat. "It's something I should have done years

402

ago. If I had, I wouldn't be limpin' around on that cane now like some three-legged donkey."

"You plan to kill Lathe?" Ethan asked then shifted his weight to one leg and crossed his arms over the sharp pain squeezing through his chest. He had expected Zeb's plan to have to do with his helping him get away again.

"Sure, it would solve all our problems," Zeb said, glowering down at his leg with an expression charged with hatred. "With Lathe dead, we could all be happy again. The captain could get that information he wants and I could finally quit all this blasted runnin', and *you,* you wouldn't have to keep chasin' after us anymore. We could finally get on with our lives."

Ethan stared at him with a perplexed frown. "The captain could get *what* information? I thought the reason he was after Lathe was because Lathe killed his little brother."

Zeb looked at him and paused for a moment before he quickly wet his lips and looked down at the paper still in his hands. "That's right. That is the reason. But he also needs certain information from me in order to finally put the man away for good."

"So what's your plan?" Ethan asked, feeling so sick inside he could hardly breathe. He knew he wanted no part of whatever it was Zeb had in mind; but at the same time, he realized he could never help Lathe stay alive unless he knew exactly what Zeb intended to do.

"With your help, and the captain's, I plan to ambush Lathe in broad daylight." A strange gleam glinted from Zeb's dark eyes. "With any luck, Lathe will live just long enough to get a good long look at who shot him."

"With help from the *captain?* The captain is coming here?" Ethan felt something cold and immense grip his chest. "When?"

"I suspect he could be here as early as tomorrow mornin'," Zeb answered, glancing at him curiously.

403

"Why? Don't you think he has a right to be here for something like this?"

"Well, sure I do," Ethan said, hoping to sound convincing. "Fact is, I sent a wire to him myself just a few days ago telling him how I would be ready to make a move on Lathe myself sometime later this week. I just didn't know he intended to come on to Texas before then."

"He probably didn't until I had Carlito send that telegram to him late Saturday," Zeb admitted. "And I'm not all that sure he's on his way even now. I didn't want nobody knowin' I was still around, so I had Carlito put only my initials on it and just to be extra safe, I didn't give the captain no way to get hold of me in return. I'm just assumin' he got my message on Saturday and responded to it by catchin' the next train headed this direction."

Ethan prayed that would not be the case. "So? What is this plan of yours?" he asked, thinking it would be wise to pretend to go along with whatever Zeb had in mind—at least for now.

"Here, have a look at this map I stole from the Martins and see what you think," Zeb said, moving the lantern to one side so he could lay the page flat. "Lot of it has to do with perfect timin'."

The hotel clerk looked up when he heard the footsteps headed in his direction. He set his pen aside when he noticed a man dressed in white just a few feet away. "May I help you?"

"I certainly hope so. I need to know where I might find either a Mr. Zeb Turner or—" he paused, trying to remember the name Ethan had used. "Or a Mr. George Ethan Parkinson?"

"Don't have any Turners staying here, but we do have a Mr. Parkinson. Won't find him upstairs though. Already been one fellow stop by the desk looking for him today. Came by about an hour ago wanting to know when he'd left."

"Oh?" the captain said, sounding only casually interested while he brushed a piece of lint off the white hat he held in his hand. "And did you answer the man?"

"Just to tell him that I didn't actually see him leave. But I did explain that he might find Mr. Parkinson over to Stegall's Mercantile. Mr. Parkinson tends to spend a lot of his time over there with Miss Stegall."

"Miss Stegall?" he repeated, knowing she had the same last name and that Ethan had originally come from Little Mound, he realized she had to be either a sister or a cousin.

"Yes, Miss Leona Stegall. Has her Mercantile just down the street." He pointed in the general direction. "Up across from the courthouse at an angle."

"Thank you," the captain said, with a pleased smile, then he adjusted his white summer coat with his free hand. "I'll see if I can't find Mr. Parkinson there. But before I do, could you tell me where I might find the Golden Eagle Saloon? I'm supposed to meet a gentleman there at ten."

"Well, you'd sure better hurry. It's after nine-thirty now," the clerk said, then gave the directions he needed.

After writing the directions on the back of the telegram Zeb had sent Saturday, Captain Potter slipped the paper back into his pocket then pushed his hat back onto his balding head and stepped outside. Although he was eager to find Ethan, he first wanted to have that talk with Zeb. He was curious to see if he had carried out his plan yet and if it had been successful.

Following the directions exactly as given, Potter arrived in front of the saloon just as it opened. When he noticed that Zeb was not yet there, he sat down at a small table near the door so he would see Zeb the very minute he walked in.

When Zeb did not arrive immediately, the captain ordered a whiskey so as to have a reason for being there, not wanting to be tossed out as a vagrant. By eleven, he had drunk three such whiskeys and, deciding he had waited long enough, he pushed his chair back and strode toward the bar intent on asking the bartender if he happened to know Zeb. While waiting for the burly man to turn around from the tall stack of glasses he was polishing, he saw a small Mexican man enter the room and head straight for him. He waited to see why the man acted as if he had recognized him.

"Are you Captain Jeremiah Potter?" The man slipped his straw hat off his head and held it awkwardly across his chest.

"Yes, I am," he answered with a raised brow, still wondering how the man knew him.

"I was told you would probably be wearing all white," he said, grinning, obviously pleased he had found him so easily. "I have a message to give to you."

"From Zeb?"

The man's eyes widened then he nodded. "Yes, sir, it is from *Señor* Turner." He then reached into his pocket and pulled out a sealed envelope. "He said to give this to you."

Annoyed that Zeb had not bothered to meet him in person as indicated in the telegram, the captain snatched the envelope out of the man's brown hand.

"This had better be good," he muttered as he tore open the outer covering and quickly unfolded the letter inside. His expression changed from clearly annoyed to extremely intrigued while he read the message within. "Tell him I will do exactly what the letter says."

The Mexican shook his head. "But I think I will not see him again today. He left in the dark of the morning and said it might be days before he returns. He gave me this letter to give to you just before he left."

"I see, then perhaps he is already out there," the captain said, quietly refolding the paper and tucking it into his pocket. "I'd better hurry. Where can I get a horse in this town?"

Because the livery was so close, he did not have to write down the directions this time. He hurried first to hire a horse then headed straight to the Stegall Mercantile. Stopping to check the directions on the back of the telegram, he soon had the brightly painted sign of the Mercantile in his sight, and glanced around to find a shaded place to tether his horse.

It was then he noticed Lathe standing in the doorway talking to a pretty young woman in an apron who looked to be in her midtwenties. He wondered if she might be Leona Stegall.

Furious to see Lathe still alive, he glared angrily at the pair for several seconds, then spurred his horse on past.

In Saturday's telegram, Zeb had said Lathe was as good as dead and if all went well, he would take his last breath before noon Monday. Well, it was nearly noon now and Lathe was still very much alive — and very much interested in Ethan's sister, or cousin, or whoever the hell she was.

Angrily, he snatched Zeb's drawing out of his pocket and headed in the direction indicated. He wanted to know what had gone wrong this time, and he wanted to know *now*.

Within the hour, he had found the house designated on the map and, after reaching into his coat pocket to make sure his derringer was still in place, he climbed down from the horse and called out Zeb's name.

When he heard Ethan respond from inside the house, he headed in that direction and began his angry tirade just as soon as he had cleared the top step and spotted both men leaning out the window.

"I want to know why Caldwell is still alive," he said, marching angrily toward the window where both Ethan

407

and Zeb stood, eyes wide. He glared furiously at Zeb when he came to a halt just a few feet away. "I thought you said that man was to have reached his demise by noon today. I paid good money to make sure he did just that."

"And I fully intended for him to be dead by now," Zeb admitted, stepping back when he realized how angry the captain was. "But that was before I decided to wait for you. I thought you might want to be here when it happens."

The captain's anger visibly drained from his face and in its place remained a slight, distrustful frown. "Why? What do you have in mind?"

"Ambush," Zeb answered, grinning. "Come on inside and I'll fill you in on the whole thing."

After the captain learned more about Zeb's plan to lure Lathe into the perfect trap, his anger fully abated. Sitting in the only chair, staring up at the other two, he nodded his approval. "So Ethan here has managed to become friends with the scoundrel. Quite clever. Quite clever indeed."

"That's right," Zeb added, glad to see the captain smiling at last. "That's why all we have to do is send Ethan into town to summon him out here. I figure all he'll have to do to get him to follow him is tell him he thinks I might be hiding here. That should bring Caldwell at a high gallop. All I have to do is wait until his back is to me and shoot him dead center. It won't matter then how heavily armed he is when he gets here. If hit from behind, he'll never have a chance to get off a single shot."

Standing back away from the others, Ethan shifted his weight and kept his head bent forward. He knew he could never see such a cowardly plan through but did not want either of them to read that in his eyes.

"So, what do you think?" Captain Potter asked, leaning forward and nudging Ethan with an outstretched finger in an effort to make him look up. "Will he follow you out here like Zeb says?"

"I don't know. Maybe." Ethan glanced at him only briefly then returned his gaze to the dusty floor.

Aware something was wrong, the captain came out of his chair and stood directly in front of him. "What's the matter with you? You act like you don't want to do this."

"I'm just not too sure it will work," he said, shaking his head while continuing to avoid the captain's probing gaze. "What if he decides to bring the sheriff in on this? After all, he's had Sheriff Lindsey in on this ever since he first hit town."

"Then we shoot the sheriff, too," Zeb put in and glanced down at his injured leg with an angry glower. "I'd like to give him a taste of his own medicine."

"But what if they want to bring in a whole posse?" He finally lifted his face to meet the captain's stern gaze.

"You will see that he doesn't," he responded calmly, as if that should have been a foregone conclusion. "Because, my friend, if you don't pull this thing off just the way Zeb wants it pulled off then I will see to it that Leona is the one who pays for your mistakes."

Ethan's eyebrows notched at the unexpected mention of her name. "How did you find out about my sister?"

Captain Potter's mouth leveled into a satisfied smile, "Well, until now, I didn't know if she was a sister or a cousin, but I found out about her when I went to the hotel to ask around about you. Fact is, I've even had the opportunity to see her. Very pretty, your sister. How come you turned out so ugly?"

Ethan let the insult slide. He was too worried about his sister's safety to care what anyone thought of his appearance. "There's no need to bring her into this."

"No, there's not," he answered agreeably. "At least not as long you do exactly what you're told. Whether your sweet little sister ends up a part of any of this really depends on you."

Ethan let out a defeated breath. He knew the captain meant every word he said. If he did not cooperate, Leona would suffer the consequences. "I'll do whatever you ask."

"Too bad," Zeb said with a cruel sneer as he leaned heavily on his cane. "I'd like to be the one to put a bullet through that blasted woman's pretty head. If she hadn't jumped off my horse the way she did, that sheriff never would have had the courage to take off after me. It's just as much her fault as the sheriff's that I got shot."

"How bad *is* your leg?" the captain wanted to know, turning a shoulder to Ethan to give Zeb his full attention.

"Hurts like hell, but at least I can get around on it now, thanks to the Martins. But don't worry. It won't be any problem for me to climb up into that loft when the time comes."

"Good. You wait for him in the loft. You should have a clear shot at the front porch from there. I'll stay here in the house and make enough noise, for him to hear it outside and think you're in here."

"And, Ethan," Zeb said, stepping toward him to face him squarely, "if you fail to do exactly what you're told, Leona is not the *only* one who will suffer. Since the first day I laid eyes on her I've had a burning itch for that pretty little Sarah Martin you seem so sweet on."

Ethan's body tensed with a desperate desire to smash his fist into the very middle of Zeb's smirking face; but he kept his temper in check.

"I already told you I intend to do exactly what you want," he repeated in as casual a tone as he could muster, then turned his attention back to the captain. "But you have to keep your promise that as soon as I have helped you take care of Caldwell once and for all, I will

410

no longer be in your debt. I will be free to do whatever I want with my life."

"That's sounds reasonable," the captain responded vaguely, then reached into his coat pocket for a cigar, already trying to figure out ways to spend all that money.

When Ethan entered the Mercantile a few hours later, he saw Lathe before he saw his sister, and, feeling very much like a callous murderer, he headed directly for him. If it were not for the fact that Lathe had killed a man and—whether by accident or not—he deserved to answer for that, Ethan was certain he would never be able to follow through with Zeb's plan. As it was, it was either the life of a killer, or the life of his sister.

"Eth—" Lathe started to say then remembered that Leona's brother did not yet want his true identity known and changed it. "George! We've been looking all over Little Mound for you. Where have you been?"

"Out for a ride," he answered vaguely. "And I think I may have found something while on that ride that should interest you."

"Well whatever it is, it can wait. Leona and I want to talk to you. Right now, before I leave."

Having spotted her brother when he first entered, Leona quickly finished with the customer she was waiting on, then hurried to lock the front door and pull down the shades. "Come on into the back where we can sit down."

Ethan followed, puzzled by the serious expressions on their faces. He waited until they were all three seated around a small work table in the back, then asked, "What's wrong?"

"That's what I want to know," Lathe answered, leaning forward in his chair. "Leona said there is a captain out there who claims I killed his brother and that

411

Zeb witnessed it. I want to know more about that."

"Like what?"

"Like who this man is and why he's spreading such vicious lies about me." He curled his hand into a hard fist and slammed it against the table to emphasize his anger.

"Lies?" Ethan asked, confused by the sincerity in Lathe's determined expression. It was every bit as profound as the captain's had been. "Then you *didn't* kill his brother?"

"You know he didn't," Leona admonished. "He never even knew about the accusation until I mentioned it to him."

"I've never killed a man in my life," Lathe stated calmly, not as insulted by Ethan's willingness to doubt him as Leona had been.

"But I don't understand. If you didn't kill Captain Potter's brother, then why are you trying so hard to catch up with Zeb?"

"Because *Zeb* killed *my* brother," Lathe explained, already reaching into his pocket for the proof. "Right after the war was over, Zeb Turner murdered my brother in a small town in Alabama called Mill Run. There was a witness and Zeb was sentenced to hang as a result; but he managed to escape just hours before. As you can see, there's a reward for his capture, though I couldn't care less about the money. All I want is justice."

While Ethan studied the wanted poster, he felt the last of what little resolve he had gathered slowly drain out of him. "Then you didn't do anything wrong? You didn't kill nobody?"

"No, Zeb is the only murderer I know," Lathe answered, then went on to tell him more about the incident, but Ethan was too distracted to listen.

"Lathe, we got problems," Ethan said, unaware he had interrupted anything.

412

"What sort of problems?" Leona asked, frightened by the sudden pale coloring in her brother's face.

"Zeb has sent for the captain. And the two of them have in turn sent me here to try to convince you to follow me back out to the Conway place where they are all set up to shoot you in the back the second you step on the front porch."

Leona let out a startled gasp then reached for Lathe's hand, her heart hammering with brutal force. "But that can't be. Zeb was spotted just this morning a few miles outside Daingerfield. Sheriff Lindsey received a telegraph only a little while ago telling him all about it. Lathe was just about to leave."

"Couldn't have been Zeb," Ethan told them. "I just left him and the captain, not more than an hour ago. They're out at the old Conway place right now waiting for me to bring Lathe back."

"Then we have to tell the sheriff," Leona said, pushing her chair back, but not yet letting go of Lathe's hand.

"They said they'd kill him, too, if he came along. Fact is, Zeb is just itching to get back at that man for the hole he put in his leg."

"Well, we have to do *something*," she wailed. "Those two are not about to wait out there forever. Eventually they will realize you two aren't coming and decide to come into town after you."

"Who said we aren't going?" Lathe asked, resting his other hand on top of hers to help reassure her in some way. "The only way we will ever be safe from those two is by confronting them directly. Since Ethan obviously has heard their plan, we have the advantage of knowing right where they are and what they expect to happen after we get there. That's an advantage we won't have later if we let this thing slide."

"That's true," Ethan stated. "If we don't get them now, there's no way for us to know how and when they

413

will strike later on. Right now, I know their plans by heart. The captain intends to be in the house making lots of noise while Zeb positions himself up in the barn loft. Zeb is the one who is supposed to do all the shooting."

"Then while you sneak up on Zeb the back way, I will come in the front as planned. Hopefully, Zeb will be concentrating on me so he won't notice when you come up from behind. Then as soon as you indicate you've gotten the drop on him, I'll confront this captain face to face. I want to know why he's been spreading such vicious lies about me."

"But what if the captain doesn't want to come out and face you? What if instead he decides to shoot you where you stand?" Leona argued, thinking the two men fools for trying such a thing.

"I don't think he's the type to do his own killing. If that were true, he never would have sent Ethan after me. He'd have come after me himself."

"That's true," Ethan said, trying hard to keep their fears at bay. "That's why Zeb is the one who'll be climbing up in the loft, even though he's still got that injured leg. The captain doesn't like to bloody his own hands."

"But then it could be he's just lazy," Leona argued. "It could be that he doesn't have any qualms at all about killing, he just prefers to make someone else do all the work."

Lathe frowned and looked at Ethan. "Is the captain armed?"

"Not that I know of. I was adamant enough about wanting my rifle with me in case something went wrong, so they let me bring it along. But on the other hand, I didn't take the time to check the captain's saddlebags. He could be carrying a pistol I don't know nothin' about. So could Zeb for that matter."

"Then I'll approach the house under the assumption he has a weapon," Lathe said with a resolute nod.

"Lathe, don't do this," Leona pleaded, already knowing it was a lost cause. She could tell by the determined gleam in his blue eyes that he meant to do it.

"Leona, we have to," he said quietly. "If I'm ever to have peace of mind again, I have to see this through. Until I have finally brought Zeb Turner to justice, we can never be married."

Leona blinked several times, startled by what had sounded very much like a marriage proposal. "But then again, I cannot marry a dead man. The judge in this town just won't allow it."

Lathe smiled, aware she was trying to wear him down with humor.

When he leaned forward to stroke her cheek gently, it sent a strange contrast of warmth and chills down her spine.

"That could be to your advantage. I've been told I'd make a lousy husband—even alive." His tone then turned serious. "Leona, we have to go."

"If we don't," Ethan put in. "They will eventually find some way to kill us all, you and Sarah included."

Having heard that, Lathe stood so abruptly, his chair fell back and clattered to the floor. "Then let's go. I have to stop by the hotel and get my other pistol and my rifle. I want to have as much protection as possible before I go riding in there."

Chapter Twenty-three

Lathe waited a full eight minutes before urging his horse out of the woods and back out onto the road. Ethan had claimed he would need only six minutes to get into place, but Lathe wanted to give him the extra time just to be sure nothing went wrong.

A few minutes later, Lathe caught his first glimpse of the house and yard from the road when he came over a small hill. Within seconds after he turned off, he spotted his burly friend hiding behind a huge water trough only about fifty yards from the barn, right where he was supposed to be.

Lathe then noticed the barn door. Because of the slight wind, one side rocked precariously from its top hinge while the other stood wide open, Ethan should have little problem entering unnoticed — at least as far as Zeb was concerned. The only way Ethan could be spotted now was if the captain had found himself a clear view of that particular area through the narrow crevices of the boarded windows. But Lathe was confident that if the captain was indeed looking out a window, he would be watching the front gate for him.

As he entered the main yard, he kept his head pointed toward the house, but he cut his gaze briefly at the loft and noticed the door there ajar. It was open to where a man could get a clear shot of the house, but not much else — parted just enough for the barrel of a rifle to ease through practically unnoticed when the time came.

But that time should never come, not if Ethan did exactly what he was supposed to do.

Lathe's blood stirred at the realization that if everything went according to plan, he would finally have Zeb Turner firmly within his clutches, and Ethan would finally be free of the captain's control. Even if there was no way to prove the captain had broken any laws, by the time Lathe got finished making a few threats of his own, that poor excuse of a man would know better than to try to extort any more of Ethan's life.

Cutting his gaze from the barn back to the house, he stopped just inside the main fence and turned around in his saddle, as if searching for someone. He hoped they would think he had truly expected to find Ethan. Looking both perplexed and alarmed, he pulled hard on his reins and slowly backed his horse away from the house, all a clever ploy to hold the attention of both the captain and Zeb long enough for Ethan to make his move.

While glancing around, trying to appear deathly worried when in fact there seemed absolutely nothing worth worrying about yet, he glimpsed Ethan just seconds before he disappeared into the barn. He continued to back slowly away and appear flustered, all the while waiting for the all clear sign from the loft.

When Ethan did not appear in the opening during the next few seconds, Lathe's heart rate began a steady climb. Something had gone wrong. While wondering what he should do next, he heard hurried footsteps from inside the barn and glanced over in time to see Ethan burst into the yard, his face filled with alarm.

"Lathe, get out of here," he shouted after coming to an abrupt halt several yards away. His panic-stricken gaze darted about as if in desperate search of something. "Zeb wasn't in the loft."

417

"Nor will you find the captain in the house," they heard. At that same instant, Zeb appeared from behind the barn door, his rifle already aimed at Lathe's head. "Ethan, old boy, we had a feeling you would break down at the last minute and warn your new friend of our clever ploy. Isn't that right, Captain?"

"Exactly right," came a response. "I could tell just by looking at him, he was going to turn tail on me." The voice had come from somewhere in the front yard. Ethan and Lathe turned in time to watch Captain Potter emerge from behind the oak tree closest to the house, his white coat splattered with bright patches of the sunlight that splashed through the young leaves. In his left hand, he held a small derringer, pointed down; but in his right, he held a large revolver, pointed directly at Ethan. "I could tell by the way you refused to look at me."

Ethan turned to glance back at Lathe, his dark eyes round with apology. "I said for you to get out of here!"

In the second that followed, a shot rang out, hitting Ethan's back with such force that it caused him to stumble forward. He grimaced when he realized he had been shot, though he had yet to feel much pain. Glancing back to see which of them had fired, he noticed that Zeb's rifle was still aimed at Lathe. It was the captain's bullet that had cut through him.

Lathe watched in horror when Ethan turned to look at him again. Ethan's face was filled with disbelief when he reached behind him to feel for the wound and his hand was quickly covered with blood. "Lathe, they done killed me. You get the hell out of here."

Ethan then turned to face the other two, raising his rifle as if intending to shoot back, but slumped before he could get off a single shot. Folding more at the waist than the knees, he curled forward at an angle and fell into the thick grass with a sickening thud.

Not about to leave Ethan behind in the hands of

418

these two ruthless men, Lathe kicked his horse sharply in the flank and sent him rearing forward. Reacting on sheer instinct, he then rolled backward over the horse's rump and dropped to the ground, at the same time drawing his pistol out of his holster.

Landing sharply on the side of his shoulder, he bit back a yelp of pain and scampered quickly for the same water trough Ethan had used earlier to shield himself from the house.

Keeping low while he hurried through the tall grass, he heard several shots. He knew they had to be aimed at him, but had no way to judge how close the bullets had come to striking him until one splintered the front of the trough just as he wriggled in behind it. The next three shots also struck the front of the trough, barely two feet from where he lay on his side, waiting for the opportunity to take a quick shot back at them.

"Did you get him?" the captain called out just as Lathe prepared to rise up from behind the trough and take his first shot.

"Can't tell," Zeb answered. "I think I may have winged him, but I can't be sure."

Stopping himself in time, Lathe fell back to the ground and did not move, wanting them to think he might already be dead.

"Can't you see him from there? You're only about fifty yards away."

"No, Captain, I can't see nothin' from here. There's too much grass in the way."

Lathe listened carefully to the footsteps that followed, aware Zeb was cautiously moving toward him. He waited until he felt certain Zeb was in the open, then quickly rose up and fired. He stayed unprotected just long enough to see Zeb's body jerk, indicating he had successfully hit his mark, then fell back behind the trough. In the next instant, he heard Zeb's body hit the ground — *hard*.

"Zeb!" The captain sounded like he was still near the house. "Zeb, you all right?"

Lathe took the chance that the captain would be looking toward the barn, where Zeb had fallen. In one quick movement, he lifted his head just high enough to peer over the top and he took a shot in the captain's general direction, hoping the man would do something in return to give away his exact location. He did. The next shot came from behind that same tree. The captain had not moved.

"Zeb! Can you get to him from where you are?" Potter called out, his voice filled with a combination of anger and fear.

When Zeb offered no response, the captain realized he now faced Lathe alone. Squatting carefully to remain protected by the tree, he picked up a stick near his feet then stood again. He hoped to distract Lathe just long enough to make a run for the house, so he threw the stick as hard as he could toward the barn, wanting Lathe to think Zeb had made the resulting noise.

But Lathe had expected him to do exactly that and he kept his gaze trained on the broad trunk of the tree, waiting with his pistol poised in midair. When the captain made his wild, stumbling dash for the house, Lathe fired two shots. He cursed under his breath when he realized both had missed. The captain clambered up the steps and disappeared behind the thick shrubbery surrounding the front porch.

Knowing he had little choice but to charge the house and hope for the best, Lathe slowly rose to his feet, all the while holding his Colt in readiness. When he started to ease around from behind the large drinking trough, the captain suddenly ducked out from behind the thick bushes and took a wild shot in his direction.

Lathe reacted swiftly and, fanning the hammer, fired three shots before dropping quickly behind the trough again.

420

Aware he had emptied his pistol with those last shots, he reached to the back of his holster for six more bullets. His chest constricted with instant alarm when he discovered that only three remained. At some point during all that commotion, the remaining bullets had worked their way out.

With no time to search the tall grass for the other bullets and with his other weapons still on his horse, he quickly slipped the three he still had into the proper chambers and prepared to make his assault on the house. To find out exactly where the captain had gone, he slipped out of his vest and rather than stand up himself, he wadded the vest and lifted it high above the trough. When no shot rang out, he peered over the trough toward the house, puzzled.

"Hey, Captain, you may as well give up," he shouted, hoping to draw a verbal response. "Without Zeb, you don't stand a chance."

After a lengthy, nerve-racking silence, Lathe decided to take the risk and slowly stood. When nothing happened, he began the long, cautious trek toward Ethan, anxious to see if he might still be alive.

While keeping his gaze trained on the front of the house, ready to drop to the ground the instant he spotted any movement, he continued to cross the yard, half-crouching, half-standing, but constantly moving. Although he could not actually see Ethan's body through the crop of three-foot weeds and dead grass that surrounded him, he could tell where his friend lay by the large indentation where the foliage had fallen flat.

Lathe was about halfway there when he first noticed a sound from somewhere behind him. He spun around just as the next shot rang out. This time, a bullet grazed him in the left leg, a few inches below the knee. He ignored the stinging pain when he spotted Zeb kneeling in front of the barn, his Spencer rifle still raised to his blood-soaked right shoulder. He was wavering slightly but ready to fire.

Before Lathe could drop into the grass, Zeb fired again. This time the bullet missed him, flying just past his neck. After rolling until he faced the barn again, he rose up on one knee, just high enough off the ground to see through the tops of the wind-wavering grass. When he saw that Zeb had stood to try to get a better shot at him, he fired all three of his remaining bullets. The first shot splintered the barn wall several yards away. The second whizzed within inches of Zeb and struck the barn door, causing it to slam back against the wall with a sharp whack. But the third shot met its mark. Zeb screamed with rage just before he clutched his side and crumpled forward into the dirt a second time.

Lathe's pistol was again empty and knowing Zeb could still be alive and threatening, Lathe turned and headed toward Ethan again. Remembering Ethan had never gotten off a shot, Lathe knew the rifle beside him should still have all seven bullets.

Running like a madman, despite his injured leg, Lathe reached Ethan's side within seconds. Just as he bent forward and scooped the rifle off the ground, another shot sounded, scattering grass and dirt just inches from his feet.

Aware that the shot had come from the direction of the house and not the barn, he spun about to find his next target, but did not immediately see anyone.

"Toss the rifle," he heard, then finally spotted the captain down on one knee near the back of the house, his long-barreled pistol held steady in both hands, aimed right at his heart.

Aware the odds were definitely against him this time, Lathe did as told, but tossed the weapon only a few feet away.

"Zeb? You all right?" Potter asked while he slowly

rose and moved in Lathe's direction, never taking his gaze off his intended victim.

Grimly, Lathe realized there was not a mark on the captain. He had missed completely.

"Hell, no, I ain't all right," Zeb responded in a deep, guttural voice while he slowly forced himself back to his feet. "That fool damn near shot my shoulder off."

Lathe glanced at Zeb and frowned when he noticed that he had opened his shirt and was busily examining his two wounds. Although the injury to the front of his shoulder appeared serious, the other was merely a surface wound. That last bullet had barely clipped his side. Zeb had fallen to the ground that second time as a bluff to make him stop shooting. Lathe felt like an idiot.

"Okay, Caldwell, it's time for you to come away from over there," the captain said, effectively recapturing Lathe's attention. "I want you well away from that rifle and whatever other weapon Ethan may have on him."

When Lathe glanced at Ethan, he was surprised to see his eyes open and his chest moving just enough to indicate life. Although nothing else moved, Lathe felt there was a very good chance he could be lucid. Taking a carefully planned step, he kicked the rifle closer to him when he then headed toward the captain, his hands raised high into the air. But when the rifle struck Ethan's hand and he didn't flex as much as a facial muscle, Lathe knew the cause was hopeless. Ethan might still be alive, but he was not responding to physical stimuli.

"Now what?" Lathe asked the captain when he stopped a few dozen yards away, aware that he was positioned about halfway between the two men.

"Now I want you to take off your pants."

"You want *what?*" Lathe asked, not certain he had heard him correctly.

"Your pants. Take them off. I want to have a gander at that famous scar of yours."

423

When Lathe did not immediately oblige, the captain moved a few steps closer, letting Lathe see that the hammer of his pistol was already cocked, ready to fire.

"I said take off those pants. I want to see that scar."

"How do you know about my scar?"

"Jonathan told me," the captain said, then chuckled when the mention of his brother's name caused Lathe's whole body to tense. "That's right. I know all about the family treasure. Jonathan told me everything."

Suddenly, Lathe did not care that the captain was now less than a hundred feet away and still held a pistol on him. He would not allow the man to lie about his brother like that. "Jonathan wouldn't do that."

"Oh, but he did. The lad was a talker, especially whenever he had too much to drink. Fact is, he told me all about how the two of you sold everything you owned in exchange for gold just weeks before the war got started. He told me how you then put that gold and some of the family jewelry into a large steamer trunk and buried it deep in the ground for safekeeping. He also told me your plan for recovering everything after the war was finally over. He explained how the two of you carved the nearest longitude and latitude directly into your own flesh, deep enough to leave scars so you wouldn't forget the location, knowing the special rocks you placed nearby could eventually be cleared away. Pretty sound thinking, I'd say. I applaud your good sense."

"Is that why Zeb killed him?" Lathe asked, keeping his hands raised as high as his shoulders but wishing he could use them to smash their faces instead. "Just to get the information off his leg?"

Zeb chuckled and limped forward for his moment of glory, dabbing at his bloodied shoulder with his wadded shirt. "You are right, Captain. This one's pretty smart. He figured that all out on his own."

424

Lathe's anger flared, and the muscles in his jaw pumped rhythmically.

"Of course part of the reason we decided to go ahead and kill him instead of just knocking him senseless was to get him out of the way," the captain went on to explain. "Didn't want him finding all that gold before we did."

"Speaking of gold," Zeb said, taking another step in Lathe's direction. "I want that ring. Your brother's ring just like it brought over a hundred dollars in Alabama."

Lathe turned his hands so Zeb could see them better. "I don't have it anymore. I left it with someone."

"Probably Ethan's sister," Zeb commented, then grinned. "Doesn't matter. I'll just get it from her when I stop by to pay my respects." His grin turned into a lurid sneer when he added, "And that ring is not *all* I'll get from that wench before I'm through."

Lathe took an angry step toward Zeb but was quickly reminded of the captain's advantage when a bullet struck just inches from his feet.

"I wouldn't if I were you," he cautioned then laughed. "Now be a good boy and drop those pants."

With bitter hatred glinting from his eyes, Lathe refused. Instead he faced the captain with his chin high and his body rigid, ready for the shot that would end his life.

Aware Lathe had no intention of doing as told, the captain shrugged then moved closer to get a better shot. "Then I'll just take them off myself after you're dead." He chuckled as he made a big production of stretching his arm out to take perfect aim. "So, Zeb, where should I shoot him? In the head or in the heart?"

Aware Zeb was unarmed at that moment and the captain now stood only a dozen feet away, Lathe considered rushing the man. Although he knew the captain would get off at least one good shot before he reached him, it was really his only hope.

"So long, Caldwell," the captain said, then closed his left eye to assure a perfect aim but popped it back open when the next gunshot sounded. Blood shot from his chest when he turned to look at Ethan. His expression registered total disbelief just before collapsing, with the gun still in his hand.

Cursing with rage, Zeb turned and made an awkward dash for his rifle, which he had left several yards away. Ethan tried to stand, to get a better shot, but stumbled and fell weakly back to the ground. Aware Ethan did not have the strength to lift the weapon and shoot again, Lathe set himself in immediate motion but was unable to get but a few yards before Zeb had his rifle again and had swung it around.

Aware of the danger, Lathe made a mad dive into the grass just as a shot sounded—but it was Zeb who screamed as he jerked back and fell to the ground.

Astonished, Lathe turned to see how Ethan had ever managed to gather enough strength to fire that shot and was stunned to see Leona standing near the main road, a rifle poised in her hands and a look of utter amazement on her face.

Lathe blinked several times, unable to believe Leona had managed to hit the man at such a distance. Confused, he did not know whether to chastise her for having put her life in danger like that or sing her praises for having just saved him from certain death. Although what he wanted was to go to her and find out what on God's green earth had possessed her to follow them—aware she was still in shock over what she'd done and very well might faint—he knew Ethan needed him more and Lathe quickly returned to his friend's side.

An immediate examination of both Ethan and the area where he lay revealed how very much blood he had lost. He knew that the bullet might very well have pierced his lung. Bending forward, he pressed his ear to

Ethan's chest to listen for gurgling sounds, a sure indication the lung was damaged. But all he heard was a deep, rattling wheeze, which was really inconclusive.

Ethan was still awake but in shock, though aware he had killed the captain and saved Lathe's life. Weakly, he smiled while Lathe rolled him onto his side and ripped his shirt to get a better look at the wound. "Maybe I helped undo some of the bad I've done by killing the captain when I did."

"You won't hear me complaining," Lathe admitted, forcing a return smile before glancing up when he felt Leona's presence. "And I don't think you'll hear Leona complain much either."

"Leona?" Ethan asked, then squinted to get a better look at the shadow standing over them. "What are you doing here?"

"Who do you think shot Zeb that last time?" she asked, then held out their father's hunting rifle so he could see. Although she tried to appear very calm and composed about the whole matter, her hands trembled so violently, the rifle shook. When she first came over the hill and found some man holding a gun on Lathe, while Ethan was nowhere in sight, her fear had been overwhelming.

"You shot Zeb?" Ethan asked and tried to chuckle but the sound instead came out as several short rasping coughs.

It was after her brother had finally stopped coughing that Leona heard Zeb let out a low groan.

"Zeb is still alive," she gasped and rushed over to make sure his rifle was nowhere within his reach. After tossing it well away from them, she bent forward and felt Zeb's neck for a pulse. She did not know whether to be relieved that she had not actually killed the man or angered to find him still alive.

Hurriedly, she snatched up the rifle she had tossed aside and carried it and her own to Lathe's side, where she deposited both before heading over to see if the captain might still be alive. When she again returned to Lathe's side, she reported, "The captain is dead but Zeb is still alive, though barely."

"Is he unconscious?" Lathe asked, holding Ethan in position with one hand while he probed the bullet wound with the little finger of the other, hoping to find the bullet near the surface where it could be easily extracted.

"For now he is," Leona answered, then nodded toward her brother, who was also unconscious. "Can you save him?"

Lathe pressed his lips hard against his teeth while he eased Ethan back down to let him lie flat. "Not without the proper instruments. But then, even if I did have the instruments, I doubt I could save him. That bullet had to have hit his lung or his heart."

"But if you had the right instruments, there'd be a chance?"

"There's always a chance," he admitted, though he did not want her clinging to false hopes.

"Then we'll take him to Dr. Owen's office. Everything is still right where it was the day he died, even his instruments."

"But how do we get him there? Did you bring a carriage?" he asked, glancing at her hopefully.

"No," she answered, not ready to admit she had stolen her neighbor's horse and ridden out there bareback. "But we are only half a mile from the Martin farm. I know I can get a wagon or a carriage from them," she said, already heading toward the nearest horse, which was Ethan's. "I'll be right back."

Sarah was the only one home when Leona arrived in a panic-stricken state. She rushed outside the moment

428

she heard the frantic shouts begging for someone's help.

"What's wrong?" she asked as she hurried into the yard, wondering what had happened to cause Leona to behave like that. She was like a madwoman.

"Ethan has been shot. So has Zeb. At the Conway place. I need a wagon," she said, flailing her arms wildly, already headed toward the barn.

Aware that whatever had set Leona off, causing her to talk out of her head like that, it had to have been something very serious. Sarah followed and asked no questions while she hurriedly helped Leona hitch their best horse to her father's wagon.

As soon as they had the animal secured, they both climbed into the wagon, and with Leona driving, they headed out of the yard, leaving Ethan's horse behind.

By the time they had the Conway house in sight, Leona had become calm enough to explain a little of what had happened, but to Sarah it still did not make sense. Leona kept claiming that *Ethan* had just been shot, when they both knew Ethan was already dead.

It was not until they came closer and Sarah saw that it was *George* who had been shot that she, too, became frantic. To Lathe's amazement and relief, the women proved to be very strong physically. Knowing time was essential, they helped him get both Ethan and Zeb into the wagon and within a very few minutes, they were all on their way into town, this time with Lathe driving.

Making the trip in record time, within a quarter of an hour they pulled to a clattering halt in front of the doctor's office. Realizing they did not have time to hunt for whoever might have the key, Lathe hopped down and broke the door open with a resounding kick then hurried inside to assure himself that the promised instruments did indeed exist.

By the time he arrived back outside, a crowd had gathered and he had plenty of help getting the two men

429

inside. There were two patient rooms in Dr. Owen's office and he had some of the men carry Ethan into the first and Zeb into the second. Iris Rutledge appeared out of nowhere and immediately did what she could to stop Zeb's bleeding while Lathe, Leona, and Sarah went to work on Ethan.

It was while Lathe was hard at work trying to dislodge the bullet and Sarah and Leona were holding Ethan's arms flat against the padded table, so he could not fight the pain, that Sarah finally found the courage to ask, "So, he is Ethan, isn't he?"

Leona was in no state to tell her the entire story, but did nod that it was true. "He finally admitted it to me." She pulled her tearful gaze away from Lathe's work and looked at Sarah. "I am scared to death I'm going to lose him again."

Overwhelmed by all she had just learned, Sarah began to shake uncontrollably and stepped away from the table to sit in a nearby chair. Tears filled her eyes as she clasped her hands against her cheeks. "Oh, Leona, if he dies now, a part of me will surely die with him."

Chapter Twenty-four

"Here it is," Lathe said as he deposited the tiny lump of metal into his blood-splattered hand. "The good news is that this bullet did not pierce the lung or the heart. The bad news is that it did do some pretty severe damage to one of his ribs and his condition remains critical. Only time will tell whether he'll live or not."

Leona decided it was to everyone's advantage for her to appear as brave as possible when inside she was terrified. "He'll make it. I know he will."

Lathe smiled, proud of her courage. "We'll soon see. After I put a couple of stitches in that wound and tape a pad of gauze down to keep it clean while it drains, I will have done all I can for him. At least for now."

"What about Zeb?" Leona asked. "Are you ready to have a look at him?"

Lathe's face hardened with such intense hatred it surprised even Leona.

"I guess I should at least have a look."

"I'll stay here with Ethan," Sarah volunteered, coming out of her chair to rest a gentle hand on Ethan's bare shoulder. The determination was back in her voice and the color had returned to her cheeks. "I'll call if there is any change."

When Lathe followed Leona into the next room, he discovered that Iris Rutledge was still there, though it had been hours since their arrival. In that time, she had managed to stop two of Zeb's wounds from bleeding and, while holding a thick pad of gauze over the still oozing wound, she busily cleansed away as much dried blood as possible from around the other two.

"Doctor, he has not as much as flinched a muscle since they brought him in here," she said, then quickly backed away to give them room.

With Leona still at his side, Lathe lowered the overhead cable lamp Iris had lit and noticed the bullet that had struck Zeb's shoulder had gone straight through. But clearly one bullet was still inside the man—the one Leona had placed just inches above his left hip.

Lathe knew he had two choices. He could leave the bullet right where it was and let the man die—and be through with the whole ugly ordeal at last. Or he could try to save his life and take him back to Alabama to hang, as he had originally planned. The decision was solely his and was a hard one to make.

Despite the fact that this man had willingly admitted having killed his brother and very well might have killed Leona's brother, too, Lathe's allegiance to the Hippocratic oath finally asserted itself. When he turned to gather the needed instruments, he found Iris already placing them on a small tray in the proper order.

"Are you a nurse?" He arched his eyebrows inquisitively.

"I was many years go," she admitted. "But I gave it up the day I married Harry Rutledge. Harry was one of those men who thought it was an unforgivable sin to have a wife who worked." She paused to hold up a small brown bottle labeled *ether*. "Will you need this?"

"Not unless he starts to wake up and thrash around," he answered, then turned to look at Zeb again.

Knowing that Iris would be more helpful, Leona stepped

back and let the other two work. She watched with clasped hands while Iris handed Lathe the instruments he needed to extract the bullet. Finally, after twenty minutes, Lathe stood erect and deposited the bullet on the tray beside several of the instruments he had used.

"If you don't mind, I'll let you clean up," he said to Iris, already headed for the door. "I want to get back in the other room and see how Ethan is coming along."

Iris's eyes widened when she heard the name Lathe had used, but she did not ask any questions. Instead she set about putting all the bloodied instruments in a small basin to be boiled and replaced in their airtight containers.

It was not until Lathe had again examined Ethan's wound and found it had finally stopped bleeding that he relaxed enough to realize his own pain. He pulled up his bloodied trouser leg and studied the wound.

With Leona's assistance, he tore off part of his trouser leg and tended to his own injuries, letting her apply the clean bandages after he finished. It was not until Lathe, too, had been patched and suddenly there was nothing more for her to do that the seriousness of what had happened finally hit Leona and she started to weep uncontrollably.

Aware of all she had been through, Lathe quickly took her into his arms and held her close until she finally stopped crying, then he held her several minutes more simply because it felt so good to have her there.

Of Lathe's two patients, Zeb was the first to wake. He came to shortly after midnight, screaming and thrashing about like a wild man when he discovered his hands tied directly to the examining table. Because the sheriff had felt it would a good idea to have a lawman in the room with him at all times, it was a deputy who came running into the back room where Lathe rested and told him the news.

433

Leona and Sarah heard the commotion from Ethan's room and hurried to see what had happened.

With Leona right on his heels, Lathe hurried to administer just enough ether to calm Zeb, then after checking for fever or renewed bleeding, decided his least-wanted patient was well enough to be transported to jail. Despite the malicious comments Zeb flung at him, he promised the deputy he would come by to check Zeb's wounds again sometime later that morning.

Ethan did not open his eyes again until nearly noon. When he did, he found himself face down on a very firm, padded surface. Finding his position most uncomfortable, he quickly pushed himself up and turned over, closing his eyes and gasping aloud at the resulting pain. When it finally eased enough so that he could open his eyes again, he was very pleased to find Sarah standing beside him like a beautiful guardian angel, her cool hand upon his forehead. "Where am I?" he asked and attempted a smile. "In heaven?"

"Why would a man who tells such terrible lies be in heaven?" Sarah admonished playfully, tears glimmering brightly in her blue eyes while she continued to stroke his forehead with her fingertips.

Ethan's face paled, not certain which lies she meant. Unable to face her now that she might know the truth, he glanced away, vaguely aware he was in Doc Owen's old office. "I guess Leona told you all about it."

"Only that you are really Ethan," Sarah admitted. "I never did get the opportunity to ask her *why* you decided to tell us you were someone else. I do hope you had a good reason."

"Where is Leona?" he wanted to know, trying to push up on one elbow only to be reprimanded with another sharp stab of pain. He decided it would be wiser, and a whole lot less painful, to lie back down and stay flat.

434

"Leona went with Lathe to the jail to see how Zeb is getting along. They left just a few minutes ago."

Ethan's forehead wrinkled when he looked back at her, clearly confused. "Didn't Leona kill him?"

Sarah's eyes widened at such a question. "You mean Leona is the one who shot Zeb?"

Aware Sarah still had a lot of questions that deserved answers, Ethan took her hand in his and started at the beginning. He started by admitting all the foolish mistakes he had made and how ruthlessly the captain had treated them, and asked her not to breathe a word of it to her parents. When he finished by telling her what had happened at the Conways' old house, he looked at her pleadingly. "Can you ever forgive me?"

"I don't understand. What is there to forgive? You just told me that the captain killed my brother to keep him from interfering with his horrible plan to steal Lathe's gold. I don't see that what you did was all that wrong."

"But I lied to you and Leona," he reminded her.

"And you did that to save our feelings," she explained, smiling to show she held no grudges. Truth was, it felt good to have so many of her questions finally answered. "You wanted us to go on believing that George had died a hero's death and that possibly you had, too. But I really think my parents deserve to know the truth. Father already suspects that something like that happened."

"But they might hold all those lies I told against me and not let you marry me," Ethan argued, not wanting to do anything that could jeopardize his chances.

"*Marry* me?" Sarah's eyes lit with joy. "You want to marry me?"

"More than anything on this earth," Ethan admitted and smiled when he reached up to caress her cheek with his hand. "What would you say to becoming Mrs.

435

Ethan Stegall and trying to help me get my life back on the right track?"

"What would I say?" she repeated, unable to believe he did not already know her answer. "Why I'd say, *yes*. A thousand times, *yes!*"

Ethan grinned, pleased by her obvious excitement. Moving his hand to the back of her neck, he pulled her gently forward for their first kiss. "I don't need to hear it a thousand times. Once was plenty."

Leona hated to watch Lathe leave, but she knew he had to go. He had spent far too many years and made himself far too many promises. It was important *he* be the one to deliver Zeb into the hands of the sheriff whose duty it was to hang him. And it was important he stay long enough to see justice finally done.

"Don't take too long," she said, forcing a smile when he stepped forward to give her one last kiss before leaving. "And take special care of that leg. It has only been four weeks since you were shot."

"Don't worry about me. I told you I'm practically good as new."

"That may be, but I still worry. I want you to promise to be careful."

"I told you, the sheriff has hired two deputies to go with me to make sure we both arrive safely. And I plan to stay right in the sheriff's office helping them watch Zeb until they finally do hang him. He's not getting away this time."

"Just hurry back. Ethan needs you."

"*Ethan* needs me?" he asked, glancing at her with a raised brow. "I doubt that. With Sarah, you, and Iris around to look after him, I think he'll do just fine without me. In fact, I estimate he'll be up walking again by the end of the week. He's already sitting up most of the day and demands more food than any one man really needs."

Leona laughed, knowing that was true. "Still, you need to hurry back just in case something goes wrong."

"Oh, while I'm thinking about it, I have something for you." Reaching into his coat pocket, he pulled out an envelope and handed it to her. "I want you to read this after I've gone. I think it will explain exactly how I feel."

Leona's heart fluttered with eager expectation, anxious to read his words but she was not about to waste any of their last precious moments together by actually doing so. With eyes glittering, she set it reverently on a nearby table, freeing her hands so she could hold him one last time.

Although it was already ten-twenty and Lathe had told the sheriff he would be at the jail ready to leave no later than ten-thirty, he took Leona into his arms for one long final goodbye kiss, knowing it would have to last him for at least two weeks. Then, without saying another word, not sure he could force anything intelligible past the painful constriction in his throat, he turned and walked away, still favoring his injured leg.

Blinking back a burning rush of tears, Leona hurried outside and watched with an aching heart when he paused near the gate to smile and wave, then walked over to his horse and swung himself into the saddle.

He was not even out of her sight, and she already missed him dreadfully. How could she ever bear to live through these next several days without him? Trembling, she bolted out into the yard so she could watch him until he had disappeared onto the next street.

"Glad you got back here in time," John said after he pulled the shade down then turned toward his desk.

437

"According to the sheriff, they should be leaving any minute. All you have to do is follow at a safe distance and make sure that Lathe never returns."

"Does it matter *when* I kill him?" Simpson wanted to know, still frowning over the fact there would be two deputies along.

"Not really. Just as long as it happens a good distance from here. Just like last time, I don't want news of his death to get back here. Leona has to think he's staying away because he wants to."

"Then I think I'd better wait until after he has delivered his prisoner and he and those two deputies have finally let their guard down."

"Keep in mind that those two deputies have to return here unharmed and completely unaware of Lathe's death," John cautioned. "If not, Leona might eventually come to suspect foul play."

"Then I'd better try to fix it so Lathe stays behind."

"Which he'll probably do anyway. I feel certain he'll want to stay at least long enough to see that man hang, and I doubt those deputies will want to stick around for something like that. They will probably want to get on back home."

"Any particular way you want him to die?" Simpson asked with a casual shrug as if they were discussing nothing more important than yesterday's weather.

"No. I don't really care how you do it," John admitted as he handed over the expense money he had promised. "Just bring me back some kind of proof that the job has been done."

Leona leaned heavily against the fence for several minutes after Lathe had disappeared from sight, listening until she could no longer distinguish which sounds were those of his horse and which came from someone else's. Lifting a hand to wipe away a lingering tear, she wondered how she would ever survive the following week to ten days without him. Then she remembered the letter. It was like having a tiny part of him left behind. Eagerly, she lifted her skirts and ran as fast as she could into the house to read his treasured words and was devastated when she discovered that the letter was missing.

Frantically, she searched the floor, hoping it had fallen nearby, but she could not find it. Then, gasping with horror, she hurried toward the back of the house, calling Scraps by name.

Knowing he liked to take his booty into the back room where he sometimes slept, she went there first, hoping all the while she was wrong.

"Oh, Scraps, how could you?" she sobbed when she found him lying in a puddle of shredded paper. Her hands trembled when she knelt and tenderly picked up several of the larger pieces. On one of the pieces she glimpsed the word "love" and tenderly singled it out and pressed it against her heart.

Part of the letter was still in Scraps's mouth, in one large wet wad, and there were too many other pieces to put together, so Leona quietly placed the tiny piece she had salvaged into her breast pocket, then quickly picked up the rest and set them on a shelf high enough so that Scraps could do them no further harm. Even though the pieces were no longer of any real use to her, she could not bring herself to throw them away.

"Look, Leona. He's been gone for over three weeks. When are you going to get it through that pretty head of yours that Caldwell is never coming back?" John snapped, having grown tired of her stubbornness. "That's the truth of the matter. That man is a rambler.

439

He's not coming back here for any reason, and it doesn't do you or Ethan a bit of good to believe otherwise."

"He is too coming back," she vowed with far more conviction than she actually felt, now that three weeks had passed with no word, not even a telegram. "He's just had some sort of difficulty, is all."

"What sort of difficulty could he have had?" John asked, then forced the annoyance out of his voice as he gently rested his hands on her shoulders then bent forward to look directly into her eyes. "Leona, those deputies got back two weeks ago and both admitted that Zeb Turner was scheduled for an immediate hanging. That means Caldwell should have returned right behind them, but he didn't. Nor did he bother to write and give you a reason why. When are you finally going to see that man for the scoundrel he really is? He's the type who uses people for whatever he can get, then tosses them aside."

"No he isn't," Leona said, lifting her chin, refusing to believe Lathe could be so cruel. "If he wasn't coming back, he'd have told me so." A tight knot formed in her chest when it occurred to her that it could be he had done just that. She had no way to know what had been in that letter. It could very well have been a farewell note. It was possible the reason he'd put his words down on paper instead of saying them directly to her face was that he had been unable to confront her with something so heartbreaking. And he did warn her he would make a lousy husband.

Still, she did not want to believe it. Lathe would be back. She knew it. And when he did come back, it would be to marry her.

"Leona, Caldwell is *never* coming back," John tried again, certain that by now Simpson had done his deed and was on his way back with the proof. "You have to

440

put all thoughts of him behind you and get on with your life. For your own sake."

Leona blinked back her tears and pulled free of his grasp. To avoid his attempt to touch her again, she moved to the other side of the parlor. She reached into her skirt pocket and fingered the ring she had never bothered to return to Lathe, knowing it was all she had left to remember him by. "Even if he doesn't come back, I am not marrying you."

"But I was in your store just yesterday and saw for myself how meager your stock had become. Can't you see that you and Ethan are both in very real danger of losing that Mercantile forever?"

"Only because your father keeps refusing to give us that loan," she said, clearly resentful.

"He explained that to you. Business has been bad all over. He can't afford to let out any more money right now. But, Leona, *I* have plenty of money. I can loan Ethan all the money he'll need to keep going until first harvest; but I'll only do that if you promise to marry me." Although it bothered John to know he would not be gaining control of the Mercantile as he had originally planned, he still wanted Leona to marry him. "If you can't do it for yourself, then do it for Ethan."

Leona let go of the ring to press her cool hands against her hot cheeks, wishing she knew what to do. A part of her wanted to do whatever she could to help Ethan keep the Mercantile, but another part of her wanted to wait a little while longer to see if Lathe might change his mind and come back after all. Problem was, she did not dare wait too long. If Ethan did not get the money he needed very soon, there would be no Mercantile to save.

"Give me two weeks," she finally agreed. "I'll have an answer for you then."

441

"There's no point openin' up when we got nothin' to sell," Ethan said when Leona wanted to know why he was still seated at the kitchen table nursing a now luke-warm cup of coffee. "To tell you the truth, I've been givin' some serious consideration to Roy Porterfield's offer."

"And *sell* the business?" Leona asked, unable to believe Ethan would even consider such a thing.

"Just the building and what stock we got left," Ethan said, hoping to make the situation sound better than it really was. "If we decide we want to open up again at some later date, we can turn around and do just that. We'll just have to do it in another building, is all."

"No, I won't allow you to do that." Leona curled her hands into tight fists until her knuckles were as white as her dress when she turned away from him. Lifting her chin proudly, she stared through the open window into the back yard, oblivious to the cheerful sounds that came from the two fat robins perched on the back fence. "I can get the money we need to restock."

"By marrying John Davis?" Ethan asked, scooting his chair back but not yet standing. "I won't let you do that."

"Why not?" She turned to face him again. "It will get us the money we need."

"*Why not?*" he repeated, unable to believe she could even ask. "I'll tell you exactly why not. Because you still happen to be very much in love with Lathe Caldwell, that's why not. And although you seem to have given up all hope, I happen to believe that man still has every intention of coming back here for you."

"If that were true, he'd at least have written to me by now, or he would have sent a telegram. He's done neither."

"And I figure that's because that letter he left you explained it all. Lathe has no way of knowing that mangy mutt got hold of that letter and destroyed it before you could ever read it." His eyebrows arched when Scraps suddenly barked in the distance, as if he had actually heard the derogatory comments and wanted to voice a protest.

"Still, he should have been back by now," she argued, aware she was repeating John's own words. "He's been gone for five weeks and Zeb has been dead for at least four of those weeks. You know that as well as I do. You had Sheriff Lindsey check that fact yourself."

"Maybe he had something else to do before heading back."

"What else would take that much time?"

"I don't know," he admitted but leaned forward to show how sincere he was. "Just don't give up on him yet."

"But we need the money *now,*" she stated with a firm nod, although she was already weakening. "Besides, I promised John I'd give him an answer in two weeks and it has been exactly that."

"So give him an answer. Tell him no." Ethan grimaced when he pushed himself out of the chair, still finding sudden movements a little painful. He reached out to take his sister into a gentle embrace. "Leona, even if you did decide to marry him, I wouldn't accept his money. I refuse to have any part in your unhappiness. I have already caused you more than enough sorrow."

Leona smiled, tears glimmering in her eyes as she pressed her cheek against her brother's strong chest. "I'll give Lathe one more week."

"One more week for what?" The question came from just the other side of the back door.

Startled to hear Lathe's voice, Leona turned to see if it could be true, and she squealed with delight when

443

she noticed him standing just a few feet away, arms open. Breaking immediately from Ethan's embrace she ran into his, stretching up on the very tips of her toes to meet his parted lips halfway.

After several minutes of eager, hungry kisses, Lathe broke away, laughing at such a warm welcome. "So, what is it you plan to give me another week for?"

"To come home," she said, too overjoyed to do anything but laugh right along with him. "Where have you been?"

"I told you. I had to go visit my aunt."

"Your aunt?" she asked, looking puzzled. "Whatever for?"

He studied her bewildered expression for several seconds then looked at Ethan. "Didn't she read my letter?"

Blinking back a few tears of his own, Ethan laughed then looked at Leona with a raised brow. "Didn't I tell you? It was all in that letter." He then walked over and patted Lathe soundly on the shoulder. "I'd love to stay and chat, but I'm late as it is. I should have opened that store half an hour ago."

Realizing that Ethan was letting them be alone, Leona stayed cuddled in Lathe's warm embrace and waited until her brother had left before explaining what had happened to the letter.

"Then you *didn't* know," he said with new understanding then bent back to look at her while he explained. "After Zeb was finally hanged, I went to Florida to visit my Aunt Carole so I could get the information I needed. While I was so close, I decided to go ahead and get that gold Jonathan and I buried at the beginning of the war. When I arrived at her house, I discovered she had been very sick, so sick it had affected her memory and she could not remember what she had done with the letter. It took us two days of searching through her belongings to find what I needed. Then when I returned to Mill Run, I still had a hard time locating the exact spot. I eventually had to hire a surveyor to find it for me."

"But you did find it?" she asked, sensing that it was important to him to reclaim what was rightfully his.

"Yes. But then I had to exchange the gold for money and after that, have the money transferred here so I can use part of it to buy Dr. Owen's office and equipment. Another reason it took so long for me to get back is because I also spent two days in Montgomery purchasing some new equipment Dr. Owen didn't have. While I was at it, I made a few purchases for the Mercantile. The first shipment should be arriving in a day or two and by the time it all arrives, you and Ethan will have all the stock you need to put Porterfield out of business once and for all."

He gazed at her disbelieving expression for a moment. Aware of how thrilled she was by what he had just told her, he took a deep breath before telling her the rest. "And then there was that incident with the man who tried to kill me."

"Tried to kill you?" she asked in a strangled voice. Any protest she might have made over his having purchased all that merchandise died on her tongue.

"Yes, just before I left Mill Run that first time, a man tried to shoot me in the back. Fortunately, he was a poor shot."

"But why?"

"Didn't know at first. I'd never seen him before. But another man saw him getting the drop on me and took a shot at him. *He* proved to have much better aim and shot him right off his horse, knocking him out cold. Since he was unconscious and couldn't tell us anything, we searched his pockets to try to find out who he was and realized right away his motive couldn't have been to rob me of all my money. He had plenty of that on him."

"Then why would he try to kill you?" she asked, forcing the words through a tightly constricted throat.

"At the time, I figured he was someone working for Captain Potter, like Ethan was, and hadn't yet found out the captain was already dead. But, shortly after we carried him to the local doctor he came to, and right after that, the sheriff showed up to question him." He paused before continuing, knowing how angry the next part of it would make her.

"And?" she prodded, wanting to know why the man had tried to kill the man she loved.

"And he confessed everything. He'd been hired by John Davis to kill me."

Leona felt her whole body grow weak, unable to believe such a thing. "John hired him?"

"That's another reason I was so long in getting back here. It took a few days for the sheriff to arrange for a U.S. Marshal to accompany me back here. John Davis has already been arrested for the part he played in all this and is sitting in Sheriff Lindsey's jail. He'll have to stand trial."

Leona shuddered while she thought about how very close Lathe had come to being shot. "It's just horrible. You were almost killed."

"I'll admit, it did put a damper on my day," he agreed, laughing at how large and round her brown eyes had become. "But it's all over now and it didn't prevent me from going on to my aunt's house and then back to Mill Run to get my gold. Nor did it keep me from having what money I had left after making all those purchases sent here."

"Then you are really planning to make your home right here in Little Mound?" she asked, her heart soaring.

446

"Of course I am. Even if you didn't get the chance to read my letter, you should have known that," he admonished, then bent to kiss the tip of her nose. "As I recall, you indicated that if I could only keep myself alive long enough, you'd eventually marry me."

"But that was before you told me you'd make such a miserable husband," she cautioned, tilting her head and gazing at him lovingly, so full of happiness she was certain her heart would burst.

"Are you backing out on me?" he wanted to know, stooping to press his nose firmly against hers with playful intimidation.

"Not at all. I am fully prepared to spend the rest of my life in complete misery."

Lathe chuckled then bent to nip playfully at her ear. "And I'll be sure that you do," he vowed, then returned to capture her mouth in a devouring kiss meant to bond them for an eternity.